Cancel
the
Wedding

Cancel the Wedding

A NOVEL

Carolyn Dingman

HARPER

NEW YORK . LONDON . TORONTO . SYDNEY

HARPER

CANCEL THE WEDDING Copyright © 2014 by Carolyn Dingman. All rights reserved. Printed in the United States of America. No part of this book may be used or reproduced in any manner whatsoever without written permission except in the case of brief quotations embodied in critical articles and reviews. For information address HarperCollins Publishers, 195 Broadway, New York, NY 10007.

HarperCollins books may be purchased for educational, business, or sales promotional use. For information please e-mail the Special Markets Department at SPsales@harpercollins.com.

FIRST EDITION

Library of Congress Cataloging-in-Publication Data has been applied for.

ISBN 978-0-06-227672-8

14 15 16 17 18   OV/RRD   10 9 8 7 6 5 4 3 2 1

For Scott, Tempel, and Parker

Cancel the Wedding

PROLOGUE

August 1956
Huntley, Georgia

The strap from the overloaded canvas satchel dug into Janie's shoulder as she made her way down the well-traveled path to the river. She could feel that George was already there before she could hear him and long before she could see him. They were only ten years old but they had been tuned in to each other like that for as long as she could remember. As she jumped over one of the small creeks that fed into the river, she glanced at the wild blueberry bushes growing on its small bank. They had all been picked clean, so she didn't bother to stop.

Janie left the cool shade of the treelined trail and burst into the blazing sunlight on the bank of the water. She was at the Hitch, a bend in the river where the Dunk Pool formed every spring, which was what they called the slow, swirling pond of water that was deep enough for swimming. There were a hundred secret places on this river, and they knew all of them. She had sensed correctly that George was already there jumping off of the Overlook, an enormous granite outcropping over the frigid waters. Janie watched as he jumped high into the air before diving into the water.

The soda bottles clanked together as Janie put her heavy pack right next to George's. Strewn about in the mud were the contents of Oliver's bag. Oliver was George's twin brother. He had probably tossed the bag carelessly over his shoulder while running into the water. As Janie gathered his scattered belongings she noticed a handful of cherry bombs. She groaned thinking of the near catastrophe the week before when Oliver blew up a soda bottle with firecrackers. One glass shard had sliced his forehead open, requiring six stitches. He just missed his left eye.

Making sure the boys couldn't see her from their vantage point, Janie dunked the cherry bombs in the river, soaking them through. Then she tossed them back on the ground where she had found them.

George waved to Janie from the Overlook. "Get in already!" He dove again, and Janie jumped into the chilly water and swam to the deepest part of the Dunk Pool where her feet couldn't touch. George's head popped up next to her, and he grabbed her hand, pulling her through the water until she could stand.

They climbed onto the Overlook, the baking stone hot under their feet. Janie shielded her eyes and looked across the sparkling river for some sign of Oliver. George pointed to the far bank at the rope swing, which was tied to the overarching limb of an ancient water oak.

Oliver ran down the path and vaulted from the rocky ledge, his arms flailing until he connected with the lowest knot in the tattered, unraveling rope. When the rope swept up to its highest point, he let go. The rope whipped back as Oliver curled his sinewy body into a tight ball flipping through the air with no effort before landing with a graceful dive into the deepest portion of the Dunk Pool.

George and Janie watched this feat together from the Overlook. Like Oliver they were a vision of pointy elbows and gangly legs strapped with the tight muscles and scabbed knees of childhood.

George asked, "How can he be like that in the water but such a mess on land?"

Janie thought mess wasn't a strong enough word. She lay down on the hot rock, resting her head on George's leg. "He had cherry bombs."

George tossed small stones and acorns into the river below. "I know. He bought them with his bottle-return money." He didn't have to ask if Janie had already sabotaged them, and she didn't have to answer. Sometimes it was exhausting keeping Oliver safe from himself.

Janie said, "I brought extra food and some sodas."

"Oh good, Oliver ate most of his food on the hike down here."

"I figured."

George asked, "What'd you bring?"

Janie rattled off her list of provisions: fried chicken, biscuits, potato salad, homemade pickles, peach hand pies. She trailed off before even listing the two kinds of cookies she had brought: chocolate chip for her and George, peanut butter for Oliver. It suddenly occurred to her what a spectacular feast had been prepared for them.

George sensed what was wrong. All of that food could only have come from Maudy, and today was Sunday. If Maudy was at the house on a Sunday, then Janie's mother was getting worse.

George said carefully, "Well . . . it'll be neat to be up at Sunset Rock by ourselves."

Janie sat up, nodding slowly. George silently gathered up more stones and acorns and handed them to her. Together they tossed them into the water below for a while. Sometimes being with George was the only thing that made Janie feel that she could live through her mother's illness.

Janie, Oliver, and George spent the day in the water just as they had a million other days in their summers on the river. When the sun started to drop below the treeline, they gathered up their packs and put their shoes back on to make the long hike up to the top of the ridge.

While they walked, George and Oliver recounted the Red Sox game from the day before in excruciating detail. Whenever they mentioned Ted Williams, all three proclaimed in unison, "The greatest hitter of all time!" That was Oliver's rule and it was always obeyed.

The evening had turned cooler once they reached the ridgeline, but the face of Sunset Rock still radiated heat from the warmth of the day. Janie unfurled the maroon wool picnic blanket that Maudy had rolled up and attached to her pack. That blanket had accompanied every outdoor meal that Janie had ever had, but Janie hated it, especially the way it made the backs of her legs itch.

Oliver helped Janie unpack all her food. It was by far the largest stash they'd ever had for a picnic at Sunset Rock, but this was the very first time they had been allowed to come alone so it was a special occasion. Oliver looked at the spread and waved his hands over it like a shopkeeper presenting a lovely display. "Janie, is this their way of making you feel better about your mom dying?"

"Oliver!" George shoved him.

Janie didn't say anything, but anger bubbled up from inside her. She grabbed the stupid, awful, itchy, picnic blanket and hurled it off Sunset Rock with a scream. It fluttered down very slowly and unsatisfactorily to the trees below.

The three of them stepped carefully to the edge and stared down at the heap. Finally George said, "I always hated that thing."

Oliver said, "Sorry, Janie. I didn't mean it."

"I know." She turned her back to the ledge.

They stared out over the valley below, which changed with every slight dip of the sun. When they had finished eating, they all lay on the ground with their heads resting on their arms waiting for the pale blue sky of day to gasp white just before the red and orange of sunset burst through. Janie held one hand in front of her face. She had her mother's hands, exact replicas. It was the only thing about Janie that resembled her mother, and when Janie looked at them she wondered if she would someday grow to hate the sight of her own fingers out of sheer heartbreak.

Oliver spotted the first star, bright and low on the horizon. He jumped to his feet. "Star light, star bright. First star I see to-night." His eyes were closed as he recited the incantation, concentrating on this wish. "I want to play for the Boston Red Sox just like Ted Williams—"

And the chorus chimed, "Greatest hitter of all time!"

Oliver continued as if uninterrupted. "And travel all over the world playing baseball."

Janie understood why he loved baseball, but she never could understand his need to escape home. "Why would you ever leave Huntley?"

Oliver just looked at her with a confused expression as if he didn't fully understand the question, because he couldn't understand why anyone would stay.

Janie popped up next. "My turn. Star light, star bright." Janie clasped her hands together and closed her eyes as tight as she could. She wanted this wish to count. She considered wishing that her mother wouldn't be sick anymore, but Janie had wished that on every star and every candle for the last two years, and it didn't seem to be working. "My wish is to become a lawyer when I grow up like my daddy and to someday marry George."

As soon as the words were out of Janie's mouth, Oliver was howling. George turned a little pink in the cheeks, but he would never hurt Janie by acting like it embarrassed him that she had said that. And really the idea of marrying Janie someday didn't bother him; it was just the way Oliver was acting that was bugging George. Oliver doubled over laughing, hitting his knee, and pointing back and forth between George and Janie.

Janie stomped her foot one time before punching Oliver in the stomach. He went down hard, the wind knocked out of him. George debated stepping in, but it seemed that Oliver had had his fun, Janie had taken care of it, and in the end the score was tied.

Changing the subject, Janie asked, "Aren't you making a wish, George?" She glared at Oliver, still on his knees, daring him to make a comment.

George shook his head, laughing a little to himself.

Oliver croaked out, "Why not?"

" 'Cause you guys just made a wish on a planet." He pointed to the pinprick of light in the sky. "That's Venus."

As dusk turned to night the children made their way back down the dark path toward home. Janie was moving more slowly than the boys, in no rush to get back to the house. Her flashlight cast a dim yellow circle of light on the trail. A bobbing beam of light turned back up the path toward her as George ran uphill, backtracking to where Janie was walking.

George moved his flashlight to his far hand and reached out for Janie. Their fingers locked together. Oliver had stopped walking and waited on the dark trail for George and Janie to catch up. When they reached him, Oliver fell in line, walking with the same cadence. Janie tried to release George's hand so that Oliver wouldn't tease them, but George held tight, not letting go. Oliver was walking on the other side of Janie, hitting his busted flashlight on his thigh hoping to shake some life back into it. He had broken another one; his mother would be so angry. Janie handed hers to Oliver, and she took the broken one.

Oliver put his arm around Janie's shoulder, and the three of them walked the rest of the way home. Silently holding on to each other.

ONE

I took the sharp curve too fast, causing the urn to tumble off of the backseat and roll across the floorboard. My niece, Logan, threw her arm back to grab it.

"Oh my God, Olivia. Be careful!" I was being scolded by a fourteen-year-old. "You almost spilled Grandma out in the backseat."

"It won't spill. The lid is screwed on." At least I thought it was. "Maybe hold it in your lap or something."

"What? No! Gross."

I glanced at the urn containing the cremated remains of my mother. It looked to be undamaged. I said, "At least buckle it back in."

The narrow two-lane highway leading into Tillman, Georgia, was bordered on both sides with a suffocating canopy of trees. In the dark, with no streetlights and just the beams of the car allowing a glimpse of the shoulder, it looked like we were about to be swallowed by a tidal wave of thick, green water. There was no way I was pulling over to properly secure our cargo. I had seen that movie and I knew better than to stop the car on the dark shoulder of a deserted country road.

My phone rang. It was my sister, Georgia, calling. I put it on speaker and Logan made a face at the screen. Being fourteen she often hated her mom for no particular reason. I said, "Hey, Gigi."

"Livie, you left your ring at my house."

I was hoping it wouldn't be discovered quite so quickly. "I know, sorry. I meant to tell you. Can you just hang on to it for me?"

"I can FedEx it down to you if you want."

"No . . . that's not, I mean you don't need to bother."

"Why?" I could hear her tapping her foot at me over the phone line. Georgia was my older sister in every conceivable way. It didn't matter that we were now adults. She would forever view me as the baby who needed constant reminders, nudges, and prompts. Otherwise there existed the very real possibility that I might forget to get dressed before leaving the house.

"Jeez, Georgia, just hang on to it for me will you? It's no big deal." I thought, *Don't tell Leo*. But I didn't say it. I was ten hours into a poorly planned, spontaneous road trip and I was too tired to fight with her. When I had picked up my niece that morning I slipped the ring off and put it in her bathroom. For some reason I didn't want to wear that noose when I fled, but I didn't feel like trying to explain it to Georgia.

Leo and I had been engaged for almost three years. He asked me to marry him right after my father died. Last year, when my mother died, we bought a house together. With each death, Leo and I ratcheted up our commitment level. I was in a race to keep the houseplants alive for fear of ending up pregnant.

I kept my eyes on the road as I spoke toward the phone's speaker. "Look, I'm driving. I gotta go. Logan, hang up on your mother."

She clicked the phone off and put her bare feet up on the dashboard. "Finally, something we agree on."

I merged right. "What's that?"

"Hanging up on my mom." Logan was now picking at the peeling polish on her toenails. "Why'd you ditch the ring?"

"I meant to have it cleaned." I lied. "It's no big deal." I lied again.

"Are you going to cancel the wedding?"

"What? No, I just . . . no."

"It's cool, Livie. Whatever. But you know sometimes you talk about marriage like it's the Bataan Death March."

I looked at her. "The Bataan . . . ? Can't you just read zombie love stories like a normal teenager?"

"Can't you just wear your ring like a normal fiancée?"

I stole a Twizzler from the bag she was holding and bonked her on the head with it.

This impulsive little escapade, driving from our home in the DC area to a strange town in the northwest corner of Georgia, had materialized the day before.

My fiancé, Leo, had picked me up at work so that we could rush over to my sister's house for a family supper. I wish I could say that I didn't usually work on Saturdays, but that wouldn't be true. I just really wish I could say it.

Leo was waiting for me in the circular drive in front of my office building as I hurried to roll up the last set of blueprints, which were incredibly heavy but not in fact blue. I dropped one copy on my boss's desk with a note telling him that the project was finished, that he was a jerk for making me drag my team in over the weekend, and that I was taking Monday off. I may not have actually written that middle part.

I pushed through the heavy glass doors to the outside and was engulfed by the thick, wet summer air. It instantly smothered the chill I had from being in the air-conditioned office all day. My mom, whose name was Jane but who everyone called Janie, referred to air conditioning as "store-bought air." My sister and I would get into trouble if we wasted it by leaving the back door open. The familiar wave of grief swept through me as I thought of my mother.

I got into the car and buckled as Leo pulled away from the curb. I glanced around to see if he had remembered the wine. He knew what I was looking for and pointed to the floor by my feet. After so many years together we didn't need many words. I tried to see that as a comfort instead of a toxic premonition.

Leo didn't mind that I had to work all the time. He was an attorney and was under the mistaken impression that this was a normal number of hours for one to spend on the job. There was no use arguing with him about it.

Sometimes I wondered if we had accidentally backed into

our engagement simply because the timing had worked out. We got engaged at a time when I was in the process of losing both of my parents; I think Leo felt understandably a little bit sorry for me. It also happened to coincide with Leo's consideration for a junior partnership. The senior partners at the firm liked for the junior partners to be stable and solid, which roughly translated from legal jargon meant "married."

We left Tysons Corner and headed north around the Beltway to my sister's house for dinner. It was the one-year anniversary of my mother's death, which in my opinion was a bizarre thing to celebrate, but no one asked me. I missed her and my dad every day and I couldn't shake the rudderless feeling of being orphaned. It wasn't something I liked to mark with cocktails and grilled meat.

I sighed a little, which made Leo ask, "What're you thinking?"

"I just can't believe it's already been a year. And we haven't even scattered her ashes yet. I'm irritated with Georgia that it's taking so long."

Leo patted my leg. "Filter." He said it in that type A, slightly controlling, but well-meaning voice he used on me when he thought I should keep my thoughts to myself.

Our mother left very specific instructions for the scattering of her ashes. We just couldn't figure out why she had requested it. The letter our mother had given to her attorney with her last will and testament was frustratingly brief. It read:

My daughters know that it is my wish to be cremated.
I would like for the two of them, together, to scatter

*my ashes. Please lay half to rest in Lake Huntley
and half over plot 34B in the old section of Huntley
Memorial Gardens. ~Janie*

Our mother, Jane Rutledge Hughes, grew up in Huntley,
Georgia, but she never once talked about it. Her personal code
of silence was on par with a mafia omertà. We had never visited
her hometown, we knew nothing of her childhood, and she had
no living relatives.

But now this, she wanted to be laid to rest there, in the place
of which she never spoke. If her hometown meant so much to
her that she wanted to be there *permanently*, then why had we
never visited Huntley? Why hadn't she ever talked about her
past? The people, the town, her life there? None of it made
sense. This was probably why her urn had still been sitting on
the mantel in Georgia's living room a year after her death.

We pulled up to Georgia's house, a bungalow sitting just outside DC's city limits, safely tucked into the jurisdiction of
Chevy Chase. My nephews were playing in the front yard.
Will, the ten-year-old, was sitting on Adam, his younger
brother, and hitting him repeatedly with a lacrosse stick. Without breaking my stride I confiscated the lacrosse stick from
Will as I walked by. I figured Adam should at least have a fighting chance. We younger siblings had to stick together.

Leo and I let ourselves in the house. "Gigi, we're here."

I found Georgia in the kitchen. A door slammed overhead
and she flinched. That would be Logan. I came up behind my
sister and hugged her shoulders. "Sorry we're late. I had to finish that project this weekend."

"You're working too much."

"I know." I raided her liquor cabinet and made myself a stiff drink.

She waved to Leo as he passed quietly through the kitchen on his way to help William with the grill. "Are you two fighting?"

"No, we don't fight." I wondered if we had come to a place where neither one of us cared enough to get into a decent argument anymore. You really only have a passionate row if you feel completely confident that you can get through it, or if you're using it as the hand grenade tossed over your shoulder on your way out the door.

Georgia was hacking at a head of lettuce. She pointed her knife at my glass. "Then why are you drinking so much lately?"

I took the knife out of her hands, deciding that preparing the salad myself might be safer. "Why are you judging so much lately? Relax."

Logan had appeared out of nowhere and let out a snide laugh at my comment. "See Mom? You're too judgey." She was already walking out the back door, throwing a "Hey, Aunt Livie" over her shoulder before Georgia could respond.

Georgia stole my drink from me. "I need this. Logan is being impossible."

"She's a teenager. It's kind of her job to be impossible."

We all sat down to dinner, which was its usual bout of lovely chaos. My nephews were kicking each other under the table relentlessly as Georgia gave a sentimental speech about our mother on this one-year anniversary of her death. The kicking was very distracting. I finally kicked them both back simultaneously. To eight- and ten-year-old boys, getting kicked by your aunt is hilarious apparently. Milk came out of Adam's nose. It landed on Will's plate. I was in trouble.

Logan hardly touched her dinner. Either she was still mad at Georgia or she was protesting the steaks. Sometimes she was a vegetarian.

I was finally starting to relax, no doubt the effects of my second vodka tonic. My brother-in-law, William, was finishing a story about some baseball game and then just like that, with no warning or hint that it was coming, Leo stood up and demanded everyone's attention.

"I have an announcement to make." Georgia glanced at me to see if I knew what this was about. I shook my head slightly and shrugged. I couldn't imagine what he would have to announce. But this was just Leo. He liked to control situations and conversations. I very rarely bothered to step in or protest.

Once everyone at the table had quieted down and the boys had stopped fidgeting, Leo said it. "The scheduler for Trinity Chapel called the house today and there's been an opening." He paused for dramatic effect. I felt my stomach drop suddenly knowing what was coming next. "So I booked it. Olivia and I officially have a wedding date. Mark your calendars for the last weekend in September." He took my hand, smiling down at me. "Surprise!"

I could feel the blood drain out of my face. I felt like I was falling, rushing toward something, and I needed to make a drastic move quickly before I hit. My sister and her husband were happily congratulating Leo and me.

Through the clamor I heard Leo explaining everything, but the words were taking a while to make their way to my brain.

"The timing couldn't be better." He was explaining that the end of September was perfect, logistically, for a wedding. He should be finishing one of his cases by then, it was always a slow time for me at work, and the firm's off-site in Kauai wasn't until the beginning of November. I had not been to any of his firm's off-site conferences yet because they were strictly "spouses only" and so far I had not qualified. I knew Leo felt it was bad form for me to miss another one. The timing for the end of September worked nicely into his schedule.

My nephews were taking the distraction this offered to feed their vegetables to the dog. Logan was staring at me with the strangest look on her face, a hybrid of amusement and empathy.

My vision went slightly fuzzy and gray around the edges and without thinking I jumped up, nearly knocking my chair over. "I have a surprise too. I've decided to leave in the morning and drive down to Georgia to see where Mom wanted us to spread her ashes."

Leo dropped my hand. "You're what?"

I started making plans as the ideas popped in my head. "It's the one-year anniversary of her death. I have a million vacation days saved up at work and this is a good time for a break. It would be so easy to just drive down there. We could all use closure, right? Right?" I was babbling, my voice trying to keep up with the excuses my brain was feeding it. Leo looked concerned but kept quiet. I knew he hated it when I blurted out every single thought racing through my mind, but I wasn't in control enough to stop it.

That was not the reaction Leo had expected from me, clearly. He turned me by my shoulders until I was facing him and spoke quietly. "We shouldn't keep putting this off. This was the chapel you wanted to use; it was your parents' chapel and it's available, finally. Let's stop waiting and move forward."

Leo looked so sincere. I did love him and I did want him to be happy. "I know. And you were right to reserve it. I just . . . before we plan too much . . . if I could just . . ." I hoped he would understand my need to do this first. "I think I need to go do this, to put her to rest." I looked at Georgia, hoping she would back me up.

Georgia said, "You can't spread the ashes without me."

"Then come with—"

"You know I can't just leave." Her arms moved around the table pointing from one kid to the next. "Why can't we just fly down one weekend?"

"No, you're missing the whole point." The trapped feeling that had materialized when Leo dropped the wedding-date bomb was still holding firm and the urge to flee was palpable. I sounded a little more frantic than I meant to. "I want to go down there and find out who Mom was and where she came from. It's been a year since she died. How long are we going to wait to do this? I won't actually spread the ashes without you, not until you can come down, but don't you want to know why she picked those two places from her past?" I could feel myself clinging to the idea of my mother, as if she were the rip cord for my chute, and if I didn't pull it right that second I wouldn't survive the impact. "Maybe we could investigate Mom's childhood. Finally learn something about her family and where she came from. Aren't you dying to see where she grew up?"

"You don't understand, Livie. I don't want you to have to do that by yourself and I don't have time to go on a vision quest with you right now."

Logan stood up. "I do."

TWO

A mere twenty-four hours after jumping up at dinner and surprising myself by announcing this little road trip, Logan and I were taking the exit to Tillman, Georgia.

Tillman was the largest town in Huntley County, Georgia. Technically it was the only town in Huntley County, Georgia. Our mother had told us she grew up in Huntley. That was really all we knew. I had every intention of finding out more. Huntley County was tucked up in the northern corner of Georgia and it was a nearly eleven-hour drive from DC.

When Logan volunteered to come with me, I wasn't so sure I wanted a drama-filled fourteen-year-old girl riding shotgun for my sabbatical. But having her along for the ride felt right, she was a good traveling partner. Mostly she just texted on her phone and stayed plugged in to her earbuds. It was like having a younger, quieter, tech-savvy, and non-hypercritical version of my sister with me.

I had hastily printed out what I could find about Lake Huntley since that was one of the "burial" locations, but I hadn't done more than browse the headlines: where to rent canoes, where to have lunch on the water, and where to buy a fishing license. There was an inordinate amount of information about obtaining a fishing license. If they were that weird about fishing I wondered how they would feel about the scattering of human remains in the lake.

I also printed out a map showing the outline of Lake Huntley. It wasn't a smooth, round body of water. It had a long, jagged main body that seemed to snake through the mountain range. And from there, countless ragged fingers forked off on all sides and at strange angles. It was an odd little lake.

We passed a highway sign that read: TILLMAN—6 MILES. Thank God. I had to get out of this car. It was almost eight o'clock and I was starving, my knee was killing me, and I had a headache from trying to follow these dark country roads.

The road widened as we got closer to town. At the first big intersection there was a Walmart Supercenter on one side of the road and a Super Target on the other. The road leading toward town was lined with strip malls of fast-food joints, dollar stores, nail/tan salons, and Mexican restaurants. It was Anywhereville, America.

Logan pulled the information and directions to the inn where we were staying out of the seat pocket. "This says the town of Tillman is 'a lovely and charming town on the banks of Lake Huntley.' This does not look lovely and charming."

"Well, we're not quite there yet." I tried to sound optimistic but I wasn't staying long if this was all Tillman had to offer.

We came to another intersection and turned left following the signs to the historic district. The street changed slowly from commercial to residential. As we approached the center of the historic district the streets began to be arranged in a grid.

The streets farthest from the center of town were filled with newer midcentury ranch-style houses. They had long green lawns and straight driveways that led into carports. Then there were the bungalows from the twenties and thirties fronted with buckled sidewalks and picket fences dripping with jasmine vines. Driving down the street took us back in time until we arrived at enormous Victorian homes with wrought-iron fences and gravel paths that led to detached garages. These were clearly built before cars were a consideration. And then finally, nearest the town square, there were a few remaining stately antebellum homes with intricate columns, porches, and railings. This was more like it.

I was pointing out things to Logan as I crept down the street. The elaborate fences, the enormous porte cocheres with deep first steps nearly three feet off the ground built in a way that allowed a lady to get out of her carriage without having to step in the mud. The triple-hung windows, which would create cross ventilation throughout the houses in the time before air conditioning.

Logan was completely ignoring me. Our last turn brought us into the town square. It was lively for a Sunday night. There were several restaurants with tables spilling out onto the sidewalks and diners sitting at Parisian-style tables under red umbrellas. There was a small trio playing jazz in the square with a little cluster of people milling around them.

The town square had a lush green lawn with meandering gravel paths snaking through it. In the center of the square, surrounded by blooming crape myrtles and azaleas, was some sort of nondescript war monument honoring a soldier riding a bucking horse atop an enormous stone plinth. I rolled the windows down as we made our way through town, breathing in the damp summer air. I was waiting for Logan to complain about the humidity, and the potential for cataclysmic hair frizzing, but she surprised me by rolling her window down too and letting her arm dangle in the night air.

"There's the inn." Logan pointed to one of the larger buildings facing the main square. The James Oglethorpe Inn was a redbrick, three-story building on the western edge of the square. It featured a two-story, white-columned porch on the front façade with hanging baskets overflowing with geraniums.

I pulled up and a man, well actually a teenager, in an oversized valet jacket ran out to meet me as I opened the door.

"Good evening, ma'am. Are you checking in?"

"Yes, we are. May I leave the car here while I register?" The boy didn't answer me, as he was very busy checking out Logan. With his mouth hanging open ever so slightly. Logan was returning the favor.

I plopped the keys in his open hand. "Come on, Logan. Let's grab some dinner before they stop serving." I meant before they stop serving alcohol, but I didn't elaborate. I could really use a vodka tonic, or three.

I woke up the next morning with a raging headache and a desperate need for coffee. Maybe an intravenous drip that I could wheel around with me on an IV stand. And aspirin. I needed coffee and aspirin, stat. If there were one thing I had become an expert at recently it was the quick eradication of a hangover. I was reminded again of my sister's comment that I was drinking too much lately and decided that she would probably view this latest skill as a bad sign. I knew I was overdrinking because I was stressed and confused and maybe a little bit depressed. I just didn't need her to know it too.

I knocked on the bathroom door again. "Logan? You are *literally* killing me. I have to get coffee. Now. Please stop with the hair. You don't even know anyone around here." I leaned my head against the hard, cold wooden door as I spoke to her. That felt good.

Logan threw the door open and I nearly fell over. "You shouldn't have had all that vodka last night, Livie. It's not my fault you feel sick today."

Logan was all scrubbed and straightened and polished and smelled like some kind of tropical fruit blend. "You're right, Lo. I'm sorry." She smiled a little and I tucked her hair behind her ear. "You look very pretty. It was worth the wait."

I think she was planning on continuing the after school special. I could see she had all sorts of things spooled up in her head, but mercifully she stopped herself.

Logan grabbed her purse. "Let's go get you some coffee."

We walked down the street to an indie coffee shop tucked into a row of brick buildings facing the town square. As we stepped inside we were immediately swimming in the lifesaving aroma of deep, rich coffee. The ancient heart-of-pine floors were newly scrubbed, making the morning sun explode off the shiny surface. I put my sunglasses back on.

The shop had the skeletal layout of the pharmacy it had once been with the long counter still running the length of the side-wall. The mirrored surface behind the counter was pockmarked with age and the silvery glass took on the quality of mercury.

The far end of the rectangular coffee shop had floor-to-ceiling shelves stacked with an odd assortment of candy and fishing gear, art supplies and artisanal teas. The highest shelves were accessed by a wooden library ladder, which rolled back and forth on casters. It had long ago carved its own track on the floor. I did not immediately spot any aspirin.

A few mismatched tables with accompanying mismatched chairs dotted the open space at the front of the shop near the door where several people were eating breakfast. There was a long, low-slung blue velvet couch by the storefront window overlooking the sidewalk. The coffee table facing it was smothered with piles of magazines and well-used boxes of board games.

The long wall opposite the counter was covered from floor to ceiling with original artwork. Black-and-white nature photographs, abstract oil paintings, funky found-art folk collages, and more than a few watercolors of different species of dogs. Under each piece of art was a small tag bearing the artist's name and a price pinned to the wall with a thumbtack.

We sat down at one of the tables and I looked around for a waiter so I could order my coffee. I put my hand over the screen of Logan's phone to get her attention. "What do you want to eat?"

Logan rolled her eyes at me for rudely interrupting her trolling of status updates and then scanned the menu written on a chalkboard at the front of the shop. "Um, you know I'm not eating meat, right?"

"Yes, you make that abundantly clear every time I bite into a hamburger." Logan had an alarming recall of appetite-curbing facts related to the methods of commercial cattle farming. It was all really gross and I didn't want to hear it at the moment, especially when the delicious smell of frying bacon was coming from somewhere in the back.

Logan said, "I'll just have a biscuit and hash browns." She went back to her phone.

I rubbed my head. "You are the worst vegetarian ever."

"You sound like my mom, Livie."

I read over the menu. "Try the tofu thing." She opened her mouth to protest. I stopped her. "If you don't like it you don't have to eat it."

"Fine."

I rested my chin on my hands. "Where. Is. The waiter?"

Logan looked around and then motioned with her thumb over her shoulder toward a man who had just appeared from the back of the shop. He had stopped to chat with the man behind the counter. The newcomer had a dish towel slung over his shoulder. His hair was a bit wavy and he kept raking his hand through it, trying to make it behave and stay out of his eyes.

He was wiping the towel over the counter as the two men laughed about some shared story, then his eyes swept the room. When they landed on me, they stopped. Because I had been caught in the act of staring at him, rather blatantly. I did a tiny wave and smiled, implying that we were ready to order.

He seemed a little confused. He glanced behind him to see if there was someone else there that I could have been waving to. When he didn't see anyone he looked back at me and smiled as he approached the table. "Can I help you with something?"

"We were just, um, ready to order. I mean if you're ready." I glanced at Logan, hoping she'd jump in quickly.

Logan smiled up at the waiter. "Sorry, my aunt needs coffee, like now. She's hung way over."

"Logan!"

She shrugged.

I pretended to laugh. "Ha, kids. So funny." The waiter still seemed a bit confused as I told him what we wanted. At one point he grabbed a pen from another table and wrote our order down on the palm of his hand. I guess we were all having a rough morning.

The waiter looked at me and said, "It's weird. I almost always have a notepad on me."

Well sure, I thought. *You're a waiter.*

He held his hand up, confirming our order that was written on it. "I'm Elliott by the way."

"Okay. Thanks, Elliott."

In no time he was back with our food and a whole carafe of coffee. I couldn't quite soak my entire body in it fast enough.

He said, "You can pay Jimmy at the counter when you're finished."

Elliott waved to Jimmy behind the counter, who was laughing at our exchange for some reason. I watched as Elliott walked out the front door and made his way across the square.

While my head was turned Logan stole the bacon off my plate. As she stuffed it in her mouth I said, "Really?"

"What?"

"I thought you weren't eating meat."

She looked at me like I was a crazy person. "Well, yeah, but I didn't mean bacon."

The food was helping to wake me up and so was the coffee. When I went to pay the check I asked if I should leave the tip on the table for the waiter or leave it with Jimmy-behind-the-counter. Jimmy seemed like the kind of guy who would never snake your tips.

He shook his head. "No, we don't have a waiter. You're supposed to just order at the counter."

I was confused. I looked back at our table as if it would explain the phantom waiter to Jimmy.

"But I thought—" I held my hands up in obvious confusion.

"Nah, Eli was just here for breakfast. He was probably trying to be helpful since you didn't seem to know any better." Jimmy shrugged. "Didn't want to embarrass you."

Oh great, so I had accosted some poor customer and demanded that he take our order and wait on us. Mission not accomplished. I was embarrassed.

Logan and I made it safely outside before she started laughing at me. "You're such a dork, Livie."

"You're the one who made me think he was the waiter." I made a conscious decision to change the subject. "What should we do today?" The slightly cooler temperatures of the morning were long gone and the day was heating up. I asked, "Research? Go by the cemetery? Visit the lake?"

Logan looked around. "I don't get it. How come Grandma never talked about her childhood? This town is totally cute." We were walking along the sidewalk looking out over the green lawn of the town square. There were booths for a farmers' market set up on one side and some kids playing soccer on the other. It was, in fact, very cute.

"I don't know. Hopefully we can find out. I was thinking we could go to the library and the local paper. See what they have in their archives."

"It's too nice today to be stuck inside."

"Good point." We weren't planning to scatter her ashes until Georgia could fly down, but we had a lot of information gathering to do before then.

And this was the crux of our adventure. Research. Long hours at a library table reading through years and years of old newspaper articles until your eyes were seeing double. Leafing through countless legal documents until you stumbled on something that actually told you more of the story. Digging up old maps and plats and deeds to track the location of homes and property. I loved the idea of trudging through all of that. But I was absolutely not up for any of it today.

We began walking back toward the inn. "So that leaves us with the cemetery or the lake."

"Do you think it's her parents' grave that she wants to be left on?" She asked me without looking up from the screen of her cell phone as she typed.

"Probably." I didn't really know. But who else would it be? "Who are you texting?"

"My mom. I'm telling her how you're ordering random townsfolk around to do your bidding."

I snatched the phone away from her and threw it in my purse. I was putting her in cell phone time-out. She was not allowed to make fun of me via electronic media.

That same boy from the night before was standing at the va-

let stand in front of the inn in his oversized maroon jacket with
the James Oglethorpe Inn logo embroidered on the pocket. He
was waiting for a car to park or a person in need of an open
door. He seemed pleased to see us. That's when I realized why
Logan had spent so much time on her hair.

"Morning, ma'am." I wished they'd all stop calling me
ma'am. It made me feel very old.

"Good morning."

He asked if we were planning to spend the day shopping. I
glanced around at the few stores in the square. They were ad-
mittedly adorable but it didn't really feel like a shopping Mecca.

I said that we might shop later but asked him if he could tell
me where the cemetery was. Apparently it was a quick drive
and just outside of town. And the lake was even closer as the
town actually sat on it. But to reach the marina, you had to drive
through thirty minutes of winding back roads to get to the other
side of the lake.

I wasn't thrilled about the winding roads to the marina, but I
decided on the lake instead of a visit to the cemetery. It sounded
like a good way for us to spend the day.

I asked, "Would you mind drawing me a map to the marina
then? We just want to spend some time on the lake today."

"Well, if you don't want to rent a boat or anything you don't
need to go all the way to the marina. You're welcome to just use
our dock. We have a path straight down to the water and a floating dock on the lake. It's only three blocks away. It's on a nice
quiet cove for swimming."

The inn should have mentioned in their materials that they
have a waterfront dock. I had no idea the lake was within walking distance. The valet boy's name was Graham, and he gave us

directions to the path down to the lake. He seemed to be a sweet kid who was clearly trying to get Logan's attention. In the few minutes we stood there talking to him he had managed to share with us that he was going to be a junior in the fall, he dropped hints about his football and baseball prowess, and then mentioned that he was hoping to go to Johns Hopkins for college.

Logan and I went to our room to gather our bathing suits and some gear for a nice day on the lake. And then I waited while Logan reapplied her makeup.

"What are you doing?" I asked.

"What?"

"Why are you putting on eyeliner to go swimming?"

She was ignoring me. "Graham seems really nice. He's totally cute. Didn't you think he was cute?"

Well played, Graham, your plan is working. I sort of missed the days when it was just that easy.

THREE

Logan and I walked down the ancient broken sidewalk in the direction of the lake. There were a few old oak trees whose roots had jumped the man-made confines and were spilling out over the edges of the concrete. The little bungalows on both sides of the street were well kept. There were a lot of additions, new roofs, and new second stories. There were flowers in bloom everywhere making the entire block look like an ad out of a real estate brochure. In the distance to the west you could see the blue tinge of the mountain range. The Appalachians were old and gentle mountains. Worn down through time in a way that was emphasized by their blue mist.

The directions Graham had given us led down a pathway between two houses and across a wide back lawn. I felt like a kid cutting across the neighbor's yard. They probably got a lot of traffic through there from guests of the inn but you'd never know it to look at the grass. It was lush and thick and meticulously edged. A gravel path, lined on both sides with rough-cut granite stones, took us through the stand of trees. Then after climbing down a small flight of wooden steps we were on the banks of Lake Huntley.

It was a calm, clear lake. The ragged edges I had seen on the map made more sense down here on the water. The landscape was hilly and rugged with the water filling in the low spots. It looked as if the rains had come one day filling up the basin in the valley and allowing the water to slowly climb up the mountains. The endless fingers snaking off the main body of the lake made up these coves. There was a shadow on this side of the lake, cast from the rise on the opposite bank.

Looking across the lake there were several islands jutting up out of the water here and there. Each one had blue-green water lapping up to a thin strip of red Georgia clay, which was then topped by a mass of green trees, mostly pine and bald cypress.

We walked out onto the floating dock and sat in some of the old Adirondack chairs facing the water. The surface was alive with skimming water bugs and swooping dragonflies. The sound of birds singing was everywhere.

This particular narrow cove in the lake had houses backing up to the water on both sides. All of them had some form of stairway down to the water. Some were wooden, some were made of very elaborate stonework, and some were just crude steps cut into the hillside. At the base of each stair was a dock. There were simple floating platforms like this one and then there were gargantuan two-story boat garages, floating deck mansions on the water to pull your boat into and tuck it in for the night. Those deck mansions were topped with covered decks and outfitted with teak seating groups and custom bars. One of them had a hot tub on one side of the top deck and a diving board off the other.

I said, "This is beautiful." Well, the hot tub was a little tacky, but the lake and trees and rocky outcroppings were lovely. A slight breeze was coming off the water, cooling us considerably, and with it came the faintest sound of a song from a distant radio. I couldn't quite make it out.

The sun had risen high enough in the sky to peek over the opposite ridge and bathe us in light. We both sat with our eyes closed and our heads back, soaking it in.

I said, "You know those houses we walked past are probably from the nineteen thirties or forties originally. They would've been here when my mom was here." I was trying to picture my mother as a young girl walking around the town.

"Where do you think her house was?" Logan asked without opening her eyes.

I shrugged. "Maybe we can find out when we hit the library."

There had been a fire in my mother's childhood home when she was in her twenties. The house and all of its contents burned to the ground one night. This event explained the lack of physical mementos from her childhood, but the lack of stories from her was something we had just had to get used to. Mom never talked about her childhood and after a while we stopped asking.

Logan was putting sunscreen on her face. "In a town this small there must have been a bunch of stories about the fire."

"You're right." She looked pleased. "We'll try that," I said. "And old property deeds. I'm not really sure. Hopefully the librarian will be good at research and willing to help us out."

"It's weird being here, you know?" Logan shielded her eyes and stared out at the lake. "Grandma hated the water."

"What? I never thought she hated it. She just never, I don't know, had an interest in it."

"She told me she hated it."

Sometimes I forgot how close Logan and Mom were. "Really? What did she say?"

Logan remembered a story of the two of them having lunch discussing her summer plans. Logan was trying to choose between a landlocked summer camp and one on a lake in Upstate New York. My mother gave Logan a glimpse, as she did on occasion, of someone we never knew, of the person she had been before she became our mother. She said that there was nothing quite like being on the water. The way it made the dirt smell in the evenings, the way the fog drifted over it on fall mornings, the way the dragonflies hovered over it at sunset in the summer. There was a time, she said, when she didn't feel alive if she didn't dip her toes in every day. "But then Grandma said I should always stay landlocked because nothing can break your heart the way water can."

"What's that supposed to mean? That doesn't even make sense. How can water break your heart? And then why would she want to be buried in the lake?"

Logan threw her hands up, exasperated with my ignorance. "That's what I'm saying. It's totally weird."

We sat there for a long time with our eyes closed, telling each other stories about my mom. Awful things she used to cook. Funny things she used to say. I felt like I needed to tell Logan everything I knew about Mom so that the spirit of Jane Rutledge Hughes could go on living. And there were a lot of stories to tell.

When someone did or said something particularly stupid, instead of arguing back my mom would shake her head very slowly and say, "Bless her heart." As if it wasn't worth getting upset over, clearly God had made that person stupid and all you could do for the ignorant was feel pity and pray for a jump in their IQ. I think that phrase might have meant something else to other people, but my mother had adopted it to mean "dumbass."

The horrific meals she used to cook that always had cream of something soup as a major component. That woman had not grown up learning the finer art of cooking. Maybe that was a byproduct of losing her mother at such an early age; she was no more than ten when her mother had died. But then who cooked for her and her father? So many questions.

"Hey Lo, who'll be the manners gestapo now?"

Logan laughed. "You know my thank-you note after Christmas was late one year so she wrote out the whole thing for me and left it taped to my door. She was all, 'Dear Grandmother, I am absolutely appalled by my lack of courtesy in writing to thank you for my lovely monogrammed stationery.'"

I had always thought of her quirky mannerisms as old-fashioned. Now I was starting to wonder if they weren't just a product of this small town. I had been getting "yes ma'am" and "no ma'am" since we drove in. She was at the heart, after all, a small-town girl. I just had to figure out why she decided to hide it from us.

The sound of very loud footfalls on the wooden staircase behind us startled me. I turned around to see Elliott, the non-waiter from breakfast, making his way toward us. He was carrying a fishing pole. A surprised sort of smile edged across his face as he spotted us on the dock. I could tell he hadn't expected to see us here.

Well, this was embarrassing. I leaned into Logan. "We're being stalked by Opie Taylor."

Logan looked at me. "Who's Opie Taylor?" Then she turned in the direction I was facing and saw Elliott. She waved. *Ugh! Don't wave at him.* I was hoping I wouldn't have to see that guy again after the stunt I pulled at breakfast. Logan lowered her sunglasses. "He's super cute, Livie."

"I think he's a little old for you, Lo."

Logan was whispering now so that Elliott couldn't hear her as he reached the bottom of the stairs. "Gross! Not for me. He's so old. He's like your age."

"Nice, thanks. " I stood up to greet our random visitor.

"Well, hey ladies. What are you doing here?" Elliott said.

"Us? We're just—what are you doing here?" I blurted out. "Why didn't you tell me you weren't a waiter?"

He winced or laughed I wasn't sure. "Sorry. I was just trying to help out. Jimmy's shop can be so confusing." He said it with a fair amount of sarcasm. "And you looked a little bit like you might drop dead without a quick injection of coffee." He winked at Logan and she laughed at me.

Great, now they were in cahoots with the whole "Olivia's an

idiot" thing. As if Logan didn't already think everyone over the age of twenty-five was a moron. I said, "It wasn't . . . You should have said something. I felt awful. I didn't mean to make you serve us."

He stepped out on the floating dock, making it wobble a bit. "It was no problem."

Elliott came over and sat in the chair right next to me. It felt a tad too familiar, him sitting so close.

I asked again, "So what are you doing here?"

He held up the fishing rod like it was pretty obvious what he was doing there. "But please stay. You won't bother me."

I was confused. Who was this guy? "Are you staying at the inn?"

"What? No, why?"

Hang on. I had a bad feeling about this. "Isn't this the inn's dock? Is it open to the town or . . . ?"

"No. This is my family's dock. That's our house. Well, my parents' house." He was pointing up at the house whose yard we had cut through to get here.

I felt like the universe was handing me new and different ways to embarrass myself today. "I am so sorry." I jumped out of my seat. "The boy, Graham, up at the inn sent us down here." I was throwing things into my bag and scrambling to find my sunglasses. Logan was still just sitting there smiling at Elliott. I kept tripping over myself apologizing. I could not get out of there fast enough. "I didn't realize it was a private dock." I felt like this guy Elliott had just walked into his house and found me eating food out of his refrigerator.

"No, you don't have to leave." Elliott stood up. "I'm sorry.

Graham should've explained better. It's fine that you're here. We don't mind at all."

"I don't think so." *Where are my stupid sunglasses?*

Logan put her hand out to him. "I'm Logan."

He shook her hand. "Nice to meet you, Logan."

I mumbled, "I'm sorry. We'll be out of here in just a minute."

Logan pointed to me. "That's my aunt Olivia."

He held his hand out. "Nice to meet you, Olivia." I shook, sheepishly. He kept talking. "Really, please just sit down and we can start this over. I have to be back in the office by two o'clock and I don't want to waste the whole day having you apologize over nothing." He opened his tackle box and began poking through some lures. Without looking up at me he said, "Your sunglasses are on your head. If that's what you're looking for."

I stood there like a disheveled idiot, my hastily packed bag overflowing with my towel and lotion and magazines. I was staring at the back of their two heads waiting for someone to realize the absurdity here and let me off the hook so I could slink away. But no, I was stuck. I dropped my bag on the dock.

Logan was unfazed. "So is Graham your nephew or something?"

"He's my brother actually."

She nodded, tucking away this new bit of information. "Cool."

Elliott looked at me as I sat, defeated and embarrassed, on the edge of the dock. He said, "Can you believe kids still say the word 'cool'?"

Can you believe I've been in this state for less than twenty-four hours and I've managed to make an ass out of myself in front of the same man twice? I put my sunglasses back on to give me some semblance of invisibility and kicked my feet in the water.

While Elliott readied his fishing rod Logan threw me a series of frantic gestures and facial expressions ordering me to find out what I could about Graham from his brother. Elliott cast his line in a smooth arc, landing the lure in the muddy waters bordering the shore. He sat down on the dock next to me and sighed as his feet hit the cool lake. "So, what brings you guys to Tillman?"

I was staring out at the water watching the small ripples the breeze was stirring up. "Actually"—there didn't seem like any other way to put this—"we're here to bury my mother."

"Oh." He ran his hand through his hair. "I am so sorry. And here I am acting like a jackass."

That made me laugh. "I thought I was the jackass."

"No. That was me. I shouldn't have made that joke about—" He cut himself off. "I'm sorry for your loss. Was it recent?"

Elliott the nonwaiter was so genuinely empathetic about my mother that I thought I might cry. "No. It wasn't recent. Actually she passed away last year. She was cremated and we've come to scatter the ashes."

Elliott just nodded his head as he reeled his line back in and cast it out again. We sat there quietly for a long time, swinging our feet in the water in unison. Logan eventually tracked down an inner tube and floated out into the lake. She would glance up at me occasionally and nod in Elliott's direction. She could be really demanding when she wanted to be.

It was fact-finding time. "So . . . Graham's your brother?"

"Yes. He's the baby."

"I'll say. What is he? Sixteen?"

"He just turned seventeen, actually." Elliott opened a small cooler he had with him and handed me a bottle of water.

I took it with a nod of thanks. "That's quite an age difference."

"I know. I'm the oldest of five. I was sixteen when Graham was born. I can't tell you how traumatizing it is to know that your parents are still doing that when you're sixteen."

That made me laugh. "I can imagine. Actually, I don't want to imagine." I lowered my voice conspiratorially. "So listen, I'm not very good at being subtle about these things, but I think Logan would like to know if Graham has a girlfriend."

"Wow, is that the best you've got? That wasn't sneaky at all." He shook his head in mock disapproval.

"I said I wasn't good at this. What should I have done?"

Elliott slowly cranked the wheel on his fishing rod, bringing the glittering lure back to the surface before casting it out again. "You should have done what I did." I held my hands up, questioning. He explained, saying, as if it were obvious, "I don't normally go fishing on a Monday in the middle of the day." I nodded, understanding, as he continued. "Graham sent me out here to find out about her."

"Aw, that's so cute." It did seem odd that he would just show up. I hadn't seen another person on the lake. "But then why were you so surprised to see us out here?"

He looked sort of puzzled that his surprise had registered with me. "Oh, well, I just didn't realize that it would be you guys."

I looked over the water at Logan to make sure she was out of earshot. Her head was kicked back on the edge of the inner tube. It looked like she might be napping out there. She had the right idea being in the water; it was starting to get hot on the dock.

I said, "You cannot tell Graham that she was asking about him."

"Ditto. And no, he doesn't have a girlfriend."

"Excellent, I shall report back to my superior with the information that I so cagily extracted from you without you even being aware of it."

"Yes, you were very sly. I didn't suspect a thing. So what about Logan?"

"No boyfriend. She'll be a junior in the fall, same as Graham."

Elliott took a sandwich from the cooler and handed me half in a way that told me declining the offer would be pointless. It turned out he was a nice guy and very easy to talk to. And yes, I suppose he was good-looking, as Logan had mentioned, but I wasn't really in the habit of noticing that anymore. But I did notice his very slight Southern accent. It was so charming. He had an easy manner and effortless self-confidence. Elliott was simply the kind of guy that you really wanted to like you back.

I was staring out over the water trying to remember how I had gotten here. I was engaged in a conspiracy with some strange man to set my niece up with some boy we didn't even know. It was all a futile flirtation for her really. I mean how long would we even be in Tillman? But I would do it for her because she asked. I would do anything for her. I used to be the fun aunt who always had candy in her purse; now I was the fun aunt with a cute boy in her purse. Wait, that made me feel a little bit pimpy. I took a long sip of the water. Was I the pimp in this scenario or was Elliott?

I could feel Elliott watching me out of the corner of his eye. "What are you thinking?"

I surprised myself by answering honestly. "I'm thinking how odd it is that I'm sitting out here on a dock in the middle of no-where with a stranger setting up my niece." I pulled a tiny piece of crust from the sandwich and tossed it in the lake. "And eating half your lunch."

Elliott laughed and leaned back on his hand. "This is a small town. There are no strangers. Just people you haven't met yet."

I was wondering how my sister, Georgia, would view this turn of events. I turned toward him. "Your family could be a whole clan of axe murderers for all I know."

"Now, why do people always pick the axe? I mean why not machete murderer or hacksaw murderer? It's always the axe."

"Not making the girl alone on the lake feel better."

He laughed and finished his sandwich. "I promise I'm not a murderer. Of any kind."

"And neither is your brother?"

"Not as far as I know."

"Very comforting."

Elliott reeled the line back in. There weren't any nibbles in the middle of the day. He asked, "How long will you two be in town?"

"I'm not really sure." I was watching Logan. Maybe we'd be in town long enough for her to go to a movie with Graham or something. I wondered what kids her age did on dates these days. I probably didn't want to know. "We're just going to be here long enough to do some poking around in Huntley before we scatter my mom's ashes."

Elliott was carefully securing the lure to the hook keeper near the rod's handle. He asked, "Huntley?"

"Yes, she grew up in Huntley. She never talked about it much. Actually, not at all. And it's weird because she wants her ashes scattered here."

Elliott became quiet, in concentration or concern, I wasn't sure.

I continued. "So that's why we came down here. We wanted to see where she grew up. Find out what we could about her life before. Before she met my dad I mean." Our mother's stories only traced back as far as October 1977 when she married our father, Adam Hughes. Anyone could see that she loved him. She did it gently and with a lot of quiet restraint, but fully. He positively adored her. But there was an underlying sadness to our mom that we could never quite figure out. It had to have been bred in her childhood. Losing her mother at an early age must have been devastating. And the complete destruction of her childhood home must have been difficult. But there was something else, some other reason for her refusal to ever speak of the past.

Elliott's eyebrows were furrowed together as if he was struggling to ask a delicate question. "Where exactly in Huntley did she want to be . . . put to rest?" I noticed that people didn't like to use the words "scattered" or "sprinkled" when talking about human remains. But there really was no other good description.

"She requested that half be put over a grave in the cemetery;

we're thinking that's probably her parents, and the other half in Lake Huntley."

"And all you know is that she's from Huntley?"

I nodded.

"So not Tillman? I mean you're here, in Tillman." His voice had gotten very quiet.

"No, it was definitely Huntley. But this is the biggest town in Huntley County so I figured this was the best place to start."

Elliott turned his whole body toward me, getting my full attention. "Olivia, how much do you know about Lake Huntley?"

I shrugged, "Nothing really. Why?"

"Well, it's just that . . . Where do I start? First of all, there are no natural lakes in Georgia. None of any size anyway. All of these lakes were created by dams. You know, for power production or reservoirs. Especially as the population grew after the war. They would dam up a river and create the lakes. Like this one. This lake was built in the nineteen sixties by the TVA, and sometimes, when creating these lakes, property got flooded. This is one of those lakes. Lake Huntley actually has a whole flooded town underneath it."

I pulled my feet out of the water, suddenly feeling terrified of what could be underneath me floating just out of reach.

Elliott put his hand on mine the way someone would when preparing to deliver bad news. "The town of Huntley, Georgia, was flooded when they built the lake. It's not here anymore. It's under there." He pointed to the water. Where Logan was floating. I wanted to yank her out. It seemed as if this were a mass watery grave, a whole town with streets and houses and churches flooded with water and inhabited by fish and mud beneath her floating body. It felt ghostly. As if something could reach up from the murky water and grab her.

"Logan! We need to get going."

Elliott said, "I'm sorry. You didn't know." He was trying to soften the blow. "The town was really small I think. I'm sure the residents were all relocated and any gravesites were moved. I mean I know they moved a church." He glanced over and saw the horrified look on my face and backpedaled. "I think what they flooded was mostly farmland."

I was completely freaked out. Logan was slowly kicking her way toward the dock. Suddenly I was seeing all of the bodies rising up out of the ground in the movie *Poltergeist* and Craig T. Nelson was screaming, *You son of a bitch! You moved the cemetery, but you left the bodies, didn't you?* I really wanted Logan to move faster and get out of the water.

Elliott was still talking, but I couldn't process what he was saying. I interrupted him. "Sorry, I'm just a little bit shocked, that's all. Logan, hurry up!" I was shoving all my things in my bag again. "I just never knew. Never imagined. How . . . I mean how could they do that?"

He shrugged. "It's the government. They can do whatever they want."

"Right. But why—" I just sighed. Now the frantic feeling of fleeing was waning and the urge to cry was creeping in. "Why didn't she ever mention any of it?" Of course that was nothing new. The woman could keep her secrets.

FOUR

"God that is so bizarre." Georgia had said the word "bizarre" three times since our phone call began two minutes ago. Logan and I were in our room at the inn on the speakerphone with her.

I agreed. It was bizarre. And disheartening. Maybe this is why Mom never wanted to talk about her hometown. Because it was underwater.

I sat down on the edge of the bed. "What do we do now?"

Since we had pulled into Tillman I had this feeling that I was walking in my mother's footsteps. That I was just one block away from finding the street where she grew up. The school she attended. The diner where she sat with friends.

Georgia's voice floated up from the phone. "How can they just flood a whole town?"

"I don't know. Apparently it was a really small town."

Georgia asked, "What does the lake look like again?" I think she was feeling a little bit left out now that our adventure had taken on a murky-depths quality. I mean a drowned town? That's a peculiar turn of events.

Logan had already showered and changed into clothes for dinner. I asked her to go downstairs and find out about the Internet access in the inn.

Her hair was still damp and was at least an hour away from being ramrod straight and she didn't have any makeup on. Of course she didn't need any makeup and when she was caked in it I thought she looked a little bit silly. But she was busy reminding the world that she was *almost* fifteen and would be a junior in high school in the fall. It took a lot of smoke and mirrors and subterfuge to make the world see you the way you wanted them to. It had always been difficult for Logan to look like her peers. She had one of those late summer birthdays that people were always using as an excuse to hold their kids back in school. But Logan had started kindergarten on time, one week after turning five. Then she skipped the second grade. Now she was about two years younger than most of her classmates.

Logan whined about having to go to the lobby unpolished but finally gave in and left the room. The disembodied voice of Georgia barked at me. "Take me off speaker, Livie."

"Okay, you're off. What's up?"

"Is Lo okay down there? Are you keeping an eye on her? Does she want to come home?"

"Georgia, we've been here for like five minutes. She's fine; she hasn't said a word about home." I knew when total silence followed that remark that it had been a mistake. I quickly added, "I mean she seemed a little blue last night. I think she may be a little homesick, but she's putting on a brave face." I wouldn't call that last bit a lie, more like an exaggeration.

Georgia sounded very small. "Oh, well good. I hope she's having fun." Those two could barely get through a conversation without screaming and yet Georgia was heartbroken by her absence. Why are relationships between mothers and daughters always so complicated?

The door opened. It was Logan. "I've got to hang up, Gigi. Lo just got back and I have to shower before she decides she wants to straighten her hair for six hours in the bathroom."

Logan stuck her tongue out at me as I hung up the phone. Apparently the only place to get Internet service was the lobby.

I suggested, "How about we just eat dinner downstairs tonight and then set up our mobile HQ in the lobby?"

"Our what?" Logan's raised eyebrows should have told me not to elaborate for fear of sounding foolish.

I hardly ever take heed of the raised eyebrows. "Our HQ! Our headquarters. We can bring our laptops and notebooks and good pens to take notes and do research about the town and the lake."

Logan was laughing at me. "You are such a dork, Aunt Liv. Good pens?"

She could act like I was a loser for wanting to dig in right away and find out more about Huntley but she was a fourteen-year-old girl who just found out she was staying on the banks of an underwater town. That had a cool factor that she couldn't ignore. It was, in her words, pretty trippy.

The lobby of the James Oglethorpe Inn was not exactly what one would expect to find in an early-nineteenth-century building. Especially one with such an interesting provenance. The building was originally built as a tavern and inn in the mid-1800s and then had served as a hospital and morgue for several years during the Civil War. There was even supposed to be the ghost of a Confederate soldier wandering around the third floor somewhere looking for his boots. I was making a point of avoiding the third floor.

Over the years the building had also served as a post office, an office building, and then finally had gone back to the inn it was originally intended to be.

I had been expecting overstuffed chintz furniture and lace curtains with the obligatory curio cabinet filled with Civil War memorabilia. And maybe for the floor to be covered in needlepoint rugs and the walls filled with mounted deer heads and trout.

Instead it was stylish, elegant, and modern. Not in a cold way, but in a very comfortable yet lush way. The Belgian linen couches and well-worn saddle leather armchairs cuddled up to the fireplace. The floors were a beautiful distressed wide-plank pine with seating areas corralled by thick cream squares of carpet. The walls were a mottled Venetian plaster in a deep rich caramel color.

Logan and I made our way to the dining room and were seated at a table near the window. The triple-hung window had the old pulley and weight system in the wall and the glass was warped and wavy.

I pointed it out to Logan. "Do you see how the glass has

slowly, over time, melted down slightly and become thicker at the bottom of each pane?"

She was not impressed. "Yeah, 'cause that old glass is more like a liquid. You told me that before." She was perusing the menu.

I ran my finger over the glass. It's strange to think of something that appeared to be solid like this as actually being a liquid, but that's what it was. A very thick, very slow-moving liquid. I was starting to think of my mother like that. She seemed solid. She seemed to be exactly what you saw. But now as I looked back at her I realized that she was morphing before my eyes. Why did she want to come home again after she died? She wasn't what I thought she was. Then what was she? Who was she? Maybe she was the same, but it was my perception of her that was changing.

The waiter was standing there staring at me. I hadn't heard him pop up. We ordered our food and then chatted about the strange reality of mom's hometown being underwater.

I was getting anxious about digging into the history of the place. "I wish the library was open late. We could go there to research." I loved—I mean *loved*—starting a new research project. At first the wedding planning had started that way. I had a new notebook and a new three-ring binder. I had torn pictures of dresses and cakes and flowers out of magazines and filed them all appropriately. I had taken notes from caterers and event facilities and florists. I was having a ball planning a big party, picking out favors, deciding on color schemes. In all that time doing party planning I hadn't given much thought to the fact that an actual marriage was the inevitable conclusion of the festivities.

It was all so frantic and rushed. Leo had a very small and nonnegotiable window in his work schedule where we could fit in time off for a honeymoon. Between his schedule and mine, finding the perfect wedding day was a little bit like negotiating the moon landing. Then my mother got sick and it all fell apart. We put the planning and the wedding on hold.

My mother's illness was quick, not the drawn-out heart failure that my father endured, but a swift painful cancer. Stomach cancer.

I would never forget the look on her face when we went to the doctor to hear the results of the biopsy. Georgia was in the chair on my mom's left and I was on her right. The three of us sat silently staring ahead, afraid to make too much noise or touch anything in the doctor's office, as if our behavior while we waited could somehow impact her diagnosis.

Georgia was reading through the doctor's pedigree on the wall as I browsed the obligatory family photos on his desk. His children were painfully ugly. Pug-nosed, fish lipped, and mousy haired. They looked alarmingly like our family's old French bulldog, Chloe. I pointed at the line of photos and nudged Georgia. She gave me her "shut up this is serious" face.

My mother turned to where I was pointing and said, "Oh dear, that poor man. Those children have been absolutely beaten to death with the ugly stick."

We couldn't stop laughing. Especially because we knew we shouldn't be laughing. Once you try to contain it, it just bursts out of you. When the doctor came in he thought we were crying and handed us a box of tissues.

Once we got ourselves under control he told us the results of the biopsy. Georgia started crying for real and I started asking him about the next course of action. My mother was utterly calm. Almost like she was looking death in the eye and saying, *Thank God. What the hell took you so long?*

She smiled and stood up, thanking him for his time, and then announced that she wanted us to go out for a nice lunch. She refused to talk to the surgeon or the radiologist about treatment options, saying she wouldn't waste her time with that nonsense. Her husband was already gone and she didn't intend to make her daughters go through several more years watching a parent get weaker. She only did pain management with her general physician, and even that she kept to a minimum. As if suffering through the pain was part of her necessary final journey.

Maybe, if we could find out enough about her childhood, I would finally understand why she acted the way she did at the end. So ready to die and end this life. To me she was an amazing, complex, loving mother. I just couldn't understand why it was so easy for her to accept her fate and leave us. I needed to be careful that I didn't forget who she was to me while I tried to figure out who she was before me.

Logan was thinking back to my comment earlier. "Why do you need a library?"

I took all of the abandoned beets off her salad plate and added them to mine. "So we can look things up like maps and old newspaper accounts of the town being flooded."

"Jeez, you can find all of that online."

"You don't even remember a world before Google."

"There was a world before Google?" She teased.

"Be nice to me or I won't tell you anything else that I learned about Graham."

She gave me a snide look that reminded me so much of her mother that I had to smile. Why do we always turn into our mother?

After dinner we settled into a very cozy corner of the lobby and each started our laptops to begin searching. I ordered a cocktail, which Logan made a point to comment on.

I could see Mrs. Chatham, the innkeeper, sitting at the bar talking to an older gentleman. He seemed to be holding court at his perch on the bar. People were obviously eager to have an audience with him, so Mrs. Chatham didn't stay with him long.

While I was glancing up to see whom he would receive next, Mrs. Chatham materialized right next to me. "I have been meaning to come meet you. My name's Mrs. Chatham. We are so pleased to have you here at the inn."

Mrs. Chatham made me believe that she was genuinely thrilled to have us here. I wondered if she meant it or if it was just her job as a hostess to be polite.

I shook her hand. "It's nice to meet you. I'm Olivia and this is my niece, Logan." Mrs. Chatham sat down with us. I said quite sincerely, "Your inn is lovely."

She crossed her legs and leaned in like we were old friends. "Thank you so much! We just did the renovation last year, and I really thought it'd be the end of me." She looked at Logan and said, "I have never met a girl named Logan before." Then Mrs. Chatham addressed the next comment to me. "You know, because Logan is a family name. But I guess people just don't hold to that like they used to."

"My sister always liked the name so . . ." I wondered what it meant for something to be a family name. Whose family? I was about to ask her when she turned her charms on Logan.

"Well, you're such a beautiful girl you can have any name your mother wants you to have." Mrs. Chatham was smiling and shaking her head at Logan. "I mean look at that skin. Like silk. My daughter had such a hard time at your age with her skin." She sighed, "Bless her heart."

Logan and I looked at each other and smiled. *Bless her heart.* It was the exact same tone and inflection my mother used to use.

There was no stopping Mrs. Chatham. "So what are you two doing in town? Are you shopping or just visiting?" Where exactly did all these people think we were shopping around here?

"We're just visiting. My mother is from"—I paused for a second not wanting to say "the town under the lake" then continued—"around here. So Logan and I just wanted to come see it for ourselves."

"Well, isn't that nice. Is she anyone I would know?"

It had never occurred to me that there could still be people living here that had known my mother. But Mrs. Chatham looked to be about the same age as my mom. I held my breath for just a second as I said, "Her maiden name was Jane Rutledge."

"Was? Has she passed?" When I nodded, she sighed a little and put her hand on her heart. We accepted her sincere condolences. She seemed legitimately distressed that my mother had died. She was twisting her pearls and tugging at the sleeves of her twinset while knitting her brows together and resting her hand on my knee. She really felt our pain. That woman had a gift.

She gave one last consolatory pat on my leg and then composed herself. "I didn't know her, but you must be one of the Huntley Rutledges."

"I'm not sure exactly. I guess that's what we're here to find out." It occurred to me in an instant how much easier it would be to find out about my mom's past if we could meet the people who had known her. And then, just as quickly, that there may not be anyone left from Huntley to ask.

Mrs. Chatham was thrilled at the prospect of some old family bloodline returning to its roots. "Isn't that exciting? You'll have to let me know everything you discover. I'm not sure if there's anyone around here who remembers having Rutledges among us."

Logan finally chimed in. "Excuse me, what did you mean when you said that Logan is a family name?"

Well, that sent Mrs. Rutherford Chatham into a sort of fascinating lecture about how one should name their children. Apparently there were a lot of rules that I had never heard before regarding naming a child.

Logan and I sat patiently as she explained lineage and first-borns and monograms. "One should never ever use the husband's name for a monogram. Good Lord, I don't know who decided to start mixing up the names. That just undoes me. Traditions are traditions and are there for a reason." As she said that I noticed the monograms on the pillows and napkins in the lobby and bar area and asked her about them.

"Those are the initials of Lady Elizabeth Wright, James Oglethorpe's wife. Like I said, always use the woman's initials. Everything in the house belongs to the woman." She pointed at Logan. "You remember that."

That sounded like a lot of baggage. I was starting to get that prickly feeling again about not wanting to get married. It occurred to me that if I had been home on Saturday instead of the office I could have intercepted that call from the chapel and politely declined the time slot. I had a fresh wave of loathing for my job.

One didn't have to be very present while Mrs. Chatham was speaking; she didn't require much in the way of response. At the moment she was retelling the family tree of nearly everyone in town. It seemed as if everyone was knotted together in one way or another as she went through the names. Coming from the transient world of DC, I couldn't help but wonder if it was hard for people in this small town to always be surrounded by the same families.

I was having a hard time keeping up with Mrs. Chatham as she explained the pedigree of someone named "the fourth."

"It's a shame," she said wistfully. "Of course people used to get married so much earlier and have babies so much earlier. It gave you a better shot at the older generation still being alive when the great-grandbabies came. I think Jimmy may be the only fourth left in town."

I was trying to give the impression that I was following her. "Mm hmm, Jimmy? The fourth?"

"The story goes that Jimmy's mother, Sarah, was in labor in one room and her husband's grandfather was dying in the next room, so Dr. Mathews was running back and forth trying to get Jimmy to go ahead and be born while trying his best to keep that old man from dying."

I finished my drink, careful to put the empty glass on a

coaster. "That's awful. Although I suppose there's a lot to be said for living a long life and—"

"Well, you know to be named a fourth, James Tillman Calhoun *the fourth*, he had to be born while James Tillman Calhoun *the first* was still alive."

Logan piped up. "Who makes up these rules?"

But Mrs. Chatham was patently ignoring questions she deemed unworthy of an answer. She was on a personal mission to impart some tiny bit of proper naming pedigree to us poor ignorant souls.

She waved her hand in the general direction of the front door and the town square beyond it. "You probably met Jimmy at the coffee shop."

Oh my gosh, I actually knew someone in her story. "We did meet Jimmy. He doesn't seem like a *fourth*." I had a very clear mental image of Thurston Howell the third in my mind when I heard "the fourth" and Jimmy—that skinny, bearded man with an easy smile and an arm full of tattoos who was laughing at me in the coffee shop—did not seem like he belonged in an ascot with Lovey on his arm.

Mrs. Chatham said, "No? Well, looks can fool you. Jimmy owns half that block. Maybe the whole block." She laughed at her own joke.

She wished us luck on our search for the Rutledge family line and then glanced over her shoulder at the gentleman at the bar who was surrounded by a pack of men in suits. There was clearly something about him she found distasteful. She leaned in to us and said pointedly, "Names are important. Name and family are the only things a person can't buy."

I wasn't sure what she meant by that but then again I wasn't sure of much about this place. It was a town of contradictions. The lake was hiding a town, the bearded slacker behind the coffee counter was James Snooty Something the fourth and owned a huge chunk of the town, and we outsiders may be the long-lost Huntley Rutledges. Whatever that meant.

We said our good-nights to her and she made us promise we would call on her if we needed anything. I didn't tell her about scattering the ashes or that most of what we were looking for was probably under a whole lot of water.

Logan and I packed up our things to head up to the room. I checked the time to make sure it wasn't too late and then I called Leo. I hadn't been able to get hold of him all day.

As soon as he answered I knew I'd woken him up. I practically whispered, "Hey, it's me. I'm sorry. You're asleep. I'll call you in the morning."

I could hear Leo rubbing his face. "No, it's fine. How's it going?"

"Good, sort of. Maybe weird is a better answer. It turns out the town of Huntley is underneath the lake. They drowned the town so it's not even here anymore."

"Hmm. That is weird." He sounded unimpressed. "When are you sprinkling the ashes?" I heard him yawn. He probably wanted an exact time and date that he could put into his schedule and then check off once the chore was finished. The thought irritated me.

"I'm not sure, but I'll let you know. Go back to sleep; we can talk tomorrow." I was absentmindedly following Logan up the stairs.

"Okay, 'night."

I disconnected the call and found myself staring at the phone. I'm not sure why. We got into the room and I threw my phone into my open suitcase.

Logan watched my beloved cell phone fly precariously through the air and when it landed she gave me a knowing look. "Are you and Leo fighting?"

"No, we don't fight."

"Maybe you should start."

I ignored that. How could picking a fight help matters? She and I got ready for bed and then climbed into the tall four-poster queens. I sighed and kicked my foot out so that it wasn't being trapped by the sheet.

"What?" Logan asked me.

"What d'you mean?"

"You did that moany thing. My mom does it when she's thinking about something."

"I think I'm just frustrated about today. I'm beginning to realize just how much we don't know. If that makes sense."

"What do you mean! We found out there's a super creepy underwater town, and that Grandma got all of her weird stuff from growing up here. I mean the 'bless her heart' thing and the monograms all over the place? These people put their letters on anything that sits still. They are totally wiggy about names." She yawned. "I bet that's why she named my mom Georgia, 'cause it's where she was from."

"I wonder why she named me Olivia?"

Logan shrugged. "Maybe we'll find out tomorrow."

"Maybe. Good-night, Lugnut."

" 'Night, Livie."

All night I had dreams of my mother. She was swimming in the dark lake late at night. I was trying to follow her but she kept turning a corner into one of those jagged coves, going just out of sight. I could see the splashes of water being kicked up by her feet and sparkling in the reflection of the moonlight. Then the dream changed and I was in a boat chasing her and I was finally catching up.

FIVE

I woke up to the realization that it was Tuesday, a workday, and I was not on my way to work. That's a pretty great Tuesday. I tossed a pillow onto the sleeping lump in the next bed. It moaned. "Hey, Logan. There's no work today!"

"Ibmsleepingoway."

"What?"

Logan sat up in a huff. "I said I'm sleeping. Go. Away." She put the pillow over her face and went back to sleep.

Not that a teenage girl isn't a little slice of joy in the mornings, but I decided to start my day without her. I got ready quickly and then headed down to Viscount James Something the fourth's coffee shop to redeem myself after the whole waiter fiasco of the day before. I went straight to the counter to place my order and then waited there like a local until the food was ready. I cleared all of my work e-mails and returned a few calls while I was standing there.

Jimmy passed my order across the counter and winked as he said "good girl" for figuring out how it was supposed to work.

I decided that we needed to hit the cemetery at some point and at least see if they had any conditions regarding the deposit of my mother. I called Huntley Memorial Gardens while I ate my breakfast. The sweet woman who answered the phone had such a thick country accent that we had a hard time communicating. She didn't really understand what I was asking for and I didn't really understand her answers. This was a conversation that would need to take place face-to-face, so I thanked her for her help and hung up.

I went back up to the counter to get some food to take to Logan. While I waited I asked Jimmy about the library and the local paper. The library wouldn't open until eleven o'clock, so he told me where the newspaper office was as he handed me the to-go bag. There weren't quite as many people out and about in the square this morning. Hazy rays of sunshine were breaking through the trees overhead and there were distant sounds of sprinklers bursting to life.

I followed the directions Jimmy had given me across the dewy grass to the other side of the square. The newspaper's office was located in an old house that must have been rezoned at some point as a commercial building. I was hoping the archives were digital because there was no way they could store much in the way of paper copies in that small building.

The old, white house had a tiny front patch of a lawn with a wrought-iron post announcing that this was the *Tillman Free Press*. The post was dripping in gnarled vines of star jasmine to the point where you could barely read the words on the sign.

To my great surprise Elliott was sitting in a rocking chair on the front porch of the small office with his feet propped up on the porch rail typing away on a laptop. His eyes never left the computer screen as I climbed up the stairs, but a small playful smile appeared on the side of his face.

I didn't bother trying to hide the fact that I was surprised to see him. "What are you doing here?"

He finished typing something and then looked up at me, amused. "Every time you see me you ask me why I'm here. You do realize that I live here, right?"

"Sorry, that did sound rude. I'm just surprised to see you again." I peeked through the window to see if there was anyone official looking inside that I could speak with. I could hear a phone ringing incessantly but no one seemed to be around to answer it. "Do you know when someone from the paper will be in?"

Elliott closed the lid to his laptop. "Yes, right now. I'm the paper."

"You're the what?"

"I am the paper. I own the newspaper."

"Oh, you do? That's weird, although I guess that explains what you're doing here."

He looked at me with a sort of delighted confusion. "Do you say everything that pops into your head the second it shows up there?"

I sighed. "I do." I sat down on the rocking chair next to him. "It's a really bad habit. I have no filter. Sorry."

"Actually, I find it incredibly refreshing."

The phone began ringing again. I waited for a moment, thinking he would rush in there to pick it up, but instead he just rubbed his face and sort of grumbled. I pointed toward the phone. "Aren't you going to answer that?"

"No." We waited for the ringing to stop before he spoke again. "So how are you today? I mean about everything? The lake and Huntley."

"Okay, I guess. It wasn't really what I was expecting to find." I shrugged because there wasn't anything else I could say about it.

"Holy drowned town, Batman."

That made me laugh. "Exactly. That's why I'm here. I was hoping Logan and I could go through the newspaper archives to see if we can start doing some research about the town and my mom."

"Sure. I'd be glad to help you. Do you know what you're looking for?"

"No, not really. I just need to start looking." The phone started again. My eyebrows rose at him, questioning.

He crossed his arms in a tight knot and pursed his lips, holding his ground. "I'm not supposed to be in the office today, which she knows, so I couldn't possibly answer that. And my cell phone doesn't work out here. I am legitimately and innocently unavailable."

"Oh, got it. Girl trouble. Women love it when you avoid their calls." I pointed back and forth between the office and his rocking chair. "Nicely done." The racket finally stopped. She'd given up, whoever she was.

Elliott gave me an exasperated look. "Do you want my help or not?"

"Yes, I do want your help. I won't make any more comments about the way you're treating your lady friend." I changed the subject. "So how long have you been the official face of the *Tillman Free Press*?"

"We just had our second anniversary."

Oh no, they were a brand-new publication. There may not be any archives to go through. I didn't want to waste his time. "The paper's brand-new then. So, uh . . . what were you doing before you started it?"

"I didn't start it. I just reopened it. So yes, there are archives that you can access." *Busted*. He leaned back in the chair. "I was an engineer for years but just decided it wasn't for me."

"Really? That's funny. I work for an engineering firm." That was another thing that had snuck up on me out of nowhere and imposed its squatter's rights on my life.

When I finished my undergraduate degree in art history, I imagined myself in the depths of some museum somewhere restoring great works of art. Probably in one of the smaller more remote cities of Eastern Europe, because I was oh so tragically hip. Or maybe teaching? I thought I could work at the university with my mother, mentoring brilliant but misguided youths. She in the history department, me in the art department. But then again I could barely manage my niece and I had known her for her whole life. And Logan could be a real pain in the ass. Maybe mentoring wasn't really up my alley.

But there would definitely be coffee. In my mind I was always holding a steaming mug of coffee while inspiring the minds of today's youth or clearing away the dust from long-forgotten masterpieces. Hopefully I was someplace cold while OD'ing on all this fantasy coffee.

Fantasy was a good word for it because a BA in art history roughly translated into "unemployable, slightly pretentious asshole."

After graduating I worked in a coffee shop for almost a year, which was not nearly as mind-altering as one would expect. Then I entered law school. I figured if I was going to be an asshole I might as well get paid for it.

My first summer break during law school found me interning with a large international construction firm. I was assigned to the Due Diligence Department. It was mind-numbingly boring work researching various codes and ordinances particular to the local area in which a new building was being constructed. They always needed the information yesterday and the pace was insane. And I was really, really good at it. At the end of the summer they offered me a job making a stupid amount of money so I packed my soul into a little shoebox, along with my BA diploma and one year of law school, and tucked them all under my bed. Then I got myself a fancy new wardrobe and a lease on a Range Rover. Full asshole transformation complete.

That had been almost ten years ago and although I had moved up through the department the only place left to go was the department head. And since that position was currently held by the devil, and the devil wouldn't die, I was pretty much out of options in that particular firm.

Elliott said, "I was a structural engineer. What about you?"

"I'm in due diligence with a construction firm in DC. I think I've grown to hate it. What made you decide to leave?"

"It just wasn't what I wanted to be doing, the work wasn't interesting anymore, and I hated the deadlines. And I was living in Chicago, so far away from my family." He shrugged not wanting to elaborate. "I don't know. The pace of life was just wrong for me. I was miserable." I felt like he was channeling my reality at the moment.

"But how did you just up and walk away and then do"—I waved my hands at the house that the newspaper inhabited— "something completely different?" I wasn't being polite; I really wanted to know how one did that. I was looking for a road map.

He started slowly rocking his chair. "It wasn't easy."

We talked for over an hour sitting there rocking on his porch. Everything he said about being miserable with the deadlines and the inconsequential work hit a little too close to home. The way he hated Sundays because they were always followed by a Monday, and a job that you hate will always destroy a Sunday. The way his boss would make ridiculous demands and then never acknowledge his team when they were able, somehow, to pull it off. The way the job was intensely boring. I wondered if Ms. Missed Call was playing a role in his discontent but I managed to stop myself before asking him. I did ask him why the newspaper though. Had he always wanted to run a paper? Be a journalist?

He kind of laughed. "No. I don't see myself as a journalist. I'm just . . ." He thought for a second trying to put into words what he thought his role was. "I guess I just think a town needs a paper. A community has so many small things that happen that need to be reported and no one else will do it. Like the baseball scores. Or the club meetings, the little accomplishments, the births, and deaths, and marriages. It's important for the people of the community to feel connected to each other and that's the role I think we play. We try to broaden horizons a bit beyond just this little town too. I don't know. Maybe it gives the kids an idea of what else is out there." He shook his head at that. "Although with the Internet it's so much easier. I don't think kids feel as isolated today as we did."

"Plus they can access porn whenever they want."

Elliott laughed out loud. "Literally no filter. It just falls out of your mouth." He shook his head, amused. "So yeah, other than porn we pretty much cover the life around here. Someone had to do it. The paper had been out of print for a few years before I came back and opened it up again."

Thinking back on all of the history in this town reminded me of something that Mrs. Chatham had said. "Do you know anyone around here named Rutledge?"

He nodded. "The Huntley Rutledges?"

"You're the second person that has referred to them as the Huntley Rutledges. What does that mean?"

"They were an old family in the area, some of the founders. There's even a Rutledge Reading Room at our club. I don't think there are any of them left, though."

"Actually, we're back. My mom was a Rutledge."

He ran his hand through his hair then he looked at me. "Really, now that's interesting. We love articles about the old families. Maybe I can help you dig up some family history and we could see if there's a story there."

"You mean for the paper?"

"I wouldn't print anything without your permission, of course."

My cell phone pinged. It was a text from Logan: *can u get me food*

I showed the screen to Elliott. He said, "It drives me nuts the way they write when they're texting. All those abbreviations and lack of punctuation."

I teased Elliott as I typed a note back to her. "Okay Grandpa. Do you have a hard time keeping those whippersnappers off your lawn too?"

Elliott tilted my rocking chair back hard and I almost fell over. "Whoa!" I laughed. "Quit it."

Logan sent me her response: *can cu from here. STARVING! stop flirting w/E.*

Elliott said, "You know I'm right. What did she write this time?" He tried to lean over to see the text but I shut the phone off quickly to hide the message from him. She was being ridiculous.

"Apparently she's starving and she can see me from the inn holding this bag of food. I better get going." I stood up. "So, can Logan and I come back to start researching? You really don't mind?"

"I don't mind at all." He seemed to be thinking of something. "Actually, let's meet at the library. They open at eleven and their computers are faster than mine."

I stood up. "And your cell phone doesn't work there?"

"Something like that."

"Sounds good. And thanks again for helping us with this."

"You're welcome." He looked a little guilty. "Although, I'm actually being a little selfish. Anything about the drowned town, especially involving one of the founding families, is always so interesting." His voice took on a tone of apology. "It sells papers."

My family, and especially my mother, were a lot of things, but interesting was never really one of them. "Well then, mutually advantageous research." I held my hand out and he shook it.

Elliott said, "Besides, I feel responsible since I was the one who broke the news to you about the lake. You're kind of my problem now."

I laughed. "Sorry about that. I can be a lot of trouble."

"That's the impression that I'm getting." He teased. "See you in a bit."

SIX

Logan and I got to the library as soon as it opened and Elliott was already there sitting at a long table in front of a laptop computer. I set up my stash across from him and organized everything around my seat to my very specific liking. I looked up and saw that Elliott and Logan were staring at me.

"What?" I asked.

They both started laughing. It's not like I had researcher's OCD or anything. So I had a few pens and some paper? Maybe a notebook, with some pockets and dividers. I didn't pull out a label maker or anything.

Elliott poked at the pens, unsettling their straight line. "Do you ever get a wild hair and write outside the lines?"

"Oh okay, mocking from the guy who writes notes on his hand." I lined the pens back up.

Where was the old librarian saying shush when you needed her? This particular librarian, whose name was Bitsy—yes, Bitsy, swear to God—couldn't have been older than thirty and never once told either one of them to shush. In fact, at the moment she was shouting directions about the wireless printer from her desk at the front of the room.

Logan plopped down next to me and booted up her laptop. "I think we should look for stuff about the lake first, right? I mean that's just like so weird that there's all that stuff under there. Graham said there's an old church steeple from the town that's still floating around in the lake."

I glanced over at her. "When did you talk to Graham?" She ignored me.

Elliott shook his head. "That thing sank to the bottom years ago. It's become a bit of a local legend and ghost story. Kids on the lake say they can hear the bells ringing at night."

I shuddered involuntarily at the thought of some haunted church steeple floating around the water ringing its bells. Or even worse, sitting at the bottom of the dark lake looking up at you through the silty, green water.

Logan and I searched the Internet for information while Elliott dug into the newspaper archives. After a few hours we had an emerging picture of the lake and its formation.

In the 1930s Franklin Roosevelt created the Tennessee Valley Authority as part of the New Deal. The TVA was tasked to develop solutions to problems occurring down the length of the Tennessee River valley. They were innovative in finding new ways to deal with power production, river navigation, and flood control.

The creation of man-made lakes along the river and its tributaries provided jobs in that desperate time of the Depression. The dams also provided power production and ushered a vast number of people into the modern world with electricity.

The dam at Lake Huntley was the last one built before the TVA switched their efforts to nuclear power plants. Poor Huntley, the last kill before the carnivore went vegetarian.

In 1963 the dam was approved and construction began on the diversion tunnels. There were some poignant photographs of the town of Huntley after it had been abandoned. Although to call it a town was a bit of an insult to the word. Huntley was merely a crossroads with six or seven buildings near the intersection. The largest was a hardware store, which seemed to double as the town's soda fountain and possibly the post office. There were also two churches and an old storefront that looked like a dress shop. A few other buildings rounded out the tiny town but we couldn't make out what they had been.

In the black-and-white photos the signage was being taken down, and in the foreground one of the wooden churches had been jacked up onto a flatbed truck and was in the process of being moved. In the next set of images the church was gone, carted off somewhere, and the few buildings that remained had been razed. The only proof of their existence being the concrete foundations left behind. I wondered where that other church had been, the one that wasn't torn down so that its steeple could haunt the lakefront. It wasn't in any of the pictures we found of the town.

I held up the printouts of the photos of Huntley side by side. Before and after. I hated to admit it, but there didn't seem to be much lost. Huntley wasn't much of a town.

I had a long queue of pictures spooling out of the printer and Elliott went to pick them up for me. After about the fifth print he started laughing.

"What?" I asked.

He held up the pictures, all of them black-and-white images of the dam, the diversion tunnels, the water slowly filling in the valley. "You're being kinda weird about the lake."

I went over and snatched the papers from his hand. "I am not." Then I hit him on the shoulder with the stack. "You have to admit it's very odd. I feel like I can't wrap my head around it, and it's so creepy." I peered down at the pictures. "It would be so strange to watch your home being gobbled up by water."

I held up one of the oldest photos. It was taken inside the Huntley General Store in the late 1930s. There were three men in the photo standing in front of the rows of merchandise. They had waxed mustaches and bow ties and their hair was parted and greased right down the center of their heads. One man was standing on the middle rung of a tall wooden ladder. There were rows upon rows of glass jars holding all manner of who knows what lining the walls. The way the men stood—solitary, staring into the camera—was haunting.

When I looked at the image I could imagine a wall of water exploding into the center of town, knocking the men off their feet and washing them down the length of the valley. Turning them over and over in the rapids until they could no longer stand it and they simply let go. Drowned. I imagined each parcel and jar and sack being tossed and thrown by the force of the raging water. Rushing downstream and being slammed and battered until it all came to rest at some distant location. Mismatched and wrecked. Shoes hanging from tree limbs. Grain sacks drained of their contents and lapping at the shore of the newly created lake. Broken shards of glass twinkling in the sun on the granite outcroppings in the water.

I knew that none of this had happened. I had a thirty-four-page report from the TVA listing the measures taken to clear the town of all of its people and contents. I had an article in the local newspaper describing the warning sirens that blew every fifteen minutes for half a day before they shut down the diversion tunnels and began to fill the reservoir and then continued to sound sporadically throughout the summer. I had pictures of the water very slowly and methodically climbing up the wall of the mountains over a series of eighteen months.

But when I saw the pictures of the old town of Huntley, as it was, it all appeared in my mind to happen in an instant. With no warning and no measures in place to outrun it.

Logan found some information online in a blog about recreational lake diving. There was a whole group of hobbyists who went to these man-made lakes to scuba dive on the ruins of the towns. I had no idea there were so many drowned towns out there. There were pictures of one that had an entire cemetery still intact underwater. I wondered why the people had chosen to leave it there and not move it when the water came.

The blog showed a series of pictures of the rows of tombstones, covered in moss. Seeing the fish swimming around the gravesite was a bit disturbing.

The marina on Lake Huntley even offered diving tours. There were some pictures posted of one of their dives. They were grainy images of the murky, muddy bottom of the lake.

There was a shot of those same building foundations we had seen before they had been drowned. The now-underwater concrete was covered with muck and moss. It sent a chill down my spine. There was a picture of a few tree stumps and even one half-buried truck that had been abandoned. It was hard to see much in the photos. They were dark and had that distorted uniform green quality of underwater pictures. But just knowing that all of this was still sitting there—motionless, drowned under the waters of Lake Huntley—was eerie.

Elliott found photographs of the lake as it was being filled after the construction of the dam was completed. The photographer had been standing on a rise shooting images of the water as it methodically crept up the hillside. You could track the progress of the water as the hillside slowly sank beneath the surface. The images seemed to be taken over a series of months. The leaves were changing color, and then dropping from the limbs, marking the passage of time.

There was one last picture in the set. Apparently whoever was documenting the rising water had at one point turned the camera around on the crowd surrounding him. There was a large group of people gathered there, perhaps to watch the water flood the valley. There were picnickers on blankets and some were sitting on those woven vinyl patio chairs from the sixties. There were small children running around the green lawn and a huge barbeque pit was set up on one side, which trailed a steady stream of gray smoke. In the background, at the crest of the hill, was a big white house. I squinted my eyes to try and get a better view of it but it was out of the depth of field and slightly out of focus.

There was something familiar about that house.

I showed Elliott the picture. "Do you know where this house is?"

He stared at it for a long time. "I'm not sure. I don't think so, but something about it . . . Huh. I can't put my finger on it. Something's familiar. Let me go ask Bitsy."

I closed my eyes and tried to rack my brain about where I had seen that house. Maybe we had driven by it on the way through town. Or maybe I had seen a photo of it earlier in the day. But I just felt like that wasn't it.

I looked at the picture again: at the two-story porch with the white railings and the vines creeping up all sides of it. There were blurry images of people standing on the second-floor balcony leaning on their arms and looking out over the lawn. The dormer windows lining the roof were open to catch the breeze. I looked down at the porch again. The way the people were leaning on the rail . . .

"That's it!" I shouted and Logan jumped. "This was Mom's house!"

Logan rushed over and looked over my shoulder. "How can you tell? We don't have any pictures of her house."

Elliott had heard me shout and was back standing behind me looking at the photo with us. I said, "There is one. Sort of. That one picture she had of her and her parents when she was little. And they were all leaning on the rail of the porch. I would swear this is the same one."

Elliott said, "God I hate to keep bringing you bad news—"

"It burned down. We know."

He looked relieved. "Oh good. No, not good that it burned

down. You know what I mean. Good that I didn't have to be the one to tell you. But I knew I recognized it." He pointed to the top of the house. "Those chimney stacks are still there. When we were kids we used to have parties up there. We called it the Ruins." He was talking to himself now. "I had no idea that was the Rutledge house."

"Nice," I teased. "Partying on the remains of my ancestral home."

Logan stood up. "Can we go see it, Livie?"

"Of course." I thought about all of the work e-mails on my phone that I had to deal with. "It might have to be tomorrow, though."

Logan pouted a little. I forgot how much kids needed instant gratification. She turned to Elliott and asked, "So can you take us there tomorrow?"

"Logan, don't be so pushy." I turned to Elliott and said, "Sorry. Maybe you could just give us some directions though."

Logan was on some kind of mission; there was no stopping her. She was looking at Elliott now and ignoring me. "Graham's not working tomorrow. Maybe he could go too."

Elliott and I shared a look. I shrugged. Elliott yielded. "She's good."

I agreed. "She really is. I'm kind of shocked."

"Maybe being with her pushy aunt is rubbing off."

"You're hilarious."

He smiled at Logan. "We'll go out there tomorrow." I felt bad about dragging him into this but he was trying to research a story and maybe seeing the old homestead would help him as much as it would help me. He rubbed his hands together, making a plan. "Let's go by boat. It'll be fun and you can get a better feel for the lake."

I guess we were all in this together now although to be honest I wasn't thrilled about going back out to the creepy lake. I asked, "Are we going to run aground on the top of a bell tower or anything?"

Elliott narrowed his eyes at me. "Very funny, but no. I will be very careful. No shipwrecks, no capsizing, and no swamp things."

Logan said, "Oh good. So can we go eat lunch now? I'm starved."

SEVEN

I woke up the next day after dreaming, of course, about my mother. In the dream it was my birthday and I was finding my birthday notes. My mom used to write tiny notes to us on our birthdays and hide them everywhere: lunchbox, pockets, backpack, inside cereal boxes, and under pillows. You never knew where one would be tucked away and half of the joy on your birthday was discovering them all. In my dream the notes were there, as always, but the pieces of paper were all blank.

My mother's silent past, which had always just seemed private, was now beginning to feel like a mystery. I hadn't expected to find a drowned town, and I couldn't help but wonder what other things were out there hiding in the depths of the water and the passage of time.

Elliott and Graham met us at the inn after breakfast and we all walked down to the lake together. The sidewalk was narrow enough that we could only walk two astride. I was only next to Logan for a moment before she slowed down to walk with Graham. Elliott and I took the lead, a matched set of third and fourth wheels. As we walked, he filled me in about his memories of the Ruins. They used to sneak up there on the weekends with kegs of beer and have bonfires. It sounded like what any good American teenager would do with a place so aptly named.

The partying had stopped, however, when the local historical society began enforcing the park hours of sunrise to sunset and running the kids off after dark. The TVA owned the shoreline up to one hundred feet back and the local historical society now owned the rest. Apparently the land housed a private graveyard that held the remains of one of the founders of the county.

So now it was a protected site. No more parties. No alcoholic beverages, no open campfires, no digging, no dogs off leash, no hunting. There were a lot of things one could *not* do on the site of my mother's home. And even though I had absolutely no connection to it whatsoever, I was relieved to see that someone was protecting it.

We walked down to the lake via a different pathway than the one we had taken the first time. This one led to one of those massive two-story floating docks and a beautifully restored wooden Chris Craft Sportsman from the 1950s.

Elliott untied the lines to the boat. "This is Jimmy's house and boat. He won't mind if we use it."

I stopped before stepping off the dock. "You're stealing his boat? Did you ask him?"

Elliott said, "I haven't seen him yet this morning but when we get back I'll tell him that we used it. He won't care." Graham held the lines and waited for me to climb aboard.

"Should we call him first?" I looked around, for help or witnesses I wasn't sure. "Should we leave him a note or something?"

Elliott started the engine. I noticed that the key was just sitting in the ignition attached to a plastic floating key chain. Graham took my hand, insisting that I climb in already and telling me that I didn't understand how things worked around here.

Elliott shook his head at me. "You worry way too much, Liv."

I sat down next to Logan in the back of the boat as we pulled out of the dock. *Liv? Did he just call me Liv?*

I answered him back. "Okay, *Eli.* I'll just sit back here and not worry about the fact that we're committing a felony in the company of minors." He pretended like he couldn't hear me but I could see his shoulders move as he laughed.

I was having a hard time reconciling the murky green images of the dead town under the lake with the gorgeous body of water we were cruising across. The shoreline was filled with amazing new lake homes, which were systematically replacing the smaller, older brick ranch houses. The water was dotted with pontoon boats and a few small fishing boats that were tucked into coves here and there.

Elliott took us on a long tour of the lake before heading out toward the Ruins. I made a mental note to think of some other name to call that place. The lake was so confusing. Elliott was making a series of turns across it and all of the branches and coves looked exactly the same to me. I had no idea how he was navigating. Maybe it was just an innate knowledge that the people who lived here were born with.

We stopped at the marina to load up a picnic for later and to fill the boat with gas. The marina was clearly fashioned after the grand lake lodges of the Adirondack region. It looked just like those opulent lake resorts of the Gilded Age with its strong stone base and soaring timber-peaked roofline. I was standing on the flagstone patio with my back to the water staring up at the main building when I heard someone approach me. I turned to see the same pompous man who had been holding court at the inn the other night.

The man came up to Elliott and shook his hand. "Eli. I'm glad you stopped by. Are you planning to go to the meeting on Tuesday?"

Elliott ignored his question and held a hand out to me. "Emory Bryant, this is Olivia Hughes. She's in town visiting and we're showing her the lake." Apparently Elliott wanted proper introductions to take place before discussing business.

Emory barely glanced at me and said, "Nice to meet you. Enjoy the lake." He spit that all out by rote and then turned his attention back to Elliott to get a better answer to his question about the meeting. Emory was not originally from around here. I could tell by the stark contrast in manners and civility between the two of them.

Elliott was still looking at me as he explained. "Emory owns the marina." He threw a thumb over his shoulder. "And the golf course."

I said, "It's a beautiful marina."

Emory nodded his approval, not in a way that seemed to be bragging but more as an acknowledgment that it was in fact a beautiful building. "Have you been to Tillman before?"

I said, "No, this is my first time."

"Cruising the lake a bit?" He asked the question while he glanced around the patio.

"We're actually headed to the Ruins."

Elliott nodded and added, "Olivia's family is from the area so we're doing a bit of research and touring. She's one of the Huntley Rutledges."

Something in Emory's manner changed and he turned his full attention to me. He looked me up and down slowly as if trying to make sense of my appearance. "Are you staying long in town or just passing through?" Now he was staring intensely at me, trying to get a better look at my face under my sunglasses, and it was making me uncomfortable.

This sudden interest in me was unnerving. I took an unconscious step closer to Elliott. "I'm just here to find out some things about my mother. I'm not really sure how long we'll be here."

"We?" he asked. "You said your mother is from the area? Is she with you?"

"No, she passed away recently." Now he looked a little bit queasy. I waved toward Logan, who was waiting with Graham in the boat, and said, "I'm here with my niece." He glanced at Logan and then back to me, staring silently. I said, "Well, it was nice to meet you." It was more a way to break the tension and walk away than a statement of fact.

As Elliott and I walked down the long dock to the boat I said, "Emory seems a little intense."

Elliott helped me into the boat. "It would be hard for me to explain him."

Plenty of words came to my mind that would explain him. Rude, crass, abrupt, pompous. I went with the most obvious impression. "Big fish in a small pond?"

Elliott pulled the bumpers in to the boat as he backed away from the dock. "There might be a bit of that. He's definitely the biggest fish around here. It took him a while to break into society. Maybe he still has a chip on his shoulder about that." Elliott noticed the quizzical look on my face when he said "society." He continued. "There are some things in this town that only your name, not your money, can get you into. Of course Emory's all in now. But with Emory you can just tell his mind is always working on the next big thing. Solving the next problem. Every time we have a conversation I feel like he's ten moves ahead of me in a chess game that I didn't even know we were playing."

We moved back out onto the lake. The day was hot but as we sped across the water the breeze cooled us off. My hair was whipping around my face. I kept trying to hold it back with my hand but the wind would grab it from me and smack me in the eyes with it.

The boat started to slow down as Elliott turned in to the last cove. On the low rise above the bank of the river were two elaborate brick chimney stacks. We docked the boat on a nearby pier and climbed up the bank.

I knew from the pictures we had seen that the house had once sat high above the surface of the river. But as the lake filled in the valley the water level rose to meet the house. Now, even though it sat far back from the bank of the lake, it was only at an elevation of about ten feet above the water.

The site was nothing more than a gradual sloping green lawn that led to the ruins of the house. And then behind them and on a slight rise was an ancient oak tree and a small wrought-iron fence. I assumed that the fence was enclosing the graves that allowed this land to be owned and protected by the historical society.

Elliott finished tying up the boat and Graham was wandering in Logan's wake as she ran up ahead. I made my way across the lawn. It was beautiful. The thick green grass was newly mowed and framed on one side by the neighboring property's woods and on the other by the edge of the golf course. I felt a cold chill run down my spine as I approached the ruins of the house. The granite steps were still there, leading to the ghost of the wide back porch that would have faced the river, and then later the lake. Part of the granite foundation was intact so that you could still make out the perimeter of the house.

The interior of the house was now filled with wild flowers. There was a small plaque that read: PLEASE DO NOT PICK THE WILDFLOWERS. ~TILLMAN GARDEN CLUB.

Logan was in the far corner picking handfuls of the wildflowers, of course.

I stood in the center of where the house had been, surrounded by wild poppies, and looked around. It felt like I owed it a reverence normally reserved for places of worship. This was my mother's home, where she had grown up, where she had lived with her mother and then watched her die. Where she had cared for her father. Where she had done homework as a kid and carved pumpkins and decorated Christmas trees. A whole life gone and forgotten.

I walked over to what would have been the front door and climbed up the small foundation wall and tried to imagine where the rooms would have been. As I entered there would have been a foyer with a grand stair of some kind. Was it a double stair or single? Curved or rectangular? To my right (or perhaps my left but I was imagining it on the right) would have been the parlor or receiving room. Maybe a private office for her father, the judge?

As I worked my way toward the rear of the house there would have been the formal dining room. Was there a chandelier? Were the walls plastered? Wallpapered? Maybe a hand-painted mural?

From there one would pass through the butler's pantry to the kitchen. Who did the cooking in there once her mother died? I knew it wasn't my mother or she and her father would have starved. I laughed to myself as I thought again of my mother's awful cooking.

Elliott was walking up the small hill to the oak tree and the graveyard. I think he was trying to give me some time to absorb all of this.

I called my sister, Georgia. When she answered I said, "Guess where I'm standing."

"Um, at our grandparents' grave in the cemetery?"

"Nope. At the ruins of Mom's house."

"Oh my God! No way! You found it?"

I filled her in on our day of research at the library and how we had come to find the site of the house. I described it all to her as best I could. I really wanted her to be here with me to see all of this. I glanced over at Logan, who was still picking the wild-flowers.

I called out to her. "Lo! Stop picking the flowers."

Georgia asked, "Why can't she pick the flowers?"

"They were planted by a garden club or something. There's a sign that specifically tells you not to pick them. I can't wait for you to come down here, Gigi. You need to see all of this."

I could hear her flipping paper and could see her clearly in my mind's eye standing in her kitchen, looking through her calendar. "I know. Should I try to come down this weekend? No, Adam has a baseball tournament. Maybe Monday? William's trying to get out of that sales trip to San Diego." She let out a big breath. "I don't know."

I knew she was feeling left out. "Don't worry, really. There's no rush. This place isn't going anywhere." The image of Georgia thumbing through her calendar reminded me of the date. "Mom's birthday! That's when we should scatter her ashes." It was in a few weeks. I knew from watching my father's birthday loom over us the first year after he died that it would be a bad day anyway. Why not pile all the depression into one really aw-ful horrible bad day?

"Aw, that's a good idea, Livie. You and I can fly back down there and spend the night. You can show me the town."

Hearing Georgia say "fly back down" made it sound like I would be leaving Tillman any minute, heading back home. Something in my stomach lurched at the thought; for some rea-son that I couldn't quite grasp I was in no hurry to leave Till-man.

Elliott was standing under the tree on the hill. He called out from the small family graveyard. "Hey, I found something!"

Georgia asked, "Who's with you?"

"Elliott and Graham brought us out here by boat."

"Oh, Graham is the one Logan likes?"

I whispered into the phone. "Don't tell her I told you!"

"I won't. And Elliott, is he the old newspaper guy?" *Yes, the Wilford Brimleyesque newspaperman. He managed to climb up here with his walker.*

"Yeah, he's helping us with the research, in case there's a story there for the paper. And he's not really that old." I walked over to Logan and said, "Do you want to talk to Lo?" Then I handed her the phone.

I wasn't lying to Georgia about Elliott. She had come up with the idea that he was older all by herself. I didn't give it to her. I just wasn't correcting her. She would just worry unnecessarily if she knew that Elliott was, through no fault of his own, very good-looking. I didn't see the point in bringing it up.

Logan immediately asked her mom if she could speak to her little brothers. After a beat I heard her voice change to a sweet and caring tone. She was asking Will about his little league game and how his skinned knee was healing. I think she missed her pesky little siblings.

As I walked up to where Elliott was, he knelt down and wiped some dirt off one of the headstones and wrote down what it said. He folded the page back on the small spiral notebook he was holding and then tucked his pencil behind his ear. He was sweating from the heat of the afternoon and it was making his shirt stick to his back. I could see the outline of his shoulders clearly as I got closer. I slowed down a bit and watched the way his body tensed and moved as he balanced himself. One single bead of sweat trailed down the length of his darkly tanned neck and as I watched it I forgot for just a moment what exactly I was doing there.

Suddenly he popped up on his feet, snapping me out of my trance. I shook myself back to the present as I approached the small gate. It creaked as I pushed it open and then it stuck so that I had to squeeze through it. I closed it behind me for some reason. Who was I trying to hold in here anyway?

Elliott wrote something else in his little spiral notebook and then put it in his pocket. I asked, "So what did you find?"

The graveyard held about thirty plots. Most of the headstones were simple granite pieces carved with names and dates. There was one large obelisk on a dais that was clearly someone important. A few of the newer markers had more elaborate dedications with Bible verses and carved motifs of the life lived. Crossed cavalry swords, bouquets of flowers, hands in prayer.

Elliott said, "I've never even been in here. Isn't that weird? All the times I've been up here and I've never come in the cemetery."

I squatted down to run my finger along the dates of one of the more weathered stones. Died in eighteen seventy-five. "Well, they probably didn't put the keg in here, so you had no reason to open the gate."

He pushed me over. "Oh look at that. You seem to have fallen."

"Elliott!" He was like a kid. I put my hand out and he took it to help me back up, redeeming himself.

"Olivia, this is your family's graveyard." His arms were

spread out wide. "These are the Huntley Rutledges. Well, and a few other names thrown in for good measure." He grabbed my hand and led me to the far side of the fenced-in graveyard. "I think this must be your grandparents."

We stood together as we read the inscription on the double headstone. On the right was my grandmother:

MARTHA CALHOUN RUTLEDGE
BORN 1910, DIED 1956.
LOVING WIFE AND DEVOTED MOTHER.

On the left was my grandfather:

HON. WINCHESTER TILLMAN RUTLEDGE
BORN 1906, DIED 1967.
HONEST, TRUE, AND A FRIEND TO ALL. LOVING HUSBAND
AND DEVOTED FATHER.

I realized I was still holding Elliott's hand and I let go. I cleared my throat. "It's so strange to be here and see this."

Elliott gestured to the surrounding headstones. "Your people go back to the early eighteen hundreds. The big one—"

"The obelisk."

"Right. That's George Howell Huntley. Huntley County was named for him. He was a Revolutionary War hero. And over there is a whole line of Calhouns and more than one Tillman."

Howell, Calhoun, Tillman: these were all the names I had heard from the innkeeper Mrs. Chatham when she was blathering on about the family lines in the town. Now I wished I had paid more attention. Maybe I had the provenance to be one of them. I was starting to understand what it might mean to be one of the Huntley Rutledges.

I wandered around the small graveyard reading the headstones as Elliott continued to take notes, writing down every name and the date of each headstone. There were so many babies and young children buried here. It was a reminder of how difficult it had once been just to make it to adulthood.

As I read through all of the names I realized I was recognizing half of the street names in the town. These people, "my people" as Elliott had called them, were an integral part of this community. They had obviously helped to build this area, these towns. It was strange that we never knew about any of it. That we had never been a part of it.

My sister and I had grown up like nomads. Both of my parents had been only children and both were so much older when they had us that their parents had long since died. We were a family with no ties, no strings or tethers to anyplace or anyone. We were utterly adrift. That had never bothered me. We had our little unit and we were solid. When other people had to endure family gatherings and dinners I just felt sorry for them. And extended family reunions? I would shudder at the thought. All of those strangers that you pretended were family just because you shared a name? Absurd.

But as I stood there looking at a spot rooted with generations of my family I suddenly felt a little bit lonely. I wanted to have a place that was home. A place that had ties to things that made me who I was before I was ever even a consideration. I wanted a connection to the generations behind me.

I made a conscious decision to force out any anger I might have felt toward my mother for keeping all of this from us. She had her reasons. I may never know what they were but I had to remind myself that I loved her and trusted her. I may never understand her, but I had to trust her.

Logan came over and hopped the gate and plopped into the graveyard.

"A little respect for the place please, Logan."

"Sheesh. Sorry. So who are all of these people?"

"These"—I waved my hands at the headstones—"are your relatives."

"Cool."

Yes, it was. I would have to see it that way instead of seeing it as something that had been denied me. I had all of this now and that would have to be enough.

I took some pictures with my cell phone camera and sent them to Georgia and Leo. Logan wandered around laying her illegally picked wildflowers on the graves of the babies and kids.

I took the paper bag that was holding our picnic lunch and ripped it open until it was a smooth sheet of brown paper. I placed it flat against the carvings of flowers on my grandmother's headstone and used Elliott's pencil to do a rubbing.

I was staring at the image of huge mop-headed clusters of flowers that had been transferred to the paper. Elliott stood behind me and looking over my shoulder said, "Hydrangeas."

We left the graveyard and spent some more time wandering around the ruins of the house. Well, I wandered around the ruins. Graham and Logan were sunning themselves at the edge of the water and Elliott was fixing a broken cleat on the boat.

Eventually we spread out our picnic at the dock on the lake. We ate our sandwiches with our feet dangling in the cool water.

Elliott was flipping through his notebook. "I'll make you an ancestral chart when we get back. I have a program on my computer we can use. You just plug in the names and dates and it creates the chart."

"Thanks. I would really love that." I turned my attention back to the house and looked at the chimney stacks rising from the ground. "I can't quite get over being here. Seeing that we're related to all of these people. I can't explain what it's like to go your whole life thinking you don't have any family and then . . . you stumble across this whole history. It's just weird." I thought back to the grace and charm I had encountered since arriving in Tillman. I may be related to them from some long-ago line of people, but I wasn't like them. "I feel like I don't really fit in here though."

Elliott agreed. "You really don't." I was kind of offended, which I think he could read on my face because he started laughing at me. "I meant that as a compliment. It's nice to talk to someone who actually says what she's thinking. Sometimes people are so polite that they stop saying anything of any value. It can be tedious, so much civility."

"Well, that's the same everywhere. People here are just a lot more charming about it."

Graham butted into the conversation. "We are super charming." He nudged Logan with his shoulder and she giggled.

He was a funny kid. I tapped the notebook where Elliott had written all of the names in the cemetery. "How many people were in there?"

Elliott counted the names. "Thirty-four. I wonder if we can find any photos of them now that we know their full names."

Logan said, "Thirty-five."

"What?"

She said, "There were thirty-five graves."

Elliott went back through his notes. "Are you sure? I only have thirty-four. I must have missed one."

Logan was putting on lip gloss. She smacked her lips. "It didn't have a name. It was that rock at the edge, like over by the fence. It just has an *O* carved in it. But why would it be there if it wasn't a grave?"

Elliott looked at me and I just shrugged. He flipped to the next page in his notebook and wrote: "O? Date?"

We finally climbed aboard the boat to head back. As we cruised over the water, I stood with Elliott at the front of the boat because Logan was sitting in the back with Graham.

Elliott leaned close to me so that I could hear him over the sound of the motor and the wind. "So, what are you two doing tomorrow?"

"I promised to teach Logan how to drive."

Elliott winced. "You might need a drink after that."

I laughed. "Definitely."

Elliott leaned back into his chair steering the boat effortlessly with two fingers hooked over the edge of the steering wheel. There was a thin, straight tan line from his sunglasses running along the side of his face. The wind whipped around his head, blowing hair in his eyes but he made no move to tame it. He tapped his hand on the edge of the boat; he had made up his mind about something. "I know where we need to go."

We? I said, "Has Logan been orchestrating another date?"

Elliott made a face as if he hadn't considered Logan and Graham. "Sure, they should come too."

We pulled the boat back into the dock where we had stolen it and Elliott parked it easily. Graham jumped out to tie it to the cleat. Elliott said, "So seven o'clock?"

I smiled and got ready to answer him when Logan cut me off. "What's at seven?"

I pulled my eyes away from Elliott with some effort and spoke to Logan. "Elliott thought of a place we all need to go tomorrow night."

Logan said, "Cool." And just like that we had a double date.

EIGHT

Logan and I spent the next morning driving slowly around the parking lot of an abandoned grocery store. She was getting the feel of steering and turning, accelerating and stopping.

Leo called while we were having our illicit driving lesson. I was a little giddy with the freedom of breaking the rules and gushed about how quickly Logan had picked up the basics. Then he heard me tell Logan to stop pushing the gas and break at the same time.

Leo was not pleased. "Don't let her drive your car, Livie. Do you have any idea how much it will cost to replace your transmission?"

I didn't want Logan to have her confidence shot so I ignored that. "Yes, she's doing really great. I'll call you later."

Once she got comfortable and was consistently using only her right foot, I let her go out on the back roads a bit. She was actually a pretty good driver. She attributed it to being forced to play video games with her brothers. I attributed it to Logan just being naturally accomplished at everything she tried. I reminded her about seven million times that she could not tell her mom and dad that I had let her drive the car.

As we followed the winding roads out of Tillman I took over in the driver's seat. She wasn't ready for the switchback roads that climbed the mountain. We rolled our windows down to let in the cooler air at the higher altitude.

I was aimlessly following the road up to the higher points. I was trying to get close to the top of the ridgeline so we could look out over the valley, the town, and the lake below.

We turned off the main road and began to follow a small gravel street, which continued up the mountain. My hands were gripping the steering wheel as I slowly ascended the road. There was a sheer granite face on my side and a harrowing drop on Logan's. We were both completely silent in the car, putting all of our mental focus on getting safely up the incline.

I stopped the car at the first point where the road widened. I decided to turn the car around so it was facing downhill. I wasn't sure if I would have another chance to do it and I knew there was no way I could reverse all the way back down.

Once we were safely pointed down the mountain, we climbed out to look for a vista. Logan spotted an overlook, which consisted of a large granite rock cantilevered precariously over the edge of a cliff face, and decided it was a perfect spot to take in the view.

I said, "Really? This is where you want to sit?" I inched as close to the edge as I dared and looked down at the treetops below me.

Logan plopped down at the rim of the stone and swung her feet over the edge. "Look at that view, Aunt Liv. Don't be such a chicken."

"Fine, but you are not allowed to plunge to your death." I moved back as far away from the edge as I could while still being on the rock. "That's a rule."

From this vantage point we could see the entire eastern end of the lake below. I located the marina and then the golf course. I followed the fairways around the lake until they ended at the property known as the Ruins. I pointed it out to Logan. A few boats were tying themselves together in the nearest cove to form a party flotilla below.

My phone pinged with a text from Leo: *Sorry about the car lecture. I'm sure it was fine. Have to catch the overnight to SFO. Be out of pocket till Sun AM. Will call you then. xo*

If he hadn't signed off with "xo" that text could have gone to anyone. We weren't communicating very well lately.

Logan pointed up to her right at the house clinging to the crest of the hill. It was an impressive spread, definitely the largest house I had seen in the area. From where I sat on the rock I could see that there were actually several buildings making up the estate all surrounding an expansive infinity pool pouring out into nothingness. As day turned to afternoon music began to waft out from the house.

She asked, "Who do you think lives there?"

I shrugged. "Someone with a lot of cash and a four-wheel drive."

I wanted to get off that deathtrap of a rock, but Logan didn't want to leave the view. I had to lure her away with the promise of adventure at the end of the road.

As we followed the footpath up the hill I was losing pace with Logan. I called out to her, "Slow down!"

She never broke her stride. "Come on, Livie. You're way out of shape."

I grabbed a pine cone from the ground and threw it at her. It missed. "I just wanted to walk up to the ridge, not have an Outward Bound experience." Logan finally stopped and waited for me then made a point to walk at my pace.

After a while of walking in silence she said, "You know what's weird about you and Elliott?"

Me and Elliott? "There is no me and Elliott, Logan." I kicked a rock and watched it scuttle into the underbrush. I couldn't imagine what she had conjured in her imagination.

Logan continued, as I knew she would. "You're all silly with him. Like playful. You two are always laughing about something."

I wasn't sure how to respond to that. "He's just a nice guy and we're very busy playing matchmaker for you and Graham."

She made a sarcastic sort of grunting noise. "Yeah right, this is all about me. You should see the way he watches you. And when—"

"He doesn't watch me. He's just being—"

"Don't say polite, Livie. It's totally different. You guys find ways to touch each other, like constantly."

"What? We don't touch each—"

"You do. You're always shoving or smacking each other. It's cool. I mean it's kind of sweet."

"I do not smack people." To make my point I smacked her on the shoulder, which made her laugh.

"I mean with Uncle Leo . . . you're more like grown-ups, like my parents."

"Leo and I have been together for a long time. We've already moved past the stage where you're silly or fun or whatever."

Logan stopped and looked right at me. "Was Uncle Leo ever fun?"

Was I really having to stand here and defend my fiancé to my niece? "You love Leo. He's always been so great with you. What is going on here?"

"You haven't been happy for a long time, Livie. I don't think I noticed it till I saw you laughing the other day with Elliott. That's all I'm saying. I think it'd be great if you could be happy again."

I was taken aback by her comments, or maybe by her perception. I mumbled, "Out of the mouths of babes."

We walked easily on the path as crickets sang in a wave of rhythm under the trees, low to the ground. I checked my watch, wanting to make sure we turned back toward the car before too long. Finally I said, "Elliott is just a fun person, who happens to have a girlfriend . . . I think. And I'm just someone in need of research assistance, who has a fiancé. That's it."

Logan didn't respond.

We came around a bend and spotted an abandoned house set back from the path. The house had weathered to a uniform gray and the front walk was overgrown in gnarled vines. The rusted metal roof had long since caved in and was leaning at a strange angle into the second floor.

"See Lo? An adventure!"

We walked carefully up the broken front steps, across the rotted boards of the porch, and through what was left of the front door. Most of the windows had been broken and the inside of the house had a blanket of leaves and pine straw that had blown in over time. There were still pieces of furniture here and there, most of it knocked over or ransacked. Logan went over to a sideboard that was still standing against the wall and opened a drawer. She held up a stack of papers. They were old letters.

She put them back where she found them and we walked to the next room. Logan was heading for the stairs but I pulled her back and shook my head. I didn't think the floor was safe to stand on up there.

We held hands as we walked to the kitchen. The cupboard doors were missing but the contents of the cabinets were there. Plates and bowls, napkins and tablecloths, all stacked in their proper place and covered in dust.

I realized that neither of us had uttered a word since crossing the threshold, the only sounds coming from the creaking floorboards under our feet. The house had an eerie foreboding to it and I felt like we had seen enough. Logan seemed to agree and we made our way back out to the front porch.

Tchck-tchck. Even before I knew for certain what direction the sound had come from, or had fully processed what it was that I was hearing, I was in terror. Sheer terror. Logan and I both froze, our feet planted in the last step they had taken before that unmistakable sound.

Tchck-tchck. I had never heard a shotgun being cocked or

loaded or pumped or whatever that was, in real life, but I had seen enough movies to realize it was a bad sound. It was the sound the villain makes to instill fear, to make a point. I turned slowly around toward the direction of the noise with my hands where he could see them. Point taken.

Standing between the path and us was a very old weathered man in greasy blue jeans and a denim work shirt pointing his shotgun in our direction. I felt absurd doing it, but I slowly put my hands up.

"Hi . . . um, my name's Olivia and my niece and I were just out hiking." I slowly stepped in front of Logan and pushed her behind me with my foot. I kept smiling at the man but he didn't make a move to lower the gun.

I kept talking. "I'm sorry is this your house? We uh, we didn't mean to intrude." He was still standing there staring at us with a look of complete incomprehension. I was wondering if perhaps he was profoundly deaf. I was wondering how I would explain Logan's untimely demise to my sister. I was wondering if I was actually going to wet my pants.

Logan peeked out from behind me and in a tiny voice said, "Sir, could you please lower the gun? You're scaring us."

He looked at Logan and then propped the gun over his shoulder. He didn't look menacing anymore, just sort of tired and irritated. I realized I had been holding my breath and blew out the air. The man spit on the ground, a long brown sticky spit, which I assumed was from chewing tobacco.

He motioned to the house with his head. "You're trespassing."

I put my arms down, took Logan's hand, and began to back

slowly away from the house. My eyes never left the shotgun. "I'm really sorry. And we didn't realize we had gotten so far from the road. It seemed completely abandoned."

Before I could reach the tree line he asked, "You one of Bryant's people?"

I had no idea what he was talking about, but I was glad at that moment that I was not, in fact, one of Bryant's people. "No sir, we were just out walking. We didn't mean to intrude." I took a step backward, pulling Logan with me.

The old man walked a few feet closer to us and squinted at me. "Goddamn, you look like a Rutledge." He spit again, this time narrowly missing my shoe.

Logan was gripping my hand so tightly that my knuckles were aching, but this man seemed to recognize me. He must have known my mother, and if so he was the first person from this town I had run into who had known her. "Did you know Jane Rutledge, or her father Winchester Rutledge?"

The gun moved back into firing position. "Get off my property."

He didn't have to ask us twice. Logan and I began to back slowly out of sight from the gun-wielding mountain man. As soon as we reached the path we ran as fast as our legs could manage down the rocky, uneven terrain. I fell twice and Logan ran head-on into a wasp's nest, getting stung several times on her shoulder. None of this made us stop. We ran until we got back to the car.

Gasping for breath I looked us over as I locked the doors then started the engine. We were both filthy and sweaty with scrapes and scratches from running through the stiff, sharp brambles. My left knee was already bruised and bleeding badly from where I had fallen. Logan's shoulder was red with welts from the wasp stings.

I asked, "Does it hurt?"

She wiped the dirt from her hands before pulling out one of the stingers. "Yeah, but getting shot probably hurts more. Let's go."

NINE

After a recklessly high-speed getaway back to the town of Tillman, and a very long, hot shower, Logan and I went down to the lobby to meet Elliott and Graham for dinner.

Elliott looked us up and down, noticing the scratches on our arms, the bleeding gash on my swollen knee, and the angry red welts on Logan's shoulder from the stings.

As Graham opened the door leading us to the waiting car, Elliott asked, "What happened to you two?" I went to get in the backseat, with Logan, but Graham beat me to it. I climbed in the front with Elliott.

On the way to dinner Logan gave a hilarious recount of our narrow escape from the mountain. She made that poor man defending his property from two nosy girls sound like the security guard of the *Deliverance* clan. Elliott was laughing so hard his eyes were watering.

It all seemed very exaggerated now that we were safe and sound and back in civilization. But when I remembered the sound of the shotgun behind me I still shivered.

I said, "I think he recognized me, or I mean I think he recognized my mom in me. I look a lot like her. He must have known her."

Logan piped up from the backseat. "Yeah, and he clearly didn't like her."

We pulled up to something called the Circle J, parked in the crowded parking lot, and Graham and Logan jumped out. Calling this place a roadside shack would be a generous description.

Elliott said, "Hang on." before I could climb out of the car. He leaned over me, leaving a trail of the scent of soap from his skin, and opened his glove compartment retrieving a first aid kit. He took out a piece of gauze and taped it to my bleeding knee.

Graham and Logan walked toward the restaurant leaving us alone in the car. Elliott gently rubbed the edges of the bandage over my knee to make sure it would stay put. I said, "Thanks. I can't get it to stop bleeding."

Elliott took his hands off my leg and sat back. "No problem." He smiled, making the car seem as if it were getting ever so slightly smaller. Then he teased, "It's pretty nasty. I don't think I want that thing oozing out while I'm trying to eat dinner."

I climbed out of the car. "Oh, are you telling me they prepare food in this dive?"

"You better be careful. If anyone hears you talking about the J that way they'll take out your other knee."

I followed him into the Circle J, which looked like it had once been a gas station. There were large bay doors that were rolled up and open to the terrace where a patio had been created using potted plants to delineate the edges. The chairs were plastic and so were most of the tables.

The patio was full of families with young children, so we elected to sit inside. This was obviously more of a bar area so Logan and Graham were very happy to be allowed at the adult's table.

The walls were covered in rusty old road signs and gas station logos. It looked like the kind of place that had slowly and lovingly been built out of garbage over the years. The resulting pastiche was actually pretty charming.

The long bar had three televisions above it all tuned to different baseball games. The floor was covered in a slight layer of sand; I wasn't sure why.

Elliott said that a visit to Tillman would not be complete without dinner at the Circle J, which supposedly had the best food in town. This was one of those dives that locals always adored. It made one feel terribly authentic to think the "best food in town" was served at an old gas station.

The place was pretty crowded but most of the bodies were at the bar so we didn't have any trouble finding a table. Elliott seemed to be either related to or good friends with half the patrons in the bar. I was trying to listen for familiar names. I was starting to wonder if I was distantly related to any of them too.

It looked as if Logan and Graham were on a date and that Elliott and I were serving as chaperones, which technically we were I suppose. So it was all legal in my opinion.

We ordered food and then the waitress dropped off a bowl of peanuts. Graham said something that sounded like "bald peanuts." I went to take one and Elliott snatched the bowl away from me.

"Have you had these before?" Elliott had a mischievous smile on his face.

"Peanuts? Uh, yeah."

"No, boiled peanuts." *Oh, boiled not bald.*

"Why would you boil peanuts?" I asked.

Graham butted in, saying, "Because they're awesome," grabbing some from the bowl.

Elliott picked a few peanuts out of the shell, turned to me, and said, "Open up."

"What? No. You're not feeding me."

"You have to trust me. These have to be experienced cold the first time without knowing what you're in for."

"Eww. You're not making it sound very—" he popped it in my mouth. It was cold and wet and salty and mushy. It was, in a word, disgusting. "Good lord! That's foul. Why would you do that to a peanut?"

I don't think anyone at the table heard my protestations about the blasphemy that had been done to that poor little nut. They were all laughing at me.

Elliott said, "Those are a Southern tradition."

"Yeah, like marrying your cousin. Not all traditions are good things." I washed away the taste with the last of my drink.

A band started playing in the corner. The lead singer was a red-faced, potbellied man wearing a multipocketed, khaki fishing vest. He got about two slurry lines in to some country song when I turned my head slowly toward Elliott, eyebrows raised as if to ask, *What's with the band?*

Elliott leaned in to me so he could speak into my ear. "It's karaoke night."

"It's kind of loud."

He said, "What?"

I just shook my head.

I limped up to the bar for another round and as I waited for the drinks I was surprised to see Graham and Logan take the stage. This seemed so unlike her. For so long she had been the quiet girl in the corner trying desperately to be invisible. I guess when you're in a place where no one knows you, you're free to reinvent yourself. She looked so cute up there with her little sunburned cheeks and a smile plastered across her whole face.

Ben, the drummer from the band, came over to our table and sat with us between sets. I was losing track of which ones were Elliott's cousins and which ones were just old friends. I had never been in a place where so many people were so interconnected.

The drummer stood up to head back to the band and looked around our table. "Which one of you is going next? Eli?"

Logan slapped my back causing me to choke on my drink. She said, "Aunt Livie is next." I was coughing and shaking my head. Logan looked at Elliott and said, "She won't shut up in the shower and she practically lost her voice singing on the drive down here."

I politely declined the offer to sing. "No thanks, Ben. I'll just watch." Then I kicked Logan under the table.

Ben let me off the hook and made his way back to the stage,

scooping up one of the waitresses on his way. He twirled her toward the microphone, and the crowd broke into rowdy cheers. She was obviously a local favorite.

I used to love to go to places like this, joints out off the highway. When was the last time Leo and I had been to a dive bar? We had to attend so many dinners for his work. And they were usually at some pretentious restaurant. Some new "it" place. Leo had become such a food snob in the last few years.

I tried to think back to the last time I had been someplace that made me feel this comfortable. Not just this bar, but this whole town. I felt like it was my choice that brought me here and there was so much contentment in that. How had that feeling of driving my own life just slipped away? Without a struggle or a fight or even a whimper? It had just vanished.

I was realizing more and more that I was just letting life happen to me. Letting it flow downstream and take me with it. I wasn't participating in its course correction anymore.

The waitress had a deep, raspy voice and was singing soulfully about the end of an affair, the loss of desire. I missed having desire. Maybe it was because of what Logan had said earlier but I was suddenly very aware of what I *didn't* feel about Leo. I was lost. And discovering that my mother's entire childhood was sitting underwater somehow made everything in my life just feel—shaken.

The whiskey-soaked lyrics that the waitress was belting out were hitting a little too close to home, and I realized I was getting choked up. Dammit, who gets emotional while listening to karaoke? I closed my eyes and took a deep breath, trying to settle myself so I didn't actually start crying like an idiot.

The waitress finished the song, lamenting about the loss of love, the lack of desire, the fading away of any need to keep going. She was singing out the exact thought that had begun to trouble me about Leo. I just hadn't been able to put my finger on it. Until now.

I had to excuse myself. I needed a minute away from the noise. What was wrong with me? I went outside the door and stood off to the side, gulping in fresh air. The muffled sounds of the band and the bar clatter were drumming in my head.

I really was a mess. Maybe this was some kind of posttraumatic stress thing. I did lose both of my parents in the space of two years. And I had stood in the burned-out remains of my mother's mysterious childhood one day and been chased down a mountain at gunpoint the next. Maybe that was it. My breath caught as I finally started crying.

I heard someone come up behind me and turned to see Elliott. "Are you escaping?"

I wiped at my eyes, trying to pretend like I wasn't wiping at my eyes. "Sort of. It was getting a little smoky in there."

He noticed that I was crying. "Hey? You okay?"

"Yeah, I'm okay. Maybe. I don't know." I rubbed my eyes and smiled at him. "That's not much of an answer." He stayed silent, waiting for me to continue. "I just—I'm just feeling like everything is a little bit messed up right now." Then I did that really embarrassing thing where a sob sneaks up on you and chokes out without you knowing it was coming.

"Oh man. You are a mess." He pulled me into a hug and let me cry on his shoulder.

See, Logan, I thought. *He's just a nice guy.* Just a nice guy who's easy to talk to. One of his arms was wrapped around my shoulders, holding me tightly as my head cradled into his neck; the other was slowly and gently stroking my back.

The part of my brain that handles the reasoning function was scolding me right about now and urging me to pull away. But the more primitive part of my brain coldcocked the reasoning part and I sunk into him a little bit more. Now Elliott smelled like smoke and fried food from being in the bar. I stayed there just a beat too long I think.

I finally pulled back and laughed a little at myself, embarrassed. He wiped my cheek with his thumb and stared down at me. We were standing close, too close, and I surprised myself by not moving back.

Then the door to the bar opened and we jumped away from each other.

I apologized. "God, sorry. I'm fine. It's just been a long day." I began to fidget and rub at my eyes.

"I understand." He ran his hand through his hair.

Out of habit my right hand rubbed at the pale white circle of skin on my left hand where my ring should be.

He asked, "Do you . . . want to talk about it? Tell me anything?"

Then I said something that was probably a mistake. "No. I mean, let's just . . . not. Not tell each other all of our . . . stuff." We were just research partners looking for a good story, right?

There was an unspoken understanding. He wouldn't have to explain the unanswered phone and I wouldn't have to explain, well, anything. He nodded and said, "Alright then. Let's get back in there before Graham drinks all our beer."

TEN

Elliott and Graham dropped us off at the inn after our dinner at the Circle J. I sent Logan to the room while I sat in the lounge for a minute to decompress. At some point during the evening I had come to realize that I didn't want to leave Tillman anytime soon. I wasn't ready to go home and walk away from the possibility of understanding my mother and this place she came from. There were probably some other things I didn't want to walk away from too, but I wasn't able to see any of that very clearly. As far as dealing with the reality of my job and Leo and even Logan, I had no idea how to make all of that work, but I knew I could figure it out.

I ordered a drink and called Leo. It was late and his phone went straight to voice mail. I rubbed my eyes as I left him a message: "Hey, it's me. You might be on an airplane right now.

Listen, I know this is a crazy time at work, but do you want to come down here for a few days?" I didn't realize I was going to say that until it was already out of my mouth. Which was classic Olivia. I needed to figure out what was happening between Leo and me. "I know you don't get back from San Francisco until Sunday, but maybe after that. I mean I'd really like it if you could see all of this. I want you to see the ruins of Mom's house and the family graveyard. We need to spend some time together. It's just a thought. Talk to you soon. Love you."

I squeezed a few more limes into my drink and then looked across the bar. My eyes landed on Emory, the bigwig from the marina. Why in the world was he here? He was staring at me. He held his glass up and smiled a hello. I smiled back and then pretended to be very interested in reading the menu of aperitifs served at the bar.

Emory suddenly appeared on the barstool next to me. "Olivia, isn't it?"

"Yes. Hello, Emory. It's nice to see you again."

"Are you having a nice time in Tillman?"

I had a fake smile on my face as my eyes darted around the bar trying to figure out why he was talking to me. I couldn't shake the memory of the way Elliott had described him. Ten steps ahead.

"We are having a nice time, thank you. It's a great little town. Are you from Tillman originally?"

A man attempted to approach Emory but a small flick of the hand made him walk back the way he had come. "I didn't grow up here, but I've been here long enough to call it home. Where do you call home?"

"Maryland, outside of DC."

He nodded. "Lovely up there. I bet you can't wait to get back. I'm sorry again about your mother. Is your father still living in DC?"

"No, actually he passed away a few years ago too."

Emory said, "Oh. I'm sorry to hear that." Then he asked, "Were they happy?"

That was an odd question coming from an odd man. I wasn't sure how to answer it, or why he was asking me in the first place. I asked, "Did you know my mother?"

He didn't answer me. He seemed captivated by the melting ice in his bourbon as he swirled the glass.

I kept talking because that's what I do when I get nervous about a long, silent pause. "I've come down here to try and find out about her childhood, about her growing up here. Her name was Jane Rutledge."

Emory didn't say anything to that either. He did not seem to be the type to say something for the sake of filling the void, like me. At length he stood up to leave. He turned to me with one last comment. "I'm sorry that all of Huntley is under the lake. There may not be much here for you to find."

I wasn't sure what to say to that. I just dumbly nodded my head as he walked away. Something bothered me when he made the comment about Huntley being under the lake. It took me some time until I realized why. I had not mentioned to Emory that my mother was from the now dissolved town of Huntley. Maybe he did know her. I looked around the bar to see if I could ask him how he knew that, but he was long gone.

The unsettled feeling I had vanished when Mrs. Chatham worked her way over to me. She sat down next to me with a huge smile, which I tried to mirror with one of my own. She made me feel safe.

She patted my hand. "Don't mind Emory. He's more bark than bite."

"I just can't imagine why in the world he would take any interest in my visit to Tillman."

She put her hands up as if resigned to the fact that Emory had his own reasons for everything. "He was here to talk to me about my garden club. He was all bent out of shape before you even showed up."

I envisioned Emory wearing a big sunhat and apron tending to a rose garden and I laughed. "He doesn't seem the garden club type to me."

Mrs. Chatham answered, "Oh no, not for him. He wants his wife to join. She would kill me if I put her up for the club; it's not really her thing. He just wants her in there for the status."

Status? In a garden club? What a funny world it was in this little town. But that reminded me of something. "Speaking of that, I saw a garden club sign the other day."

She perked right up. "I know! I hope you don't think I was eavesdropping, but I overheard you talking on the phone about a family graveyard."

Okay, so technically that was eavesdropping but she was so sweet I didn't care. "Yes, we found my grandparents."

"You must be talking about the cemetery up on the ridge, at the historical society's land on the lake. I was just thinking today that you might have some luck at that graveyard finding some of your relatives. I'm the president of the Tillman Garden Club this year." She said that in a way that hinted to me that I was to be dutifully impressed. "We maintain that graveyard as a part of our community service. I knew I was seeing that name somewhere in my mind but I couldn't quite get my hands on it."

I smiled at her as I finished my drink. There was something motherly and calming about Mrs. Chatham. Her mannerisms were so like my mom's. "It was strange to be there and see the ruins of the house that my mother grew up in."

She patted my hand in sympathy. "So that was her house? You've never been out there before?"

I didn't feel like telling sweet Mrs. Chatham that my mother never spoke of her childhood and that we had certainly never been there to visit. I just shook my head.

"That's a shame. You know, I used to have a landscape plan of the gardens up there before the house burned down. Rutledge Ridge was known for its hydrangeas." She hopped up and motioned for me to follow. "Come on. Let's go take a look and see if I can find it."

As I followed Mrs. Chatham to her office I remembered my mother planting hydrangeas in our yard growing up. She would save our tuna cans and bury them at the roots of the bushes, I regretted never asking her why she did that. She must have been planting them because hydrangeas reminded her of home, of her mother.

Mrs. Chatham's office was as elegant and lovely as the rest of the inn. One long wall was covered in family photos from floor to ceiling. I estimated it to be twelve feet by nine, so roughly a hundred-and-eight-square-foot photo documentary of the Chathams.

One little girl was featured the most frequently. "Mrs. Chatham, is this your granddaughter?" The picture I pointed to showed a toddler covered in red spaghetti sauce and noodles. "She's adorable."

"Yes, she is! But, oh, is she a pistol. Spit and vinegar, that one. And you must call me Betty."

I didn't understand the social currency of the garden clubs and she was trying to explain it to me as she shuffled through the papers and books on her shelves.

There were three garden clubs in town and apparently Betty's was the most prestigious. It sounded a bit like a sorority. A candidate had to be put up for membership by at least five current members in good standing and then be approved by committee. The garden club did community work and met for tea and dinners monthly. They had an exclusive garden party every year, which Betty called the event of the season. That reminded me of my mother too. She was always referring to the string of social engagements in the spring as the "season."

Becoming a member of these garden clubs was a mark of honor for any of the society women in town and apparently Emory decided he needed a foothold in one of them. Knowing that Emory's wife seemed to want nothing to do with it all made me think I might get along with her.

Betty said, "Ah-ha!"

"Did you find it?" I had forgotten what she was looking for at this point.

"No, I can't find that darn thing anywhere. But I know it's here. I'll lay my hands on it in a few days. But I found these." Mrs. Chatham was the poster child for undiagnosed adult ADD. She was holding up a series of books.

I walked over and took the books from her. They were small press printings of local historical society and garden club guides.

"Thank you? That's . . . that's really kind. I'll get these back to you after I read through them."

"Oh no, you keep them. I have loads. There'll be something in those about your family's house and gardens."

Oh, that actually did sound interesting. I thanked her again, more sincerely this time, and headed up to our room. I found Logan in her pajamas typing on her laptop while talking on her cell phone and watching TV.

I closed the door behind me and simply asked, "How?"

"What?" She hung up the phone.

"How do you do all of that at the same time?"

She didn't even answer me. It was like asking her how she keeps remembering to breathe.

"What are those?" She was gesturing at the books I was carrying.

"They're local garden guides that Mrs. Chatham gave me. And I'm supposed to call her Betty now."

Logan closed her laptop and sat up. "Well, you better remember to thank Betty properly or Grandma will roll over in her grave."

We both looked over at the urn on the dresser that was currently acting as the "grave" of my mother. I said to it, "I know, ivory cardstock with a monogram." I turned to Logan, "Do you know why Mom used to plant tuna cans under her hydrangea bushes?"

"Yeah, the aluminum in the can keeps the blooms blue instead of pink. Something about soil acidity."

"How do you know that?"

" 'Cause I asked her. Duh."

As I got ready for bed I plugged my phone into the charger and read through my text messages.

The first one was from Leo. It read: *You know I can't come down right now. Sorry! We'll talk Sun. Can you make the dinner party next Tues? Need you to make nice with his wife.*

The second one was from Elliott. All it said was: *You two want to play Nancy Drew tomorrow?*

Just reading that made me smile. I responded to Elliott: *Yes please. Library?*

As I got my feet freed from the trappings of the sheet I heard the ping of my phone.

I grabbed it and saw the reply from Elliott: *Thought I'd take you & Logan to the club. You can see the Rutledge Reading Room. It's anal-retentive office supply heaven—they even have a dedicated paper shredder, you'll love it.*

I sent back: *Ha ha. Will you be picking us up in a stolen car?*

It went on like that for about ten minutes. Which was about nine and a half minutes longer than it took to make plans.

ELEVEN

Elliott drove us up a slow, winding pebbled drive toward his club, which he called the Fells. I was staring out the window, hypnotized by the bright green canopy formed from the rows of ginkgo trees standing sentinel on both sides of the road. I was a little out of sorts this morning after getting very little sleep the night before, which was becoming a habit.

Elliott had whispered, "hey," for the third time before it registered with me. I looked over at him and he gestured to Logan in the backseat. She was lying down, eyes closed and listening to her music, her feet sticking out the window tapping to the beat. She had become unusually comfortable here.

I took the cold remnants of Elliott's coffee and drained the cup out my window. There was something so delicious about tormenting my poor niece. The wind took the liquid and splattered Logan's feet with a stream of brown droplets.

She screamed, startled, and jumped into sitting position. "Gah, Olivia!"

"Whoops. Sorry, Logan." Elliott and I were both laughing.

"You two are worse than my brothers." She pulled a travel-sized packet of wet wipes from her bag and tidied up.

I loved that kid. I mean what kind of teenager travels with wet wipes?

We pulled into the portico of a grand colonial revival building, which served as the main clubhouse for the Fells. The club's full name was the Huntley Fells Clay and Sporting Society, so I could understand why they had given it a nickname.

The stately, whitewashed building looked to date from the early 1900s based on the style of the deep veranda and the hand-turned balusters that lined it. Before I could open the car door a valet appeared out of thin air and was standing with his hand ready to help me from the car.

Elliott led us through the enormous carved mahogany entrance and into the dark, plush lobby. We turned down a wide hallway and stopped in front of a heavily carved, black-painted door with a small brass plate that read: RUTLEDGE READING ROOM. STAG MEMBERS ONLY.

I looked at Elliott and asked, "Stags?"

As he opened the door he said, "Kind of a club within the club."

I walked past him. "Ah, the Fells exclusive club has an elitist men-only enclave. Nice."

Logan followed me into the room, "How do you know it's

men only?" Then she answered her own question. "Oh, stags. Right." She held her hands up like antlers on the top of her head.

Elliott rolled his eyes at both of us. "It's not that exclusive."

Logan put her laptop on the table and looked up at Elliott. "Is it okay that we're in here? I mean it said members only, plus we're girls."

Elliott was turning on lamps and opening the heavy shutters on the windows letting the early yellow light of morning pour into the room. "Of course it's okay. You're my guests."

The room looked like a typical gentlemen's clubroom in a hunting lodge. The rich wooden floor was layered with thread-bare oriental rugs and there were a few clusters of mahogany card tables and chairs. The room smelled faintly of whiskey and pipe tobacco. The focal point of the room was the large fireplace, above which hung an oil portrait.

I asked, "Why is it called the Rutledge Reading Room?"

Elliott pointed to the portrait. The room had been named in honor of Judge Winchester Rutledge, a third-generation Stag and my grandfather.

So here I was, in the forbidden room of a restricted club, in the town I had never heard of, staring at an oil painting of my grandfather above the fireplace. He bore a shocking resemblance to my nephew Will.

Elliott put his bag on the table. "I meant to give this to you in the car." He pulled out a sheet of paper. "Surprise."

It was my family tree printed in landscape orientation. On the far left-hand side it listed my name and Georgia's name. Then connected by a line, my mother's name and my father's name. My father's side had no lines connecting him back in time but my mother's side did. It had every name listed from the graveyard with the dates of birth and death, the connecting lines to marriage, and then scribbled in at strange angles was any more information Elliott had found out about that person.

I ran my hand over the family tree. All of these people, all of these lives lived. Who were they? What traits did they pass on to Georgia and me? To Georgia's children?

At the bottom was a note: "Who was the 'O' grave marker for?"

"Thank you so much for this." My voice was barely above a whisper. "I can't tell you how much this means to me." I was choked up for some reason seeing all of this order applied to something that had at first been a mystery and then was merely a jumble of names and gravestones.

"It was no big deal. Like I said, the computer program pretty much just spits it out."

It has been my experience with computers that they never really just spit anything out. I knew he was downplaying however much work he'd put into this. I glanced up at the image of my grandfather staring out into the room from his perch above the mantel.

Elliott continued. "And we have a lot more to find out."

I decided to be clinical about this too. I tried to think of it as just research and I wondered what angle his story would take. The old "town under the lake" edge or more of a "long-lost Rutledge returns home" bent. I thought I would just follow Elliott's lead. "Okay chief, what's on our agenda today then?"

He did that cute thing where he rubs his hands together like he's making plans for a great caper. "It seems only appropriate, since we're in the Rutledge Room, to do some research about your grandfather." Elliott pointed to the four walls of bookshelves. "These were his books. Most of them are law books, but there are some journals in here too. Maybe we'll find something."

I asked, "When were they donated to the club?"

"I thought you'd ask that. It was shortly before the house burned down. I think donating the books to the club saved them from being lost."

I wondered what had prompted my mother to donate the books. I would probably never know, so it was pointless to speculate.

Elliott continued. "We can search through the newspaper archives too. There's got to be a lot of information about your grandfather because he was a judge in this county for seventeen years."

Logan raised her hand, which was so cute and endearing. It reminded me that she was still just a little girl. "I'll do the newspaper archives." She looked at Elliott. "They're online, right?"

"Yes, they are. I'll log you in and you can start going through them. A lot of the back editions have just been scanned, so word searches and queries don't work very well. There's a lot of hunt and peck."

She was nodding at him. "Cool. I can do that. I'll just do some quick searches online first and then start in on the papers."

Logan was fourteen, but she had an almost photographic memory and she read like the star pupil of the Evelyn Wood Speed Reading academy. She had picked the right task.

I looked at the floor-to-ceiling stacks of books all bound in dark shades of leather or linen. It seemed a daunting task to go through all of them. I said to Elliott, "We need a plan of attack."

He agreed. "I'll start on one end you start on the other? We'll meet in the middle."

I stood up, ready to dive in. "I say we ignore the law books and just look for personal journals."

"Deal."

Within ten minutes we were all hard at work and the room was silent except for the tapping of Logan's keyboard and the flipping of pages. The judge kept copious notes about all of his cases and rulings. There were more journals than I was expecting, but so far all of the ones we had found dealt with his professional life and not his personal life.

It was interesting reading through them and having a peek into a different time and into the mind of the grandfather I had never met. He was very clearly on the side of integration and social justice. His notes told the story of a man with a sharp mind and a sense of humor in the courtroom. But they gave absolutely no insight into his private life, so they really weren't helping me to discover anything new about my mother.

After a few hours of scanning through very hard to read scribbled journals with ink-blotted pages, my eyes were starting to blur. I hadn't found a single mention of my mother or of anything related to the judge's personal life. I checked the front page of the book I was reading again; it was dated 1964. I asked Elliott what year he was reading through and he checked the front of the book in his hand. It was from 1958.

I said, "I haven't found anything." I was sitting on the floor with several books around my outstretched legs. "You?" I asked Elliott.

He held back a yawn. "I'm finding a lot of notes in this one about changing his will to include a stipend for a woman named Maudy and her son. He paid off the mortgage on her house and put aside money for her son's college tuition."

"Maudy? Do you think he had a girlfriend?"

Elliott closed the book and reshelved it. "No. I think Maudy was probably his maid. That's what it sounds like anyway. She was probably more like a member of the family than just a maid."

I stood up and gathered all the books I needed to put back. I said, "I know. I know. I read *The Help*."

I heard Elliott laugh behind me at that. "That's a terrible example. They were awful to their help."

I turned around to face him. "They weren't all bad, were they?" He was still laughing as he nodded his head. I tossed a ball of paper at him which he caught mid-flight.

Logan defended me. "The kids were always good to the maids, right?"

I felt vindicated. "Ah ha! See?"

Elliott acquiesced. "Okay, okay." He shelved the book he had been reading. "Well, at least in this case it sounds like your mother and her parents were kind to Maudy."

I had always wondered who had helped to raise my mom after her mother died and now I had a name for the faceless woman. Maudy.

As I put the last book back on the shelf, I double-checked the numbers on the spines. The journals went from volume 64 to volume 68. There were three books missing. I checked the rest of the bookcase to see if they had been misplaced, but they weren't there.

"There are three missing. They would be the end of nineteen sixty-five and all of nineteen sixty-six." My imagination ran wild and I was quite sure that the missing volumes were full of tidbits about my mother and anecdotal stories about her life. I even imagined photographs tucked into the pages that would come fluttering out if you opened the books. I was always imagining that I would stumble across a collection of photos of my mother's early life. They were the stuff of legend to Georgia and me, as mythical as unicorns. Of course there was no evidence to support the idea that these missing journals held anything of interest. All of the books we had found contained only notes about his work, but because they were missing I had an urgent need to find them.

Elliott and I searched quickly through the shelves running our hands along all the spines looking for the missing volumes. They were not misplaced; they were gone.

He could see the frustration on my face and tried to make me feel better. "You know they're just more of the same."

I sat back down at the table with Logan. "You're probably right." I picked up the small stack of papers that Logan had printed out. Elliott rested a comforting hand on my shoulder for a moment before sitting down with us.

The first thing Logan had found was my mother's birth certificate. It didn't tell me anything I didn't already know, but I couldn't stop staring at the signatures from her mother and father. My grandmother's writing was elegantly formal. It looked like calligraphy, especially compared to my grandfather's scrawl that I had been trying to decipher all morning. They were starting to seem like real people to me for the first time in my life.

The next printout was my grandfather's death certificate. I had never known he had died of complications due to gastric cancer, the fancy name for stomach cancer. So he had died of the same thing as my mother. A cold chill shot through me as I read that.

What was it like for her to watch her father die of stomach cancer and then develop the exact same disease? Did he suffer the way she did? Did he fight it the way she *never* did?

I sighed and chewed on my pen. This was a depressing line of inquiry. I glanced at the next printout; it was my grandmother's death certificate. She died of lung cancer in 1956 when my mother was ten years old. I knew this event had forever changed my mother. I knew that seeing that coffin lid clamp shut was the reason she could not tolerate small spaces. But I only knew that because our father had told us when we were little so that we would stop teasing her about it and stop hiding under the bed. I rested my chin on my hand and found myself staring off into space. Elliott was accidentally in my field of vision.

He wore glasses when he was reading through the books but not when he was reading on the computer screen. He had to keep putting them on and taking them off. When he needed them again his hands would go through a well-practiced pat down: head, pocket, table, until he landed on them. Sometimes when he was concentrating on what he was reading his eyebrows would furrow and he would purse his lips. Elliott looked up and caught me staring at him. He kicked me lightly under the table. "Get to work, missy. No pay for slackers."

I smiled at that and asked him, "What are you reading?"

Elliott scooted his chair slightly closer to mine and showed me the filings for the judgeship campaigns that Logan had printed out. There were well-documented lists of his campaign staffers and we found my mother's name on each list starting when she was twelve years old.

As we flipped through the pages he said, "What do you think a twelve-year-old girl was doing on an election campaign?"

"Knowing my mother she was probably knocking on doors and demanding that people vote for her father."

He smiled. "So you get your feisty spirit from your mom?"

"I am not feisty."

"I beg to differ."

I showed him the copies of the death certificates from my grandparents. Elliott put his hand on my knee under the table in a show of concern. "Is this hard for you? I mean do you feel like you just lost your mom and now here you are, in a way, losing the whole rest of the family?"

"Not really. It feels a little bit like we grew up in a place that isn't real. I can't really explain it." I just shrugged. "But it also feels like I'm getting to know a part of my mom that I never knew before." I pointed to the printout of the campaign boundary map. "I never knew she worked for her dad's campaigns."

I found myself leaning into Elliott as we traced the map showing the boundary lines of the 1958 state judge election. I was having a hard time concentrating. I was thinking that I didn't really care one bit about the boundary lines of the 1958 election, but I didn't say that. Actually, I didn't say anything. I was sitting so close to him that we were touching down the entire length of our legs. He smelled like soap and old books and there was black ink smudged on his thumb. His hand was still on my knee. I was having the urge to brush his hair out of his eye.

He squeezed my leg a little and said, "Or that her hometown was under a lake?"

I smiled and looked at him. His eyes were so green, I hadn't noticed that before. My heart was racing and I hoped he couldn't sense it. I said, as casually as I could, "Yeah. Or that."

He leaned in a tiny bit closer and said in an almost whisper, "Olivia, I wanted to talk to you about something."

Logan, who I forgot was even in the room with us, shouted, "Whoa!" I jumped away from Elliott as he simultaneously slammed both of his hands on the table.

My heart was pounding as I looked at her and waited for her to fill us in on whatever was so important that it ruined the little moment we were having. Or maybe saved us from the moment we were having. I started chewing on my pen again.

"What, Lo!"

She looked back and forth between Elliott and me. "I found an article about that floating church steeple and there's a picture of it in the lake. You know, the haunted one? Guess where the church used to be." She looked back and forth between us again. I didn't really care where that church used to be. I wanted to know what Elliot was about to say to me. Logan read from the article: "On the disputed line between the Forrest property and Rutledge Ridge. That's us, right? Rutledge Ridge."

I said, "Yes, it was called the Rutledge Ridge in the garden club books too. That must be what they called the hilltop where the house was." I couldn't think of anything else to say. My mind was stuck a few seconds back in time and Elliott's hand was on my leg and I felt like he was getting ready to tell me something. Or ask me something.

I glanced at Elliott and we both suppressed a nervous smile. I said, "It's getting kind of late and I know you had work to catch up on today. And Logan and I"—I tried to sound casual to the point of complete disinterest—"are going to look at some lake houses for rent. I have some things I still want to . . . figure out . . . around here."

Elliott's mouth moved into a tiny smile on one side. "So you're going to be here a bit longer?"

"Yes. Well, you know, I'm thinking about it. Georgia and I want to spread the ashes on my mom's birthday. It's at the end of the month. I was thinking I might stick around till then, see what I can find out."

He rubbed his hand on the back of his neck; he looked nervous. "I'm glad to hear that." He nodded, as if he seemed to be deciding something. "And I may have to go to Atlanta for a few days. Actually, I know I do. I'll call you when I get back? Is that okay?"

"Sure. Of course you can." I felt tense for some reason. Why did he suddenly have to go to Atlanta? For a few days no less. I tried to sound nonchalant as I said, "Logan and I are just planning to take it easy for a few days. See what rental houses we can find on the lake."

"Good. Okay. Good." Elliott stood up. "Let me just tell them to pull the car around."

I was chewing on my pen as I watched him walk out of the room. Not sure what any of that meant.

My mental dilemma was interrupted by Logan. She said, "Gah, Liv." She leaned over the table toward me.

"What?"

Logan put her pen to her mouth and started sucking it then chewing on it. She was making fun of me.

Oh that. "I know it's a bad habit. I chew on my——"

She cut me off with a look on her face that told me I had completely missed her point. She leaned in farther and said, "I don't think Elliott can take it."

"Oh my God, Logan. Inappropriate." I was trying to act sufficiently horrified but I had to stop myself from laughing. She was only fourteen. I wasn't sure if she even understood her innuendo. I threw my pen at her. "Shut up."

I walked over to the heavy French doors and opened them up to the small balcony overlooking the rear of the club. I stepped outside and was momentarily blinded by the sun reflecting off the water in the pool. It was obviously time for adult swim; a band of small children was lining the edge of the water all staring at the lifeguards and waiting for them to blow their whistles.

I could hear the *thwack* of tennis balls being hit somewhere out of sight to my right. I leaned out to try to catch a glimpse of the courts. They were beyond my reach, but on the side of the building I noticed a trellis-covered loggia leading away from the clubhouse and out toward the low grassy hills. The trellis was smothered in huge purple wisteria blossoms. As I was staring at the trellis a familiar shape walked out into the sunlight. It was Emory.

He caught me staring at him and waved up at me. I felt like I had been caught someplace I shouldn't be. I raised my hand in a small wave and went back into the room.

I was gathering up my things when the door opened behind me. I turned expecting to see Elliott, but it was Emory.

He smiled at us and walked straight over to Logan. "Good morning, ladies." He put his hand out. "And you must be Olivia's niece."

Logan limply shook his hand and nodded as I introduced her to Emory Bryant.

I said, "Hello again."

He looked around the room, scanning the shelves, glancing at our piles of papers, taking it all in. "Researching, I assume? Any luck?"

"We're finding out bits and pieces." I didn't want to lay all my cards out with Emory for some reason. "I did want to ask you something, though. How did you know that my mother was from Huntley?"

His face was completely still but he seemed to pause longer than was customary before answering. "It was Elliott. He referred to your family as the Huntley Rutledges when he introduced us at the marina."

"Oh, right. I suppose he did."

Logan piped up. "Can I ask you a question, Mr. Bryant?" He raised his eyebrows, waiting. "Your golf course is right by my grandmother's old property. How long have you owned that? I'm just wondering because we read an article about this little church that was on the disputed line between the Rutledges and the Forrests. Do you know anything about that? Or anything about the old church that used to be there?"

Emory responded without actually answering her question.

"That dispute was never really settled. The property line was delineated by a stream that apparently used to change course frequently when it would flood."

I asked, "So when, exactly, did you buy the property?"

Emory kept talking, ignoring me. "I actually donated that parcel of land where your mother's house was to the historical society to create a buffer between the Forrests' property and my golf course."

I said, "You didn't want a Hatfield-McCoy feud on your hands either?"

He looked at me pointedly. "I didn't want anyone making false claims on the property that I spent a lifetime creating for my family."

Elliott returned and Emory took that as his cue to leave. When he was gone Logan said, "That guy makes me nervous. He's like super intense."

Elliott shrugged it off. "He's not technically supposed to be in the Reading Room. Maybe it made him seem a little off."

I moved over to the table and helped Elliott pack up our things. "Emory's not a Stag? You mean there's a club in this town where he's not a member?"

Elliott answered, "You have to be a bachelor when you're put up for the Stags and he was already married when he became a member of the club."

Logan closed the door and looked visibly relieved to know that she was safe from Emory. She let out a breath and said, "Super creepy dude."

TWELVE

We were all three quiet as Elliott drove us back to Tillman from the Fells. I would imagine we all had our own reasons for the silence. We pulled up to the inn and Logan hopped out. I made a show of collecting my things so that I could have a minute alone with Elliott.

He smiled at me and said, "I'm sorry I have to leave town so suddenly. But I need to go take care of this. I'll call you as soon as I get home."

"You don't need to explain anything to me." I had a feeling he was heading off to answer that ringing telephone. But what was he planning to say to her? "We'll um, I mean Logan and I, we'll just see you when you get back."

He nodded and smiled. Then we sat there for a second unsure whether to hug or kiss or high five. I just laughed at myself and waved dumbly and then climbed out of the car.

I caught up to Logan and we made plans for lunch. She was chattering away endlessly while I pushed the food around my plate. We meandered through the town, stopping in a few shops. I bought a scented candle for Betty Chatham as a thank-you gift for the books she had given me. When we got back to the inn Logan went up to take a nap. I found a secluded bench off the town square and sat there, thinking.

It was an hour before I finally dialed Leo. When he answered I could tell he was busy; he was pacing in some faraway office in San Francisco or Silicon Valley. I wasn't even sure where these meetings were taking place. I could hear his shoes tap over a hardwood floor then disappear onto lush carpet before turning around and retracing the journey.

I was hoping he would spare some time. "I can tell you're in the middle of something. I hear you pacing. I just, I thought we should talk . . . about everything that's going on."

Papers were being shuffled and flipped. "I know, Livie. I want you to tell me how it's going but I'm really pressed right now. Why don't you send me an e-mail later and flesh it out for me. Send me some more pictures of that church you found."

An e-mail? Seriously? I said, "It was a cemetery at my mom's house, not a church."

"Right. Listen, I'm sorry but I have to run."

"Leo, we really need to talk."

"Olivia"—when he used my full name I knew he was getting irritated—"you're down there with no schedule and no dead-lines and you want to chat, but try to be respectful of my time." That was a line he had cribbed from the therapist we used to go to. It was one of his favorites and he used it all the time. "I'm do-ing real work today and I'm about ten minutes away from hav-ing to deliver some bad news to these people. I can't talk right now. I will call you later." Click.

Another half hour went by before I dialed Georgia. She an-swered without a greeting, as we always did with each other. "Is Lo with you? I can't find the remote for the movie thing in the car and I need it for—"

I cut her off. "She's not with me."

"You sound weird. Are you okay?"

The words all just spilled out of me. "I honestly don't know. I'm feeling confused about a lot of things. I'm . . . I'm having a hard time thinking about Leo. And marriage. I just don't know if this is the right thing for us. And I keep calling to talk to him but we can't even have a conversation about today let alone get far enough along to talk about the future."

"What are you saying? Are you thinking about canceling the wedding again? Because I honestly don't think he'll handle that very well."

"Oh my God, how many times do I have to tell you people I did *not* cancel the wedding last time? Mom got sick. She was dy-ing! It wasn't a great time for a party."

"Don't yell at me! You did postpone it. I'm not saying it wasn't for a good reason, but don't rewrite history. I'm just re-minding you how excited Leo was when he booked the chapel; that's all."

"I know. It worked out so nicely, tucked in there between the end of the Feldman case and the firm's trip to Kauai. So per-fect!"

"You sound like a lunatic. What is going on?"

"It's a long story."

"So start at the beginning. And don't cry; you're an ugly crier."

That made me laugh and cry at the same time. I started telling her everything I had experienced with the burned-out house and the strange reality of the drowned town. I told her what it felt like to be standing in the family graveyard. And about the ties to a vanished family we had never known about. I wondered, out loud, if Leo and I should really go through with this wedding.

Georgia said, "You're practically married anyway. The wedding is just a formality, a celebration. With jewelry."

"Not funny, Gigi." I wondered if things would change, get better, once we were married. But when he surprised me with the date and had booked the chapel it sent me reeling. Instead of feeling excitement or relief at having the date looming I went into a panic and fled. I knew that was a bad reaction. I just had to figure out what it meant. "I don't think we should get married just because it's what comes next. If it's not right we shouldn't go through with it."

"How long have you been feeling like this?"

"I don't know. A while." I could pinpoint it to the day we canceled our therapy session because he had the draft for his Fantasy Baseball team. It wasn't the draft that bothered me; it was the fact that we were going to a therapist and we weren't even married yet.

Georgia was using her most calming mother voice with me at this point. "You'll be back in a few days. You can talk to him when you get home."

"Actually, I'm thinking of staying longer. I want to stay down here until Mom's birthday when we scatter the ashes."

Her calm demeanor vanished. "Olivia, that's weeks away. You can't hide out down there and avoid your life."

I shook my head, as if she could see me. "I'm not avoiding it. I'm trying to understand it. I want to stay here. I want to find out about Mom. I'm not ready to leave." And here comes the kicker. "And I think I might have a tiny crush on Elliott."

Georgia sounded baffled. "You mean the old newspaper guy?"

I got up off the bench and started to wander the streets of Tillman. "Did I give you the impression he was old?"

"Yes, you did. Deliberately."

"Actually, he's my age. Well a year older."

"Olivia."

"What?"

"Really? You can have a crush, but that's it. You can't act on it. And if you're having this many second thoughts about Leo then you need to talk to him."

"I've been trying to talk to him. I tried for weeks before I left. I've been calling him since I got here. I even asked him to come down here, but he's busy."

She was silent on the other end for a long time. Finally she said, "Do you think it's just you? I mean just what you're going through with everything about Mom because you took that really hard. Or do you think it's really that you're not happy with Leo?"

That was the million-dollar question, wasn't it? "Losing Mom was horrible and seeing everything down here has been unsettling but . . . I don't think that's it. I really just wonder if I'm supposed to be with Leo at all. I just need some space to figure out if this is real or if I'm just——"

"Completely nuts."

"Thanks, Georgia. That's very understanding of you."

"Look, I just think if you do this to Leo it will be awful. Awful for him, awful for you, awful for us. He's been a part of our family for a long time. He knew Mom and Dad. But no matter how awful it is, if it's what you need to do . . . then I'll stand by you. Of course."

I was crying again. "Thanks."

"Feel better?"

"No."

"I'm sorry, sweetie. I know this is hard. But you know I'm on your side. Whatever you decide."

"Thanks. I know."

"And you know you sound like an idiot, at your age, saying you have a crush on this guy, right?" I could feel her doing air quotes around the word "crush."

"Yes, but thanks again for spelling it out for me and making me feel stupid."

She felt bad for scolding me. "I'm not trying to make you feel stupid, but try to remember how bad it was when Leo had a crush on that girl at work."

She knows we don't talk about that. "I can't believe you brought that up."

She paused for a second and then her voice got tight; she was getting to what she thought was the real problem here. "You know, not everyone gets to have what Mom and Dad had. That

was just special. You shouldn't think that because you and Leo
are different that it's not good enough."

That was meant to make me feel better. It didn't really work.
"I'll call you later, Gigi."

I thought back to when our mom got sick and I decided to
postpone the wedding that first time. When I told my mother
my plan she was not pleased. We had been digging through her
attic in search of my sister's wedding veil when I broke the news
to her that I felt like we should wait on the wedding. She paused
for a minute then got right back to work finding the veil.

My mother dug down to the bottom of one of the cedar chests
tucked under the dusty eaves of the roof. "Livie, don't delay
your life because I'm sick. If you love Leo then get married,
have children, or adopt a dog, whatever. Live your life."

I held the lid of the chest up while she pulled out old Raggedy
Ann dolls and Girl Scout uniforms. "Mom, I just don't want to
have to deal with a wedding, with a giant party, right now."

"He's a good man. He's very, what's a good word for him . . .
stable. And he loves you. Ah-ha! I found it." She pulled out the
enormous piece of tulle, folded and wrapped in tissue. She
snapped it out to its full length.

"Stable? That makes him sound like a Chevy."

She cocked her head to the side, which told me not to make
light of a serious conversation. "Do you love him, Livie? That's
all you need to know. If you love him and you need him then get
married. Start living. Don't wait for it, not because of me."

"I don't *need* him. I mean I don't need anyone to take care of
me." I lowered the lid of the chest and stood my ground with
her.

My mother took me by the hand guiding me to an old cracked mirror leaning against a rafter. She stood behind me putting the airy veil on my head, testing different positions. She said, "It's not a weakness, Olivia." She kept trying to pat down the voluminous veil to make it lie more flat. "It's a good thing to need and to be needed in life. You should need him so much that without him you can't breathe."

All of my instincts recoiled. How weak a person do you have to be to need another person in order to breathe? "I don't need someone to rescue me like that, Mom."

She shook her head the way she always did when I didn't understand something. "Olivia, I loved your father, but he never rescued me from anything. I rescued myself. You don't need someone to hold you up, but you could use someone to hold your hand. I was holding my breath for a long time before I met your dad and when he came into my life, well, I could breathe again."

She and I both stared in the mirror at our reflection. I had always looked so much like her, just a younger version with lighter hair. But now she was losing weight and had an unnaturally pale pallor to her skin. Now we resembled a before and after ad.

"What does that mean, Mom? I wish you'd tell us some of these things you keep hidden." I was never good at pushing her for answers, even before she became frail and sick, but I could feel our time running out.

She put her hands on my shoulders. "I really miss your dad." There were tears in her eyes, which made me feel horrible for pushing her, even ever so slightly. "There will always be things you can't know about a person and that has to be okay. But I loved your father. I never once questioned it. I was supposed to find him . . . after everything." She stopped herself from saying more. "If you love Leo that way, if you need him and want to be with him, then let's do this."

The veil was really beginning to puff out now and with every movement it managed to get bigger. It was hideous. She tried to push it down again and it sprang back up.

She hugged me from behind, silently ending that conversation, and pulled the veil off my head. "We are telling Georgia that we couldn't find her veil. You will have to wear something else because this is the God-awfulest thing I have ever seen. I don't remember it being so big when she wore it. On you it looks like some kind of volcanic ash is erupting from your head."

I smiled remembering her like that, and I wondered if maybe I had missed her point about the way and the depth that you could need another person.

I pulled myself back to the present and made my way slowly back to the inn, clearing all of the work e-mails and messages off my phone. When I got to the inn I waved to Graham, who was manning his post at the valet stand. He was getting ready for the dinner rush at the inn's restaurant. There would be three, maybe four cars pulling up within the hour. He straightened his collar in preparation and I had to laugh. I sat down in one of the rocking chairs lining the wide porch.

Now that I had decided to stay I needed to deal with the office. I called my team first to tell them I was trying to get a leave of absence for a few weeks. They were supportive, as always. Then I had to do the difficult task of calling my boss to actually get permission.

He was strangely amenable to the idea. In fact, it almost sounded as if he'd been making plans for my departure. When I made a joke about it he said, "Well, I need to see if Jeremy can handle that team while you're gone. Now that you're getting married you'll probably be pregnant any minute and we'll need someone to step up. You women don't always come back once the baby comes."

I was too shocked to have an appropriate response to that so I just thanked him and hung up. His comment probably violated several different human resources rules, but I was too relieved to have gotten permission for the leave of absence to care about that.

My phone pinged. It was a text from Leo: *Sorry I couldn't talk. Have to have dinner w/J. I'll call you tomorrow. Love you.*

THIRTEEN

I dragged myself back up to our room at the inn, flopped down on my bed, and crossed my arms over my face. I was exhausted. Emotionally and physically.

After a few minutes of blissful, quiet darkness Logan threw a pillow at me. I didn't move, but I said, "What?"

"Are we going to dinner or can we just chill?"

"Oh yes, by all means, let's just chill." I had a splitting headache and a tiredness that had seeped all the way down to my toes. I kicked my shoes off and stared at the ceiling. I heard a crunching sound and looked over at Logan. "What are you eating?"

"Doritos."

"Where'd you get them?"

She handed me a tote bag and said, "They're left over from the car ride."

I dug through the bag and found some Fritos and strawberry Pop-Tarts. I said, "Excellent. We'll have road trip snacks for dinner."

She was licking her fingers. "Do you want a drink? I could go to the soda machine."

I thought I needed something stronger than soda. I put my shoes back on. "I'll go. I need to drop the thank-you candle at the front desk for Mrs. Chatham anyway."

I left the candle and note with the woman at the front desk, then went to the bar to get a drink to go. I got back to the room and opened my dinner of Fritos and Pop-Tarts. That covered corn and fruit. And there were limes in my vodka tonic. A well-rounded meal.

Logan and I sat on her bed while she filled me in on all the drama happening with the rising junior class. It was a nice distraction from the drama happening in my head. A lot of it also sounded annoyingly similar. Great, now I was acting like a teenager in heat.

She seemed to have forgotten all about the boy she had been dating at the end of the school year and was focused solely on Graham. It was so easy to fall in and out of love at her age. I wondered if it were just as easy at my age. Maybe what made it so difficult was just the complexity of extricating yourself from all the trappings of an adult relationship.

"I need another drink."

Logan said, "No you don't. What's up with you and the vodka?"

I thought, *It's not as fattening as beer and I like it more than wine*. I said, "I'm on vacation and I'm having a cocktail. There's nothing wrong with that."

"You're burying your dead mom and you're sitting in a hotel room with your niece. It's not like you're on the lido deck."

I patted her on the back. "Nice. More and more like your mom every day."

Her phone beeped that she had a text message and I was mercifully ignored. She was busy with her cyberlife so I spent some time tidying up the room. There were clothes scattered all over the place. It was as if Logan selected her outfit by flinging several things into the air and then choosing whatever hit the bed. While I was in the bathroom brushing my teeth, Logan asked, "What are we doing tomorrow?"

I came back in the room and just shrugged my shoulders. I had no idea what we were doing tomorrow. I checked things off on my fingers. "Let's see, drowned town? Check. Burned-out house? Check. Random family graveyard full of people we've never heard of? Check. I guess we could hit the cemetery. I might look at some houses to see if there's something I can rent for a few weeks."

She rolled her shoulders up to her ears like she used to do when she was little and wanted ice cream. "Would you care if I went out on the lake with Graham? A bunch of his friends are going water-skiing tomorrow and he asked if I could go." Then she raised her little eyebrows. *Pwease Aunt Lib, pwease can I hab some ice cweam?* I kind of missed her little speech impediment.

I figured Georgia would let her go, so I gave my permission. "Sure. That sounds fun. Of course you can go. Just no drinking, drugs, or sex on the boat. Or off the boat. Or really any-where." I couldn't remember all of Georgia's rules, but that probably covered most of the bases.

She was immediately texting on her phone again. "Okay. And no drinking, drugs, or sex for you either tomorrow."

"You're hilarious."

The next morning I helped Logan get ready for her day on the boat with Graham and his friends.

When we went downstairs to meet up with Graham I felt the need to act like a parent. I asked who would be on the boat and who was driving it. I made him assure me there would be no al-cohol, which horrified Logan. I waved to them as they walked down the sidewalk toward the lake.

I walked to Jimmy's and spent an hour just sitting in a chair staring at the wall. It's amazing how completely still the body can be when the mind is racing. I felt like I had to decide: Do I really stay here for a few weeks researching my mother's life, and incidentally run the risk of seeing Elliott every day? Or do I just sprinkle the goddamn ashes already and go home to my life? Yesterday I had felt so sure, but today I was waffling.

Jimmy eventually came over to refill my coffee mug. "You okay?"

I laughed a little. Was it that obvious? I said, "No, not re-ally."

"A lot of that going around this week. Anything I can do?"

Some part of me knew this tiny window was precious and I shouldn't waste it. I was in this strange bracket of time between the anniversaries of my mother's death and birth. Right here, right now I had to find out what I could about her. This opportunity wouldn't come again. Before my brain realized that it had made up its mind I said to Jimmy, "Yes, actually. Do you know of any lake houses for rent?"

"The resort section of the marina has rental lake cottages. I think they call them villas." Jimmy said "villas" in a way that led me to believe he found the name ridiculous.

I didn't want to be anywhere near that marina and run the risk of seeing even more of Emory. I probably needed to stay in town. "I was thinking maybe something closer to the square."

Jimmy sent me to the real estate office on the next block where I met with an agent and got the list of everything that was open for the next few weeks.

I spent the day looking at property. I drove by all the houses available. I crossed off all of the brown cedar mountain houses. They looked somehow depressing to me. I needed light. I needed open. I wanted a bright open space.

At the fifth house on my list I found what I was looking for. I parked the car on the street in front of the little white house. It was an old lake cottage just one block off the town square.

The front yard was awash with blue hydrangea bushes. It felt like a sign.

I checked the flyer again that the agent had given me. The house was very small with just two bedrooms and one bath. But the galley-style kitchen was newly renovated and the entire rear of the house held a screened-in porch that looked out over the lake.

It was perfect. I signed the rental agreement to lease it for a month starting in a few days.

When Logan got back from water-skiing I drove her by the

little cottage. I told her that she was welcome to stay with me if she wanted to. We could race toward the finish line of my mom's birthday together.

She was chewing on her fingernail. "Do you think my parents would let me?"

"I don't know. Couldn't hurt to ask."

Logan was nodding her head slowly. She looked as if she were already going over her argument and counterargument of why she should be allowed to stay with me. She seemed to have worked it all out. "Hey, a girl that I met today works at the summer camp at the marina. She said they need like three more people to help with the preschool day campers."

"Are you thinking about applying for a job?"

She shrugged. "It might be cool. It would look good on my transcripts."

"And you could be here all summer flirting with Graham."

"Yeah well, I *could* flirt with him all summer because *I* don't have a boyfriend."

"Be nice to me Lugnut or I'll ground you or something."

When I called Georgia that night to break it to her that I had actually done it—I had rented a house and would be staying longer—I made Logan talk to her first. I knew that arguing with Logan about staying with me would wear her out. But Logan was so excited about the idea of having a job and spending her summer on the lake that it was hard not to get caught up in her enthusiasm. When she finished describing the toddlers getting dropped off at the dock by their parents in their little life jackets there was nothing Georgia could do but agree to let her stay.

By the time Georgia got to me she was just tired. Another plan perfectly executed.

I couldn't sleep that night, which was becoming a theme lately. I was staring at the ceiling considering the possibility that the floor above me was haunted when I heard my phone ping. I had a text message from Elliott.

Elliott: *How was your day? Wanted to call but couldn't.*

Me: *It was good. Busy. How was yours?*

Elliott: *It was—can I call you?*

Me: *Y—*

My phone rang immediately and I snuck into the bathroom so I wouldn't wake up Logan. "Hi."

He sighed into the phone and some part of me melted. He said, "Hey. I'm sorry. I just saw the time."

"Don't worry about it. I was up. How's Atlanta?"

He spit out a laugh. "I'm burning it down again."

"What? I don't know what you mean."

"I know. I just wanted to check on you, see how you were doing."

"I'm good." I wasn't sure what he was asking me. Maybe he just wanted to know how things were going with my little research project. "I haven't found out anything new since I was with you."

"Oh." There was a pause and then he said, "I guess I just wanted to hear your voice, make sure you weren't hightailing it out of town while I wasn't looking."

I said, "Actually, I think the town is stuck with us for a while."

"It is?"

"Yes, I rented a lake house today."

"For how long?"

"A month."

I could hear the smile in his voice. "And here I thought you didn't like the lake."

"It's growing on me."

"I'm so glad to hear it."

I asked, "When will you be getting back?"

"Tomorrow night. I'm hoping anyway. It might be a bit late, but maybe I can see you when I get to town?"

"I'd like that."

We sat on the phone in silence for a moment. I was trying to stop myself from saying a whole host of embarrassing things. He sounded tired.

Finally he said, "I'm so glad you decided to stay."

"Me too. So I'll see you tomorrow?"

"See you then."

I hung up and went back to bed with absolutely no chance of getting any sleep.

FOURTEEN

Logan and I started the morning packing our things to get ready to move into the lake house the next day. Well, I packed up our things. Logan went out on the lake again with Graham.

I wandered through the square after lunch and called Leo to tell him I was staying longer. When I told him that I had already rented a house for the month he barked, "Why didn't you consult me before committing to that? Did you sign anything?"

I became instantly defensive. "I've been trying to talk to you since I got here but you've been too busy. Do I need permission from you to stay?"

"Yes!" Then he backed off. "That's not what I mean, Olivia. You said you and Georgia were flying down on Janie's birthday to scatter the ashes. You haven't said one thing about staying there the whole time."

I said sarcastically, "I sent you an e-mail."

"You know that's not productive."

That was something else we learned from our therapist. Sarcasm is not a productive means of communication. "Look Leo, I need to do this. I'm sorry that we didn't get a chance to discuss it before I rented the house."

I stopped talking so he would have an opening to speak. He was trying to be understanding. "Livie, honey, I don't mind you being down there. I want you to find out about your mom. I know this is important to you. I just don't think this is the best time. We have some important things coming up." I knew he was worried about planning the wedding but I really couldn't think about that at the moment. He continued. "I have four dinners in the next ten days." Or maybe he was just worried about making the right impression at work. "You're expected to be there and you're putting me in a bad position."

"I'm sorry." I was sorry. I felt horrible for everything I was doing, saying, and feeling toward Leo right now but I wasn't going to heel just so he could have a date to his work dinners.

He said, "Me too."

We hung up and I wondered what exactly Leo was sorry for. I looked at my phone. I thought, *That was a very unsatisfying conversation.* My phone didn't console me in any way.

Logan finally came back from the lake and I took her to buy a one-piece bathing suit for her new camp counselor job at the marina. Being with her was the most satisfying distraction. She had this unencumbered view of life that made you feel like anything was possible. She was so excited about starting her new job in the morning. Even the idea of work being fun was a possibility again when Logan was around.

When we got back to our room, I was so tired I thought about getting ready for bed. But I couldn't seem to settle my head. I decided to go for a walk. Maybe I would just walk downstairs to the bar.

It was almost nine o'clock and there were only a few people sitting in the lounge. I hadn't heard from Elliott all day. I hadn't really expected to necessarily, but then again I missed talking to him.

I peeked in the lounge and looked around to make sure Emory wasn't in there lurking. I wasn't in the mood to bump into him again.

I went to the bar and ordered my usual. There was a half-empty beer and a cell phone sitting on the bar so I moved a few seats over and sat down.

I was lost in thought, stirring my drink when I felt someone sit down right next to me. The owner of the abandoned beer and cell phone was back. Before I even looked at him I knew it was Elliott.

Without looking up I said, "You're back."

"Yep."

He sounded as tired as I felt. I turned my head to get a look at him and he just seemed beaten. "Are you okay? Because you look awful."

He smiled. "Thanks." He called out to the bartender. "Mark, can we get two more?" Then he looked at me. "I'm okay. It was a long couple of days and . . . hard. But it was the right thing. I mean . . ." He paused for a minute before continuing. "Never mind."

"That bad, huh?" I was trying to be playful, but he was obviously upset.

"Yes. But . . . it's really good to see you."

"You too." I wasn't sure what to say. "I'm glad you're back."

Elliott picked up a napkin and began absentmindedly wiping down the bar. "I just drove into town and headed over here. I was sitting here trying to decide if I should call you or knock on your door. Then you just showed up."

The bartender dropped off two more drinks in front of us and looked back and forth from me to Elliott. Then he asked Elliott, "Did you just get back from Atlanta?"

Something passed between them. Some sort of understanding. Elliott nodded his head. Mark said, "Sorry dude." And he went to the other side of the bar.

I put my hand on Elliott's; I was a little bit worried about him. "What happened?"

He smiled that little half smile of his and stood up. "Come on, let's move over there. Mark loves to listen in on a conversation."

We settled into a pair of chairs by the window and leaned in so that we could talk to each other in low voices.

I thought maybe I knew what this was about. "I assume this is the same girl trouble from the other day."

He was genuinely confused. "What trouble?"

"When you wouldn't answer the phone at your office."

He nodded, understanding now. "Yes, same trouble. We haven't been in a good place for a long time."

I felt a tinge of jealousy as soon as he started talking about this other woman, which was ridiculous so I pushed it aside. "I'm sorry. I'm a good listener if you want to talk about it." I waited but he just kept staring at his hands. Maybe I wasn't such a good listener; maybe I was a little impatient because I started feeding him lines. "Her name is . . . and we've been together since . . . and we had a fight about . . ."

He laughed a little and finally spoke. "Amy. Four years. This was the last fight, the last of many fights. I just couldn't keep up this toxic thing. We started fighting before I left Atlanta and I didn't see an end to it. The things we want are just too different."

"She lives in Atlanta?"

He nodded. "We moved there from Chicago. She thought being closer to my family would make things better, but it was just the same problems in a different city. Then I started the paper and we couldn't find a way to . . ."

"Would she consider moving here?"

He made a face that told me the answer before he even started speaking. "No. She wouldn't be happy here. She needs things, to climb after things that I just can't begin to want. She needs to be at the right parties with the right people. But I just can't chase all of that; it's not important to me. But Amy, she needs to be seen and to have the trendiest bag and right car. I don't know. It just got to the point where everything was hard."

Against my better judgment I defended Amy. "You know that you don't get to decide what's important to her."

He smiled a sort of sad smile. "It wasn't that. I don't judge that she needs it." He reconsidered. "Maybe I judged it a little. But I can't need it too. We both began to realize that if it was going to work then one of us was going to have to change drastically."

I already knew how these stories ended. "People aren't really that capable of change, are they?"

"Well, we weren't. She's happy with that lifestyle. But it's not for me. I won't play that game. And she can't come here to this place with so much . . . less. So"—he shrugged—"we just stopped working."

"Sorry."

His voice was very serious and very quiet. "I'm not. I mean I'm sorry that things ended the way they did, but I'm not sorry for having been with her. And I'm not sorry that it's over now. She'll find someone else who wants the same things and she'll be happier for it." Elliott was tracing the rim of his glass with his finger in a slow circle. Round and round. "And, well, there were other . . . reasons . . . that I needed to do it now." His eyes darted from the glass to mine for a split second and in that instant I wondered if this could have anything to do with me. There was an air of calm resolution on his face. "Being with someone shouldn't be so much work." The air was charged between us. I could feel a heaviness in my chest.

It took me a moment to find my voice, which sounded strained when I spoke. "You're right. That's the one thing in life that should be easy."

Elliott smiled, breaking the tension, and held his glass up to mine. "Like breathing." We clinked glasses. I was immediately reminded of my mother and her advice to be with someone I needed as desperately as breathing.

Elliott and I sat in that dark corner for the rest of the night discussing everything and nothing. As if unspoken permission had been granted for us to get to know each other better. We talked about my job, his paper, my sister, his family. I never brought up Leo and at some point he made the conscious decision to stop discussing Amy. We talked about the house I had rented on the lake and Logan's summer job. He told me about his parents and I told him about mine.

I found myself watching his hands as he spoke. He was so expressive with them and used them as emphasis in his stories. I had to stop myself from reaching out and taking them when they were still.

As the bar emptied and became quieter we found ourselves leaning into each other even more, our heads bowed together, our voices lower. It was an intimate conversation and we didn't want to share it.

We stayed until the bar was closed and even then we didn't leave. When Mark had finished cleaning up, restocking, and closing everything down he made us get out.

I walked Elliott to the front porch of the inn to say good-night. There was a summer thunderstorm brewing and the thick, damp wind was swirling around the porch. Strands of hair broke free from my elastic and blew around my face. The low pressure in the air forced the fragrance of the jasmine to sit low to the ground, perfuming the night.

This suddenly felt like a very awkward good-night. I had to say something to cut the tension. "I'm glad you came by to-night. I hope you're feeling better."

"I am." He stood there for a moment then he smiled and held up his hand in a small wave as he turned to go. I was watching him walk down the steps when he stopped, ran his hand through his hair, and turned around. His head was down, determined, as he marched back and stopped right in front of me, standing inches from me. His head was bent low, staring at our feet.

Slowly his hand moved out and gently brushed against mine, squeezing for just an instant before letting go. In a whisper he said, "You are easier for me to be with than anyone I have ever met."

When he finally looked at me, my breath caught. He gently brushed the hair out of my face and tucked it behind my ear. His hand moved over my skin, lightly tracing the curve of my neck down to my collarbone. His palm rested on my shoulder as his thumb gently stroked the base of my throat. We stood there, eyes locked, inches apart, as his hand moved slowly to the back of my neck. He pulled me in slightly and placed a kiss on my forehead. He said, "I just wanted you to know that."

He was gone before it ever even registered with me that he had left. I was standing there, alone in the blustering wind with my hand on my neck, trying to hold on to that feeling.

This wasn't just a crush anymore. At least not for me.

All I could think was, *I am falling for Elliott. And I don't even know his last name.*

FIFTEEN

After another night of fitful sleep I drove Logan to her first day of work at the camp. It was just as adorable as she had described it. The little campers were dropped off at the marina by boat. Then they waddled across the dock in their life jackets toward the camp. I made my way back to the inn to check out of our room.

Mrs. Chatham was walking around the property with a landscape crew directing the cleanup of the debris from the storm the night before. When she saw me she waved and I waved back.

She finished with the landscapers and came over to me to say hello. I told her again how much we had enjoyed our stay at the inn and that we would be in town for a few more weeks at a lake house.

She patted me on my hand, and told me that if I needed anything I was welcome to ask her. Then she pulled out a wrapped box of locally made pralines and gave them to me. They were a small thank-you gift to me for the candle I had given her. My phone rang, so she excused herself and went into the inn.

I answered. "Hello?" It was Elliott.

"Morning." His voice sounded gravelly, as if he'd just woken up, which I found very endearing.

I wasn't sure what to say regarding the things he whispered to me in the dark the night before so I just said hi.

He asked, "What're you doing?"

I looked down at the pralines that were a thank-you for the candle that was a thank-you for the garden club books. "I think I'm in a game of manners chicken with Betty Chatham."

He started laughing. "She'll never blink. You should just re-sign yourself to losing right now."

"I'm at a loss. Do I get her another thank-you gift for the thank-you gift? Or do I just say thanks and let this thing die?"

"Definitely let it go. What are you doing right now?"

"Nothing. I just sent Logan off for her first day of work. I can't get into the rental house until three o'clock."

"Okay then, want to meet me at Jimmy's for breakfast? Ten minutes?"

"Sounds good. I'll see you there."

When I got to Jimmy's, Elliott was already there. I felt a little shy when I first looked over at him. Considering how relatively small and tiny the kiss was that he planted on my forehead the night before, the nervous excitement in my stomach was dispro-portionably large.

Elliott and I grabbed the table near the front. I asked, "How did you sleep last night?"

He got a wicked little smile on his face, which told me he thought I was asking about one thing when I was actually asking about another. I winced, embarrassed. "I meant after all of your drama in Atlanta."

"Sure you did." He leaned over to the next table to get some sugar. "I slept well. Had interesting dreams."

At that my face blushed so fiercely I could feel the heat coming off my skin and he laughed at me. "You are easily flustered, Olivia."

"No more talking until after I get coffee." He opened his mouth to say something else and I cut him off. "I'm not kidding. Go mute on me right this minute."

He laughed, nodding. We ate our breakfast like that, in silence. When he was finished eating he said, "May I talk now?"

"No."

"How long do you think it will be until I'll be allowed to talk again?"

"That depends on what you're going to say."

"I was going to ask if you wanted to head over to the cemetery today."

"Oh." This was a nice surprise. "I'd love to. Do you have time?"

He smiled and I was starting to think there might be nothing more captivating than when Elliott was smiling at you. "Of course I have time."

Huntley Memorial Gardens was a sprawling cemetery on low rolling hills that backed up to the National Forest. We pulled in and parked in front of the office.

When we opened the door a bell chimed overhead and the cold, dry air hit us like a wall. The reception area was done in shades of maroon and royal blue with dusty plastic and silk flower arrangements on every shiny faux-cherry tabletop. One wall held tiny replica coffins propped open to display their plush interiors. Each coffin had a name like Eternal Slumber or the Regent Rest in bold script letters on copper plaques.

Elliott pointed to them and whispered, "Creepy tiny coffins."

I poked him in the ribs to get him to behave just as a woman came scurrying to the front.

"Hello there. May I help you all?" She led us into an office and motioned for us to sit down as she wedged herself behind the desk.

The woman was wearing such a thick mask of makeup that it looked as though the right amount of perspiration would cause the whole thing to slide off in one piece and land with a plop on the desk. Her blond, frosted bangs were teased up and sprayed with a lacquer that held them perfectly still no matter how much she moved her head. And she was swimming in a cloud of what must have been twenty squirts of perfume. She introduced herself as Mary Frances and spoke in a delicate whisper with an air of understanding and import that must come with the position of being the first contact in the cemetery.

I explained what we were doing there, about my mother's request, and asked about searching through the old section. The whole time I was speaking Mary Frances nodded her head with a genuine look of sympathy on her face. She frequently closed her eyes and sighed.

I wanted permission from the cemetery to scatter my mother's ashes. Logan thought we could just sneak in and do what we pleased with her. But I was worried that there could be some regulation against it. Some rule or law forbidding the spreading of ashes of human remains over the open ground with the potential of getting into the groundwater. I had a million strange things go through my head about toxins and contamination.

Elliott interrupted me and turned to Mary Frances. "Olivia likes to make sure that everything is in proper order."

Mary Frances leaned in and put her pudgy pale hand on mine. "Honey, there isn't anything wrong with it. This is a cemetery for goodness sake." She pulled her hand away, making the bevy of gold bangles jingle as it went.

Mary Frances kept talking as she pushed her chair back and wiggled her way around the desk. "The only thing we can't do is leave the flowers. You know the bouquets after the funeral? You turn your back on those things for one minute and the deer come straight down from the hills and start eating them."

She was walking out of the office and fluttered her hand behind her. "Well, c'mon then. Let's go find your plot for you."

As we followed Mary Frances out of the office I leaned in to Elliott. "You make me sound like a neurotic nutcase."

He whispered back. "You are neurotic."

"I am not."

"Neurotic."

I turned to face him. "Are you planning to make fun of me all day?"

He leaned down to meet my eyes. "No. I'm actually planning on making fun of you all week."

He was awfully cute when he was being snarky.

Mary Frances pulled out a detailed map of the cemetery and

highlighted our route from the office to the old section. It felt very similar to a rental car agency directing you out of the airport, which seemed very wrong for some reason.

Mary Frances said, "Now which plot is it that you need?"

I answered her. "It's thirty-four B. But that's all I know. I don't have a name or anything."

Mary Frances had a contemplative look on her face. It contorted the features of her pudgy cheeks and made her look as if she were in a bit of pain.

She said, "If you want I could pull the files for you and see if there's anything in there that might help you. I'll need to get permission from Mr. Heard first but it shouldn't be a problem." She flicked her bejeweled hand at me conspiratorially. "It's not like it's top secret or anything."

As Elliott and I made our way across the cemetery I said, "I am not neurotic."

"Yes, you are or you wouldn't feel the need to keep telling me that."

So then would saying it one more time prove his point that I am neurotic?

Elliott looked me up and down. "I am an excellent observer of people."

"And so modest too." I consulted the map and led us farther back into the cemetery.

He ignored that little quip and kept talking. "Along with your very slight neurotic tendencies, you're an obsessive compulsive desk organizer. You gnaw on your pens like a squirrel. You like your coffee dark and sweet. You will eat anything that anyone hands you, except for boiled peanuts. You adore your niece. You miss your mom. And probably your dad although you don't talk about him as much. When anything happens the first person you call is your sister. You prefer extra limes in your vodka tonic but you seem to feel bad about asking for them. You hate your job and you want to sell your house."

I was stunned by all of these little things Elliott had noticed about me, not because he had noticed them—we had been in that bar talking all night after all—but because he felt so comfortable listing them out like that. It caused my pace to slow. When he noticed that I was lagging behind he stopped and looked at me.

My eyes narrowed in concentration as I responded. "You compulsively fix the broken things you come across. There was the boat cleat, the chair at the Circle J, the sugar shaker at Jimmy's. When you talk about your brothers and sisters you get this little smile on one side of your face. You run your hands through your hair when you're thinking. You need glasses but don't like to use them, probably because you keep losing them. You would rather be fishing with your dad than fishing alone. And I still don't know your last name."

He smiled then reached out and took my hand. "Tate. It's Elliott Michael Tate."

The thirteen-year-old girl who lived in my brain began scribbling *Olivia Tate* on the front of her three-ring binder.

My phone rang, interrupting us, and I knew before I even looked at it that it was Georgia. I picked up without a proper greeting and said, "I'm at the cemetery."

She said, "Call me when you find the plot."

"Yep." I hung up, put the phone in my pocket, and followed Elliott.

The cemetery had little paths lined with gravel and each path

had a name. It was as if they had laid the cemetery out like a little city and these pathways were the streets. We followed Calhoun Avenue until it intersected with Church Street and then
turned left. The street names were hung on signs from small
wrought-iron posts and the pathways were lined with swags of
low chain. It was just enough of a hint of a boundary to keep me
squarely on the pathways. Why wasn't I the kind of girl who
would just step over the chain and walk the direct route?

At the front of the cemetery, where the newer plots were located, the headstones were basically all the same. Rectangular
marble stones lying flat on the ground. It probably made it easier to mow the grass with flat headstones.

As we worked our way back into the older part of the cemetery the headstones became much more elaborate and much
more diverse. There were all shapes and sizes. Tall monolithic
obelisks, elegantly carved angels and lambs, granite crosses,
and then scattered about were a few memorial marble benches.
Each of the different family sections were arranged around a
centrally located large crypt made of marble or granite with a
chained iron gate. There was a part of me that wanted to break
in to one of the crypts to see what was inside. But like Elliott
had hinted, I'm not a rule breaker.

We had walked for about five minutes when we reached the
section where 34B should be located. There was a rusting metal
fence surrounding section 30. The gate was broken and hanging askew from one hinge.

We entered the section, which held about forty graves, and
walked around trying to orient ourselves. I was looking for
something familiar. Some name that would hit me so that I
could think, *Ah-ha! That's why she wanted to be put to rest here.*

The oldest headstones dated from the late eighteen hundreds and the latest one that we could find was dated nineteen seventy-three. But I was baffled. I didn't recognize a single name.

Elliott looked at me and I shrugged. I said, "I don't know any of these people."

He looked around the little family plot. "Are we in the right place?"

I consulted the map and double-checked the names on the pathways lining the section we were standing in. "Yes, this is definitely section 30."

Elliott came to stand next to me as we gazed around at the headstones surrounding us. I sat down on the marble bench and threw my hands up, frustrated. Another dead end. "Who are these people?"

Elliott sat down next to me. He read a few of the headstones. "Apparently these are the Joneses."

"Well, who the hell are the Joneses?"

I called Georgia and told her that I was standing among the Joneses. She said the same thing I had said. "Who the hell are the Joneses?"

"I don't know. I'm getting kind of irritated with Mom. What is this wild-goose chase she's sent me on down here?"

Georgia tried to calm me down. "Look, she just wanted to be left there. She never asked us to figure out why. That's our own problem."

"It's weird. You don't tell your children to sprinkle your ashes over some random grave and a lake and not tell them why."

She asked, "Who was in thirty-four B?"

I realized that I hadn't even figured out which person we were supposed to be finding. I was just so miffed about once again not knowing what was going on. Elliott was doing the same thing he had done at the family graveyard behind my mother's old house. He was writing down all of the names and dates from every headstone.

"Hang on let me check the map again." I went back to the front of the family plot and counted over until I was in front of the headstone that should be 34B.

I looked at the inscription and told my sister what I saw:

GEORGE KIPP JONES III
JULY 12, 1946–FEBRUARY 27, 1972
YOU ARE MISSED AND LOVED EVERY DAY.

Georgia was quiet for a minute. I could tell she was wracking her brain, trying to remember if she had ever heard that name before. Then she sighed. "I have no clue. Who is George Jones?"

I kicked at a clump of dandelions growing on the edge of the pathway. "Isn't he the lounge singer from Vegas?"

"Funny, but no, that's Tom Jones. I think George Jones was a country singer."

Elliott was walking back toward me so I wanted to hang up before Georgia realized I was with him. "I'll call you later, Gigi."

I pointed to the headstone of 34B. Elliott said, "George Jones?"

"Yes, most fans just throw their bras on stage but my mom is having us deposit her ashes."

"You're terrible."

"I know. I'm just annoyed that she never told us what this was all about." I pointed to the small notebook he was holding. "You wrote them all down?"

"Yes, can't hurt. Maybe we can find something that will fill in the blanks for you."

The two of us stood side by side staring down at the gravestone of Mr. Jones, who was neither a lounge singer nor a country singer. Suddenly I heard a distant whooshing sound. It almost sounded like an oncoming rainstorm or maybe a swarm of locusts. I couldn't quite make it out.

Elliott and I both turned to see massive sprinklers shooting water a hundred feet out into the cemetery. They were coming on in succession and they seemed to be working their way toward where we were standing.

We snapped a glance at each other just as the sprinklers in our section sprang to life. We started running back toward the entrance of the cemetery where our car was parked. I was trying to beat the sprinklers or we would get drenched. I realized Elliott wasn't running next to me anymore and turned to see that he had stopped and was doubled over laughing.

"Elliott!" I waved at him to keep running and get out of the deluge. He stood up and threw his head back as the water overtook him. His eyes were closed; he spread his arms out and just let the water rain down on him.

I looked in every direction and realized what Elliott had already deduced: the sprinklers were spraying the entire graveyard. Fighting it and trying to stay dry was futile. It was no use. I braced for it as the water assaulted me.

Elliott was laughing as he walked slowly over to me, splashing in the newly made mud puddles. I just held my arms up in a gesture that asked, *Why?* Why would they water the graves like this in the middle of the day? Why didn't Mary Frances give us a little warning that the irrigation system was about to erupt?

He didn't really seem to mind that he had just been attacked by sprinklers in the middle of the day, fully clothed. If this had happened to Leo, he probably would've sued someone. Elliott was just rolling with it. He held his hands up, surrendering. "There doesn't seem to be any point in fighting it."

I had to agree. I had managed to turn away from the first wave, keeping my left side dry, but it wasn't much of a victory. "That's exactly what I was thinking."

He pointed to my face. I could feel the stream of water dripping off the tip of my nose. "You have a tiny bit of water right there."

I laughed. "You look like you just fell in the lake." He was completely soaked through.

He sauntered over to me. "Oh, am I wet?"

I put my hands up, backing away. "Don't."

"Don't what?" He jumped into me and picked me up squeezing the water from his shirt into mine. The water was cold and his skin was hot. He shook his head spraying water all over me. Now I was soaked too. "No use fighting it, Liv."

No, there didn't seem to be any point in fighting it.

SIXTEEN

Elliott and I sloshed into the car and drove back to Tillman. He pulled the little notebook out of his pocket to see if it was still legible now that it was drenched.

He held the paper up to the light. "I can still make out the names." As we pulled into Tillman, Elliott offered to help me move to the rental house.

I thought that I should politely decline. I felt like I was monopolizing all of his waking time, and giving him an out for the rest of the day would be nice of me. But of course I said, "That would be great."

We each changed into dry clothes and then took our things to the rental house. I opened the door to the little cottage and walked straight out to the screened porch that ran the width of the rear of the house. I stared out at the lake as the afternoon sunlight was glinting off the surface of the water.

As I brought the last bag in from the car Logan exploded through the front door. "Hello! Cool, you're moved in."

She was home early. "Lo, I was supposed to pick you up at six o'clock."

She was quickly poking around from room to room getting the lay of the land. "Hi, Elliott." She kicked her shoes off and they landed in the kitchen. "We got out early today. They were showing the kids a movie. Cute house." She threw her pool bag on the dining room table upsetting all of the research printouts I had put there.

That girl made my head spin. "Logan! Stop running around. Talk to me. How was work? What are you looking for?"

"My makeup bag."

"It's in the—"

"Found it!" She dropped her wet pool towel on the chair. "My friend Laura is waiting for me outside. We're going to her house to hang out. Then Graham and some guys are coming over later to watch a movie."

Elliott was laughing as he watched this whole scene unfold. I went outside to the waiting car where I found a girl that I assumed was Laura, and I made her come into the house. I grilled her in a fashion that would make Georgia proud, and horrified Logan.

I walked them out. "Be home by ten, Logan."

She counteroffered. "Eleven?"

"Ten."

"Fine. Hey, what did you find at the cemetery today?"

"Not much. Another weird dead end."

Logan snickered. "Ha. Dead end. Cemetery."

"You're such a dork."

She climbed into Laura's car. "Hey, who was in thirty-four B?"

"It was George Jones. Whoever that was."

Logan was sort of mumbling to herself. "Jones, Jones from Huntley. I know it's a totally common name but I read a bunch of stuff about the Joneses from Huntley the other day in those archives. A lot of stuff about baseball and the army or navy or something." She waved out the window as the car pulled away.

Elliott sat down at the dining room table with Logan's laptop. He looked up at me and said, "We might as well start looking."

I pulled my computer out too, and we sat across from each other at the table. We kept looking over our computer screens at the other one.

I said, "I really appreciate how much you're helping me with this little mystery."

Elliott looked up from the screen. "I'm just using you for the story." He ran his hand through his hair. Thinking. "Don't let me overstay my welcome."

I said, "You can stay as long as you want."

He smiled that lopsided smile. "Good to know."

I looked back at my computer and pretended like I was able to concentrate on it. Luckily it didn't take much of my mental capacity to begin searching for George Kipp Jones III. I was operating on about a fourth-degree black belt in Googling at this point so I was able to find his birth certificate in no time. His birth weight was low, only five pounds ten ounces. That was small for a boy. Very small. But then I noticed another box, checked in the affirmative, which read "Plural Births Only." Apparently George had been a twin. In the box next to "Birth Order" was the note "1 of 2."

So George had been a twin and had been born first. George's mother was Ester Rebecca Jones and his father was George Kipp Jones Jr. His mother's profession was listed as a nurse and his father was listed as an army officer. As I zoomed in to the grainy scan of the document I thought it was interesting, especially the way it was obviously written with a fountain pen, which had splattered ink on the edges, but I still didn't see what it had to do with my mother.

The next document I was able to find was his death certificate. Birth and death and not much in between. I read quickly through the grim facts. He died February 27, 1972. Age: twenty-five years, seven months, fifteen days. Cause of death: primary streptococcal pneumonia.

I looked up and asked Elliott, "Pneumonia? Who dies of pneumonia?"

He took his glasses off. "Tolstoy died of pneumonia."

"Show off." I clicked on the next link in the search query. "But Tolstoy was old, right? Old people, especially old people in Russia, can die of pneumonia, but a twenty-five-year-old?"

Elliott snapped his fingers. "Corey Haim, he died of pneumonia too."

Now I was laughing. "Why do you know that?"

Another fuzzy scanned image came up on the screen. I squinted to read the words and "oh my God" fell out of my mouth. It was a marriage certificate.

Elliott came behind me to read over my shoulder. "What?"

"She was married to him. My mom and George Jones were married." I felt a crack open somewhere. Something shifted. My mother had a whole life I didn't know about.

"You didn't know that she'd been married before?"

I couldn't say anything. I just shook my head. Elliott was quickly digging through the papers scattered on the table. He found my phone and handed it to me. "I'm guessing you want to call your sister."

I started speaking before Georgia could even say hello. "Georgia, I found George Jones and . . . you aren't going to believe this."

Georgia was speaking in her clipped, scolding tone. "I tried to call you earlier."

"Did you hear me?"

"Have you talked to Leo today? He's been trying to call you all—"

"Georgia! Listen, George Jones and Mom were married." I was pacing the small living room.

"What?"

I read the date off the screen. "On September 4, 1966, George Jones and Jane Rutledge were married."

"What!"

How many times would I have to say this before she could process it? I spoke very slowly. "They. Were. Married."

"Well, that . . . I don't . . . I can't believe it. How could she not tell us that? Do you think Dad knew about it? But nineteen sixty-six. Wouldn't she have still been in college? She would've only been twenty-one. Wait no, twenty! I can't believe she never told us she'd been married before." Georgia's words were flying out of her all mashed together.

They had been married for about five years. Why had she never told us about him? Maybe his early death was too painful for her to talk about. I thought back to when I was twenty, how very young I was.

I mumbled it under my breath. "Twenty." I looked at Elliott and asked, "Why do twenty-year-old kids get married?" I knew it was a different time and place, the sixties in the South, but it just wouldn't be like the Jane Hughes I knew to get married before she graduated from college.

He knew what I was getting at. "Because they have to?"

My phone barked. "Olivia!" I had forgotten that Georgia was still there.

Elliott and I were already starting a new search, fingers typing frantically on the keyboard. He said over his shoulder, "We should check birth records for nineteen sixty-six and nineteen sixty-seven."

Georgia sounded breathless and angry. "Who are you talking to, Livie?"

"It's Elliott. I'm talking to Elliott." Before she could start in on me for that I cut her off. "We're going to check the birth records to see why Mom had to get married when she was twenty."

We searched for hours through every state and county website we could access but we couldn't find any birth certificates from 1966 or 1967 for my mother or George Jones. It was another dead end.

Elliott tried to make me feel better. "Logan mentioned there were stories about the Joneses from Huntley in the newspaper

archives. We could search through there to see if we find anything."

I stood up stretching my back then went to the couch and
flopped down closing my eyes. I was so tired. "I can't look any
more today. I still can't believe she was married before. And I
feel like everything I find out about my mother or her time here
involves death and endings. People dying, the town drowning,
the house burning down. It's like everything she knew here
died, so she just walked away and never looked back. It's so depressing."

Elliott sat next to me and kicked his feet up on the coffee table
next to mine. "Well, the good news is it looks like they got married because they wanted to, not because they had to. She was
probably in love with him."

My eyes were closed, and I didn't want to open them again.
"Remember when you said I was being kind of weird about the
lake?" I felt him nod his head. "Well, starting tomorrow I'm
about to go to a whole new level of weird about George Jones."

Elliott laughed and pulled me to my feet. "Come on. We're
going down to the water." We ordered pizza for dinner and ate
it down by the lake. We took some chairs from the porch and
carried them down to the small sandy beach at the edge of the
water. We stayed down there past the pale, hazy blue sky of late
afternoon and through the orange and pink wisps of sunset and
finally into the twilight hour as the black silhouettes of the trees
began to outline themselves against the pale gray sky.

I watched the water as it changed with the diminishing light.
Elliott had found a fishing rod on a nearby dock and I tried to
fish. There's a lot of waiting when you're fishing. Which is re-

ally boring. The whole time I was sitting there I just kept thinking, *How many secrets was this lake hiding? How many lives were altered by the rushing of floodwater and the passage of time? Why didn't she ever tell us she had been married before?*

Also: *What am I going to do about Leo? What am I going to tell Elliott?*

Maybe "boring" would be the wrong word to describe my experience fishing. Maybe agonizing would be better. Yes, fishing was agonizing.

Elliott went up to the house to search for something to drink and came back with two beers. He handed me one, and then sat next to me again. I hadn't bought any groceries yet. "Where did you get these?"

"I suppose they were left by the previous tenant. There are also a *lot* of coffee filters for some reason. Cheers."

We tapped the cans together. "Cheers."

Elliott took the fishing rod from me and stood at the edge of the water reeling the line back in. I suspected I was doing it all wrong, although how one could hold on to a pole incorrectly was beyond me.

My phone rang, upsetting the solitude. I groaned as I fished the phone out of my pocket. "I hope this isn't the office again." I had several missed calls on my phone and I knew that most of them were from work.

It was Georgia. She was having a hard time dealing with the fact that our mother had been married before too. She sounded unusually tired. "What exactly are you doing right now, Livie?" I think she knew the answer already. She was just waiting to see if I would lie to her or not, to gauge how completely I was messing up my life.

I looked at Elliott, who was casting his fishing line far out into the lake. He looked back at me with those green eyes and smiled.

I decided to fess up to her. "I just had dinner with Elliott." He looked pleased that I was telling my sister about him. "I think I mentioned Elliott to you."

Georgia didn't say anything. I thought maybe I had dropped the call. But then I heard her say, "Dammit, Livie." And she hung up the phone.

Elliott said, "So you mentioned me, huh?"

I kicked him lightly with my foot and teased, "Nothing good I assure you."

My phone rang again. Georgia must have been unsatisfied with her level of admonishment. I picked up. "What now?"

"Livie?" It was Leo.

Shit.

Elliott was looking at me and I just froze. Leo said it again. "Livie?"

I had to say something. I could feel a lone bead of sweat trail down my back. "Hi. I'm here. What's going on?"

"I need to talk to you. You were supposed to call me today remember? I've been trying to get in touch with you all day and you haven't answered."

"We were at the cemetery today." That seemed like the safest thing to say.

"Okay. Great. But you said you would call me. I need to talk to you. The deposit for the gallery is due by Friday if we want it for the reception."

Oh my God, this is not happening. I tried to sound like I wasn't freaking out internally. "Can I call you later?"

"No, Olivia. No, you cannot call me later. We need to firm this up. Your phone's been going straight to voice mail all day. It's been very frustrating not being able to get in touch with you."

I didn't know what to say. I had to talk to Leo but I couldn't do it right now. And I couldn't do it on the phone. Elliott was slowly reeling the line back in.

I could hear Leo's shoes clomping on the floor of the kitchen. He was waiting for me to say something. I panicked and hung up on him.

I had never hung up on him before.

The phone rang right back. I felt the blood drain from my face. I was gripping the phone to the point where my knuckles were turning white. I couldn't do this now.

I cocked my arm back and threw my phone in the lake. It was ringing as it sailed in an arc through the air and didn't stop until it plopped into the water.

I stood up and stared at the ripples. Elliott came to stand next to me and we both stared silently at the dark waters of the cell phone–eating lake.

Elliott put his arm around me. "Olivia, I am so proud of you. You just went a little bit crazy."

I couldn't take my eyes off the water. What good did that do? Now I didn't have a phone. That was just . . . stupid! My brain was reeling.

Elliott was laughing with his arm around my shoulder. "Was that your office?" I nodded, lying. He said, "I honestly didn't think you had it in you."

This is why you don't go off half-cocked and do spontaneous stu-

*pid things! This is why you plan things! This is why you do not put
yourself in situations that make you lose your mind!*

Elliott tightened his grip. He stopped laughing, probably
sensing that I wasn't finding any of this funny. "It's okay. We'll
get you another phone. We'll fix it." We watched the ripples
cast out from my drowned phone. His voice was quiet. "But I
do think you need to seriously consider more than just a leave of
absence from work."

Elliott realized that I hadn't spoken. I was just standing there
dumb struck with my mouth hanging open staring at the lake. He
moved in front of my face and bent down a little to be in line with
my eyes. He said, "Hey, really. It's okay. You just got to the point
where you snapped. It's not the end of the world. It's just a phone."

It wasn't just a phone.

"Elliott, I think I'm kind of confused right now." My voice
sounded strange and shallow. I couldn't quite get enough air.

He smiled and brushed the hair out of my face, trying to calm
me down. "I can tell. Is it because of everything with your
mom? Is it just work? Do you want to talk about it?"

I shook my head.

He laughed at what must have been a very strange and pained
expression on my face. "Okay. But remember, I've been where
you are with work. I know what it's like to be all tied up with
your job and your life and feel like there's no way out. It makes
you crazy. It makes you do insane stuff"—he pointed at the
water—"like throw your phone in the lake."

My heart was racing. He didn't realize that I had just thrown
much more in the lake than my cell phone. We were standing
there facing each other at the edge of the water.

He tucked my hair behind my ear. "Why don't you just leave your job and go off the grid. You can hide out down here with me."

He was joking, being silly, but I was about to break into a full panic attack. I could feel tears sting my eyes. "I . . . what?"

Elliott laughed then. He grabbed one of my hands and looked down at me, smiling. "I'm serious. Clearly technology is a problem for you." He was making jokes to ease the tension either because I had just freaked out and lost my mind a little bit or because he had said, out loud, that I should stay here with him. What did that even mean? Was he just kidding or was he telling me something else? At the moment he simply kept teasing me. "You may need to go full Amish. Live out your days in a cabin on the lake."

His grip tightened around my hand and I could feel myself calming down, letting go of the panic I felt moments ago. He smiled and I couldn't help but smile back. I asked, "And what will I do for sustenance in this Amish lake cabin?"

Elliott filled his cheeks with air and blew out slowly, thinking. "That's a really good question. It could be tricky, especially since you are such a terrible fisherman."

Logan was right. He did make me laugh. I took a step closer to him. "How hard can it be to hold a stick until a fish is fooled into biting it?"

He was shaking his head, disappointed in my portrayal of fishing. "You will definitely starve."

"I can always order pizza."

"No, you can't. You don't have a phone." Elliott stopped talking and something in his eyes changed, became more serious. He reached up and took my face in his hands and everything felt different. I could feel myself being drawn in to him. He bent down to kiss me and everything else seemed to vanish.

Our moment down by the lake was suddenly and abruptly cut short when Logan came home, bursting through the screen porch door and screaming down toward the water, "Aunt Livie? Are you down there?"

She was proud of herself for getting home before her curfew; I was lamenting the fact that I didn't let her stay out until eleven.

I walked Elliott out and watched as he walked down the sidewalk toward his house. I started to consider all that had just happened, all that it would mean, and then shut it off. I couldn't let my mind go there.

I went inside to the little kitchen and got a glass of water. I walked over to the mantel where the urn containing the remains of my mother had been placed and clinked the glass on it. *Why didn't you ever tell us about him, Mom?*

I took Logan's phone and called Georgia back. I had forgotten to tell her that we didn't find any evidence of a shotgun wedding. No evidence of a little bastardly bundle of joy in the mix. For the first time she sounded like she was in a near panic about not being down here with me. She started to say something about Elliott, but I stopped her. "Look, it's complicated and I don't want to talk about it right now." She was saying something else but I just kept talking over her, not letting her get a word in. "Gigi, will you do me a favor? Call Leo and tell him that my phone . . . my phone fell in the lake and I will call him first thing in the morning after I buy a new one. Don't embellish."

"Fine. But I have to say something." I just waited. Georgia's voice didn't sound angry anymore, just concerned. "You may be messing up your life in a way that you won't be able to fix."

I knew she was right. "Maybe." I hung up the phone. What had Elliott said about going to Atlanta? He had burned it down again. Throwing my phone in the lake felt like me striking my own match.

SEVENTEEN

When I woke up the next morning Logan had already left for work. She was going to be catching a ride to the marina by boat with Laura, the girl I had met. Apparently Laura lived across the cove. Not a bad way to commute.

I walked into the kitchen and was assaulted with a barrage of fluttery white paper hanging from the ceiling. It looked like a very overzealous child had hung paper snowflakes all over the place. There were dozens and dozens of them.

I stepped under the falling snowflakes suspended in mid-flight and twirled my hands around. They moved on the breeze I created. Then I noticed that some of them had writing on them.

I pulled one down. I realized the white papers were actually coffee filters and the note on the one I pulled down read: "Four o'clock." I pulled down all of the other filters with writing on them and laid them out on the counter.

I arranged them into some sort of logical message:

> *Good morning!*
>
> *Why do you think there are <u>so many</u> coffee filters? It's weird.*
>
> *I won't get to see you today. I have to be in Chattanooga for the night.*
>
> *I'm taking you to an event tomorrow afternoon.*
>
> *Four o'clock.*
>
> *I'll pick you up.*
>
> *I would have called, but you don't have a phone. Ha.*
>
> *No problem though. I found some paper and left you a note.*

I couldn't help but wonder how Elliott had managed to do all of this without waking me up. I made my coffee and stood under the shower of white papers as they danced on the current from the air conditioning vent.

I had never before had the sensation that standing under

those silly white coffee filters hanging from strings taped to the kitchen ceiling gave me. It was one of calm mixed with surprise and comfort mixed with excitement. All at the same time. They should really think of a word for that feeling.

I took my time getting ready and then headed to the store to replace my phone. And then, after all the procrastinating I could think of, I called Leo to talk to him about the wedding reception venue. He was very upset with me. For all the obvious reasons. He should have been even more upset with me, but he was unaware of those other reasons.

"Leo, I know you're going to think I'm postponing—"

"Oh my God, Olivia. Really?"

"Just listen to me. I'm down here, in Georgia. I just can't go booking reception venues when I'm hundreds of miles away!"

He spoke through his teeth. "You know what the place looks like. We've looked at it three times! You either want it or you don't."

I stood my ground. "Okay then, I don't."

He said, "I think maybe you should come home."

"What? No! I'm not finished yet."

"Finished with what? You're on a wild-goose chase. If your mother had wanted you to know all of this from her past she would have told you. It's none of your business."

I had the urge to throw my new phone into a lake too, but I resisted. "Leo, if we want to find out what happened to her then we have a right to."

"There is no 'we.' Georgia's not even down there with you."

I said, "That's because she had to stay at home with the boys."

"That's my point. She's at home, where she should be. With her family."

"You are unbelievable."

"Me?" I could hear all the anger in Leo's voice. "You're the one who ran off for the summer. And why don't you want to book the gallery? It's the only place you liked."

I wasn't mad anymore, just tired. "I don't want to argue about it, okay? I just don't want to book that place."

"Why?"

Such a small word for such a loaded question. "I'm just not . . . I don't want . . . " I kept hearing Georgia's voice in my head telling me I was messing this up to the point where I couldn't fix it. I closed my eyes as I said, "The gallery is too cold. Austere. And I don't like the echo. They can't seem to control that echo."

I could hear him plop down in his ergonomically correct desk chair in his office. "Is that really why you don't like it?"

"Yes. That's why."

Leo sighed. "Okay. I understand. We'll find something else."

"Listen, do you have time to talk right now? A lot has happened since I got here and I feel like we haven't been able to talk."

"You know I'm inundated this whole week." I could hear him already shuffling through papers as he spoke to me. That was the cue that this conversation was almost over.

"I know, Leo, but this is important. I'm having a really hard time . . . with some things."

"You'll be home soon. We can talk then." That was Leo's polite way of saying he didn't have time to talk to me. Or he didn't want to make the time.

Resigned. "Right, I'll be home after Mom's birthday."

I wandered through the square and found myself near the library. I decided to duck in and get my mind back on my quest and off of Leo. I walked in and stood for a minute in the cold foyer, taking a few deep breaths and fanning myself with my shirt, which was now damp with sweat from the heat outside. When I found Bitsy I told her that I had a new development in my little research project in the form of an undisclosed first husband.

Bitsy had some things that she had pulled and wanted me to see. She led me to the long library table and produced a large book. It turned out to be the book of plat maps from the area spanning three decades: the 1950s through the 1970s. That would mean it would show the area of Rutledge Ridge before, during, and after the lake had been created.

She tapped her finger on the oversized volume. "Someone pulled this from the shelf this week and I kept it out thinking you might want to take a look through it."

"Someone else was looking through old maps of Huntley? That's weird. Do you know who it was?"

She shook her head. "No, these are reference books and can't be checked out, so there's no way to know. It is strange though. That book hasn't been pulled for almost thirty years and now it's getting read twice in one week."

Bitsy went off to find something else while I opened the map book. The book was huge, at least two feet by three feet and when I turned to the first page I was staring at the now-familiar plan of the town of Huntley in the 1950s before the deluge.

This map was at such a tiny scale that I couldn't make out any of the names or plat numbers in the individual parcels of land.

But from this vantage point I could see the whole town situated in the valley with the mountains rising on both sides. Huntley was sitting at the bottom of the pool, hemmed in by the river on one side and a railway line on the other. I traced my finger along the topography lines as they crept up and away from the river's edge. You could see very easily how the water would fill it all in. Off to the northeast, safely perched on a plateau in the hillside, was the town of Tillman. It was about to become lakefront property.

It was hard to get my bearings when the geography had changed so much with the formation of the lake. But after orienting myself with the town of Tillman, and knowing where the golf course and marina were currently located, I knew where to look for my mother's house. I had to go steal a magnifying glass from Bitsy's desk to be able to decipher the tiny names on the map. The remains of my mother's house abutted where the golf course was now, so I followed that line in the hilltop until I was able to locate the parcel with "Rutledge Ridge" written faintly across it.

The property contained nearly fifty acres and encompassed both sides of the ridge and all of the land that rolled down toward the valley below. The piece of property to the west of Rutledge Ridge was owned by Nathan Bedford Forrest. That was the family that had the border dispute with my mother's family about the location of the property line. The Rutledges and the Forrests seemed to have had a good old-fashioned neighbor's feud. Cue the dueling banjos.

I moved the magnifying glass to the name written on the parcel to the other side of the Rutledge property. This parcel was roughly the same size and shape as Rutledge Ridge. This piece had the owner's name listed as: George Kipp Jones Jr.

So Janie Rutledge and George Jones were next-door neighbors; they had grown up together. I sat back in the chair realizing, maybe for the first time, that this man, George Jones, was my mother's first love. I was achingly sad for my father as I wondered what that meant he had been to her.

Bitsy came over. "Any luck?"

I pointed to the map. "The first husband, George, lived next door to my mom."

Bitsy loved the romantic turn of events. "That's so sweet to have your first love be the boy next door." She was obviously the kind of woman who loved a love story. She had that dreamy look on her face.

I asked, "Where did you meet your first love, Bitsy?"

As I expected, she was hoping I would ask. Why couldn't I be one of these girls who got giddy and gushy like that? As she told me her tale of dorm-crossed lovers I thought back to when I met Leo.

He and I met at a friend's wedding five years before. Leo showed up at the ceremony deeply tanned having just vacationed in Barbados. The second he walked into the ballroom he became the number one draft pick for every unattached girl in the wedding party. At one point the maid of honor, with a microtolerance for alcohol, was performing some kind of dance for him that would have satisfied a liberal definition of the term "sex act."

As I was walking by the peep show, Leo grabbed my arm, deliberately spilling my champagne down the front of his suit. He made a show of needing to dry off and kept hold of my hand while the two of us made for the exit in a fit of laughter. He introduced himself to me in the cab that we shared back to the hotel and that was that.

He was smart, good-looking, and kind. We had all the same friends. We fell into dating, moved naturally into a relationship, and were suddenly a couple. I didn't question any part of it; it just happened. It was painless. I had been in my midtwenties and everyone around me was getting married; some were already having babies. It seemed like Leo and I met at the right time in our lives. We had never had much in the way of passion, but I always considered that a good thing because it meant we never fought. Leo and I were vanilla ice cream. Consistent but bland.

Bitsy asked, "What about you? Was your first love the boy next door?"

"Ha, no." My stomach lurched as I thought of the art installation of fluttering white papers I had found in the kitchen that morning. I surprised myself with my answer. "I think I met him in a coffee shop."

I could feel my face blush, realizing I had said that, and I pretended to be engrossed in the map book. Bitsy went back to her research. I opened to the map from the sixties showing the creation of the lake. I didn't stop long on that one. All I could see from this vantage point was the hand of God turning on some colossal spigot, giggling as he extinguished the whole town of Huntley.

The next map showed the area as I knew it now. It was drawn in the late seventies and included all of Tillman and all that remained above water from Huntley, which wasn't much.

There was a legend indicating that there were some larger-scaled maps of the parcel where my mother's land had been on pages thirty-four and thirty-five. I turned to the pages in the book, anxious to see what my mother's property had looked like in the seventies. Pages thirty-four and thirty-five were missing from the book. They had been surgically cut from the spine. I ran to find Bitsy.

It took Bitsy a long time to calm down enough to stop pacing, but she was still ranting about the missing pages from the map book. She said for the second time, "It is against the law to willfully and maliciously deface any property of the public library." You would think someone had sneaked in at night and cut off her child's hair.

I asked, "Is there another copy of this? Is there somewhere else I could get these maps?"

She turned her mind away from the vandalism for a moment.

"Well, you could contact the county, of course, but the information they'll have readily available will be the most current maps, which are at most maybe five years old. They won't show any historical data, just the name of the person who owns it now or who had last filed a deed when the map was printed."

I knew she was right about that. I started thinking aloud. "Maybe I can order the older records from them." Now that the maps were missing I desperately wanted to look at them. It was the same way I felt about the missing journals from the reading room. What was in there that someone didn't want me to see?

Bitsy went back to writing up her report on the "wanton destruction of property" while she spoke.

"You should, Olivia. The county courthouse is just across the square. I know they do a lot of searches for title discrepancies and ownership disputes so they should know how to order the historical maps." She finished the report with a sigh and put it aside.

When she said "discrepancies" it reminded me of something. "Bitsy, you know that old church steeple that used to float around in the lake? Logan found an article about it that said it was from a church on the disputed line between the Rutledge and Forrest properties. Do you think there would be any articles about the dispute between those two families?"

Bitsy smiled. "That's so funny that you asked about that church."

"It is? Why?"

She put a printout from a newspaper article in front of me. "I found this when I went looking for your mother's wedding announcement. Guess where your mother and George Jones were married."

"No way!" In some part of my imagination I could hear the distant chiming of church bells float out from the bottom of the lake, bloated and distorted.

"Yes, and guess where your grandmother's funeral services were held."

Now the floating ghostly church steeple felt like it wasn't just quietly haunting me, but was literally trying to scream out at me from underneath the water. I shuddered involuntarily as I read the articles.

The first one was a story about the Rutledge family dedicating the small garden in front of the church to Martha Rutledge's memory. The fuzzy picture that went with the article showed my grandfather, the judge, standing stoic but clearly sad as he held the hand of his little girl. On the other side of ten-year-old Janie Rutledge was a little boy, slightly taller than her, holding her other hand. I stared at the picture for a long time and knew for certain that the little boy must be George.

The little girl in that picture looked so lost. She was staring through the camera with a haunting vacancy. The one detail that kept pulling my eyes down was her sock. One white knee sock had fallen and was sagging down around her ankle. It seemed like the kind of tiny detail that a mother would notice and rectify before letting the newspaper take her photograph. To me it was the personification of being raised without her mother. That sagging sock.

The article continued on another page with a second photo. It showed the judge ceremoniously holding a shovel next to a newly planted hydrangea bush. Janie was standing slightly behind him holding the hand of a black woman. I noticed that now Janie didn't look quite so lost or quite so frightened. And her sock had been pulled up, fixed for the camera. The name of the black woman was not given in the article but I knew it had to be Maudy. The woman who had worked for the judge and most likely raised Janie after her mother had died. I felt an unmistakable gratitude toward this woman I had never heard of, and would certainly never meet, for doing such a good job raising my mom.

The newspaper story focused mostly on the church. It was a tiny one-room building, wooden framed and whitewashed, built in 1893 by former slaves. The sparse little structure held eight pews and could seat about forty people. It was no longer being used by the First African Baptist Church when this photo was taken, but the community was in the process of trying to have it declared a historical site to protect it.

The second article Bitsy had found was an editorial debate about the little church. One side argued to preserve the structure by having it moved to higher ground. Apparently one of the tributaries leading into the newly formed lake had begun to flood in the springtime and was threatening to overtake the church. The other side argued that the structure was fully on Mr. Forrest's land and if Mr. Forrest wanted the building to be left alone to be swallowed by the lake, then that was his right.

The side in favor of saving the building had a photo of a very young and very angry-looking Janie Rutledge. As I examined the picture more closely I corrected myself, not Janie Rutledge. She was now Janie Jones and she was standing with George while he held up a clipboard, which he was waving at someone off-camera. Their body language was exactly the same. They were matched perfectly.

Underneath the photo was the caption: "Mr. and Mrs. George Jones, formerly of Huntley, petition to save the church where they were married."

Because we had no photos of my mother at this age I was mesmerized by it. Her skin was so smooth and her hair was thick and dark. She wore it in a long flip and she was wearing lipstick. My mom never wore lipstick. Her arms were strong and lean and her tiny waist was pinched with a wide belt over her slim cropped pants.

George was at least a head taller than her. He wore khaki pants and a white shirt. He was tan and fit and perched on his head was a pair of tortoiseshell sunglasses. It wasn't hard to see why she had fallen for him. Or him for her. They looked like a slice of Camelot, or a Ralph Lauren ad.

The picture accompanying the other side of the argument showed a man wearing blue jeans with a work shirt and no shoes sitting on a porch with a hunting dog by his side. I said, "Nathan Forrest Sr., I presume." Then I looked closer at the picture. I recognized the face. When I met him he had aged considerably, and was armed with a shotgun. But this was definitely the same menace we had run into on the mountain.

I heard Bitsy, sitting at her computer say, "Oh dear."

When I looked up she waved me over. She printed out one last piece and handed it to me. It was the front-page article covering the conflagration of my mother's house. There was a picture of the burned-out remains. Charred sticks of wood framing were bubbled up on their surface like burned marshmallows. Wisps of smoke were still billowing up, frozen gray and transparent in the still picture. One part of the roof remained intact and you could see into the maw of the attic where unidentifiable family heirlooms were melted together or burned into nothingness.

Bitsy pointed to the first paragraph. Someone had been badly burned in the fire: Nathan Forrest Jr. That must have been the mountain man's son.

The story emerged as I read the article. Nate, as he was called, was a twenty-five-year-old married mechanic working at the dam. He woke up his young wife in the middle of the night and told her that he smelled smoke. He urged her to call the sheriff while he went to investigate. Apparently, he was worried that someone could be trapped in the house, asleep when the fire broke out, and now passed out from the smoke.

He ran from his house, pulling on his work boots. He managed to run into the inferno and get to the top of the stairs before they collapsed beneath him. He was pulled from the wreckage with burns over both of his legs.

It had been assumed by the first responders that Nate had gone rushing in to try to pull my mother out of the house, but Janie Jones was nowhere to be found.

A search for the missing Janie commenced using tracking dogs, volunteers on foot, and boaters. After twelve long hours, Janie Rutledge Jones was found alive. She was pulled out of a small rowboat, adrift in the lake, unconscious. The article stated that she was uninjured, but offered no explanation about the strange fact that she was floating out on the lake in the middle of the night while her home burned to the ground.

The investigation concluded that the fire started in the kitchen and was most likely due to the ancient wiring. Perhaps a spark had gone off inside the wall igniting the cotton batting insulation allowing the fire to take off from there.

I closed my eyes, the images of shifting map lines morphing with hydrangeas and wide summer porches bursting into flames in front of a black night sky. Why was she in the lake while her house burned? Was she trying to escape the fire?

How many things had burned for her that night that she lost her house? I needed to find someone who knew her back then, someone who may be able to answer some of these questions. So far the only person I had met in this town who may have known my mother was that crazy old man wielding a double-barreled shotgun. It wouldn't be pleasant, but I was going to see if I could talk to him again.

EIGHTEEN

I retraced my drive up the switchback roads and climbed the gravel lanes that led to the top of the ridge. Before I left the safety of my get-away vehicle I checked around for a weapon of some kind. I was regretting not buying mace years ago when Georgia had told me to. My only weapon was my cell phone so I kept it in my hand as I hiked up to the abandoned house.

The path looked different this early in the day. It was steamy under the trees in the heat and the sunlight was sharp as it broke through the leaves. The house came into view and I approached it slowly, fully expecting Nathan Forrest to materialize at any minute.

I stood at the edge of the eroded path leading to the front door and called out. "Hello? Mr. Forrest?"

The house looked different in this light too. Instead of menacing it just looked sad. Lonely almost. *Thud!* I wheeled around at the direction of the bang I had just heard expecting—what? For someone to swing down from a tree with a knife in his mouth and an axe in his hand probably. "Mr. Forrest? Are you here?" *Thud!* This time the bang had come from the other side of the house. I was surrounded. I held my cell phone out in front of me, putting it between myself and the monster sound coming out of the trees.

"Hello! Who's there?"

Thud! Thud! I was hit and I screamed. It got me on the shoulder. I ducked down instinctively, thinking that someone must be throwing rocks at me. I threw my hands over my head wondering if I should make a run for it when another one hit the ground right in front of me.

It was a huge green seedpod of some kind. The size of a racquetball and just as hard. They were falling from the trees. I was so relieved that no one had been here to witness my ducking for cover from a falling tree nut.

Thud, tink! One of them hit the tin roof of the old house. I picked up the nearest green ball and threw it back at the tree mumbling to myself. "You are an idiot, Olivia. Get it together." I tried to shake off the feeling of imminent danger and walked over to the front porch.

I climbed up the broken steps gingerly and went into the shell of the house. It was hot and sticky inside and there was a damp smell of mildew. I called out again, for good measure, but no one answered me. I wandered around the house again, trying to get some sense of the people who had lived here. The only thing it told me was that they had abandoned it a long time ago.

Going up the disintegrating stairs to the second floor was tricky, but I managed it by clinging to the wall and testing each step before I put my weight on it. The house creaked with my intrusion and the trees outside continued their assault. There wasn't anything up there so I carefully went back down.

One last walk through the first floor brought me to the sideboard filled with old letters. I looked over my shoulder before taking a handful and stepping out into the sunlight to read through them.

I fanned my face with one of the larger envelopes as I sat on the splintered front steps reading through letters. Occasionally I would call out to Mr. Forrest, "Hello?" No one ever answered.

The letters dated from the forties and fifties and they were personal correspondence, but not so personal that I felt like I was intruding. They were so old and had been so obviously abandoned that it felt like they were a part of the public trust, open to anyone who cared to read them.

They were updates to the Forrests from out-of-town friends and family. Each one seemed to give a weather, health, and crop update with the occasional announcement of a birth or a wedding.

The letters didn't say much, but the way they were written told me a great deal. Calling the language in the letters racist would be a gross understatement. It felt inappropriate just reading some of the words in my head.

After I read each letter I tucked the pages back into their yellowed envelopes and stacked them next to me where I sat. My mother had been a history professor whose main focus was the American civil rights movement. As a young woman Janie had ridden buses to Birmingham, marched in Selma, and protested in Atlanta. I knew about her experiences from listening to her lectures at school and the first-person accounts she would recount to her classes. She used to end one lecture series by saying, "It's the opportunities that divide people, not the color of their skin. But some people have opportunities given to them, handed to them, and some have to go out and find them for themselves. Go out in the world and find your opportunities."

She never talked about any of it at home of course. Those events had taken place before the demarcation in her timeline. They had occurred here, in her time growing up; therefore it was all part and parcel of the same code of silence.

But comparing what I knew about my mother's views on civil rights and what these letters told me about the Forrest family, well, I could understand why they didn't get along.

"Why are you back on my porch?"

I jumped. Nathan Forrest materialized out of thin air and was suddenly standing behind me, catching me in the act.

He walked around to face me. I was relieved when I didn't see a shotgun, although I was unfamiliar with the state of Georgia's concealed weapons laws. He shook his head slowly. "Trespassing wasn't enough. You had to come back and steal my family's letters?"

I put all the letters down. "I'm so sorry, Mr. Forrest. I have no good excuse for intruding like that." I tried to make light of the moment. "Although it would be tough to say I had to break into the house." I motioned to the door, barely hanging on to one hinge. "You don't live in there do you?"

He rolled his eyes at me clearly annoyed and grabbed the letters, shoving them into his pocket. "No one lives there." He didn't end that sentence with "idiot," but it was implied. He was wearing the same pair of old blue jeans and a tan windbreaker. It was already pushing ninety degrees. Why were old people always so cold? He grumbled at me. "Why do you keep turning up?"

"I wanted to ask you some questions about my mother. And her parents. You're the only person I've met in town who knew my mother."

Nathan Forrest started walking away from me, into the underbrush. As I followed him he said, "Didn't *you* know her?"

Touché. I explained about my mother's second life, the one she shared with my sister, my father, and me. I told him that she never spoke of her time growing up here and I had come down here after her death to learn more. I wasn't expecting to find the drowned town, or the dead first husband though.

Nathan Forrest had to be in his late eighties, but I was having a hard time keeping up with him as he followed a faint trail through the woods and undergrowth of blooming mountain laurel. "May I call you Nathan?"

"No, you can call me Buddy."

"Why Buddy?"

"Because it's my damn name."

I said, "Are you tracking something or can we slow down a bit?"

He stopped and looked at me with that "are you stupid" face again. "Tracking something?"

I wasn't sure if he was repeating me because it was a dumb question or because he didn't understand what I was asking. I tried to clarify. "Are you, you know, tracking? Hunting?"

"Girl, you're about to get on my last nerve. There's no hunting season in the middle of the damn summer. If I answer your questions can I get a minute's peace from you?"

"Well, I don't have any specific questions. I just want to know who my mom was growing up. What life was like for her here."

"Don't you think if she wanted you to know that she'd have told you herself?" I was getting tired of people asking that question, but I wasn't budging. He said, "Fine. If I tell you a few things will you go away so I can check my damn trees?"

"Yes."

As we walked back to the house I asked what was wrong with his trees. He had very little patience with me. Apparently his black walnut trees were dropping nuts early because they were stressed over the drought. Well, that explained the attack of the killer green seedpods.

I assumed that Buddy was a nickname, like Bubba or Bo, but he didn't offer up that information. Buddy wasn't a man to just start talking. I found I had to ask him very specific questions to get anything other than a yes or no out of him. When I asked the right question, however, he would get on a bit of a roll.

We were sitting together on the edge of what was left of the front porch. I asked, "Did you blame my mother in some way for your son getting hurt in that fire?"

"Of course not. I blamed Nate for trying to be a damn hero running into a burning house. That was stupid; she wasn't even in there. Did you know that?" I nodded, having just learned that detail at the library. "Well, Nate grew up with them, Janie and George. He thought she was in there all alone and he couldn't just let Janie burn to death now could he? She did right by him after that though. Damn near gave him every dollar she had for his recovery." I was about to ask how long it took Nate to recover from his burns but Buddy didn't pause long enough for me to ask. "Nate didn't ask for it. The money, I mean. She just gave it to him. Guess she didn't have the need for it anymore and she wanted him to have it. Damn Rutledges always had too much money anyway. That's what made Win act so superior all the time. He was damn pushy even before he became a judge. Nate and Margaret moved down to Gulf Shores after all his surgeries were done. Bought a nice house down there." He was drifting; he started to talk about the fish he had caught down in the Gulf.

I pulled him back to my questions. "Do you know why she was in the lake? I mean it's the middle of the night, her house catches on fire, and she heads out to the lake?"

Buddy never looked at me while I asked that question, he just kept staring at his hands, checking his watch. Finally he said, "You can't know what's in a person's mind."

Um, okay. After that little tidbit of wisdom I tried to ask my questions in a way that would avoid any need for Buddy to delve into hearsay or mind reading. "What was the story with the property line dispute you had with the Rutledges and that old church?"

"Just foolishness." He spit on the ground. "Foolishness and pride." Buddy explained the way the two tributary creeks that fed into the river on either side of the small white church had begun to flood every spring. The edges of their banks would shift and change each year. "That water divided our properties.

Sometimes the church was on my side, because of the water flow, and sometimes it was on his. I didn't give a damn about the thing, I just wasn't going to let Win Rutledge come in all high and mighty and take my land using some damn colored's church as an excuse. That old thing was falling down anyway."

He rubbed his hands together, kneading the knuckles, while he talked. They were just as wrinkled as his face, and even more callused. The stiff fingers on his right hand were stubbornly refusing to unbuckle no matter how much he worked them.

Buddy was obviously still a very active man, hiking out here alone in the woods. He smelled like wood smoke and Old Spice. I mean sure he was kind of a jerk and probably a total racist, but still, the old man was kind of growing on me. He seemed, underneath it all, to be really sweet.

He barked at me. "What're you grinning at me for?"

I said, "I never knew my grandfather went by Win. And I don't think they say 'colored' anymore. I think you should call it African American."

"Don't sass me."

"Sorry. Did you know my grandmother?"

"Yes."

I waited patiently hoping he would expand that answer. He didn't. "Can you tell me about her?"

"What do you want to know? She was real active in church, the Altar Guild. Martha had a big garden out there by the house, people always out there traipsing in and out, touring her flowers." Buddy was staring off, trying to focus on some past memory. "She was so homely. I never did understand what Win saw in her. There wasn't a nicer person you could meet. That was true, but she was so plain. And fat, she was always plump. Even when she got sick she didn't thin out. We all thought it was so peculiar when Janie turned out so pretty. Martha was sick for a long time before she finally died. Win was never the same after she passed. If you ask me, that was the thing that made him turn into such an asshole."

So my grandmother was overweight and unattractive and my grandfather was a pretentious asshole. *Please, Buddy, don't hold back on my account.* "We read something about a woman named Maudy. Did you know her too?"

He nodded. I expanded the question. "Was she their maid?"

"Of course she was their maid. What the hell kind of name is Maudy anyway?"

After the usual prodding Buddy told me a bit about Maudy, mostly about the food she used to make. As he went through the list my stomach started growling, and it went a long way to explain why my mother had never needed to learn how to cook. Buddy's stories about Maudy were smattered with colorful epithets. I didn't think it was for shock value, but simply out of habit. I got the impression that Buddy still remembered feeling a certain way about those times, about the segregation, but it seemed as though his core views had evolved over time, even if he didn't have the ability to change his language to match it.

He told me that when Maudy's son Robert began applying to colleges Win offered to pay his tuition. There was only one condition: Robert had to go to school up north. Win thought Robert had a better shot at some kind of equality if he went north. He ended up attending Northwestern. Eventually Maudy got too old to work, so Janie moved her into the Rutledge family house with Win. Janie ended up taking care of Maudy more than the other way around.

Buddy was warming to me. I could tell he hardly even wanted to shoot me anymore. "So Buddy, what was it like when they dammed up the river to build the lake?"

He looked sad then, and there is nothing sadder than an old person who's sad. "I'm guessing that you don't know much about rivers. But rivers are live things. That river had a personality; she had moods. She was different every day you went down there and every mile of her length. Angry and fast after a storm. Cool and slow in the summer. Dark in the fall. Then the damn government came in and strangled her. Killed her while she slept."

"I take it you don't like the lake?"

Buddy stood up to leave. He was finished with this little interview. "That lake is just a shallow grave for a dead thing."

I stood up too and brushed the dirt from my shorts. "What about all of the life that the lake has brought here? All of the people and boats and the marina?"

"It'd do you good to stay away from damn Bryant and his marina. That man won't care that you're Janie's daughter. He'd steal from you too just as soon as he'd look at you."

"You mean Emory Bryant?" What did he mean, "steal from me too"?

Buddy shook his head, as if I just didn't understand life. "There may be reasons your mother didn't talk to you about this place. Just let it go; what's done is done. You can't get it back."

I had so many more things I wanted to ask him. "I know

you're busy today." It seemed absurd to say it, but I added, "With your trees. So can we talk again sometime? You said that your son Nate grew up with them? My mom and George, right? I would love to hear some stories about them growing up."

I gave Buddy the address of my rental house and my cell phone number. I had to stop myself from asking him if he had access to a telephone.

I hiked back down the path toward my car listening to the thuds of the black walnuts hitting the ground. I also said a little prayer for rain, suddenly worrying about the fate of Buddy's beloved trees.

NINETEEN

I woke up the next day sore from the small hike up to Buddy's property and aching from being hit by the walnuts. Who knew that unshelled walnuts could make such good weapons? I spent most of the day wrapping up some things with work, not because I wanted to necessarily, but because it needed to be done and I could do it indoors. It had become unfathomably hot outside. I would put it on par with a solar detonation. The locals were referring to it as "summer."

Elliott arrived at four o'clock, just as he had said in his note, and as soon as he was in the door I was gushing information. I told him all about the articles I had read in the paper regarding the fire and about my sojourn to Buddy's house. When I called him Buddy, Elliott knew immediately whom I was talking about. He knew all about the old man and his black walnut orchard up on the ridge. I showed him the purple-and-yellow bruise that had bloomed on my shoulder overnight.

Elliott moved the thin strap of my sundress off my shoulder and examined the bruise. Having his fingers brush on my bare skin made me shiver. He asked, "Did the tree actually fall on you?"

"No, it was this giant green pod thing."

"You know black walnut trees are really valuable. Buddy's land is worth a lot of money. I've heard that Emory was trying to buy it and get his hands on the old growth." Elliott ran his finger over the bump on my shoulder, amused by the goose bumps it was causing to sprout on my arm. "I'm not sure it's safe for you to leave the house. You get hurt every time you venture out."

"Very funny. I swear I'm not a klutz. These things just happen to me." I added, "Through no fault of my own." I headed toward the kitchen to get my purse.

He said, "All evidence to the contrary," as he followed behind me.

I pushed through the swinging kitchen doors and once again smiled at the very elaborate note hanging from the ceiling. He was surprised that I had left it all hanging there, but looking at it made me happy so I kept it.

"This is maybe the best note anyone has ever left me. How did you break in here to put this up?"

"Your door was unlocked."

"Really?" I was sure I locked the door every night before we went to bed. I looked around a bit, out of convention, to see if anything was missing or out of place. "I lock it every night." I was starting to feel like I was being watched. "And you know what else? The maps I was looking for at the library, the exact map pages that I needed, had been cut out of the plat book. The only pages I needed! Now I find out that my door was open? What if someone broke in here?"

Elliott looked like he was trying not to laugh at me. "You're losing it. Logan had unlocked the door, not the boogie man."

Oh, there goes my conspiracy theory. I said, "Did she tell you that she had opened it?"

"Yes, she had gone out to get her shoes from the front step."

"Are you sure?" I couldn't shake the feeling that someone was trying to put a stop to my investigation.

He was definitely amused by my quaint but ridiculous suspicions. "I need to make you lose that big-city paranoia."

I balled up one of the coffee filters hanging at my disposal and tossed it at his head. "I'm telling you, something weird is going on. First, the journals were gone from the reading room, then the map pages were cut from the book, and now my house was broken into."

"Your house wasn't broken into."

"It wasn't?" It was hard to feel unsafe when Elliott was standing in my kitchen.

"No, I think you're just a little bit crazy." He smiled and leaned back against the kitchen counter. I found myself staring at him, at the lopsided smile on his face, and recognizing the fact that we were all alone here. No Logan to come bursting in to interrupt us. Elliott broke the silence. "Are you ready?" He held his hand out to me.

I shook some distracting thoughts from my mind. "Sure. Where exactly are we going?"

"We're going to Betty Chatham's garden club party."

"We are?" I glanced down at my sundress wondering if it was too casual. "Is it outside? It's so hot outside."

My reaction made him laugh. "It's a garden party. You can probably count on it being in a garden." He led me out the front door. "Betty called me and said she wanted you to meet their guest speaker. She didn't know where you were hiding yourself so she called me." He glanced at his watch. "We need to be there in ten minutes."

We followed Old Post Road outside of town. Elliott turned onto a gravel drive that had been marked by a bouquet of white balloons tied to an old wooden wagon overflowing with bright pink blooming azaleas. The gravel drive led through a canopy of dogwoods and then opened up to a vast green lawn. The dark gray of the gravel cut a curving sliver through the green grass ending in a courtyard in front of a white antebellum mansion.

The art historian in me was dying to go inside. The house sat on a foundation of dark granite that matched the driveway. The steps and floor of the deep portico were painted gray, offsetting the crisp white of the house. There were six two-story Corinthian columns on the façade sitting atop raised pedestals. The hipped copper roof, weathered to a pale green, sloped gently back to meet the four brick chimney stacks that reached into the sky.

Elliott stopped the car at the front steps and a valet opened my door. I found myself just staring up at the gorgeous thing. The house, not the valet.

Elliott took my hand, pulling me to the side gate. "Come on."

I protested. "Can't we go inside for just a second?"

"We're already late."

As we walked around the side of the house I was too preoccupied with Elliott's hand to take any notice of the party. It was such a simple gesture, taking my hand to guide me through the yard, but it felt so intimate. I wrapped both of my hands around his and he squeezed mine in response. We were fully engulfed in the crowd before I even noticed that we had entered the fray.

Someone was already at the podium speaking. He was right; we were late. The party itself was set up on the rear brick patio, which was hemmed in by a low brick wall. Outside the patio, flanking it to the left and right, were formal French gardens strictly geometrical and meticulously manicured. Leading directly out from the patio was another lined pathway that stepped down to a pool and pool house.

Elliott guided me around the bar and I finally took full notice of the party guests. I was severely underdressed. The women were all wearing summer suits and elaborate hats.

Elliott was writing our names on some HELLO MY NAME IS badges as I tried to get my hair to stop sticking to my sweaty neck. It was no use. I whispered, "I should be more dressed up."

"You look great. Don't worry." He stuck the badge to my sundress and leaned in so that only I could hear him. "At least you're not the only man at the party."

We meandered through the round tables covered in starched white linens and floral-patterned china, looking for our assigned seats and trying to make as little noise as possible. It was made difficult because women kept grabbing Elliott's hand as he passed by. They were thrilled to see him there, as he was, in fact, the only man at the party. Our progress was followed with a chorus of: Why Elliott, it's so nice to see you. How're you doing, Eli? Writing an article for the paper? How's your sister/brother/father/mother? It's lovely to see you here, Eli.

By the time we sat down, the opening speaker had finished with the club's business and Betty Chatham was standing to introduce the guest. Betty winked in my direction, appearing excited to be sharing this experience with me. A troupe of waiters began to serve iced tea and tiny sandwiches in unison as Betty introduced the speaker, Mrs. Grant Baker.

Mrs. Grant Baker, or Florence, had been invited to speak to the club at the insistence of Betty Chatham. That sent a murmur of laughter through the crowd; I would imagine it was hard to turn down Betty when she was insisting. Florence was here to speak about her journey from being the premier party planner in North Georgia to the sole owner of the local minor league baseball team.

Her story was interesting. I just couldn't figure out what it had to do with me or why Betty had tracked me down to hear it. Florence's husband, Grant, had grown up playing baseball, including a one-year stint in the majors before doing two tours in Vietnam. He returned from the war, went to law school, and became a tax attorney. But he always wanted in some way to return to baseball. When a minor league franchise became available they took a chance and bought it.

I glanced around, mostly at Elliott. He looked so nice in his crisp white linen shirt. I was fanning myself with my napkin.

Why wasn't he as miserable as I was? I noticed he was taking notes, always the reporter.

I stole his pencil and wrote in the margin: *I'm melting.*

Elliott: *Heat is your kryptonite.*

He was funny. Me: *Why are we here?*

Elliott: *Not sure. Did you tell Betty you were a big baseball fan?*

Me: *Yes, I did. I told her I especially like the games in the middle of the day when the sun has exploded and*—he wrestled the pencil from me to write something else.

The two of us were giggling as he turned the paper over looking for a blank spot on which to write. A woman sitting at our table cleared her throat, an indication that she found our behavior terribly rude. Elliott and I gave our full attention back to the speaker.

Florence and Grant purchased a Class-A team, which was wallowing in low attendance at a dilapidated stadium in Mississippi. Their first order of business was to move the team to Gainesville, Georgia, where together with the state they were able to put together a multi-million-dollar funding deal for a new stadium to be built on the banks of Lake Lanier. The day of the groundbreaking ceremony Grant had a heart attack and died.

During the hushed whispers of sympathy that followed that statement I tried to dab the sweat on my forehead. I looked around at the women—some of them ancient, in their smartly tailored suits and huge hats—thinking that we were bound to have a man down before this thing was over.

Florence was going into great detail about how difficult it was when Grant first died and she was alone in the ownership of the franchise. As a minor league owner she had no real responsibility for the baseball aspects of the team. They were affiliated with a major league team that had full authority over which players were sent down and brought up, who would be playing, the coaching staff, all of it. As the construction on the new stadium was coming to an end and her financial woes were coming to a head, one of the coaches said something that changed everything. He told her, "You just have to get bodies in the seats, Flo, and make sure they have a good time. You're in charge of the experience."

Florence realized that this was no different than planning a great party, and she knew how to throw a great party. The crowd murmured their agreement at that, her reputation preceding her. She turned the Gainesville team into the most financially successful franchise in the South Atlantic League.

There was a round of applause and then everyone began to chatter at the tables. A few people stood up and began milling around the white tent set up at one end of the patio, carrying their iced teas with them. The woman at our table who had shushed Elliott and me asked him what he had been writing.

He smiled at her. "It's for the paper."

She wasn't buying it and didn't approve. "Mm hmm. Eli, *you* know better than to act like that when someone's speaking." She glanced at me, making it clear that she viewed me as the bad influence here.

She turned her back to us. I whispered to Elliott. "You have to teach me some manners. I was just scolded at a garden party." Stifling a giggle. "My mother would die." The pun was unintentional.

Elliott tapped my nose. "You're perfect. Don't change a thing."

He was really too nice to be an actual male creature. "Have I thanked you today?"

"For what?"

"For helping me with all of this."

"I'm happy to do it." He leaned in, our faces too close for this public venue. "Besides it gives me an excuse to hang out with you."

"You don't need an excuse." I gave him a very chaste kiss on the cheek causing the ancient Emily Post at our table to huff in disapproval. I ignored her and turned back to Elliott. "What's in the tent?"

"Shade. You want to go?"

I was already standing up.

Betty Chatham was standing under the tent with Florence Baker introducing her to various mad hatters. When Betty saw me she interrupted the receiving line and dragged Florence straight over to us.

Betty said, "Elliott, thank you so much for bringing Olivia! Florence, *this* is Olivia Hughes."

Florence was dabbing under her eyes with a tissue, trying to stop the perspiration from destroying her makeup. She put her hand out to me and then for the first time looked at my face. She looked shocked. It was obviously the reaction Betty had been hoping for because Betty was thrilled.

I held my hand out. "It's nice to meet you."

She didn't shake my hand so much as hold on to it for support as she leaned in to my face. "You look just like a girl I grew up with."

My breath caught in my throat. "Did you know Jane Rutledge?"

I was immediately assaulted. Florence let out a sort of laughing howl and then grabbed me, hugging me, squeezing me, and crying.

Florence whispered, more to herself than to me. "I'm so glad she made it."

I felt awful having to be the one to tell Florence that Jane hadn't actually made it, that she had passed away last year. But when I said it Florence didn't stop smiling. She kept staring at me with tears in her eyes, shaking her head at my apparent misunderstanding of her comment.

She pulled herself together but never let go of my hand. "I meant she was able to move on." Patting my hand. "I'm so sorry to hear that she passed though. Oh, it would've been so good to see her!" Florence turned to Betty. "No wonder you insisted I come today!" Then back to me. "We need to get into some store-bought air and have a nice long chat. It's too damn hot out here and I want you to tell me absolutely everything about Janie." Florence was looking around for someplace to duck off where we could talk. She looked me up and down again, shaking her head. "Aren't you just the most gorgeous thing?" She glanced at her watch to check the time, apparently not liking what she saw. "I wish Grant were here. He would have loved to meet you. You know he played ball with George and Oliver starting when they were about three years old and all the way through high school."

She was a dervish and was talking so quickly I was having a hard time following her. I asked, "I'm sorry. Who's Oliver?"

That question seemed to grab Florence's full attention and

she finally became still. The transformation was alarming. She immediately stopped talking, pausing as if to figure out what to say. "Janie never told you about Oliver?" I suppose the look on my face answered that question for her because she just kept talking. "Oliver was George's twin brother."

Elliott and I shared a look, nodding. *Ah, the twin.* We knew from the birth certificate that George had been a twin. Now the twin had a name: Oliver.

I turned back to Florence, explaining, "We literally just found out about George. We saw on his birth certificate that he was a twin but we didn't know the name."

Florence sounded stunned. "Your mom never told you about George?"

"No, nothing about George or even growing up in Huntley. She never talked about her past. I mean the time before she married my dad. We're just starting to learn some things about her younger years."

Florence looked sad about our ignorance of Oliver but devastated about our ignorance of George. She had stopped the maintenance of her brow and sweat began dripping down her temples. She looked back and forth between Elliott and me, assuming that the "we" I kept referring to was us.

Elliott seemed to clue in to that. "I'm sorry. I didn't introduce myself. I'm Elliott Tate, from Tillman. I'm helping Olivia research her mother's story."

Florence had managed to compose herself and was adjusting to the fact that I was clueless about my mother. She was backing out of any shorthand or quick name-dropping, knowing that anything she mentioned would require an extensive back story.

Her voice sounded drained. "And what about your father, dear?"

I told Florence about my dad and gave her the *Reader's Digest* version of my mother's life with him. When they got married, the places we had lived, her teaching at the university, a tiny bit about Georgia and myself.

She was genuinely happy to know that my mother had managed to endure George's death. Happy and surprised. The impression Florence gave me was that one of them could barely survive without the other.

Florence checked her watch one more time, angry for what it was telling her.

"I'm so sorry, Olivia, but I have to get back to Gainesville. We're in the middle of renegotiating our concession contract."

I deflated. I finally had someone in my grasp who had been a friend of my mom's growing up. Elliott put his arm around me sensing that I would not take this well. I was getting ready to ask for her phone number.

But Florence saw my face and smiled. "Honey, you can't get rid of me that easily. I can come back tomorrow." She grabbed Betty's attention from the crowd surrounding her. "Betty, can you spare a room at the inn tomorrow?"

I wrote down the address to my rental house and we made a date for the following afternoon. Florence hugged me three more times before she left and kept saying, "You look just like her," and shaking her head in disbelief.

TWENTY

I had a hard time sleeping after meeting Florence. Finally I went out to the dining room and sat down among the papers and articles we had found since arriving in Tillman and made lists of the things I wanted to ask her about my mother. If I could just get everything out of my head and onto a piece of paper I might get some sleep.

An hour later I was back in bed and having a dream. My mother, Florence, and I were sitting around a table talking. My mother was a young girl; she sat there angrily pouting with her arms crossed high over her chest, furious that I was interrogating Florence. She stared straight ahead with a scowl on her face. Florence looked exactly the same as she had at the garden party. She was talking nonstop, her hands waving around wildly as she spoke. Sometimes she would say something she found funny and she would laugh, playfully hitting my mom on the back, old friends. I was trying to read her lips as she spoke because there was no sound coming out.

I woke early the next day feeling not at all rested. I had nothing to do while I waited so I cleaned the little rental house. I scrubbed and dusted and polished until it was shining. Logan was finally dropped off from work and rushed to her room to change before Florence was due to arrive. Elliott showed up with a pad of paper to take notes and a little tape recorder. I looked at my watch again. It was one minute later than the last time I had checked it.

At exactly four o'clock Florence rang the doorbell. She breezed in, as much of a force as she had been the day before. She gushed over Logan and then me and then the view of the lake from the porch. She emanated so much energy the little house felt smaller with her inside of it.

We had a nervous few minutes where we all four stood in the small living room making bits of small talk about the weather and the house, not sure where to begin. Logan cut through it, not one to bother with such formalities; she just wanted to dive in.

"Mrs. Baker, would you mind if I set up my computer to record you? I promised my mom we would try."

Florence sat down, looking relieved at the idea of getting down to it. "I don't mind at all." She looked at me as Elliott and I sat across from her. "And I want you to know that I will answer every question you ask, fully and truthfully, but I was thinking about this all night. There must have been reasons that your mom didn't want to talk about her life here, and I need to respect that."

I looked up from my notes. "I'm not sure I know what you mean."

Florence's gaze was firm. "I mean I'll answer what you ask, but I won't offer up information if you haven't asked about it."

Logan looked at me and then to Florence. "Is there something we don't know about?"

Florence sighed as she sat back crossing her legs, our interview apparently beginning. "Honey, I'm meeting Janie's daughters"—she motioned between me and the computer that represented Georgia—"who don't even realize they're named after George and Oliver Jones, so yes, I'd say there's a fair amount you don't know about."

Of course. We must be named after them and I didn't even see it. What else wasn't I seeing? I said, "It hadn't occurred to me that we were named after them." I felt stunned, not the best way to begin an interview. And now I knew that if I didn't ask about something, she wouldn't talk about it. I pulled out my list of questions, which seemed completely inadequate. Did I really care what the house at Rutledge Ridge looked like? My eyes were going back and forth between the list and Florence as she waited expectantly for me to ask her a question. I was at a loss. "How could she just keep all of this from us?" That wasn't on my list of questions.

Florence sounded sympathetic about my frustration, but it wasn't the kind of question she could answer. All she said was, "People always have their reasons."

Right. I looked at the first question on my list. "Did you

know my mom when you were little? Did you know her when her mother died?"

Florence and Janie grew up together. There wasn't a time she could remember when she didn't know Janie. And yes, everyone knew Janie's mother, Martha, not just because the town was so small, but because Martha was so kind.

Florence explained that the illness had been hard on Janie; she hadn't really understood how dire the circumstances were. "People didn't talk about things like that the way they do now. And we were just kids." Florence shrugged. "Mrs. Rutledge coughed a lot. That was really all we knew."

Then she told us her fragmented memory of the funeral. Janie, just ten years old, had become hysterical when the lid to the coffin was closed. She began crying in the church and screaming that her mother couldn't breathe. Janie was so bereaved they had to carry her out.

She obviously wasn't able to comprehend the fact that the coffin held the body of her mother but her mother was gone.

I knew the closing of that lid was the event that created my mother's claustrophobia and suddenly I felt horrible for every time Georgia and I had hidden under the bed and dared her to come in after us. The first days after the funeral were the worst for Janie. She couldn't be in any confined space; she couldn't even sleep in her canopy bed.

The week following the services Janie camped out in her backyard with George and Oliver every night. She needed to have nothing but air above her head. George set up the pallets and built the campfire; Oliver provisioned the food. The memory of that made Florence laugh a little. "I tried to get my parents to let me stay with them, but they wouldn't hear of it." She affected an old Southern accent. "Young ladies do not camp out for days at a time with young men."

Logan spoke up. "But they were just little kids, right? I mean it's not like they were dating when they were ten years old."

I jumped in. "When did they start dating?"

Florence shared the story. It was Margaret's birthday party; she was turning fourteen. I remembered Margaret's name from talking to Buddy. She was the girl that Nate Jr. married. She was the young wife who had called the sheriff when my mother's house caught on fire.

The birthday party was being held in the deliberately dim basement with the long brown plaid couch pushed to one side and a small table against the wall stacked with bowls of chips and pretzels. In the background a long-playing album was scratching out ballads on a record player.

Grant and Florence were already dating at this point. They stood against the far wall with George, the three of them looking on at the latest party game. Someone, probably Oliver, had suggested a game of spin the bottle. The players were all in the center of the room sitting in a circle atop a dusty oval braided rug, tugging at collars and smoothing out skirts. Everyone was nervously picking at their nails or playing with their hair trying to look as if they weren't nervous. Except for Oliver, of course. Oliver was never nervous.

Florence could tell that George wanted Janie to leave the circle. He was staring at the back of her head with an intensity that he thought could bring on mind reading. *Leave. Quit this stupid game.* Everyone could tell they were starting to like each other, starting to see each other differently. They weren't just best friends anymore or neighbors who had known each other their whole lives. There was a new tension when they were together that anyone could feel. And watching Janie sit there and potentially get her first kiss with some other boy was about to undo George.

With a flick of Oliver's wrist the thick green bottle whirled around and finally came to a slow wobbling stop right in front of Janie. Florence remembers hearing George gasp a little and then Grant said, under his breath, "This ought to be good."

Janie's back became ramrod straight and she was visibly fighting the urge to turn and catch George's eye to see his reaction. She didn't dare turn around. Everyone knew Janie wouldn't want to kiss Oliver of all people. He was like her brother. Everyone's eyes were darting back and forth between Janie and George, knowing something was about to blow.

Oliver didn't seem to care about the growing tension or maybe he just wanted to get George's goat. He made a big show of licking his lips as he leaned in to the center of the circle to kiss Janie. Janie sat there frozen to her spot. She was supposed to meet him in the middle for the payoff. Oliver glanced up at George and raised his eyebrows like, *I bet this is gonna bug you.* George got across the room in two steps, pulled Janie to her feet and announced, "Janie and I are going out."

George dragged Janie up the stairs and out the front door. The wolf whistles and laughter followed them all the way outside. There was a horrible screech as someone dragged the needle off the record so that everyone in the room could better hear the fight outside. Everyone ran to the tiny windows at the top of the basement wall to eavesdrop. Florence could see Janie's feet as she paced back and forth, stomping occasionally. How dare he do that to her. He had no right, the nerve! She went on and on and poor George was just standing there like a fool staring at her, taking it all, saying nothing.

She finally realized he wasn't fighting back and she stopped yelling at him. Florence couldn't hear what George whispered to her at that moment, but the next thing you know Janie was walking over to him and they were kissing. Just like that. That was the night they officially started dating.

I could picture the whole scene in my mind. I imagined the embarrassed look on her face when he dragged her away in front of all of their friends. The look in George's eyes when he whispered something so sweet to her that she stopped yelling and started kissing. I decided that this was each one's first kiss. Whether it truly was or not seemed irrelevant. How sweet that George didn't want anyone else to have Janie's first kiss? This was the exact kind of sappy romantic crap I usually hated, but I just couldn't help myself. It was flowing effortlessly out of my subconscious. The whole vision was causing me to feel heartbroken for young Janie and perhaps a little bit infatuated with my dead mother's dead first husband.

I glanced over to Elliott to try to snap myself out of it. The bridge of his nose and cheeks were sunburned; he brushed the hair out of his face. He caught my eye and gave me a complex look that said, *Isn't this great? But I know it's probably making you sad. Sorry.* And just like that I was cured of my infatuation with the past and fully reengaged in my infatuation with the present.

I asked Florence about the house at Rutledge Ridge and what

it looked like. She relayed a vague report of the house itself, but the elaborate descriptions she gave of the way it smelled when it was filled with Maudy's cooking were painstakingly detailed. Florence reinforced the impression I had gained of Maudy when I had spoken to Buddy about her.

I asked about the school they attended. The first through eighth grades of their schooling occurred in a three-room schoolhouse in the town of Huntley proper. Florence mentioned apologetically that the school was segregated. The school for the black students was located up the mountain. When it came time for high school, the townie kids all went to the prestigious Country Day School, which was a short bus ride through the valley. The country kids had had enough schooling and went to work, and the black kids remained at their school up the mountain.

Florence said, "You know what's funny? The lake took those segregated schools for the white kids in the valley, wiped them both out. But that little school up the hill where the black kids had to go? It's still standing. I think it's a Friends School now. I always thought of that as poetic justice. So much disappeared when they built the lake. The house that my husband, Grant, grew up in"—Florence was counting it off on her fingers—"our school, the church Grant and I got married in, the baseball fields where he, Oliver, and George spent every minute of daylight growing up . . . they're all under the water now. When people asked Grant where we were from his answer was always Atlantis."

I knew from Florence's presentation to the garden club that Grant had played professional baseball, served in Vietnam, and gone on to become a lawyer. I didn't know anything about George or Oliver.

I said, "I know my mom went on to college. What happened to George and Oliver after high school?" The three of them, George, Janie, and Oliver were apparently one system, one unit. They did everything together, Oliver always screwing something up, George coming in to fix it, Janie smoothing things over.

Florence took her glasses off again and wiped them down with a handkerchief. I think it was more out of habit than a necessary cleaning. No one's glasses needed that much attention. "George was in school with your mom. They went to college together." She didn't pause long enough for me to process the feeling of surprise at that comment. Florence continued. "I think it was hard for all three of them when your mom and George went off to school. It wasn't long after that when Oliver left for Vietnam."

Florence gave me the impression that George and Oliver, although identical twins, were complete opposites. George was apparently the steadfast intellect and Oliver was the lovable delinquent.

I asked her about this and a smile bloomed on Florence's face. "You couldn't help but love Oliver. I mean you wanted to beat him silly one minute and then hope he'd bless you with his presence the next. You never knew what might happen when you went out with him, but you knew it'd be a good story if you lived to tell about it."

I asked, "So what happened to Oliver?" Now I was curious about Oliver too. Add it to the list.

Florence explained that Oliver felt his time to be called up in the draft was imminent. He didn't want to be conscripted into the army so he enlisted in the navy. Florence confided that George had actually been the one to take Oliver's aptitude exams that allowed him to earn a commission.

Logan asked, "They looked that much alike?"

"Well, not if you knew them like we did. But if they were strangers to you, they were identical."

I asked, "So was Oliver unprepared to be in the navy? I mean if George took his tests?"

Florence shook her head like I had it all wrong. "There wasn't anything Oliver couldn't do in the water, but he would never have passed those written tests. Nowadays we would've recognized it as dyslexia or some other diagnosable disorder. Back then it was just that Olivier wasn't very good with tests. And there wasn't a thing George wouldn't do for him so when Oliver asked him, George said yes. I think George might've regretted it later, after Oliver was shipped out to Vietnam. But he was going somewhere anyway, the army or jail or a ditch after being caught by someone's husband. He just ran too hard and too fast for anything good to come of it. George probably did the right thing. Must've wrecked the two of them when Oliver died though."

"Did he die in Vietnam?"

Florence was staring out the window toward the lake. The light had changed while we had been sitting here drifting back in time. She said, "Well, I think it was probably the war that killed him, but he didn't die over there." She began to rummage around in her oversized bag. "He came home, but I guess he was changed by everything." I wanted to ask her what she meant exactly, but she kept talking. "I wasn't here during that time." She couldn't seem to find what she was looking for and dumped the bag out on the coffee table. "Where is that darn thing?" Florence looked up briefly. "Grant and I were married and we were living in Florida when Oliver came home. Grant had been playing ball and then he got drafted in the army. I lived on base with the other army wives. When he came home we moved to Birmingham. I worked while he went to law school. I never did come back here, and by then of course 'here' was underwater." She pulled a bundle out of the pile on the table and shouted, "Ah-ha!" Then she held up an old envelope yellowed with age and stamped with a red-and-blue "Par Avion" across the top.

She handed it to me. "These are some letters we got from Oliver when he was in the navy. There're some pictures in there too. You're welcome to keep them."

"Are you sure?" I asked. I pulled out the letters, wanting to read them right there, but also not wanting to be rude.

Florence waved that away. "You're Janie's family so I guess you're his too. You keep them. Besides, what good are they doing him or me stuffed in a box somewhere? All of my old pictures and letters are still in storage from when I moved to the condo after Grant died. This was all I could find in his desk."

Florence described them for us as I held them up. The first one was a photo of Oliver sitting on a squat green-gray river patrol boat with four other men. Oliver looked just like the pictures we had seen of George. The men on the boat were all smoking; one held a can of beer in his hand. They were smiling at the camera. They looked tan and relaxed and completely unaware of what the next few months probably had in store for them in the Brown Water Navy, as they called the naval forces patrolling the rivers in Vietnam. I flipped the picture over and read the names written on the back: Me, Whitey, Johnnie, Turk, and Slim.

The second picture was obviously taken sometime later, perhaps years later. It showed Oliver standing alone on the bow of his small boat. His hair was long and shaggy. He no longer looked much like George. He was wearing an olive drab flak vest with no shirt underneath to hide his much thinner chest. His camo pants were loose on his waist and cut off above the knee with long strands of threads hanging down and sticking to his tan sweaty legs. He stood there alone staring out at the flat brown river, loosely holding a machine gun at waist height. The sky behind him was gray with the threat of rain.

Elliott spoke up, breaking the spell that had fallen over the room. "Florence, may I get you something to drink?"

TWENTY-ONE

The clatter of Elliott mixing drinks in the kitchen allowed Florence the opportunity to move around the room looking at the piles of printouts and articles stacked on the dining room table. A few images caused her to recall things and she shared a few unsolicited stories about George, Oliver, and Janie. Each snippet seemed to have the three of them woven together. The car the three of them bought together when they were fifteen that they could never get to run. The time George almost drowned in the swollen river going after Janie's dog, and how Oliver had had to jump in and rescue him. The huge summer birthday party the three of them always threw together at the barn on the Joneses' property. The way Janie and George were always bailing Oliver out of some trouble with the principal, or the coach, or the sheriff.

Elliott, Logan, Florence, and I took our drinks out to the screen porch. Logan brought a tray of food and repositioned her laptop to keep recording. Dusk was beginning settle on the lake as we indulged in our cocktails. Florence didn't sip; she drank. In no time Elliott was mixing her a third gin and tonic and Florence's self-imposed restrictions were waning.

Logan was nursing a lemonade, her feet tucked underneath her in the rocking chair. She looked over to Florence. "How come they got married so young?"

Florence laughed—her laugh being considerably louder soaked in gin—saying she thought they waited as long as they could. She was inferring that the two of them were having a hard time remaining virgins until the wedding night. I had to resist the urge to put my fingers in my ears and hum loudly.

Florence sounded wistful and nostalgic. "It was a strange time; everything changed that summer, the summer of sixty-six. It was the last year that we were able to be on the river." She wasn't slurring her speech but it was much looser now, slower. Her accent became much more exaggerated, she sounded more and more like Betty Chatham with each sip. "The dam was under construction and Huntley was being evacuated; most people left to find houses or work somewhere out of the valley." She was staring at the trees across the lake, but that's not what she saw. She was looking back. "Grant was in Florida playing Triple-A ball. Oliver was getting ready to join the navy. It was the beginning of the end of that time for us. Janie and George just wanted to get married before it all vanished."

Logan asked, in almost a whisper, "How did they get engaged?"

Florence blinked lazily as she shared the story of the day that George asked Janie to marry him.

AS JANIE AND FLORENCE WALKED the last few hundred feet toward the river they could already hear voices being carried across the water and echoing off the rise of the mountain. Janie stopped in the middle of the overgrown summer brush, her hands out by her side, grazing the tops of the wildflowers and bushes. "It's hard to believe this will all be gone by next summer."

They reached the Dunk Pool and could see a few friends on the river. Nate was already in the water, swimming toward Margaret on the Overlook, but where was everyone else? Last summer the Dunk Pool had been so crowded that first weekend home from college.

Margaret spotted them. "Hey girls! Janie, where's George?"

Janie looked around the Dunk Pool. "I don't know. I thought he'd be here by now. Where is everyone?" Oliver had been out of sight underwater and he jumped up suddenly, splashing Janie and Florence as they stood at the bank of the river. It was his way of greeting them. He dove back under before they could retaliate.

Florence wiped off the droplets that had landed on the new scarf she wore on her head. "Well, there's Oliver. Nice to see he hasn't changed."

Nate helped Janie and Florence climb onto the Overlook and then Margaret pulled them into a welcome home hug. Nate explained that this was it; all of their other friends had already left the valley. Everything was changing. Their friends, their town, their river.

Janie sat down on the hot rock, sighing, saying that even her father had changed. When Janie returned from school she was shocked at the physical transformation that had taken place in her father, the Honorable Judge Winchester Rutledge, since winter break. He had become so sedentary and was obviously in so much pain. And Maudy was having heart problems and trouble with her breathing. Janie found the two of them at Rutledge Ridge bickering like an old married couple.

So Janie spent her first days back for summer break making some changes. She moved Maudy out of her house in town and into the guest bedroom, hired a new maid to take care of the cleaning and cooking, and moved a hospital bed into her father's room to make him more comfortable.

Nate laughed. "Janie, only you would hire a maid for your maid." He gave Margaret a kiss on the top of her head and then plunged off the Overlook and into the Dunk Pool. The cold splash of water provided a moment of relief to the three girls sunning themselves on the blistering rock.

Margaret insisted that Florence tell them absolutely everything about Grant. Did he like Florida? Would he be called up to the majors? Had his shoulder healed properly? As Florence gave her girlfriends the latest news, Janie put her hand to her face, shielding her eyes from the sun. George was nearby. She couldn't see him yet, but she could feel him. She sensed that he was on the far bank of the river.

Janie called out to the seemingly empty bank. "George, you're late!"

Janie jumped into the chilly water and was halfway across the river when George materialized out of nowhere. Margaret shook her head. "How do they do that?"

Florence said, "Who knows."

George grabbed Janie's hand and pulled her through the water toward him, hugging her tight, holding her up. She rubbed her hand over his newly shorn buzz cut making water splay off it.

He kissed her. He hadn't seen her in a full day and that had been far too long. "Do you think I did the right thing?"

Janie wasn't sure if he'd done the right thing. None of them were, but she knew what he needed her to say. "Yes, of course you did." Janie's skin was slippery from the silty water; her arms were around his neck and her legs were intertwined with his under the surface.

George and Janie disappeared under the cascading limbs of the weeping willow on the far bank. Janie's feet could touch the bottom there and she used the leverage to pull George into her, kissing him with a newfound confidence that unhinged him. Her skin was prickly and cold from the icy river; his hands worked their way down her back, across her hips. She arched into him.

Their friends were suddenly talking very loudly on the other side of the narrow river. They busied themselves watching a red-tailed hawk circle above their heads, making a point to look anyplace but the far bank where George and Janie were indulging in one of their intimate hellos.

With a moan George pulled back. "Janie, I have to stop."

She groaned, complaining. "No, you don't."

He shifted uncomfortably in his bathing suit. "Yeah, I do."

Nate grew tired of waiting and called out from the Overlook. "You get enough of him at school, Janie! Let us see George for a minute."

Janie dropped her hands from his shoulders. "Fine."

Margaret finally got a clear view of George as the two of them made their way back across the river. She said, "Oh my gosh, George, with that buzz cut you really do look just like Oliver."

Janie rubbed George's fuzzy head as he pulled her through the deeper part of the pool. "It'll grow back." She nuzzled her face into his neck. He kissed her forehead.

Florence called down from the rock. "Are you sure that was a good idea?"

They had no secrets from each other, these old friends. George answered honestly. "I have no idea, but it's what Oliver asked so I did it."

Without warning Oliver sprang up through the surface of the water and tackled George, nearly knocking Janie off her feet. The two brothers wrestled all the way down the river, following its curve around the Hitch and eventually out of sight. They were never closer to their scuffling, brawling, childhood roots than when they'd been apart for a long time.

Oliver finally settled down and managed to ask George about the aptitude test he had just taken in Oliver's place.

George never hinted that he had concerns about the scam they had just pulled. "Piece of cake. I'm pretty sure they'll start you off as an admiral."

Oliver laughed. "Sure, because I'll smoke everyone at the PRT next week."

That was all they would ever say about it.

In time the two of them joined Margaret, Nate, Florence, and Janie on the Overlook. The boys were out of breath and dripping wet. Oliver gave all the girls a proper hug and then flopped down on the warm rock, exhausted. George collapsed with his head on Janie's lap and closed his eyes. He was worried about his brother. Leave it to Oliver to want to enlist in the military as war was heating up.

The rest of the afternoon was spent with everyone trying to pretend like their whole world wasn't shifting imperceptibly on its axis. They were all swimming and chatting like any other summer. Oliver held court like a minstrel regaling them with the stories of his latest exploits. The facts left them all shocked speechless one minute and screaming with laughter the next. If it had been anyone else spinning these tales they would never have believed him, but for better or worse they knew Oliver was telling the truth. The old friends stayed there the whole day, a skeleton crew of survivors on the brink of a lost civilization.

Suddenly a distant alarm screeched through the valley, shaking them from their pretense of normalcy and reminding them that this was all temporary.

Janie looked to Nate. "What in the world was that?"

Nate worked as a mechanic at the dam and had become their resident expert in all things related to it. He explained that the alarm was being installed and tested. Next spring when the diversion tunnels were finally shut down, the river would begin to fill the reservoir and the alarm would sound for days.

As evening approached, Florence went home to wait on a phone call from Grant. Nate and Margaret began gathering up all of their things so they could get back for supper with her parents. George checked the sky, anxious to get going so he and Janie would be to the top of the ridge by sunset.

Janie grabbed Oliver's hand. "We're going to Sunset Rock. Come with us."

A glance passed between Oliver and George. "Sorry, can't. I'm meeting Pauline at the Roadhouse."

Margaret shook her head disapprovingly as she folded her towel. Janie cringed and said, "God, Oliver. Pauline? You're going to catch something from that girl that will require fifty shots to get rid of."

George laughed. Oliver pushed him. George shoved back. Janie rolled her eyes.

Oliver, unshaken, said, "George, I gotta take a leak."

George knew that Oliver wanted to say something to him privately so he followed Oliver off the path. Nate was right behind them, unaware of the ulterior motive and genuinely needing a bathroom break. Nate patted Oliver on the back. "Janie's right, man. Use a rubber with Pauline."

Oliver laughed at Nate, unaffected by everyone's low opinion of Pauline. He said, "Not all of us have girlfriends. I must go where the promise of loose women takes me." He pulled something from his pocket. "Here." Oliver opened his hand to George.

It was their father's wedding band. George didn't understand. "What is this?"

"It's Dad's ring."

"I know, but where'd you get it? Why are you giving it to me?"

Nate, realizing he was intruding on a family moment, said good-bye, and headed back to walk Margaret home.

Oliver hated it when people acted like everything was just fine when it really wasn't. How was that any different from lying? "Look, George, the judge is about to drop dead from that cancer and Maudy's right behind him. That's the only family Janie has left. And you're convinced that I'll end up getting shipped to Vietnam, so in your eyes I'm half dead too. I know you guys wanted to wait till graduation but the way I see it, you and Janie should just get married now, this summer, while we're all still here, while that little church she loves so much is still above water. If you don't, you'll regret it. And you can be a real pain in the ass when you're living with regret."

George didn't even respond to what Oliver was saying. He was too surprised by the ambush and, as always, in awe of how well they could read each other. George pulled the small box from his duffel bag and opened it to show his brother.

Oliver laughed, pleased with how right he'd been. He recognized Janie's mother's ring. He'd seen that image a million times in the oil portrait hanging in the front hall at Rutledge Ridge. Oliver smacked his brother on the back in congratulations. "You're asking her at Sunset Rock, though? That's kind of lame don't you think?"

"Shut up. It is not."

They were walking back toward Janie. Oliver said, "Lame." Then he waved to them over his shoulder as he climbed up the path toward home.

George and Janie climbed the familiar trail to Sunset Rock and he kept checking the duffel for the tiny box, making sure he hadn't dropped it along the way.

The sun was taking forever to dip down behind the mountain range to the west. George was quiet, which Janie didn't really notice. She didn't notice the way his foot was tapping nervously and constantly either, waiting for the sun to set. She was staring out at the valley below, trying to commit it to memory before it was completely underwater.

The sky finally burst into a stream of hot red as the sun dripped out of sight.

George took Janie's hand and let out his breath, trying to sound nonchalant. "Do you remember the first time we got to come up here by ourselves?"

Janie knew which trip he was referring to, not just because it was the first time they had gotten to go by themselves, but also because her mother died four days later. "I remember."

George turned to her. "Well, I've been thinking about it for a long time, since that night, actually. And my answer is yes."

Janie was confused. "What are you talking about?"

George rolled his eyes, feigning offense. "How can you not remember? We made wishes on the first star as the sun went down. You said that you wanted to marry me when you grew up. Remember? Oliver started laughing at you so you punched him in the stomach and he cried."

When Janie retold the story of this proposal to Margaret and Florence, even with the million tiny details she included, she was never able to find the words to express the way her chest had tightened up at that moment. With her skin heating up even as the night air was cooling down.

George continued. "I've been thinking about it, and I've decided that my answer is yes."

Janie could feel the tears rolling silently down her cheeks.

George stood up, pulling her to her feet. Then he got down on his knee. "Jane Martha Rutledge, I have loved you my whole life and I will love you until the day I die. I've been calling you my girlfriend since we were kids and I don't want to anymore. I want to only and forever call you my wife." He put her mother's ring on her finger. "Will you please marry me?"

Janie threw herself into him, kissing him with a salty mix of tears. Of course she would marry George. He was the rest of her, her other half, her whole reason for everything.

George kissed her softly. "I love you, and all I want is to make you happy and to be with you every day." They spent the next few hours huddled together on top of Sunset Rock, kissing, whispering, and making plans. Ignoring the cool darkness and racket of the crickets.

I DIDN'T REALIZE HOW SILENT we had become until Florence stopped talking and the bleating of bullfrogs screamed all around us.

Logan broke the spell. She put her hand gently on Florence's. "What was the wedding like?"

Florence looked suddenly much older. She turned to Logan and seemed almost confused. She sat up straight, remembering where she was and pulling her mind out of the past. She said, "I'm sorry. I'm very tired now." Her smile returned and she playfully tapped Elliott on the knee. "I may have been over-served."

Elliott gallantly took the blame for the amount of liquor she had consumed and offered to walk her back to the inn. I showed them out, thanking her profusely for the stories she had shared. There was so much more I wanted to know. I asked if I could see her again the next day, but she was getting up early to head to Daytona for an owner's meeting.

We exchanged numbers, but I was worried that Florence would wake up the next day and regret telling us as much as she did. I thought, *That font of knowledge may have just slipped away.*

They got to the end of my walkway and Elliott turned to me. I motioned to the ground as if to ask if he would come back after getting her safely to the inn. He nodded. Of all of the discoveries I had made in this town he was definitely my favorite.

Logan uploaded the interview video. She explained what she was doing while her fingers moved across the keyboard. Then we called Georgia and Logan told her how to view it.

I said to Georgia, "Guess who you and I are named after?" She was just a silent expectant breath on the other end of the line. "George Jones and his twin brother, Oliver."

"No. Way. Oliver?"

"Yes, can you believe that? How weird is it that they meant so much to her and she never told us anything about them? How could she not tell us about George?"

Georgia said, "It makes me sad when I think about Dad. Do you think he knew about all of this? Do you think she loved him as much as she had loved George?"

I had been having the same thoughts. "I've been thinking about that all day. I have to believe that she did. It was different maybe, but you can love two people. And you said it yourself. Mom and Dad had something special."

Georgia said, "Yeah, maybe. But now it makes me question

everything. I mean it could never be the same, could it? Would you always love one of them more?"

I thought, *Well, that really seems to be the question for everyone lately, doesn't it?*

Logan took over the call with Georgia to walk her through watching the video and I went out front to wait for Elliott to return from the inn.

I thought about my mother and George and their first kiss at the party and their last swim in the river. I thought about the church where they were married and about Oliver dying after returning from Vietnam. I made a mental note to search for Oliver's death certificate too. I was curious about how he had died. I thought again about my mother floating in the lake while her home burned to the ground. That seemed so strange.

Elliott turned the corner, walking with his hands in his pockets. When he saw me sitting outside he smiled and I reflexively smiled in return. The first day I saw him I had thought of him as the kind of guy I really wanted to like me back. And every once in a while I was caught off guard by the fact that he did. I was finding it increasingly difficult to remain seated on the porch and not run over and jump on him. I had reasons of my own to keep myself in check. I wasn't sure what was keeping Elliott so virtuous but I suspected he was taking his cues from me. It made me wonder what sort of confusing mixed signals I must be putting off.

He sat down next to me on the step. "What are you thinking?"

That was a loaded question. "I'm just, I don't know, shocked I guess. I really can't believe she never told us anything about him."

"Are you disappointed Florence didn't bring pictures of them?"

I surprised myself by laughing. "No. I don't think I could handle that and the stories at the same time. I need to digest all of this I think." My mind's eye had already gone into hyperdrive imagining an entire lifetime of snapshots, staccato home movies, soundtracks. "That's all I need—to see one more image of my mother when she was young and happy draped all over this man whom she loved more than anything, who was not, incidentally, my father. I'll probably feel differently tomorrow and will break into Florence's storage unit to search for photo albums."

He laughed. "So a very strange, but good day."

I agreed. "Yes, strange but good." He leaned back on his hands looking up at the canopy of leaves from the elm tree in the front yard. His cheeks and nose, which looked pink earlier, had gone to a full sunburned maroon color. I poked his cheek watching the place where I had touched turn white and then fade back into red.

"What?"

"You're sunburned from the garden party." I leaned back too, looking up through the same leaves. "I was fortunate that your plans to kill me with heatstroke did not come to fruition."

He groaned. "We have to do something to build up your tolerance for the heat or you'll never make it down here."

The weather down here was the least of my problems. "I think we should only do things that involve air conditioning."

Elliott stood up. "Come with me to the courthouse sometime. It's air-conditioned."

I took his hand and let him pull me to my feet. "You sure know how to woo a lady. What's at the courthouse?"

"Well, I think it's time we get our hands on more of the paper trail. We can spend some time in the records office and see if you can order those old maps that were missing, maybe get some more records about Mr. and Mrs. Jones. Even Oliver, I bet we can find some records on him there."

"You had me at air-conditioned."

He laughed. "Okay then. It's a date." We kissed good-night, for a very long and satisfying time. Then I watched him walk down the path toward his house.

TWENTY-TWO

Most of my time in Tillman was spent with Elliott either on the lake, at the house, having coffee at Jimmy's, or going around town while he did his work for the paper. The rest of my waking hours were usually filled with cleaning up after Logan and organizing all of our research. There was so much disjointed information we had discovered about Huntley, my mother, the fire in her home, George, and now Oliver. It was turning into a web of things that I had not expected and I had to get it straight in my mind. I bought several pieces of foam core and propped them up on the sideboard in the little dining nook. It looked a little bit like I was presenting a science fair project.

I began to tape and pin and note things all over those boards. I began with maps and pictures of the lake as it was now. I pinned up pictures of the ruins of my mother's house and of the family graveyard located behind it. I added the family tree that Elliott created from those names we found.

Next to that were copies of death certificates, birth certificates, and marriage certificates. I pinned up some of the highlighted parts of the TVA report regarding the formation of the lake and the town of Huntley. Copies of the garden club book describing the hydrangeas in my grandmother's garden were overlaid with images of the burned-out house. There were articles and documents and notes. So many notes. Most of them ending with a question mark.

Logan had looked over the accumulation of information one day and thrown her arms out wide, encompassing the whole table. "We shall call it the Wall of Discovery." That kid cracked me up.

I called Florence every other day and left a message. She never answered and hadn't called me back. And even though nothing actually supported this theory, I felt like I was wearing her down. There were still a few million things I wanted to ask her.

Communication breakdown was an ongoing theme in my life at the moment. Leo and I had transitioned from frequent phone calls to infrequent texts. He was busy at work, as always, but this felt different. I couldn't tell if he was sensing that something was off with me and it was self-preservation on his part, or if he just didn't want to bother anymore. Whenever I broached the subject he conveniently had to take another call or board a plane. I was wondering if he was booking flights just to get out of speaking with me.

Logan got home from work one afternoon, dropped her wet towel on an upholstered chair, and then headed straight to the kitchen. She seemed different here, after just a couple of weeks. She was calmer than I had seen her in a long time. And she hadn't straightened her hair once since we moved into the lake house. Logan would come home from her job at the marina with her hair tousled and sun streaked with blond, no makeup, cheeks pink from the sun, and not try to fix it or hide it. She seemed happy with who she was, a rarity for a teenage girl, and she was mirroring how being here made me feel about myself. I followed her and asked, "What're you doing?"

Logan's entire upper body was in the refrigerator searching for provisions. "Looking for food. I'm starved." She was always starved. She pulled the lanyard holding her marina employee badge from her neck and tossed it on the counter.

The few times Elliott and I had gone to the marina for gas, I had made a point to stay in the boat with a hat pulled low over my face. "Do you ever see Emory at the marina?"

"No, not really. I'm like on the other side by the pool with the kids. He's off, you know, running the planet and kicking everyone's ass in his office."

"Your mother is going to be so pleased with all of the colorful language you've acquired from me this summer."

She was ignoring me, as usual. "Livie, can I borrow your blue sundress?"

"Sure." I followed her into my room. "I keep thinking about what Buddy said about Emory. How he stole from Mom. I think he meant Mom's land. But how can you steal land?"

Logan said, "Ask the Lenape."

"The who?"

She changed into the sundress leaving her shorts and T-shirt on my floor. "The native Americans who had Manhattan stolen from them."

"Smartass. The Indians didn't think a person could even own land, so technically they were the ones ripping off the settlers."

"That's what I mean. There're like a million different ways you can steal something. It's all about perception."

Logan grabbed my wrist and peeked at my watch. She obviously had somewhere else to be soon. I understood why Georgia complained about hardly ever spending any time with Logan anymore. I asked, "Date with Graham?"

She nodded. "You know, Graham told me that Elliott's mom is like super pissed about him breaking up with Amy because of some new girl in town."

I threw my head in my hands. "What? They were having problems before we even met."

"Well, he told his mom and dad he had to break up with her when he met you."

For some reason that made me incredibly uncomfortable and also in some really awful petty way a little giddy. "That's not what I want to hear, Lo."

"But it's true."

"Oh sweetie, you may be too young to understand this, but the truth is often overrated." Who knew what other tidbits of gossip Logan had garnered from Graham.

She pulled her hair into a ponytail and met my eyes in the mirror. "Is that why you haven't told Elliott about Leo?"

I fell heavily on the edge of the bed. I didn't know how to explain the way I was compartmentalizing Elliott and Leo, two separate parts of my world, to myself let alone to her. And I certainly hadn't figured out how to talk to either one of them about it. But why had I so deliberately lied to Elliott about my situation?

I answered her. "I don't want to hurt him."

"Who? Elliott or Leo?"

"Both."

She gave me the same look that Georgia would have given me in that situation, disbelief tinged with disapproval. "Someone's gonna be hurt, and really angry."

For some reason I had decided that I needed to talk to Leo first and explain everything to him before I could discuss any of it with Elliott. It had made sense at the beginning, weeks ago. But Leo wouldn't talk to me on the phone about anything; he was always pushing me off. And now it had been so long. So much time had passed. So many things had happened with Elliott. I had no idea what to do anymore.

Logan had lost interest in my mental anguish and was digging through my closet for sandals.

She asked, "What're you doing tonight?"

I answered, distractedly. "Elliott." I began backpedaling immediately. "No, not doing. I mean Elliott's coming over for dinner. I don't mean that—"

Logan held her hands up to stop my babbling. "I got it. I'll be home by ten."

I plopped onto the couch waiting for Elliott and let my eyes drift to the Wall of Discovery. I stared at an old map of the Rutledge and Jones properties, which was tacked next to a current map of the marina and golf course. I could see it now: the marina and golf course complex wasn't just in the same area as the old Rutledge and Jones properties. It *was* the old Rutledge and Jones properties.

I had spent the last decade dealing in real estate and due diligence. It would be an easy project for me to figure out how those two distinct parcels of land became one piece of property that was now owned by Emory Bryant.

Elliott showed up at the house with fish for dinner. Whole fish with eyeballs and fins and tails and everything. I grimaced. "I don't know how to make it go from that"—I pointed at the head—"to the kind of fish you can eat."

He laughed. I wasn't trying to be funny. "This *is* the kind of fish you eat. Don't worry. I'll clean them."

He went to work in the kitchen hacking the heads off of those poor dead things and ripping their bellies open. I said, "Remind me not to piss you off."

He held up a bloody hand. "You're hopeless. Come here. I'll show you what to do."

"Eww, no way. I'm not ever doing that. I'll make drinks; you slaughter dinner."

"Deal."

Elliott had woken up in the predawn morning to go fishing with his dad. Elliott and his father were very close. I think it was one of the things that brought him back to Tillman. His father had been suffering from heart disease and was on his second stent. I knew that spending as much time with his father as he could was important to Elliott and I hated to think that I knew how it all would end.

I wondered what his father looked like. Did he have the same green eyes as Elliott? Or the same hair that was always falling in his face? Or that cute lopsided smile that came out when he thought I was doing something charming and/or stupid?

Elliott threw that lopsided smile at me now as I finished my argument trying to convince him that Emory had something to hide from me, which would explain why he acted so strange every time he saw me.

If Emory had done something illegal, or possibly simply improper, to obtain the land then he may have been worried that we could make a legitimate claim to it. I could tell by the look on Elliott's face that he wasn't buying my theory, but I couldn't think of any other reason for the reaction that my arrival in town had received from Emory.

I walked through it logically, spelling it out to Elliott. My mother would have been the sole heir to the Rutledge estate. George and Oliver would most likely have been the sole heirs to the Jones estate. When Oliver and George died, the Jones estate would have gone to my mother, as George's widow. So Janie Jones would have, at one time, been the sole owner of the entire piece of property.

Elliott offered up logic. "Maybe Emory bought it from her."

I wasn't buying it. "Then why did he say he never met her? And why did Buddy say that Emory stole from her? None of it makes sense. But if Emory never legally bought the land then upon my mother's death it would go to me and Georgia."

We had finished dinner and were sitting on the couch. Elliott was twisting a strand of my hair around and around, hypnotizing himself with it. He was exhausted from getting up so early and was having a hard time keeping his eyes open.

I was fully alert with a rush of energy at the moment, now

that I had some new string to pull in the unraveling of the mystery of Janie. How had I been down here all this time and never done any due diligence on the property?

I was trying to think of possibilities in my mind and explain them to Elliott. The scenario I kept returning to was a foreclosure resulting in a tax sale. I rarely had to deal with anything like foreclosures or tax sales at work. We were a multi-million-dollar international construction firm. Mostly I dealt with building codes and standards, but I had been around a long time. I knew enough, and a lot of those arbitrary details were popping into my brain. I was going from memory, but I believed Georgia was a nonjudicial foreclosure state, meaning they don't necessarily have any court supervision in the sale of the foreclosed property.

Elliott's eyes were closed. His voice was faint. "Are you actually speaking Greek right now? I have no idea what you're saying."

I just kept thinking aloud. "If there was a foreclosure against the property then there could be a case for wrongful foreclosure or maybe improper notice. He would know that. It could be making him nervous. But this would all have had to take place so long ago; surely the statutory right of redemption time period would have long since passed."

"Yep, Greek."

"I'm calling him." I sat up. "Emory. I'm calling him."

I thought Elliott would try to stop me, or tell me I was being silly. But instead he pulled out his cell phone and scrolled to Emory's number.

After an awkward preamble of pleasantries I asked him how and when exactly he bought the land. He hedged and gave me a vague nonanswer.

"Emory, I do this for a living. I'm a researcher and this is all public record so I can find out tomorrow or you can just tell me tonight."

Emory blew out a breath, which I could hear very clearly on my end of the phone. He said, "I bought it at a tax lien sale on the courthouse steps in nineteen seventy-four."

I could picture it in my mind's eye. Some lawyer out there on the courthouse steps in a polyester suit with white patent leather shoes reading out the exact conditions of the property's lien, or "crying out" the sale, as eager sharks circled the bloody mess.

I was surprised that my mother had let her property get foreclosed on. How could she have let that happen? I said, "They cried the sale on the courthouse steps? What was the purchase price?"

"About two thousand dollars, plus thirteen months' worth of accrued property taxes."

Ouch. Two thousand dollars? Generations of Rutledges had owned that land, lived and died and been buried on that land. The same must have been true for the Joneses' property. How had she lost it? How had Janie Rutledge Jones managed to lose such a substantial piece of lakefront property to a carpetbagger named Emory Bryant at a fire sale on the courthouse steps?

I was starting to feel cheated for my mother. "Did you know her, Emory? Did you ever meet her?"

Emory cut me off. "If you don't need anything else I should get back to our dinner guests."

Two thousand dollars. He did steal it. Legally maybe, but that's a steal.

I could have found that out in an hour's worth of searching. Why had I called Emory at home and rattled his cage? Now if he did have something to hide regarding the property he knew I was on to him. I was pacing the room, double-checking the locks.

Elliott came over to me and put his hands on my shoulders. He was yawning and his eyes were puffy and red rimmed. "Emory is not going to hurt you. I don't understand why you're so worried about him."

"I know you think I'm being paranoid, but there's something strange about the way he acts toward me and now he knows I'm investigating."

Elliott wasn't going to entertain my suspicion about Emory any more this evening. He spun me around and steered me toward my room. "Come on. You're exhausted. I'm tucking you in and you're getting some sleep."

I glanced at the front door. "Are you sure you locked it?"

He wasn't answering that question again either. He followed me into my room, demanded that I lie down. Elliott looked like he was about to fall over. "You're too tired to walk home. You should sleep here." I thought about all of the different things that could mean. Then I remembered that Logan would be home any minute. "I mean you know, on the couch. If you wanted. Maybe keep an eye on things? There are extra blankets and pillows in the linen closet."

That made him laugh for some reason and he kissed me on the forehead. "Sure. I'll guard the house tonight." He was talking through his yawn. "I'll be right out there; don't worry. Good-night, Liv."

" 'Night."

Several hours later I was still lying there staring at the ceiling. I strained my ears to try to hear Elliott's breathing from the other room. It was no use over the racket of the crickets and bullfrogs. It was hard to believe people thought of the country as a quiet place. I had never been to a city as loud as this lake was at night. I sat up and looked at the clock. It was after two. I tiptoed into the family room to peek at Elliott.

He was sleeping on the couch with a plastic badminton racket propped across his chest as a weapon. He had moved all of the back cushions to the floor making the couch a pretty decent-sized bed. I walked slowly and quietly over to him and gently pulled the racket out of his hand. He didn't move. I pulled the blanket back up onto his chest. He still didn't move. I poked at his hand. Then at his shoulder.

I sat down on the edge of the couch staring at him. I had to stifle a laugh. I picked up his right hand, held it aloft for a second, then dropped it on his chest. Nothing.

I leaned in and said in his ear, "You are the worst guard dog ever."

A tiny sleepy smile moved across his face but he didn't say anything.

I whispered, "We've come to steal your women."

In one groggy motion he wrapped his arm around my waist and rolled onto his side pulling me down until I was cradled in the couch with him. Tight in his grip. He nestled his face into the back of my neck, mumbling, "You can have the kid, but this one is mine."

His warm breath was tangled in my hair and he was asleep again in moments. *This one is mine.* I held his hand and pulled it into my chest. Our feet were tangled together under the blanket. I closed my eyes, feeling safe for the first time all night, and fell asleep.

I woke up the next morning to find Elliott propped up on his elbow watching me sleep. I smiled at him.

He brushed the hair away from my face and said, "Don't be alarmed but some bandits snuck in here in the middle of the night and I let them have Logan."

"You are a terrible bodyguard." I hit his elbow making him fall on me. Now he was at my mercy.

I wrapped my arms around him, not letting him back up, and said a proper good morning. I'm not sure how that would have ended if his phone hadn't started to clamber across the coffee table, ringing and vibrating.

He groaned and sat up to turn it off. "That's my alarm. I have meetings all morning."

"Well, I can see why you need such a persistent alarm. You sleep like the dead."

"My ninja-like reflexes were ready to spring into action if there had been an actual threat."

I leaned over the edge of the couch and picked up the racket from the floor. I held it up as exhibit A. "With your plastic badminton racket?"

"When used correctly, that can be a weapon of deadly force."

I tapped him on the head with the racket and offered to make him some coffee. He followed me into the kitchen and pulled a note off the refrigerator. It was from Logan; she had already left for camp. Which meant she had seen me sleeping on the couch with Elliott. I felt a wave of embarrassment. Was there no end to the debauchery that child would be exposed to by her aunt?

At least we hadn't been doing anything. And we were fully clothed. I felt a tiny bit better.

Elliott balled up the note and swished it into the trash can like a basketball goal. He said, "I'm having dinner at my parents' house tonight. Come with me. You could finally meet everyone. Except Michael."

I knew Michael was the second-youngest sibling and was going to college at the Citadel in South Carolina. Elliott had told me that Michael's major was French literature, but I was sure that had to be a joke. I kept meaning to look that up to see if it was really an available course of study at a military college.

I pulled two mugs from the shelf. "Right, Michael won't be there because he's in Paris or something? Reading French plays?"

Elliott squinted at me. "Why don't you believe me?"

"French literature? Really?" I poured us both coffee and handed Elliott's to him. Light and sweet, just like he liked it.

"You can ask my mom about it tonight." He took my hand and started swinging it back and forth. "When you come to dinner with me."

He looked so cute all disheveled from sleep. His hair was bent down at strange angles and he had lines from the pillow on his face. I was getting ready to tell him that I would go anywhere he wanted. Then I remembered what Logan had said about Elliott's mother being unhappy about his breakup with Amy.

I put my coffee down. "I think I'll pass on the family dinner this time. Your ridiculous lie about Michael and French lit are safe for another day."

He must have known why I didn't want to go. "You have to meet them sometime."

"I think it will have to be sometime *later*."

He held my hand tighter. "They won't blame any of it on you."

"Why not? I would if I were them." I wasn't going to budge on this. "I'm just not ready for all that yet. Is that okay?"

He sighed. "No. But I can tell I won't be able to change your mind."

He had to work all day and then he would be at his parents' for dinner. I wouldn't get to see him until tomorrow. I handed him his keys from the table.

Elliott was putting his shoes on, and he looked up at me. "What are you planning to do today?"

I shrugged. "Chores, I guess. I have to clear a bunch of work e-mails. I've been ignoring them for days." Being on a leave of absence wasn't exactly the full stop I had hoped it would be.

Elliott went to the front door and turned to look back one last time. He smiled at me and again I thought, *This one is mine.*

TWENTY-THREE

It was raining the day I was supposed to meet Elliott at the courthouse to search for some documents and maps. The Huntley County Courthouse sat up on a pediment overlooking Tillman's main square. It was constructed of the same local granite as the library and the other monumental buildings in Tillman, and it was the tallest structure for miles around.

I was watching the sheets of rain hit the lake below and hoping it would let up soon so I could walk to the courthouse without getting drenched when my doorbell rang. To my great surprise it was Buddy. He had looked so strong and robust up on the ridge, but he looked small and frail framed in my doorway. Behind him the blue hydrangeas bordering the walkway were sodden with water and drooping down, limp on the sidewalk. The asphalt on the street was steaming as the rain began to evaporate on impact.

I was so shocked to see Buddy standing there that I was slow to invite him in. He said, "Are you planning to leave me out here in the damn rain all day?"

"No, I'm sorry. Come in, Buddy. It's nice to see you again." I took his umbrella from him, shaking it out a bit, and then led him into the family room. "I'm glad it's raining. Won't this help your trees?"

Buddy was wearing his uniform of old blue jeans and the tan windbreaker. He carried a brown paper sack crumpled over and darkened from getting wet. "This is too much damn rain all at once. My roots are already all pushed up to the surface."

I had no idea what he was talking about, but I regretted bringing up the weather. I wasn't sure what he was doing here or how to entertain him so I fell back on years of polite manners drilled into me by my mother and began asking him how he was doing, if he'd like a drink, if I could get him a bite to eat. I was about to invite him to stay for dinner when he cut me off.

"Damn girl, I can't stay. I've got more things to do than sit around here with you all day. I just came to drop this off." The brown paper bag fell apart when he opened it so he tossed it on the floor exposing the package inside. It was a shoebox wrapped in a plastic grocery bag. He handed the bundle over to me and said, "I found a few things of Nate's you might like to see. Not much, I didn't go climbing into the attic for you or anything."

I pulled the box from the bag and opened it to find stacks of snapshots. It was the single largest cache of photographic evidence of Huntley, Georgia, I had been able to get my hands on yet. I think I gasped a little bit. I let my fingers thumb through the pictures: some of them were square black-and-white photos on thick paper with scalloped edges and others were glossy hypersaturated color with big white borders. I couldn't help but start crying.

My emotions were making Buddy fidgety. He started wringing his hands together. I discreetly wiped my eyes and pulled one of the pictures from the stack, at least pretending to be completely composed. It was a group of teenagers swimming in the river. The river was rushing over a waterfall of rocks, maybe twenty feet tall and sloped on an incline making a giant waterslide. The bank on the far side of the river that you could see in the photo was steep and covered with granite boulders and pine trees. There were a few kids standing at the top of the rushing water, waiting to slide down. One boy was in midtrip down the waterfall with a huge spray of water splashing him in the face. Wading in the shallow pool at the base of the slide were Janie and George. I moved over to sit next to Buddy and pointed at them in the picture.

"It's my mom and George."

He squinted at the photo. "That's Oliver."

"It is? How can you tell?"

One gnarled finger pointed to a scar, clearly visible, running across Oliver's chest. "You could always tell them apart by the scars. Oliver had a lot of scars."

Buddy named the other kids in the picture. Nate was the one captured sliding down the waterfall, which was called Slide Rock. It was one of the many landmarks now sitting quiet and still underneath the lake.

I pulled out a slightly blurry black-and-white image showing a group of boys leaning on a truck. Arms crossed, faces tight, young men attempting to look cool for the camera. I tried to name them all. I managed to get Oliver, George, and Nate picked out of the lineup. The rest of the boys were people I hadn't met yet.

Buddy searched through the box looking for a particular picture and pulled it out when he found it. I recognized Nate standing comfortably with his arm around the waist of a girl. She must be Margaret. He was wearing a white jacket and a tie. Margaret had dark curly hair and she wore a yellow dress and a large purple wrist corsage. They were standing at the entrance of a barn; the huge wooden doors, dark with age, were swung open to a party. A hazy yellow light poured from the open barn, haloing the couple in a flattering glow.

Behind them the barn twinkled with strings of lights strung from the rafters. The walls were lined with rows of hay bales covered with horse blankets offering a place to sit. The barn was packed with kids similarly dressed, some of them blurry because they were dancing.

Buddy said, "This is Nate and Margaret at one of the parties. You probably don't care much about seeing them, but I put it in here because it shows the barn."

"The barn?"

"Your mother really never told you anything."

When Buddy told me about the barn I remembered Florence saying something about it. About the birthday party that George, Oliver, and Janie threw every year in the old barn on the Jones property. Buddy told me that when the kids were all little they would play party games, have cake, and bring in some of the baby farm animals to pet. But when they got older the parties got bigger with every kid in town planning whom to ask and what to wear for weeks. There was music on the stereo and dancing on the dance floor. There was plenty of food and punch, and nothing but trouble happening in the dark recesses behind the hay bales.

I was straining my eyes at the picture trying to see if I could find Janie and George in the crowd. Buddy picked up another picture and turned it over showing me that there were names written on the back. Most of the pictures had names and dates written on them, which would make it so much easier to figure out who all of these people were.

Buddy pulled another picture from the box and handed it to me. It was a faded color shot of my mom's house. "That was your mom's house before it fell. I have a few more shots of it in here; I pulled out the ones I could find of it."

It showed a crowd of people in the yard sitting on lawn chairs, and smoke from a grill was wafting off into the horizon. I suddenly realized that I recognized this picture. I glanced at the Wall of Discovery and found almost the same picture tacked up there. It was the image we had found that first day in the library when we were searching for pictures of the lake.

"Do you know what this party was for?"

"That was the welcome home barbeque for Oliver when he got back from Vietnam." He glanced at the nearly identical picture I had under the TVA research on the wall. He nodded. "Yep, that was the same day it hit full pool. I'd forgotten that." I assumed that "full pool" meant that was the day the lake had finished being filled. That would explain why there had been a photographer there from the TVA to capture the occasion on film.

Buddy pulled out a few more images from that day and handed them to me. One was another shot of the crowd. I recognized a few faces, but I didn't see Janie or George. I found Nate and Margaret sitting under a tree. Margaret was very pregnant and toasting the camera with a bottle of Coke. Nate had happy written all over his face.

The next picture was a shot of the throng attacking Oliver as he climbed out of a blue sedan. A lot of the people in the picture were out of focus as they rushed to welcome Oliver back home. His face was completely vacant. He looked strange, shocked or surprised maybe. George was climbing out of the open door on the drivers' side of the car. Janie was walking toward him and their eyes were locked. Frozen on their faces was a shared look that spoke of worry and concern.

The last picture of the welcome home barbeque was taken at twilight. The group of partygoers who remained was sitting on the deep back porch of the house overlooking the lake. The automatic flash from the camera threw them into stark white contrast to the darkening sky behind them. I looked for Janie first, as always. She was sitting on the porch swing with a cigarette in her hand and her hair pulled back from her face with a red scarf. I never knew she had once smoked.

Oliver sat next to her, in the middle of the swing; his feet were bare making him look like a small, frightened child. He had yet another scar, this one on his neck. It was still fresh and pink. Oliver looked gaunt and his face was a pasty gray color even in the wash of the bright camera flash. George sat on the other side of him, fit, tan, and healthy. They were a study in contrasts. Janie and George were doing a poor job of smiling for the camera. They looked like bookends trying desperately to keep Oliver upright.

I asked Buddy, "What happened to Oliver? How did he die?"

He didn't answer for a long time. Finally he said again, "Oliver had a lot of scars." I wasn't sure if he was being metaphorical or literal.

Sitting in the foreground of the picture, in profile, was another recently discharged sailor. He was wearing the same green-gray military issue T-shirt as Oliver. I couldn't see his face very clearly. I flipped the picture over and read the names listed on the back. The new arrival was Johnnie. There had been a Johnnie on the boat with Oliver in the pictures that Florence had given me with the letters from Vietnam. He must have come home with Oliver after the war.

I squinted at the picture, desperate to get a peek inside of the house I would never ever get to see, but the windows were black.

I thought I might start crying again. "Buddy, thank you so much for letting me see these."

He didn't like the way this was going with me thinking he was a nice guy and getting weepy every few minutes. He cleared his throat. "You can't keep them, you know. They belong to Nate. But you can look at them for a bit."

"I know, but I still really appreciate you sharing them with me."

He got up and started walking himself to the door, talking over his shoulder. "I wrote my address on the top of the box so you can bring them back to me. But don't go breaking into my damn house when you come. Knock on the door."

It had stopped raining by the time he left. I watched him throw his umbrella into the bed of his truck and climb behind the wheel. I waved to him as he drove away; he just shook his head at me.

I wanted to sit down and go through the entire box of pictures systematically, but I didn't have time. I had to meet Elliott at the courthouse. I took out my phone and snapped a picture of the kids all swimming at Slide Rock and sent it to Georgia.

As I hurried across the square, being careful to miss the puddles of red mud, I called my sister.

"Hey, I just got my hands on some pictures of Huntley. I sent you one of Mom and Oliver swimming in the river."

"Hi, Olivia. I'm glad you called."

Something was wrong, we always spoke to each other in shorthand, not in full formal sentences. "And why are you glad that I called, Georgia?"

She tossed out a fake laugh. "That's so funny that you ask. Yes, he's right here. Do you want to talk to him?" Georgia pulled the phone away from her ear and said very loudly, for my benefit, "Leo, do you want to say hi to Livie?"

Dammit. I stopped walking and hid out underneath an awning trying not to get dripped on. I said, "Hi there."

"Hi, what are you doing?" It was Leo's mad voice. What in the world had Georgia said to him? Why was he at her house?

I told him briefly about the pictures that Buddy had dropped off. I began to describe one of them when he cut me off. "Listen, Georgia and I were just talking about Janie's birthday. Do you want me to fly down with her to help you scatter the ashes?"

I felt myself flinch when he said that. What day was it? I spun around looking at the shop windows for some indication of the date. "What . . . you were what? What day is it?"

"It's the twenty-eighth, Georgia is flying down in two days."

I couldn't seem to say anything.

"Livie?"

"Um, no I . . . I think it should just be me and Georgia. But I'm not sure I'm ready. There are still so many things I don't know. I don't think . . ." How could it be here already? Time seemed to be rushing past me and I was unable to keep up.

Leo said, "You can't stay."

"What?"

"You can't stay there, Olivia. You've been gone for almost a month. You need to put your mom to rest and come home."

"I . . . I know." We sat on the phone in a long uncomfortable pause.

Leo broke first. "I've got to run. I'll call you later. Love you."

"Me too." I hung up and threw my head in my hands. I waited in the shelter of the hardware store awning for Georgia to call me back. I knew as soon as Leo was out the door she'd start dialing.

When my phone rang I picked up and began talking before Georgia could say anything. "I didn't realize it was almost the thirtieth. I'm not ready." I felt choked for time. "You can't come down here yet." That jar of ashes was my indemnity. It was the only thing allowing me to stay down in Tillman. I couldn't let go of it, not yet.

"Livie, we said we'd do it on her birthday. It's time. I've already got my ticket."

"Well, cancel it. I'll pay for it. But I'm not doing it, not yet." My voice was high and sounded panicky. "There's still too much I have to figure out."

I think Georgia might have seen this coming because she didn't sound surprised, just tired and disappointed. "Figure out about what? About Mom or about you and Leo?"

"I don't want to fight with you about this. I didn't realize how close we were to her birthday." She didn't say anything so I waited her out. I was watching the remains of the storm blow out past the square and cloak the mountains in fog.

Finally she sighed. "You need to talk to Leo and tell him how you're feeling."

"I know. I've tried. He won't talk to me on the phone. He must know something is off. I need to come home to have that conversation. We've been through too much and he deserves an honest discussion, in person. But I can't come home yet. I'm on borrowed time down here. I can feel it. I need to finish this first. Then I'll come home and he and I will talk."

"Fine. I'll postpone, but not for very long, Olivia. It's not just you in this. You have to come clean with Leo. And I haven't seen Logan all summer. You really are on borrowed time down there."

I made my way slowly toward the courthouse to meet Elliott. I could feel life barreling toward something. I just didn't know what would happen when it hit.

The long, deep staircase up to the courthouse door was wide and shallow and forced you to walk in a strange processional, always making you step up with the same leg.

Walking through the revolving oak doors assaulted me with cold, stale air. It smelled like dust and floor polish. There was a metal detector just inside the entrance; the juxtaposition of it with the old-fashioned entrance and grand foyer just looked silly.

I was lost in thought as I gathered my bag from the metal detector's conveyor belt. The booming voice of Jimmy startled me, snapping me out of it. "Don't let her in here, Knox. That girl's nothing but trouble."

I turned around to see Jimmy coming across the foyer. I put a smile on my face trying not to look on the outside like I felt on the inside. "Are you trying to get me kicked out, Jimmy?"

"Yes, I am." He came over and gave me a little hug.

"Listen, I wanted to thank you again for letting us use your boat." Elliott and I had taken it out to the Ruins on a few occasions. "Are you sure you don't mind?"

"Of course not. Eli's the only one who ever fills it with gas so you two keep using it. I just saw him upstairs." He pointed his thumb over his shoulder at the licensing office sign and said, "Are you two here to apply for a marriage license?"

"A what!"

Jimmy and Knox, the ancient security guard in his oversized ill-fitting outfit, laughed at my outburst. Jimmy said, "I'm just messing with you."

"Ha. Right. That's a good one." I said good-bye to Jimmy and headed upstairs toward the records office. It was on the sec-

ond floor right next to the license office where I assume one
would go to apply for a marriage license.

I opened the door to the small, quiet room and saw Elliott
standing at the tall counter with his back to me. Just seeing him
had an immediate calming effect. That rushing clock in my
mind slowed down when I spotted him.

Elliott turned when I came in and smiled at me. He reached
out for my hand and pulled me up next to him at the counter.
Yes, calm. I couldn't let go of his hand.

Elliott was speaking quietly, the way you do when you're in
an unfamiliar office space. "There you are. I've been telling
Maggie what you're looking for. She thinks we might be able to
find some old plat maps in the basement archives."

I smiled at Maggie. She was behind the counter and on the
phone, but she smiled back at me. I asked Elliott, "Do you think
I could get a copy of Oliver's birth and death certificates here
too?"

"Probably."

Maggie finished her phone call and gave me her full attention. I gave her Oliver's name and dates of birth and death and
asked if I could get copies of his records. She was writing his
information down on a form and without looking up asked,
"Are you next of kin?"

My heart sank. I didn't know why I wanted to gather these
things about Oliver. Maybe because I was now viewing myself
as his namesake. But I did want to know, and now I would have
to go back into the Internet searches to find it.

Elliott answered for me. "Yes, she is."

"I am?"

"You're his niece." He winked at me imperceptibly. "You and Georgia are his next of kin."

Elliott was trying to bypass some red tape, but in a way he was right. Georgia and I were the only family George and Oliver had left and I, for one, didn't want their memories forever trapped at the bottom of the lake.

As Elliott and I went down to the basement of the courthouse I told him about my unexpected visit from Buddy and the treasure trove he had shared with me. I couldn't wait to get home and show him all of the pictures.

Elliott held the door open for me. "Buddy's like your personal redneck fairy godmother."

We entered the basement armed with our approved request forms for the plat maps and Oliver's records. The basement was like that of any ancient office building. The linoleum tiles were chipped at the edges and stained with decades of shoes scuffing over them. The air felt cold and damp and the fluorescent lights buzzing overhead gave off a strange blue cast.

We walked into a small windowless room and were greeted by the usual, *Hey Elliott, how's your father feeling?* I had become accustomed to people saying that by rote when they saw him.

The woman looked at our request form and told us she would have the copies of the birth and death certificates ready shortly. The old plat map would have to be ordered, but she would pull the records from the last transfer of ownership of the property for us.

Then she pointed to the reference numbers on the request for Oliver's death certificate. "Eli, this has a coroner's report attached to it. You can get that now while you wait." She wrote some numbers on a slip of paper, gave it to Elliott. "You want to just pull this yourself?"

Elliott opened the door to the storage room and turned a dial on the wall. A series of round halogen lights overhead began to spring to life, illuminating a cavernous space stacked as far as I could see with rows and rows of file cabinets.

It took a minute for the lights to get up to their full power and Elliott explained that they were on a timer so if we would be in here for longer than five minutes we would need to reset the dial or they would switch off automatically, leaving us in the dark.

I looked at the small piece of paper with the call numbers scrawled on it. "How in the world are we supposed to know where this is?"

Elliott took the paper from me. "I come in here all the time to pull records for stories. I can find it."

I looked over his shoulder as he traced his finger along the cabinet numbers until he found the one he wanted. He opened the drawer and flipped through it, reading through the tabs, then pulled out a manila folder.

I had never read a coroner's report before and it seemed a bit ghastly. The first page was a form with blank spaces to note the location of the body, if rigor mortis had set in, time of discovery of the body, etc. The second page was equally helpful with boxes one could check if the method of death were by an apparent gunshot, ligature, drowning, knife wound, etc. How handy. I was relieved to see that the box for "photographs" had not been checked.

Elliott was reading the report with a practiced eye. He flipped through all the pages and then looked at me and said, "Suicide."

"What!" I looked at the page trying to see how he had deciphered that from the technical jargon and medical notations. "Uncle Ollie killed himself?"

Elliott raised his eyebrows at me. "Uncle Ollie?"

"I'm trying to humanize him. Where does it say suicide?"

Elliott pointed to one section of the written report. "It says 'intentional drowning,' but it doesn't say how they came to that conclusion. The last page has the eye witness's report." He flipped to the end of the stack of papers. "It's missing."

"Of course it is. Why is half the stuff we're looking for missing?" I sat down on the floor feeling tired and just a little defeated as I looked over the report again.

Elliott asked, "You okay?"

"It's nothing." I wasn't sure what to say. "My mom's birthday is in two days."

He sat down next to me, taking my hand. "I'm sorry. I should've realized." The puzzled look on my face must have asked how he could have known that her birthday was looming because he answered. "It's on her birth certificate, which I've looked at a dozen times. Are you sad?"

"Yes. I'm also . . . Georgia and I were planning to scatter the ashes on her birthday." Elliott didn't say anything but his grip on my hand tightened. "I just talked to her and put it off for a bit."

"What happens after you scatter her ashes?"

I didn't say anything, which probably told him volumes.

We sat in silence on the floor of the records storage room underneath the open metal drawer for a few minutes. He knew exactly what this all meant. It meant that once my mother was put to rest this thing was over. I would leave. Right? Wasn't that the whole reason, the only reason, I was even in Tillman? Finally he stood up. "I'll go see if the other stuff is ready yet."

Elliott went to retrieve the birth and death certificates and the land ownership information. I was holding the coroner's report in my hand. It was hard to stay caught up in your own tiny drama when you were reading through a report describing a suicide.

I turned the file over in my hands and looked at all of the doodles and scrawl on the front. There was a lunch order and a few telephone numbers on one side. The other side had a list that looked like locations. Probably the last time people had seen Oliver. One note was circled. It read: "R. Ridge. Witness—Johnnie Bryant. Questioned/released. Doc—suicide."

The hair on my arms stood straight up and a chill ran through me. R. Ridge was Rutledge Ridge; I was sure of it. And Johnnie Bryant must have been questioned about Oliver's death and then released when it was ruled a suicide. Wasn't Johnnie the man who served with Oliver in Vietnam and then came back here with him after the war? Was he staying at Rutledge Ridge? And why did they think him suspicious enough to question him when Oliver died?

I said out loud, "What's your story, Johnnie Bryant?" Just as the words came out of my mouth the light's timer on the wall clicked off and the room went completely black.

The instant darkness surprised me and I sprang to my feet. In doing so I managed to impact, at full steam, the open metal drawer above my head. There was a splitting pain. As I went to crouch down and cradle my head, my foot slipped on the file folder I had dropped. It acted like a banana peel taking my feet out from under me. I went completely horizontal before landing with a crack on my head.

Things were fuzzy and black.

Then blinding light.

Elliott was holding me and someone kept talking about blood. Was it my blood? I heard Jimmy's voice say something about head wounds bleeding like a stuck pig. That wasn't very nice. Was I the pig in this scenario?

Elliott kept talking to me, trying to make me speak. My head hurt too much to talk. I wanted them to turn the lights out. I was moving. Elliott kept pushing on my head where I had hit it. I desperately wanted him to stop doing that.

I heard another familiar voice say, "Let's take her to Maggie." But I couldn't make sense of that or figure out whose voice it was.

I came to, more or less, a minute later in the backseat of a car with my head in Elliott's lap. His clothes were covered in blood. That seemed completely illogical.

Elliott's face had the strangest look of concern. It occurred to me that I hadn't seen him look like that before. It still hurt my head when he spoke. "Liv, can you keep your eyes open for me? We're almost there."

I was so confused. "You're bleeding?"

He smiled at me. "No, sweetie. That's you. You cut your head. I think you need stitches. Hang on, okay?"

I tried to pull his hand off my head so he would stop pushing on the cut. He kept his hand in place. "I need to keep pressure on it. Do you feel nauseous at all?"

My head hurt a lot and Elliott wouldn't stop with the vice and the sun was hurting my eyes. I decided that I wanted to go back to sleep. Elliott wouldn't let me do that either.

TWENTY-FOUR

I was finally fully awake and aware of the fact that I had a "self-induced traumatic brain injury" as Elliott was jokingly calling it. Once he was assured that the cut was not that deep, and that the bump I had sustained by falling on my head was a fairly minor concussion, he had left his state of panicked concern and gone back to his usual state of making fun of me.

Elliott adjusted the ice pack he was holding on my head. "So I understand you hit your head on the file cabinet when the lights went out, but how'd you manage this bump on the back?"

I was holding his other hand in both of mine, keeping myself steady. "Don't laugh."

"I won't laugh."

"After I jumped up and cut my head I slipped on the folder and fell backwards."

He laughed until I looked like I might cry again; then he managed to control himself. We were waiting for the numbing to take effect on the area of the cut so that it could be stitched up. I looked around the room where he and I waited alone. It was a doctor's office but not an exam room. I was still fuzzy on the details.

"So where are we and how did we get here?"

"We're in Maggie's office and we rode here in Emory's car."

I was shocked. "What? How did that happen? Why was he there?" I added in a whisper, "Is he following me?"

"How hard did you hit your head? No, he wasn't following you. He was there . . . Well, I don't know why he was there. When he saw me carrying you out he practically drove his car onto the sidewalk to load you in and then rushed us here."

I was still whispering. "You don't think this is all a bit fishy? He just *happened* to be there? When I'm knocked unconscious and *bleeding*?"

"You knocked yourself unconscious." Elliott gently moved the hair off my face and looked at me. "You were white as a sheet when I found you. There was so much blood. I couldn't figure out what you had done or how you had gotten hurt. You were just on the floor in a pool of your own blood, out cold, when I came back in the room. It scared me to death. I grabbed you and was running out the front door of the courthouse, carrying you, with Jimmy clearing the way. I'm not even sure where I was going. I think I was running to get my car to take you to the hospital. Emory pulled up and looked you over. He told me to put pressure on your head to stop the bleeding and he put us in his car. You bled all over the backseat, but he didn't seem to mind. He brought us straight here and got Maggie to look at you. If I had tried to get to the ER we'd still be driving."

Well, that didn't really jive with my theory that Emory was some sort of rich, sinister townie who was out to get me. I didn't have much time to think about that though because the doctor came in to sew me up.

Maggie, the doctor, looked to be close to my mother's age. She had lovely silver hair in a neat sweeping bob and she spoke in a soft calm voice. Her cool, delicate hands worked quickly sewing up the cut and she chatted with me, as doctors do, to distract me from the unpleasant business she was attending to. I think her demeanor had more of a healing effect on me than the pain medicine and ice packs combined.

When she was finished, Elliott helped me up and took note of all of the instructions about ice and pain and not getting the stitches wet for a day.

I put my hand out. "Thank you so much, doctor . . ."

She shook my hand. "Maggie. Everyone just calls me Maggie."

Later that evening, after dinner, I was nursing my head as Logan scanned in all of the pictures from the shoebox. I said to Elliott, "I really liked Maggie. She was so nice. She kind of reminded me of my mom."

He was reading something, distracted. "Yeah, she's great."

Logan cut in. "Maggie sewed you up?" Her mouth turned up on one side, smiling.

"Yes, how do you know her?"

"Everyone at the marina knows Maggie. She's Emory's wife." Logan held up the picture she had just scanned to show me. It was Oliver, George, Nate, and Grant sitting in the bullpen at a baseball game. Oliver's uniform was covered in dirt and Grant was rubbing something into his glove.

"She is?" I was surprised. Maggie seemed so lovely. Why would she be married to Emory?

Logan was laughing now. "Yeah, and she sewed you up."

"Why is that funny?"

"She's a vet, Liv. Technically she's a large animal vet."

I looked over at Elliott. "You took me to a veterinarian?"

Elliott shrugged. "She sews everybody up. Whenever anyone needs stitches we always go to Maggie instead of driving all the way to the hospital. She doesn't mind."

Logan was laughing and calling me a large animal. I threw my half-melted ice pack at her.

I looked over to Elliott, trying to change the subject. "What are you reading?"

"The papers we got from the courthouse today. I forgot about it what with all of your dramatic falling and bleeding."

I would never live this down. First the knee, then the shoulder, and now this.

Elliott showed Oliver's death certificate to Logan. She said, "That's weird that he drowned." I was thinking the same thing. How does one "intentionally drown" anyway? Logan continued, " 'Cause remember that thing Florence told us about Oliver having to save George from the river one time? Oliver was such a good swimmer. And he was in the navy in Vietnam, right? I mean here you are, this guy that loves the water, and you chose drowning as your way to kill yourself. It's totally sad."

I knew something had bothered me about Oliver having died by drowning and that was it. By all accounts he was such a good swimmer. He must have *really* wanted to die in the lake. In the place where he grew up. I looked out the window, into the night, at the black hole in the distance that marked the boundaries of the water, and I shivered. Why did he want to die so young? My mind kept flashing back to the pictures of Oliver after he returned from the war, and I could hear Buddy's voice in my head saying, *Oliver had a lot of scars.*

I continued the thoughts in my head out loud. "Oliver must have been traumatized by the war. Actually, I think maybe he was in trouble even before the war, but that experience didn't help." I pointed to the folder. "Did you see the note on the outside of the coroner's report folder? They questioned Johnnie Bryant at Rutledge Ridge about the death. I wonder if there was something suspicious about it."

Elliott asked, "Who's Johnnie?"

I pulled out the two pictures I had of Johnnie with Oliver, one in Vietnam and one at home and showed them to Elliott. "Do you think this guy still lives around here?"

He looked at the shadowed faces. "I can't really see his face."

My head was throbbing. I didn't really care about Johnnie Bryant at the moment. "Who knows." I looked back toward the lake. "I wonder if this is why my mom wants half her ashes scattered in the lake. Because that's where Oliver died."

Elliott took his glasses off and stretched his back. We had all had a long day. "Maybe, but I think it's more likely because that's where her hometown was buried."

Logan scanned in the last of the pictures and planned to print them out after work the next day. She went off to bed as Elliott checked my head for the hundredth time.

I said, "It's fine, really. I just can't wait to wash this dried blood out of my hair. So gross."

Elliott looked at me. "You scared me to death today." He kissed my hand and pulled me in close to him. "I didn't realize . . ."

He was quiet for a long time, rubbing my back. Finally, he spoke, so low I could barely hear him. "You can't leave."

"I'm right here." I tried to make light of what he was saying, but he wouldn't let me.

He held me tighter. "You can't leave . . . me."

My heart was beating so fast, and breaking into a million pieces, all at the same time. What was I doing here? How would I manage to get to the other side of this abyss I had turned my life into? I couldn't think about any of it now. My head was splitting with pain and the fact that I had started crying wasn't helping matters.

I let Elliott hold me until I fell asleep and then he moved me into my room and tucked me in bed. All night I had dreams of Elliott's voice echoing in my head. *You can't leave.* That line rattled around in there until it bumped into Leo's voice saying, *You can't stay.*

TWENTY-FIVE

Several people from town brought me casseroles because I had been injured falling down in the courthouse. I wasn't quite sure what the correlation was between being a klutz and deserving to have food delivered. But it kept me from having to cook dinner so I just said thank you and accepted them. When the thirtieth rolled around Logan and I had a little celebration, or a small memorial depending on which minute you were referring to, for my mom. The two of us sat out on the porch overlooking the lake. A store-bought birthday cake sat between us and we were nibbling at it with forks, not bothering to slice it. One second we were laughing, remembering something about her. The next we were crying, remembering something about her. It was an emotional whiplash made more intense by the self-imposed deadline this day had once been in my mind.

A few days later as Elliott and I were cleaning up the dinner dishes Logan announced that she was going to a movie with Graham and headed out the front door. Logan was feeling the same intense contraction of time that I was feeling. Georgia's voice kept repeating in my head. *You're on borrowed time down there.* I wondered when it would crack, when the pressure would be too great and this whole construct would break down. I waved goodbye to Logan absentmindedly over my shoulder, but I noticed that Elliott followed her outside and spoke with her for a minute.

When he came back inside I asked, "What was that all about?"

"Going to a movie is code in this town for going someplace to hook up."

"How do you know they're not just going to a movie?"

"Because the closest movie theater is twenty minutes away and Graham doesn't have a car." Elliott texted something on his phone as he spoke.

His concern was so sweet; you could tell he had younger sisters. "Did you just threaten Graham with bodily harm if he did anything inappropriate with Logan?"

He put his phone down. "Just reminding him to be a gentleman."

I wondered how much was wrapped up in Elliott's idea of being a gentleman. He had certainly never tried to push me into anything and I was a grown woman. A grown woman who was definitely more willing than I was able to let on. I took the dish towel off his shoulder and dried a glass. "Good, because I'm in enough trouble down here as it is."

"Oh really?" He flicked water at me from the sink. "Just what kind of trouble are you in exactly?"

I grabbed his hands to make him stop splashing me. "I'm in big trouble for throwing this guy I met into the lake because he kept taunting me."

Elliott forced my hands behind my back and held them there, his arms circling my waist. "Oh, *you're* throwing *me* in the lake? You can barely walk across the room without breaking a bone."

"You better watch it or I'll fall on you next time."

"Promise?"

He leaned down and kissed me just as Logan came back into the house. She shielded her eyes. "Oh my God! Can you guys control yourselves for like five minutes? You are so embarrassing." She tossed an envelope on the counter. "This was in the mailbox. I'll be home by ten."

The envelope had been mailed to me from Mary Frances at Huntley Memorial Gardens. It was all of the information she had pulled from the files of grave 34B. I had forgotten all about that now that I knew who George Jones was. As I dried my hands, Elliott began to read through the papers, and as he did I could feel the mood change from across the room.

"Olivia, wasn't your father's name Adam? Adam Hughes?"

I looked over at him. "Yes. Why?"

"Because these are all letters and they're all from him."

There were six letters from my father to Huntley Memorial Gardens. The first one was a mimeograph copy from 1978. The other five were more recent, ranging from 2004 until just a few months before he died.

I pored through them reading quickly, then went back and read each one again. I wasn't sure what they all meant. They were painting a story but I didn't know exactly how it related to my mother or how all of the pieces fit together.

The oldest letter from 1978 was clearly a written follow-up to a previous conversation that my father had been having with the cemetery. And by "conversation" I mean "argument." It was an admonishment to the director of the cemetery because my father could not get permission to have a body interred in section 30. Section 30, I knew, was the Joneses' family plot. Why was my father trying to get someone buried in the Joneses' family plot?

My father wrote, "You knew full well the need to act quickly with this matter and yet you had the gall to claim that bureaucracy tied your hands. By the time we discovered the resting place of the body we had only one week to disinter it before the diversion tunnels were shut down. As a result of your most immoral behavior and dragging your feet I was forced to put the remains in a temporary grave. This will necessitate the reburial at a future date, which would have been unnecessary if you had done your job properly."

The rest of the letter was more of the same. I could hear my father's voice in the scolding. After we had read through it I asked Elliott, "What's a diversion tunnel?"

"It's a tunnel they build to divert a river when they're building a dam."

"Okay, but the dam was built in the sixties. This letter is from nineteen seventy-eight."

He was pacing the room as I sat at the table with the research and letters spread out all around me.

Elliott's hands moved around the way they did when he was

speculating. "They must have done some work on the dam in the seventies. If they needed to make any repairs to the infrastructure or if they were expanding the reservoir they would have had to use diversion tunnels."

I nodded; that made sense. "Let's assume they did that. They did some more work to the dam and rerouted the river with diversion tunnels. But what would that mean?"

"Well, part of the lake most likely dried up while the tunnels were in use."

I asked, "So when they shut the tunnels down?"

"When they shut the tunnels down, after the repair to the dam, the water would begin filling up the lake again."

We were trying to fit the pieces together. "Okay, so if they were doing some work on the dam that caused a part of the lake to dry up? Just for a little while."

He continued my thought. "And when it dried up they were able to uncover a grave?"

"Right. A grave that had previously been under the lake."

Elliott agreed. "And they had to move it quickly because they only got one shot before it was underwater again."

There were five other letters. The first of these was from the late 1980s and was an introduction from my father to the new director at the cemetery. The letter simply asked that he call my father when he had some time to discuss a "delicate matter."

Three of the letters were very short and to the point. They all basically said the same thing: "The genealogical documentation you requested is enclosed. Thank you for your time and help with this matter." But none of the documentation had been copied for us. We didn't know what my father was referring to.

There was one last letter we thought might shed some light. Again it was clearly a response from my father regarding a previous conversation.

It read:

> *I am in agreement with you that enlisting the guidance of my wife in this matter would speed up the process, but I am afraid it is out of the question. It would be too painful for her to have to deal with moving the remains. I would like to be able to put the matter to rest once the transfer is fully complete and the two bodies are together again.*
>
> *She is unaware that I had the body exhumed from its original gravesite and that it is now buried in a temporary grave. Unfortunately, due to matters beyond my control, I am now dealing with yet another bureaucratic agency to disinter the body from the temporary grave. I am hoping this one will be more sympathetic to my request for the removal. (And might I say yet again, how relieved I was when you took over at the helm of the cemetery and I no longer had to deal with that obstinate dolt?)*
>
> *In conclusion, I have enclosed the remaining documents that you requested in order for me to purchase plot 34C and I am hopeful that we will be able to have the reinterment by the end of the year.*

Elliott looked up after reading the letter. "I love that your dad called him a dolt. Great word."

I had a twinge of sadness, missing my dad.

Elliott asked, "What do you think this all means? Who was he moving around?"

"I don't know. Someone that meant a lot to my mother died. Agreed?"

Elliott sat down. "Agreed."

"So my father had this body dug up and moved without telling my mother."

Elliott continued. "And your father wanted the body to go directly from wherever it had been under the lake, straight to Huntley Memorial Gardens. But he couldn't get permission from the director."

"Right. Maybe because it's a family plot you need to be a member of the Jones family?"

Elliott just shrugged as he continued. "But because your dad couldn't bury the body there he put it someplace temporary. He just had to get it out from under the lake in a hurry before the water came back."

"Yes, but we don't know where the body was the first time or where it is now."

"No, but he said something about dealing with a bureaucracy so maybe it's in a government-run place. Like a veteran's cemetery."

I flipped through the letters. "I wish he'd said who it was."

"I wonder why your dad never told your mom he was doing all of this."

I was not surprised. "My mom was a burnt-out case when it

came to her childhood. If you pushed her on it too far she would close down on you. I can understand why my dad wouldn't have wanted to drag it out with her. He obviously wanted to wait until it was all sorted out before telling her. But it looks like he never got to finish it. Whoever he was trying to move never got there or we would've seen the grave, right? Was there anyone buried next to George? I can't remember."

Elliott looked through the papers on the table until he found his notes from the cemetery. "No, not on his left. He was kind of at the end of that row, remember? And then to his right was his brother Oliver. He was buried there in nineteen sixty-eight, so that couldn't have been who your father was talking about."

Just when I thought we were finished, at the end, all of the discoveries made, we find something new. Who would my mother have wanted to bury next to George? Did George have any other siblings? Did my mother? She always said she was an only child. But then again she said a lot of things, didn't she? And there were even more things, enormous life-altering things, that she simply never mentioned.

I added the letters to the other piles of stuff I didn't understand that were stacked up on the table. Then I let my eyes wander across the Wall of Discovery. I was thinking of renaming it: My Mother's Wall of Annoying Secrets and Untold Mysteries.

I picked up the nearest stack of papers and went out to the porch with Elliott. I flipped through them while he busied himself hanging up an old rope hammock we had found in the closet.

These were newspaper articles from the local paper about George and Janie in their younger years. I didn't think we were consciously focusing on their youth, but there was the glaring omission from the Wall of Discovery about anything concerning George's death. It was so hard to think about them being so young and happy and knowing what the future held for them. Maybe it was just easier to see them together, blissfully unaware of what lay ahead, if we left the rest of their story alone.

There were two stories about George being spotlighted for baseball. One was for being voted Student Athlete of the Year for his high school team. The accompanying photo was of George and Janie. He was in his baseball uniform with dirt down the left side where he had clearly slid into base. The picture must have been taken right after a game had ended. The stands in the background were filled with people in midcheer. George was standing on the roof of the dugout while Janie was on the other side of the rail at the foot of the bleachers. She was looking out toward the scoreboard as George, dirty and sweaty, had both arms wrapped tightly around her waist. Were those two ever apart?

Another article was about Janie registering people to vote in the "negro" neighborhoods. George was standing next to her holding a clipboard as she spoke with a pastor of one of the churches. I noticed that one of George's hands was resting protectively on her shoulder. I was proud of my mother, looking at that photo. That was the mother I remembered. I was reminded that she did manage to go on living after she lost George. That she had kept going to become an amazing mother, a wonderful wife, and a respected professor of American history. Sometimes the Janie in those old photos with George was a separate person in my mind from my mother. Sometimes she was not.

Elliott hopped into the hammock to make sure the rusted hooks in the wall would hold. I sat down on it too and tried to work my way into a horizontal position next to him. I yanked on the edge of the hammock, hoping to give myself leverage to move over, but all I managed to do was upset the entire equilibrium and we both flipped off of it landing with a thud on the floor.

We were both laughing as we got to our feet. My head was throbbing and Elliott was holding his lower back.

He saw me holding my head and asked, "Are you okay?"

I nodded, but it hurt. We stumbled into the house together to make sure it hadn't started bleeding again.

Elliott teased me as he checked the stitches. "You did that on purpose to garner sympathy from me."

That made me laugh. I gingerly touched the back of my head. "It's not bleeding again is it? This stupid thing still hurts."

"Maybe you should stop falling on it."

Elliott declared my wound okay. We spent the remainder of the evening in the safety of the rocking chairs out on the porch listening to the night sounds on the lake and talking about George and Janie and unknown gravesites.

When Logan got home from her date with Graham, Elliott gathered up his things to head home. I walked him out to the street and we made plans for him to come back in the morning for breakfast.

He said, "I have a surprise for you. I should have it all by tomorrow."

"What is it?"

"It's a surprise." He kissed the bump on my head lightly.

"Can you make it back into the house by yourself? You might trip over a crack and lose a leg."

"You're mean." I pushed him down the sidewalk.

"You're a klutz."

"I hate you."

He called over his shoulder, "Ha! No, you don't. You love me."

Elliott was walking away from me, down the sidewalk. *You love me.* Something possessed me in that instant and I closed the distance to him without even thinking. He heard me coming and turned just in time to catch me as I threw myself at him, nearly knocking him over into the bushes. I was holding on to him so tightly my feet weren't touching the ground. I couldn't keep it up. I couldn't keep maintaining a distance from him. I couldn't keep saying good-night and letting him go at the end of the evening. Elliott kissed me back with so much passion it was a wonder our clothes didn't simply fall off. He kissed me down my neck and my ear and mumbled something into my hair.

"What . . . "

He said it again. "Come home with me."

Speech was becoming increasingly difficult. As was standing upright. I just nodded my head.

The porch light burst on behind us and we stopped for a second, breathing heavily. I had forgotten about Logan.

She cleared her throat from the porch. "Aunt Liv, my mom's on the phone." I saw her put the phone back to her ear. "Just a sec, Mom."

Elliott's fingers were still digging into my back. His grip released and I slid down him until my feet touched the ground again. He laughed a little to himself and made a strange grunting sound. He kissed the top of my head, spun me around by the shoulders, and gave me a little push toward the house.

I grabbed the phone from Logan and did a cursory check of my clothing making sure that everything was securely fastened in its upright and fully locked position.

"Hi, Gigi." I sounded winded. "What's up?"

"What were you doing?"

"Saying good-night to Elliott."

"You do remember that you're chaperoning my daughter, right?"

I know, and she's making a damn fine human chastity belt if you don't mind me saying. "Lo's fine. I'm fine. Our virtues are intact."

Georgia made a noise into the phone that sounded like she doubted my statement. *Rude.*

She said, "I'm coming down there the day after tomorrow."

"What? No, wait. We got all of these letters today from the cemetery. I don't even know what they mean."

"Livie, it's time."

I felt slightly deflated. "I'm not quite ready for that yet. To spread the ashes, I mean. There are some new things, and I haven't figured it all out yet."

"Figured what out, Liv? She was married before. He died. This thing's over. You need to bury Mom and come home."

"Why are you mad at me?"

"You've been gone for over a month! I miss Logan. I'm tired of lying to Leo. You need to finish this thing and come home."

She sounded tired and angry. I didn't really know what to say to her. When I thought of leaving this place, and Elliott, it made me feel lost. Homesick. I felt like being anywhere but here, here with him, would make it hard for me to breathe. I said quietly and with very little conviction, "It'll be good to see you. I'm glad you're coming. We'll talk when you get here." Then I hung up the phone.

TWENTY-SIX

Elliott showed up for breakfast the next morning with the surprise he had promised. I didn't mention that Georgia would be driving down the next day. I didn't want to think about what that might mean and I certainly didn't want Elliott to have to worry about it. The surprise was a good one; it turned out to be yearbooks. He and Bitsy, the librarian, had managed to dig up the yearbooks from eight out of twelve years of my mother's school career. I devoured them over breakfast.

My favorite picture of my mom was when she was in the third grade. She was standing in the front row of her small class and she had a huge grin on her face exposing the gap where two of her front teeth had been. I found Florence standing next to the teacher. George and Oliver were standing in the back row. George looked neatly pressed; Oliver looked recently beaten.

When I looked at the yearbook from her senior year it seemed to me as if every image of Janie and George held a secret. I stared at the pixelated images of their eyes to see if they held any hints of what was to come. That they would be getting married in two short years. That he would be dead too soon after that.

I had marked all of the pages that held pictures of them or any mention of my mother. I flipped again to the formal senior portrait of Janie. It was still strange to see images of her so young. I had never realized how much Georgia and I resembled her until we got our hands on these pictures from her youth.

I looked at Elliott as he finished his coffee. "Thank you for finding these. You're amazing."

He smiled. "Yes, I am. I'm also late." He cleared his breakfast dishes. "Does Logan need a ride to work?"

"No, she's off today. I am going to wash my hair, again." My fingers ran over the area of stitches and the stiff surrounding hair. "Then I think we're going shopping. Will you come back after work?" I thought, *We need to talk.*

"Of course. Do you want me to bring dinner?"

"No, I actually have some stuff to cook."

He feigned surprise. "She's cooking?"

"She *might* cook. If you're a good boy."

Elliott straightened up slowly and looked as if his mind were very far away. He was staring at the wall of pictures and articles from my quixotic quest. He had just been struck by some revelation. "What did you just say?"

I tried to remember exactly what I had said so that it could trigger the thought that was clearly forming in his mind. "I said that I would cook for you. If you were a good boy."

It clicked in his brain; I could see it on his face. "Huh. I think I've just had one of those honest to God newspaperman hunches."

"What is it? What are you thinking?" I tried to follow his line of sight so I could decipher it too.

He shook his head. "I'm not sure. And you've had enough dead ends. I'll look it up and if there's anything to it I'll let you know."

I took his face in my hands. "Tell me now."

He kissed me then he pulled away to say something, but I pulled him back. He started laughing. "You're very convincing, but I'll see if there's anything to it first. See you at dinner."

"Fine." I let him go and then turned to stare at the wall. Perhaps inspiration could strike twice. But it looked the same as it always looked to me. There didn't seem to be any new information or knowledge. It was no use. I gave up and called out to Logan. "Okay, missy. Let's go shopping."

Logan and I walked into town to go clothes shopping. Her fifteenth birthday was in a few days and she wanted clothes for her present. It was not easy. Apparently the dress designers had decided that fifteen is a good age to start making girls look like hookers.

We managed to find some things that we both agreed on and were now walking through the square contemplating an early lunch.

Logan was looking past me, over my shoulder. She stopped in her tracks, and her eyes got huge. "Holy shit."

I snapped, "Don't curse, Lo. Your mom will kill me." I turned around to look in the direction she was staring, toward the inn. I saw the familiar gait and the back of his head walking toward the valet stand. "Holy shit."

Logan sounded as panicky as I felt. "What is Uncle Leo doing here?"

I was having a hard time breathing. I glanced around to see if anyone else had spotted him. Which was absurd since no one here even knew Leo.

I had an urge to run to Elliott's house and hide. Or run to my car and drive away. Or run to the lake and swim across it until I was out of sight. My heart was racing with adrenaline and mostly I just felt like running. Leo walked into the inn after finding the valet stand empty.

I took a deep breath and walked toward the inn. Logan was mercifully silent as she walked next to me. When we got there I hesitated before going inside. Logan gave me a hug and told me she was going to give us some time to talk.

I walked into the inn and took a second for my eyes to adjust after being out in the sunshine. And after being temporarily blinded by seeing Leo. I glanced around the lobby and spotted him chatting with Betty Chatham. Great. Now it would be all over town that I had a fiancé and was cheating on Elliott.

Wait, what was I saying? I wasn't a part of this town. Or these people. And I was cheating on Leo, not Elliott. Right? Either way I had a pit in my stomach at all of the things I was about to break.

I was walking over to him when Leo saw me. He rushed

toward me and gave me a familiar hug. I asked, "What are you doing here?"

"I took an early flight into Atlanta and drove up. I just got in." He sounded more sarcastic than excited as he said, "Surprise."

"I am surprised." I couldn't think of anything else to say.

He kept talking. "I was just asking the manager—"

I cut in. "Betty's actually the owner."

"Okay, then I was asking *the owner* for some directions." Leo was holding a piece of paper with my rental house address scrawled on it. "I couldn't find your house. All these one-way streets turned me around." He hugged me again stiffly and I could feel the tension mounting between us.

Betty was watching me from behind the desk while pretending to arrange some flowers. I took Leo's hand and pulled him outside to his rental car. "Let's go. We need to talk."

"I know we do. That's why I came down here." We were quiet as I directed him to the rental house.

He dropped his overnight bag inside the door and said, "Do you remember what your mom used to say? If you want to see how someone really feels about you, show up unannounced."

Clearly I had just failed his first test. "My mom never said that."

Leo stood his ground. "Yes, she did."

"No, she didn't. It was my dad. He used to say it." I probably wouldn't get any points for that parry, and now I was on the defensive. Failure number two.

There was an awkward silence as I digested the fact that he had shown up here unannounced to gauge my reaction. It was a tactic. Which meant that this was a battle. Which led me to the conclusion that we were already on stage two of the breakup without me ever even firing a shot.

I wasn't sure how to proceed from here. We both remained silent as Leo wandered slowly around the little rental house, taking it all in. I was waiting to see which one of us would crack first. Who was I kidding? I would crack first. I could never keep my mouth shut and Leo was very firm on the first rule of negotiating: the first one to talk loses.

Let the babbling begin. "I am happy to see you, Leo. I was just surprised."

His eyes were firm, not letting any emotion creep in at the moment and his guard was up. Locked and loaded. He said pointedly, "I'm here to help you put your mother to rest. I know it's important to you and regardless of . . . I wanted to be here for you. That's why you came down here." He was flipping through the accumulation of research, pictures, printouts, and maps strewn across the dining room table, shaking his head. "Before you escalated everything anyway." He looked away from the Janie Jones project and back to me.

"So . . . you're here to help me finish this?"

Leo spit out a humorless little laugh. "Finish what? Your quest about your mother or our relationship?" He was trying to use his controlled, professional lawyer voice. I wasn't sure how long he would be able to keep that up, but at the moment it was making this whole thing a lot less emotional and less messy.

I half sat and half fell onto the couch. How in the world was I supposed to start this conversation? "I'm not sure what happened, or what's been happening, to us, Leo." How was I going to put into words the things I had been feeling for the last few months? "I . . . I feel like we haven't been in a good place lately. I think that you know that as well as I do. I know you think I've been hiding out down here as a way to avoid my life, us. And maybe I was to some extent, but honestly I just needed some room to breathe, some space to figure out what I wanted."

Leo was pacing in front of me, now a bundle of barely contained nerves. "Do you have any idea how selfish you sound right now, Olivia?"

I answered honestly. "Yes."

"And you don't care? You don't care how this all affects me or how this looks?"

"Of course I care how it affects you, but no I don't care how it looks." I was staring at my hands because I was having a hard time looking him in the eye. I still couldn't adequately process the fact that he was standing in this living room.

He stopped pacing and shoved his hands in his pockets. "When were you planning to tell me how you've been feeling?"

"Are you kidding me?" My voice came out sounding shrill and maybe a little desperate. "I've been trying, Leo! I've been calling you since I got here. I wanted to ask you what you were thinking, if you were having the same thoughts, but you wouldn't even talk to me. You kept putting me off because you had a meeting or a flight or a dinner."

He was trying not to raise his voice, but I could tell it was taking a lot of effort. "This isn't the kind of conversation you have on the telephone."

"No, I know. But it would've been a start." It would have

shown me that I was a priority to Leo if nothing else. Although all it would have accomplished was a quicker breakup because that's where we had been heading for months. He was here now and it was time to start the conversation. "I've had a lot of time to think about things while I've been down here. See things from a different perspective. And it's made me realize that you and I have gotten into a routine, but I'm not sure either one of us really stopped to think about it."

He looked more impatient than mad or upset. "Why do you always make that sound like a bad thing, Olivia?"

"It's not. It's not a bad thing. If it's making us happy, but I don't think it is. We both work crazy hours, and I know you love your job but I don't love mine. It's making me miserable. Our careers are the overriding focus of our entire existence. I don't want that."

"Then get a different job." He slapped the back of the chair without much conviction and I could tell he wished he'd hit it harder.

"That's not the real problem, or the solution." I couldn't stay seated with the nervous energy running through me and I stood up too. "What I'm trying to say is that because our jobs were keeping us so busy and consumed so much of our energy we didn't have time to really stop and think about much of anything. We've just been blindly following some path, without asking ourselves if it's what we want."

"Jesus, Olivia." There was a coffee table and an armchair between us. I wondered if he would've been shaking me by the shoulders as he said that if the furniture placement hadn't been set up to block it. "You don't think we've been asking ourselves what we want? We've analyzed the shit out of this relationship on that goddamn couch for a year."

I took a deep breath. I needed to stop scooting around the perimeter of it and just say it. "I haven't been happy. I don't want to hurt you, but I don't think that's a good reason for us to keep this up."

"Keep this up?" Leo stopped and looked at me, really looked at me, for the first time since he had shown up here. He was struggling to keep his emotions in check. "Look, I can't make you happy, Olivia." He was quoting our therapist. "Only you can make yourself happy."

"I'm not putting this on you. I'm not blaming you because I feel this way. I know this is all me, all my fault. But I'm trying to explain it to you." I looked out at the thick, green blur of trees surrounding the dark, still water in the lake and the beaten-up mismatched chairs on the screen porch. I could hear the sounds of motorboats on the lake and crickets outside. "I think I've found a way to make myself happy. Here."

"So what is it that you're saying, exactly?" He wanted me to make the first offer, to spell out the terms of our dissolution.

I took a deep breath. "I'm saying that I think this is over. You and me. I don't think we've been working for a while. And I'm saying that I think we should be honest about it and admit it before we end up really hurting each other."

He was nodding slowly, as if trying to digest that before saying anything. Finally he asked, "Do you really mean that?"

"I do mean it." A tear traced down my face and I wiped it away. "Leo we aren't even married yet and we've been going to counseling for a year."

Now he just looked tired. He finally sat down. "That's the same thing Georgia said."

I didn't like the sound of that. Was Georgia talking to Leo behind my back? I moved over and sat next to him on the couch. "What did she say?" I tried to keep the anger out of my voice. Leo looked at me in a way that told me I had not succeeded.

"Look, I've known Georgia and William almost as long as I've known you. Of course we've been talking. We started out talking, and worrying, about the way you were handling Janie's death, but then we sort of moved on to other topics."

I wondered if she had said anything to Leo about Elliott. I hoped not. That was my awful horrible story to have to contend with, eventually. "Other topics?" I asked.

Leo took my left hand and squeezed my finger where my engagement ring should have been. I would need to return it to him. I said, "It's at Georgia's house."

"I know." He looked defeated, which was a look I had never before seen on him. "When I saw it there . . ."

I rushed to try to explain it all better. "I didn't plan to stay down here this long. I really didn't think I would be embarking on some life-altering trip." The tears were coming and there was no point in trying to stop them. "I honestly just wanted a break for a minute so I could find out about my mom's life. I wanted to understand where she came from. Then everything got so complicated. But the more time I spent here I felt like I got . . . I'm not sure what, maybe some clarity?" I was trying not to sob. "I love you, Leo. I honestly do, and I never wanted to hurt you. I just know that this, us, isn't working. Not anymore." I was going to have to tell him about Elliott, but I didn't know how to broach the subject without Leo blaming this whole breakup on him when it was solely my fault.

"How could you be feeling all of this and not bother talking to me about it? You're not even giving me a chance to fight for us."

Those were the words he used, but there wasn't any conviction in his voice.

TWENTY-SEVEN

Leo had flown down here knowing that there wasn't anything left to fight for. He already knew that he was always putting me off for work. He had seen the catatonic and detached way I had been wandering through life these last two years. He understood that my reaction to the idea of a concrete date for our wedding had panicked me to the point of fleeing, and that it was a bad sign. He was here for the face-to-face, the logistics meeting to iron out the details. That's really what this surprise visit was: a postmortem.

The two of us argued back and forth for hours saying all of the things that had been bottled up, but we tried to keep it civil. The sun moved slowly across the room as we dissected the relationship, pulling it apart bit by bit.

"I'm so sorry, Leo. I was trying to finish this stupid thing"—I waved my hand at the wall full of clues and hints at my mother's life—"before I began dealing with my own life."

"I know you were." There was a tone of kindness to his voice, finally. "I don't think you would've been able to do much of anything until you had gotten this behind you."

We were startled by a knock at the front door. It was Jimmy's delivery boy dropping off a casserole from the coffee shop. I thanked him quickly, sent him away, and locked the deadbolt.

As I put the food in the kitchen I noticed that Leo was struggling over whether or not to examine for himself the injury that had necessitated this extra care. He decided to resist the urge.

He fell into the armchair in the corner. "I didn't ask you to marry me because it would benefit my career."

I nodded. "I know." I had lobbed that one about two hours ago. "I wasn't using you as a crutch to get through the funerals."

"I know." I think he actually felt bad about that one. The urn containing my mother's remains was on the table next to him and he motioned to it without actually touching it. "I really did want to come here to help you put Janie to rest."

He was wringing his hands. We sat in silence for a long time. Longer than I have ever been quiet with Leo; normally I am filling every void with something. But now I just waited, waited for him to process his thoughts. Finally he said, "I know what I want for us, for me. I just—"

There was another knock at the door.

Leo threw his hands up, irritated, and yelled, "Come back later!"

There was a pause and then another knock, this one louder,

demanding. Whoever it was wasn't going away. I did not have time for this. I threw the door open and found Elliott standing there. I gasped. I stared at Elliott for a second then looked back at Leo. He was walking from the back of the living room toward me. Toward Elliott and me.

I was startled into complete brain malfunction. I said, "Elliott."

"Liv." His eyes were darting back and forth between Leo and me. He couldn't make sense of it; there was obviously a lot of tension in the air. He held up the papers he was holding as if to explain what he was doing there and said, "I've figured it out. Everything. I've figured it out."

All I could think was, *You're not supposed to be here until dinnertime. Is it dinnertime?*

Leo said rather rudely, "Can we help you?"

Elliott heard the word "we" and he looked utterly confused. He looked at me with the most pained expression. Then he looked at Leo, who just seemed annoyed by the interruption.

Elliott pointed at Leo and asked, "Who is this?"

Leo answered for me. "I'm her fiancé. Who the hell are you?"

Elliott looked at me with complete shock. "You're . . . engaged?" His expression morphed quickly into a mixture of disappointment and disgust. He threw down the stack of papers he was holding and walked away.

I wanted to call out to him. To explain. To follow him. I couldn't do that of course. All I could do at that moment was watch him go. I picked up everything he had dropped and quietly closed the door.

Leo was waiting for me to explain that. "Who the hell was that?"

So much for Leo and I having a civil, amenable, quiet little breakup. I could feel his anger spooling up as he stood there.

Some primitive territorial beast roared up in Leo. He yelled again. "Who the hell was that, Olivia!" He was consumed with rage at the ugly reality that maybe I wasn't alone down here.

"That was Elliott. He owns the local newspaper. He's been helping me find out about Mom's past." My voice was very low, barely above a whisper.

Mottled red blotches were erupting on Leo's cheeks. Those only made an appearance when the Redskins were losing or apparently when he was faced with the proposition that I was cheating on him. "Helping you!" he said very sarcastically. "Are you kidding me? Have you been cheating on me down here?"

"It's not like that." Well, maybe it was a little. "I needed help with—"

"Answer me!"

"Don't yell at me!"

"Are you sleeping with him!"

I actually felt sad when I answered that question. "No. I never slept with him." I think Leo could hear the regret in my voice.

Leo punched the wall next to the door then started pacing wildly. He looked like one of those sharks in the throes of a feeding frenzy circling frantically with the smell of blood in the water. He seemed directionless. It wasn't like Leo.

I opened my mouth to start to explain, to start at the beginning and tell him everything about Elliott, but before I could speak Leo started laughing. It was the meanest sound I had ever heard come out of him. It was a deep gurgle of a laugh and it was full of nothing but spite and anger. "You are unbelievable."

I approached him slowly while glancing at the front door half expecting Elliott to come bursting through it. "Leo, you have to let me explain—"

"You don't get to explain anything! I can see it in your face."

I vaguely wondered what in the world my face was giving away. I had to make him talk to me again. "Stop it. Listen to me."

He was looking me up and down; it was an unkind assessment. "You lying bitch." Leo never took to name-calling and in some detached way I realized how angry he must be to have called me a bitch. When the strange angry laughing had stopped it was replaced by an even stranger smile. There was no trace of the smile in his voice, however. "After all I've done for you, all I've been through. Taking care of you when you lost your parents and became this pathetic depressed weepy thing." He was on a rather undignified roll now and going to some places I never thought he would. "I stayed with you all that time because what kind of asshole leaves his girlfriend when she just lost her parents? I did all that and then you pull this shit? You have the nerve to cheat on *me*?"

Years ago, before we were engaged, before we owned property together, before either of my parents had died, Leo had what I referred to as an "emotional affair" with a woman at work. He never conceded that it was cheating because in Leo's mind if there was no sex then there was no cheat. You can't have a murder without the body. Or something like that. I held firm that an emotional relationship was more serious than a sexual one, and therefore constituted cheating. Neither one of us wavered in our definition of what it meant to cheat. For Leo it was sex; for me it was intimacy. It had been a long time since I'd thrown that in his face. "You were the one who said it wasn't cheating if there was no sex!"

"Bullshit! You can't switch sides now! That's even worse! I can't believe you did this to me!"

"Well, it sounds like you wanted out anyway! You basically just said you wanted to leave a long time ago but you couldn't abandon the poor orphan!"

"You're not a goddamn orphan, Olivia! You're thirty-two years old! And I can't believe I've wasted this much time on you!"

"Wasted?" I had to ratchet this back down to civil, or at least less vindictive. "It wasn't wasted, Leo. Just because it's ending doesn't—" He shut me up with one look.

He stormed to the front door, grabbing his overnight bag on the way. "You are a lying, damaged bitch and I'm glad I'm getting rid of you."

The door slammed behind him knocking a picture off the wall and shattering the glass as it hit the floor.

I stood there for a long time staring at the vacancy of Leo. He was just gone. Out of the house, out of this town, out of my life. How had things spiraled so horribly out of control? Leo hated me, really and truly hated me. I had honestly thought he didn't care about me enough to hate me. I cleaned up the broken glass and then wandered out to the back deck to catch my breath. I could see Logan sitting in one of the chairs down by the water. *Oh no, how long has she been stuck out there?*

I walked down the path to the lakefront where she was sitting. I tapped her on the shoulder. "Hey, kiddo."

"Hey. How'd it go?"

"It was pretty horrific, actually." I sat down next to her and stared out over the water.

"I figured. When I got back to the house I could hear you guys fighting through the door so I thought I'd just wait down here."

"I'm sorry."

She shrugged that off. Even a teenager knows how hard it is to go through a breakup. Logan glanced up at the house. "Where'd Leo go?"

"I'm not sure."

When I closed my eyes all I could see was that look on Elliott's face when the word "fiancé" came out of Leo's mouth. His eyes went from Leo, to me, to the bag in the hall. I just kept seeing it over and over on some masochistic loop in my mind's eye.

I sat up. "You can go up to the house, Lo. I'll be right back."

"Where are you going?"

"I need to talk to Elliott. He stopped by and said he had figured out everything. About Mom. But then he saw Leo and . . . I need to go find him."

I practically ran to his house. I hoped he would be there. But if he wasn't then I would try the office, the dock, the coffee shop. I would just do a hard target search of the entire town until I found him.

I ran up the steps of his front porch and then stopped for a minute to catch my breath. I knocked and waited. I knocked again. I was getting ready to leave but I could feel that he was there. He was inside; he just didn't want to talk to me.

I opened the door and let myself in. "Elliott?"

He was sitting on the couch, his hands clenched into fists in his lap. He didn't look up at me. "I don't want to talk to you."

I moved over toward him slowly. "I have to explain."

He glared at me. "Explain what?"

I opened my mouth to speak but he cut me off.

"Explain why you lied to me? That you led me to believe you were free to be with me when you weren't? When were you planning on telling me that you were engaged?"

I said, "I'm not engaged anymore." My voice sounded meek.

He stood up and started yelling, jabbing his finger toward my face. "That's not what I asked you! I asked you if you were planning to explain why you *lied* to me!"

I wasn't feeling the least bit meek anymore. I moved into the room with the same angry pointing finger. "Don't yell at me! It was complicated! You don't understand—"

"I *do* understand, goddammit! I was in the same position! But I never lied to you about it!"

How was I supposed to explain this? "I owed it to Leo to see him and talk to him first. He deserved that."

"And what the hell did I deserve?"

"I was trying to be fair! It was complicated. And you didn't even know anything about me or my life! It isn't fair of you to think I had some obligation to tell you everything."

He screamed, "Don't pull that shit! It was a lie of omission and you know it. How could you not tell me about him?"

"Don't get on your moral high horse with me! You dumped your girlfriend of four years for some girl you didn't even know! Who does that?" I was grasping at straws with that, but I was emotionally wrung dry and I couldn't think of anything better. "Would it really have been better for me to break up with Leo from hundreds of miles away before I even knew what this was?"

"Yes!"

"That wouldn't have been fair to him."

"And how was this fair to anyone? I ended things with Amy because I had feelings for you. That's *not* immoral. Lying to me, lying to that poor bastard that was engaged to you, *that's* immoral! You're right about one thing though. I don't know you."

He turned his back to me and I took a deep breath trying to calm myself down. I couldn't remember a time in recent history when I had been so furious, not even the scant minutes ago when I was breaking up with my fiancé. I thought, vaguely, *Huh, so this is passion.*

I tried to keep my voice even so this could be a conversation instead of a brawl. "Goddammit, Elliot. You're not being fair."

He spun around, facing me again. His face was red. "I don't have to be fair! I'm pissed off! Honesty is the only thing I really care about and you just destroyed that before we even got started."

"Destroyed?" Had I destroyed it? Us? What were we anyway? My mind was reeling. "Stop it! I picked *you*!" I couldn't think with him yelling at me like that. "You completely blindsided me. Meeting you . . . I was already trying to reconcile the way I was feeling about Leo when I just . . . I was overwhelmed by these feelings for you. I didn't know what to do! I didn't know what to tell him. I didn't know what to tell you. I was—"

"You didn't tell either one of us anything! Is that who called the day you threw your phone in the lake? Dammit, and you've been lying to my face this whole time."

"Jesus, you are completely overreacting. I wasn't lying to you to be deceitful and you know it. I felt stuck in a situation and I needed time to figure it out."

He crossed his arms and stood his ground, glaring at me. "Was this whole thing just some kind of joke to you? Some kind of time-out from your life? Did you think you could just come down here and do as you please, say whatever you want, act however you want, and then leave when it's over? Not giving a shit about the destruction you left behind? Is this some kind of mother-daughter thing? This secret life bullshit?"

That felt like a blow to the face and I flinched. "Fuck you, Elliott."

I stormed back to the house trying not to cry. I was not very successful in that endeavor. Elliott was being too goddamn unfair. Acting like a child. I wasn't lying to him! Well, I was, but not to be hurtful anyway. Dammit. What did I expect to happen?

I got to the house and went to my room and lay down on the bed. I could hear the water running in the bathroom. Thank goodness, Logan was in the shower. I would have a good hour before I had to speak to another human.

I had blown up Leo and pushed away Elliott. All I needed to do now was get fired from my job so that I could complete the trifecta of ruining my life. I felt physically beaten. I had a headache from the back of my neck all the way around to my forehead.

The water turned off in the bathroom and I put the pillow over my head. And I cried. I tried to cry for Leo but if I were being honest I was crying for Elliott. I felt like I had just lost something that I didn't know how much I desperately needed. Until it was gone. Life works that way sometimes. Because life revels in the idea of being a bitch.

Logan came out of the bathroom and asked, "Are you going to tell me what happened with Elliott?"

I propped my head up on the pillow and sniffled. "We got in a fight."

She looked at my red, tear-stained eyes and said, "Duh. I meant about Grandma."

I had completely forgotten that Elliott had said he had figured it all out. I went out to the main room and looked around. I found the pile of papers that he had dropped when he popped in and ran smack into my fiancé. That memory made me feel a little bit sick at my stomach.

I gathered up the papers and read through them. I was so shocked by what I was reading that I had to keep starting over again at the beginning. Without even realizing that I was speaking I kept saying, "Oh my God."

Logan was getting anxious. "What is it!"

I put the papers down and looked up at her stunned. "He figured it out. Everything."

Logan's eyes grew wide. "Figured what out?"

I handed the papers to Logan so she could read through them too. I said, "About the lake. Why she wanted to be buried in the lake. We had the right idea but the wrong dates." I picked up my phone and as I dialed Georgia I noticed that Logan's wet hair was dripping all over the printouts.

"Goddammit Lo, be careful!"

Georgia had already answered her phone. She heard me yelling at Logan and scolded me over the phone line. "Do not curse at her, Olivia!"

For Christ's sake. I didn't even respond to that. "What time will you get here tomorrow?"

She said, "I'm not sure. Maybe eight?"

"Can you make it earlier? Like six?"

"Why?"

"Because when you get here . . . we're digging up a grave."

TWENTY-EIGHT

I couldn't get any sleep that night. Every time I closed my eyes
there was some new horror looking back at me. It was the look
on Elliott's face when he saw Leo. Or the realization on Leo's
when he saw Elliott. It was my mother, ghostly white, floating
alone in the lake while her house burned down on the shore, red
and gold flames licking the sky. Or the body of Oliver bloated
and tinged blue being discovered in the muddy reeds. It was
George, frozen in time, with that same adoring smile again and
again as he looked at Janie's face.

I woke up early the next day and sat on the porch watching
the sun slowly move across the surface of the lake.

Logan finally woke up and came out to sit with me. "You
feeling any better today?"

"No. Not really."

"It'll be okay, Aunt Livie."

Ah, the ignorance of youth. "I'm sitting here thinking that it would have been difficult for me to handle things any worse than I had. Truly."

"I don't know. You could've slept with Jimmy or something. That would've been a scandal. Or you could've found out that you and Elliott were actually related, but like not until it was too late." She snapped her fingers, the ideas coming in fast now. "Oh! Or you could have discovered that you were pregnant, but not known who the father was."

"You are seriously not allowed to watch daytime television anymore." I stood up to get to work. "Come on. Let's get all of our stuff organized before your mom gets here."

While Georgia was driving down to Tillman, Logan and I spent the day going through all of our research so that it was laid out in a logical timeline. I had been sending things to Georgia as I discovered them so she had seen just about everything. But it had come to her piecemeal and now, now I wanted to get it straight in all of our minds.

Our timeline was embellished with all of our evidence and printouts and pictures that had been on the Wall of Discovery. Logan and I had everything arranged on the dining room table in chronological order. I had just finished copying the year-books that Elliott had found because those had to be returned to the library. Elliott. When I thought of him I felt such a heavy sorrow that it was making me physically ill.

Logan and I were waiting outside for Georgia by the time she finally drove into Tillman and pulled up to the rental house.

We were sitting together on the front porch tapping our feet, anxious for her to arrive. All Georgia knew was that in the time we had been out of her sight her rule-following, completely neurotic, straightlaced little sister had dumped her fiancé, consorted with some strange man named Elliott, and was planning to rob a grave after sunset.

Things had gotten a little weird.

She had a worried look on her face as she got out of the car. It was the same look she carried around when our mom got sick.

We ushered Georgia into the house without letting her have a second to stretch her legs after the long drive. I closed the door behind her and she took my hand, stopping me.

"Olivia, are you okay?"

"We can talk later, not now."

She ignored that. "Are you and Leo . . . officially over? Do you want to talk about it?"

Everything that had happened with Leo seemed like a million years ago. I could feel it telescoping into my past. I was tired to my bones about it. So no, I didn't really want to tell her about it. To relive it. To have to rehash eight months of doubts, six hours of conversation, and five spectacular minutes of shouting. But I knew saying nothing was not an option.

I said simply, "Yes, it's over. Officially. You could probably hear him screaming at me from the highway."

She had a confused look on her face when I said that. "I thought it would be a bit more cordial. More mutual. I think he'd been feeling the same way, Livie."

It had all been so very civilized, so amicable, but then I threw napalm on it in the form of an unexpected visit from Elliott. I was not faring well with unexpected visits. I didn't feel like explaining everything to Georgia so I just gave her the shortest version of events I could muster. "Leo was here at the house and Elliott dropped by. It was bad. They both . . . It was bad."

Georgia looked slightly horrified. "Oh no. I didn't see that one coming. If I had known Leo was going to fly down here I would've warned you. Is he still here?"

"I doubt it. Look, we don't have a lot of time. We need to be out of here when it gets dark in a few hours and we have so much to show you first."

She wanted to ask me more about it but I wasn't answering. I dragged her over to the dining room table where she began to linger over the timeline, slowly following the events of Janie's life as we had them laid out. It started on the left with the birth certificates of our mother and George. Then the years flowed by with the school photos, our grandmother's death, and newspaper articles, some notes here and there from the stories Florence had shared with us. Georgia would stop at an article, something she hadn't seen before, and read through it. Logan stood at her shoulder following her mother's progress and answering questions as they came up.

Georgia was shaking her head. "This is so sad. And he died so young." She looked at me. "Mom's first love."

I sat down across from her at the table and tried to explain what I thought George had been to Mom. "I feel like he was more than that. I mean he was the love of her life. He seemed to be her oldest friend. He was . . . everything to her."

"It's amazing that you were able to find all of this."

Logan said, "We were lucky Mrs. Chatham found Florence

and that Olivia recognized Buddy in that newspaper article. We got most of our pictures from him." Logan ran her hand over the long line of articles from the newspaper archives. "But most of what we found was because Elliott was helping us." Then she pointed to the copies from the yearbooks. "He got those from the library."

Georgia looked back and forth between Logan and me. "You want to tell me about Elliott?"

"No." I had made an inner pact instituting a total communication blackout with my sister on the subject of Elliott. Especially since I had basically, in one day, obliterated any need for her to know him at all.

I could tell Georgia had decided not to push me. She said, "Okay then. So we know that Mom and George got married, and we know he got sick and died."

I had finally managed to get myself to find their wedding announcement. I hadn't wanted to see it, to read the words, to feel as though some part of my mother could never have belonged to my own father. Because that part of her had always belonged to George. It felt like a betrayal to my father's memory to know all of these things about my mother. But at the same time I felt as though I finally fully understood the person that my mother truly was.

Georgia was reading over the announcement from the paper for the wedding of George Jones and Janie Rutledge. Accompanying the wedding announcement was a picture of the new Mr. and Mrs. George Jones. My mother was wearing an elegant cream silk wedding gown that had been her mother's. It was a simple bias-cut sheath that skimmed her body. Knowing what

Buddy had told me about Martha, I had to assume the dress had been altered quite a bit to fit Janie. She wore her hair in a loose bun; there were some wisps breaking free and blowing around her face on the breeze.

George was wearing a formal black suit and had his arm around Janie's waist. He had her pulled into him in a way that spoke of comfort and passion and belonging. There were no signs of a nervous groom or second thoughts. She was looking just past the camera. She seemed to be caught right at the moment of laughter when something out of the frame caught her eye. George was looking down at her, gazing at her face, with a look of complete devotion.

That look of unmistakable bliss on both of their faces was haunting. It was the most emotionally charged of all of the photos we had been able to uncover. When I looked at it I felt an immense grief that their happiness was about to be shattered and they were completely oblivious about it.

We were all three quiet for a few minutes while we took turns looking over the wedding announcement and photo. I noticed Georgia had tears in her eyes.

I said, "I know. It's really sad."

She wiped the tears. "It is. It's awful. Look how happy she looks."

Logan was looking over her mother's shoulder at the image. "You look a lot like her, Mom." Georgia squeezed Logan's hand.

Now we were all crying. *Grave robbers do not cry, people!* I had to keep us moving at a faster pace if we were going to get through all of this in one night.

I cleared my throat. "Okay, so they were married in nineteen sixty-six. I couldn't find anything about what they were doing when they first got married." I was trying to keep moving to the right on the tabletop, progressing through time in our timeline, and each step to the right was a few more years down the road. Georgia wanted to linger on the images of them in their teenage years that Buddy had given me, but I pushed her along.

We arrived in the section that held items from 1968. I showed Georgia the photographs that Florence had given me of Oliver in Vietnam. Then I showed her his death certificate. She just took a deep breath and we moved one more step to the right.

I pulled out a very bad copy of a building permit. "This was the next thing we could find. It was in November of nineteen sixty-eight."

The building permit was fairly basic. George Jones had applied for a permit to have the plumbing redone in the house, a detached garage added, and some renovations done on one of the upstairs bedrooms.

I told Georgia my theory. "I'm pretty sure they were remodeling an upstairs bedroom to turn it into a nursery."

Georgia said in a whisper, "Good God. She was pregnant?"

"Yes." I handed her a copy of the birth certificate for Oliver Winchester Jones born to George and Jane Jones in February of 1969. This was what Elliott had uncovered. This was the discovery he had made that caused him to rush over to the house, unannounced. I kept seeing his face, red with fury, yelling at me. All of that passion in Elliott was so warm when it was directed at me with longing. Too bad it was now being hurled at me with the laser focus of anger.

I looked back at the birth certificate, trying to stay focused. "We had looked for a birth certificate for a baby being born to George and Janie when they first got married, thinking that perhaps they *had* to get married when they were twenty. I mean I know it was a different time and place, but you know Mom wouldn't have gotten married before she graduated from college unless it was necessary. But we couldn't find anything to support the knocked-up theory so we stopped looking. It never occurred to me that there may have actually been a baby, only later. He was born, perfectly healthy."

Logan was even starting to tear up. "They named him Oliver Winchester after George's brother and her father." Logan ran her finger across the tiny black footprint on the certificate.

I said, "So I think maybe I'm named after *this* Oliver, the baby. But we're both named after the first Oliver I suppose." I held my hand up to the tiny footprint, dwarfing it. "I don't guess it really matters."

Georgia looked as stunned as I had felt when I first found out about this baby. She had always identified herself as the oldest, the first. And now, well, now she was the second. It would be hard to explain how life altering this discovery of another baby born to our mother was for us. A whole other life lived, lost, and forgotten.

Georgia looked up at me. She seemed to suddenly think of our father. "Do you think Dad knew?"

"Yes, he knew."

Georgia still had that shell-shocked look on her face that I had been feeling when I finally processed all of this. "How do you know?"

I said, "That comes later."

"You're killing me, Livie."

"Sorry, but I think it's easier if you just hear it all in chrono-logical order." I winked at Logan. "Plus I think Logan kind of likes having the upper hand on you."

She clapped her hands in a tight quick clip and smiled. "I to-tally do."

Georgia wiped her eyes and blew her nose. "This is tragic. I know George died but where's little Oliver?"

I sighed, "That's the worst part. He died too. When he was a baby, he had just turned two." I pulled out the death certificate and showed it to Georgia.

On the death certificate the cause of death was listed as pri-mary streptococcal pneumonia. The same thing that had killed George. They died within weeks of each other. First, baby Oli-ver and then George. I couldn't begin to imagine what it had been like for my mother to live through that.

I finally revealed my plan to Georgia. "We're going to go get the baby. We're going to dig him up and move him to Huntley Memorial Gardens to be with his father. We're going to bury him next to George."

Georgia felt the need to be the voice of reason in the room of body snatchers. She used her most stern motherly voice. "You've lost your mind. You seriously want to dig up a dead body? Why do we have to dig it up ourselves?"

"Because getting permission will take too long." I took out all of my evidence to show her how we had tracked the move-ment of little Oliver's gravesite. First, I showed her the death notice in the newspaper that listed him as being laid to rest in the tiny churchyard where Janie and George had been married. The same small, white church whose steeple now haunted the depths of the lake.

It would have been devastating to stand in that spot, the same church where they had been married just five years before, and bury their child. George must have been sick by then, probably weak from the ravages of the illness about to take his life. Janie overwhelmed with grief over the loss of little Oliver. They must not have been thinking clearly to bury the baby next to that church. They knew the location was unstable, the church in constant threat of flooding. But of course they weren't thinking clearly; their baby had just died.

Second, I pulled out the very long and dry TVA Repair and Expansion Plan of 1978 explaining the need to alleviate the flooding from one of the tributaries. There was a small creek that kept overflowing its banks in heavy rains. This was the same creek that had once caused the border dispute between the Forrests and the Rutledges. And this was the same flooding problem that had eventually swallowed that church whole and taken it back to the lake.

By the time the TVA's expansion plan had been approved, the ancient little church was long gone and its secret buried body had been all but forgotten by everyone except our father, Adam.

Georgia was still not totally on board with the idea of digging up a grave. I pulled out the letters from our father. I said, "Remember when you asked me if Dad knew about all of this? About Mom's past? Well, he knew. He's the one who found the first grave of Oliver at the church and had him moved right before the lake could swallow that land up again. Dad had the body exhumed and moved temporarily until he could get permission to buy the plot next to George Jones at Huntley Memorial Gardens and have the baby buried there. It took him a long time to get the genealogical evidence required to prove that Oliver was a Jones so that the cemetery would let him buy the plot. By then Dad was sick; he never got to finish. So Oliver is still in that temporary grave, waiting to be moved, but Mom never knew that. She died thinking he was still under the lake.

"This is the whole thing, Gigi. Mom wants to be scattered in the lake because she thinks her baby Oliver is still under there. In some unmarked grave under the waters of the lake. And she wants to be scattered over the grave of George so she can be with him again. This is it. This is the reason for all of this. She just wants to be with them again."

Georgia was reading the letters from our father to the cemetery. She flipped back to the death certificate of baby Oliver. And the wedding photo of our mother with George. She was talking to herself. "Dad must have really loved Mom to want to do this for her. I mean to do all the work to find the baby and to want to bring them all together again. It's so completely selfless, so unconditional. He really was the only person who ever knew all of her."

Georgia seemed to be feeling all of this so deeply. Probably because she had children and was trying to get her mind around the idea of losing one. She said, "Can you imagine that? I mean losing your child and then days later losing your husband?"

I sat down and moved some of the photos around on the table. "And she didn't have anyone else. Her father was dead by then. George's brother was dead. I don't know if George had any other family, but Mom didn't. She was completely alone."

I pulled out one of the last of the news articles and handed it to Georgia. "And here's the kicker. It was only two months later when her house burned to the ground."

"Damn. No wonder she never wanted to talk about her life before."

I agreed. "I know. It's amazing she lived through it at all."

We had always known in the abstract that our mother's childhood home had burned down. That there were no mementos or pictures or family heirlooms because of that fire. But knowing all that we did now, sitting among the stories and pictures and proof of her life here made it so much more painful. So devastatingly real.

I let Georgia sort through everything again, trying to digest all of it. "Livie, there has to be another way to move Oliver. We can't just go out there with a shovel and do it ourselves."

Maybe it was crazy and illegal and sort of ghastly if I really thought about it, but I was finishing this quest. Now. Tonight. "Georgia, I blew up my entire life for this and I'm finishing it. With or without you."

Finally she looked up, committed. "Okay. Where do we go to dig up a body?"

"I have a good idea, but I'm not positive." I had a hunch the body was in the Rutledge family cemetery behind Mom's old house, but we didn't have enough time for hunches. "We're making a stop on the way to find out for sure."

Logan was two steps ahead of me, as usual. "Are we going to Buddy's house?"

"Yes. I bet he knows exactly where Oliver is."

TWENTY-NINE

Logan was pulling clothes out of her dresser drawers and flinging them over her shoulder. It was almost seven o'clock and it would be getting dark outside soon. We were trying to hurry. She said, "What do you wear to go grave robbing?"

Hearing those words made me incredibly nervous. "Can we call it something else?" I was wondering if I could go through with this. But we had been over it and over it. If my father had been able to get permission to disinter the body from the historical society then he would have done it, which meant that the chances of us getting permission to do this through the proper channels were pretty slim. So if we wanted to get little Oliver moved next to his father, George, then we felt like this was the best way. And getting that family back together again, even if in death, seemed to be the whole point of this journey.

Now that Georgia was committed to our little venture she had a giddiness to her that I hadn't seen since we were kids and sneaking out of the house to break into the neighbor's pool. She told Logan to wear something dark. Well sure, black is all the rage with grave robbers this season.

We stopped by the inn and "borrowed" three shovels from the maintenance shed, and I had a flashlight in my car so we figured we were fully outfitted for our caper.

I followed the GPS's directions to the address Buddy had written on top of the box of pictures. We climbed the same switchback mountain roads that had led us to the old abandoned house, but then we were directed to take a turn following the crest of the ridge. The road ended in a large and mercifully flat plateau on which was a surprisingly grand and gorgeous mountain house.

After double-checking that I had the correct address for Buddy, we climbed out of the car. The front door was reached through a courtyard lined with pea gravel and hedged by native plants. The house itself had a steeply pitched roofline, perfectly angled to shed snow. There were massive windows facing the valley, which must frame expansive and impressive views in the daylight. The house itself was constructed entirely of cedar shingles and planks. It was much more practical for this environment than the whitewashed pine house with the tin roof that had been abandoned lower down on his property. On either side of the house stood massive stone chimneys climbing up into the darkening night.

I knocked. I rang the bell. I knocked again. The door flew open to Buddy in the middle of a rant. "About to damn near knock my door down. What are you doing here so late?"

I introduced Buddy to Georgia; he remembered Logan from

our first "visit." I returned the pictures he had let us borrow and asked if we could come inside.

"No." Buddy took the box from me. "It's late." He began to close the door.

I put my hand out before it could shut. "We need to know where the baby is buried."

He stopped. "Dammit." He left the door open and we followed him inside. He walked back to his family room returning to his spot in his recliner. "You're making me miss the end of my show."

Georgia, Logan, and I sat at the edge of his sofa. I asked, "Why didn't you tell me that Janie and George had a baby?"

"You didn't ask."

"Buddy, you must've known that we would want to know about him."

"I told you; the past is done. There's no reason to dredge it up."

"It isn't for you to decide what we should and should not know about our mother. Are there other things I haven't asked?" Buddy didn't answer; he just looked at us. I asked, "Is the baby buried in the Rutledge family cemetery?"

Buddy began his hand-wringing. "What good can come of you knowing about that baby? Does it help you to know that your mother lost so much? That you weren't her first family? I don't understand how any of this can bring her any comfort. Not now. Maybe she did things she didn't want you to know about. Did you ever stop to think of that? Or are you just so damn nosy you don't care? Maybe you'd better just leave it all alone."

We didn't have time for life lessons according to Buddy. I

stood up. "Can you just tell us if he's in the Rutledge family cemetery behind the house? I just need to know for sure. That's all." Finally, he nodded.

Logan added, "Is it the grave to the side, with the stone marker?" He nodded again.

I said, "Thank you, Buddy."

We ran back to the car and Logan decoded that exchange for Georgia. "There's this rock, like a marker, in the cemetery. It just has an *O* carved on it, no name. That must be where Grandpa had Oliver moved when he got him out from under the lake."

Georgia asked, "How did Buddy know where the baby was? It sounded like Dad moved the coffin sort of secretly."

I fastened my seatbelt. "Buddy seems to know everything that happens on this ridge."

I cranked the engine and when my headlights flashed on I was startled to see Buddy standing in front of the car. He walked slowly, casually, to the driver's side window. I rolled it down and waited for him to speak.

"I wasn't sure if you knew the law here in Georgia regarding those who've passed."

I said, as circumspectly as I could, "I would imagine there are a lot of laws regarding the deceased."

Buddy spit on the ground next to my tire. "Probably. They make laws for every breath a man takes these days." He shoved his hands into the pockets of his windbreaker. "One would need permission, legal permission, to disturb a grave."

It made me nervous that Buddy had so easily figured out what we were planning to do.

He continued. "Though I always did think it was interesting

that any person, any private citizen, is allowed to transport a body for reburial. You know you can just put it in your car"—he took in the length of my SUV—"or what have you and take it to the new cemetery. I might just be careful how I explained getting my hands on the body in the first place." Without another word Buddy walked back into his house and slammed the door.

Georgia, Logan, and I were quiet as we drove back down Buddy's driveway and made our way to the graveyard. I had only been to the site of our mother's burned-out house and the family graveyard by boat. A boat driven by Elliott. I felt my face flush and my hand absently form a fist. I got lost twice trying to find the damn house in the dark.

As we parked on the gravel drive leading to the site of the house I asked Georgia, "Do you think she loved him, well, them—" My mind had an image of George and Janie, smiling, with a small boy between them swinging in their arms. "More than us?"

"No, sweetie. We know how much she loved Dad. She did. She loved him and she loved us. But we got to have her our whole lives. Maybe she just made a deal with herself, a long time ago, to be with George and Oliver again when she died."

Logan's phone pinged in the backseat and she began to respond to the text. My voice sounded a little more desperate than I intended when I asked her who it was from.

"Oh my God, Livie. It's Graham. I promise if I get a text from Elliott I will tell you." Admonished by my niece in front of my sister. *That was embarrassing.*

When we got to the graveyard we went straight to work digging. It was so dark out there on that tiny rise above the lake that you couldn't see the edge of the water, just a huge black hole in the distance. Every once in a while the clouds would break for a moment and you could see the reflection of the moon rippling on the surface. I was grateful for the cloud cover. I felt like we could use all the stealth we could get.

We were only about two feet down when I started complaining. "Everything I have ever seen on TV about grave digging has been a complete lie."

Georgia was hacking into the dense earth trying to loosen the soil. "What in the world are you talking about?"

I could already feel the blisters rubbing their way into my palms. "On *Buffy*, when they dig up a grave, it only takes them an hour and the sides are all perfectly straight and then boom! They hit the coffin." I looked at our mess of a hole with its uneven edges and misshapen oval outline.

Georgia sounded so tired. "Oh my God, you're so lame. *Buffy the Vampire Slayer?*"

"What? What's wrong with *Buffy?*" I was resting on the handle of the shovel now looking in the dim light at my palms. Logan was moving the flashlight a lot because it was attracting so many bugs. I had to keep readjusting my hand to keep it in the light.

Georgia glanced at me and huffed a little at the fact that I had stopped for five seconds. "Well nothing, but you're upset that a show about vampires misled you about how long it takes to dig a hole."

I said, "I still don't see your point."

"Forget it." Georgia wanted me to shut up and dig or get out of her way.

I glanced up at Logan. "We should've bought some gloves at Walmart."

Georgia threw a clod of dirt at my back. "Stop bitching!" Then looked at her watch for the one-millionth time.

I threw a lump back at her. "Quit it!"

Georgia brushed the dirt out of her hair and said, "Keep digging or get out of my hole."

"Fine. I'm taking a break." I stepped out of the hole.

Logan took the shovel and pointed it back and forth between Georgia and me. "I don't want any more fighting from you two or I will turn this car around."

I sat down on the rock with the *O* carved into it and tossed dirt on her too. "Very funny, Lugnut."

As we dug down into the dense red Georgia clay you could smell the dampness of the earth. We took turns with the flashlight since we could really only fit two people in the hole at one time to dig. We had long since stopped talking to each other. We were singularly focused on getting to the bottom of this grave.

By two o'clock in the morning we had been digging for five hours and the hole was only at shoulder depth. I wasn't sure if we could finish this before sunrise. Each shovel of dirt that we dug up had to be lifted and tossed over our shoulder to get it out of the hole. Did they really bury caskets six feet underground? My right shoulder was burning in pain. We were moving more and more slowly.

I wondered what would happen if we were still here and some park ranger or sheriff came by and found us desecrating a grave on a historically preserved site. Was it a felony? What was the punishment? A fine? Jail time?

I was so filthy and sweaty and sore and my mind was completely preoccupied by mounting a vigorous defense for myself when Logan yelped.

"Logan! Don't scream like that! We're in a graveyard in the middle of the night. You scared the——"

I glanced up to see a face peering down at me from ground level. Irritated by his appearance I turned away and started digging again as I called over my shoulder, "What are you doing here, Leo?"

He said, "I came to help you."

"I don't need your help."

"Don't be stupid. You can't do this by yourself, Olivia."

"Of course I can." I stabbed the tip of the shovel into the dirt for good measure.

"You're being a stubborn asshole, Livie."

"Oh, I'm the asshole? Go away, Leo."

He said, "You *are* the asshole." He took a deep breath and made a conscious choice to change his tone. "I came to help. You have something like three feet left to dig."

That didn't sound like a helpful observation. I didn't respond. I just kept digging with a new force and energy. Funny how fury can revive your energy stores. I barked at Georgia, "Did you call him?"

Her voice was indignant. "It wasn't me!"

Leo broke in. "William called me."

I was still glaring at Georgia. "You told William?" Why did she have to tell her husband every single thing she did? I was vaguely aware of Logan and Leo saying an awkward hello on the edge of the hole we were standing in.

Georgia was tired and there is nothing more quick-tempered

than a tired Georgia. "Shut up, Olivia! Of course I told him." I started to admonish her but she cut me off. "Can you just stop being selfish for five seconds? You're the one who made us come out here and do this and we could use the help." Her voice was low, almost a whisper. "Besides, if he's here then there are probably some things he wants to say."

Things he wants to say? I wanted to tell him to go home; there couldn't possibly be anything left to be said regarding our relationship. Or lack of relationship. I said, "We've got this, Leo."

He squatted down to be closer to my face and asked me calmly, "Really? What are you going to do if there's a vault?"

The vault.

Dammit!

I threw the shovel down. I thought I might start crying. I had forgotten about the vault.

Until very recently, I had no idea that in a lot of places you could not put a coffin, by itself, in the ground anymore. More disinformation about burials courtesy of *Buffy*. When we were making the burial arrangements for our father we were told about the vault. Oftentimes, depending on the rules of the cemetery, the coffin is actually placed into a concrete or metal box called a vault and then that is buried in the grave. It was explained to us that if you don't put the coffin into a vault then eventually the coffin decomposes causing a depression in the earth. So you either have a very lumpy graveyard, or you use vaults.

Would Georgia and I have the strength or the leverage to lift a lid made of concrete or metal? This caper was falling apart.

Leo put his hand out to help me climb out of the hole. I couldn't take it. I just turned away, trying not to cry. I picked up my shovel from the ground. My arms and shoulders felt like lead. I was talking, mostly to myself. "Forget it. Let's just re-bury it. We can't do this. What was I thinking? This is crazy."

Logan and Georgia were both ignoring me completely while they had some conversation about shovels and pulleys. Logan pulled out her cell phone. "I'm going to see what's keeping Graham." *Graham? Is Graham coming? Are we having a party out here?*

I climbed up out of the hole and spoke to Leo. "Why did you come out here?"

He was quiet for a moment, gathering his thoughts. I knew there was a well-rehearsed speech in there but I wasn't sure if he would recite it or not. Leo's closing arguments always got jumbled when his temper got in the way.

"Listen, Olivia, I'm sorry for, well, most of the things I said yesterday. I was already feeling so emotionally raw about everything and then . . ." He stopped himself before bringing up Elliott. I gave him a lot of credit for that restraint. It was more than I deserved.

I led him farther away from Georgia and Logan so we could have some privacy. "Where have you been all day?"

"I've been in Atlanta. I met with—never mind. It doesn't matter."

"You squeezed in a meeting?" That was actually funny to me for some reason but I knew I couldn't make light of it or laugh at him about it. There was a fragile truce brewing.

He kept talking as if I hadn't interrupted. "I couldn't get a flight back to DC and at some point I just decided to drive back home. I was a few hours away from here when William called and told me about this"—Leo motioned toward the grave—"and what you were planning to do. It sounded so crazy. I wondered if I had driven you to do something dangerous or at least ill-advised. I felt sort of responsible."

"Please don't, don't feel responsible for any of this." The absurdity of the situation was making this conversation difficult. It was too dark to really see Leo's face so I couldn't read him at all and I was covered in dirt and sweat. I motioned to the open grave. "You didn't drive me insane and make me a grave robber or anything. I know this is nuts, but we just had to try." Taking a small step closer I said, "And everything else, everything with us, that wasn't your fault at all. It was mine."

I could tell he was shaking his head but in the dark I couldn't see more than that. "Livie, it was both of us. Look, I'm sorry for the way I acted, those things I said. I didn't mean it. And I couldn't leave things like that with us; we never fight like that. When William called me and told me what you were doing, what you had found—I know this must be hard for you. Hard to deal with this part of Janie's life. And then he said you were planning to dig it up . . . I don't know. It was the middle of the night and I was driving home on some highway and something in me just made me turn around. I wanted to come help you with this. Help you finally put your mother to rest. A proper good-bye. For us and for her."

"I don't know what to say." I was fully crying now and there wasn't a clean spot on any part of me to use to wipe my own eyes. I was crying out of sadness and relief and exhaustion. "I'm so glad you're here. I know it wasn't easy for you to come back, but I'm so glad you did. You know I never meant for this to happen to us."

"I know. I can't blame it all on you, even though I really want to. Obviously. I shouldn't have said some of those things." I didn't want to revisit that conversation. He continued, "I had hoped to handle this differently. I mean when I decided to come down here and talk to you I had a whole speech prepared."

Georgia and Logan went back to digging and I led Leo to a marble bench where we sat down. There was an opening in the clouds and the moonlight chased away some of the shadows. I asked, "What were you going to say?"

"It doesn't matter.

"Of course it does."

I could see him abbreviating it in his mind, cutting to the chase. "It was just . . . You were right. I've been feeling like we weren't in a good place for a while too. It was poor judgment to think that a wedding might fix everything."

I nodded in agreement. "A wedding wouldn't have fixed it. But I didn't know how to say it to myself let alone to you. I think that's why I ran."

"Well, it's obvious you didn't know how. That was partially my fault. I would never let you talk." I started to say something but he put his hand up, stopping me. Sort of making his point about not letting me talk. "I need to say what I really came down here to say. Olivia, we've been together a long time. We've been through a lot. But I can see now that it's not enough. We don't have, what? That fire? I don't know. I can't remember how I was going to phrase it, but we don't have it. I don't know if we ever did. I was okay with that because we had something different. We complemented each other. But now, I think maybe it's not fair for either one of us to settle. Not when we're talking about marriage." I kept opening my mouth to interrupt and he kept holding up his hand. "I realize that it may not have worked out for us, but all I really want is for you to be happy. And I want for me to be happy."

He had come to the same conclusion that I had. I said, "You don't think we make each other happy?"

He looked at me with no malice and no anger, finally. "I don't think we make each other *unhappy*. But that's not the same thing."

I put my dirty arms around his neck and pulled him in for a familiar hug. "Thank you."

He squeezed me back and nodded.

I had gotten dirt all over the front of his shirt, and trying to wipe it away only made it worse. "I still can't believe you came out here."

Leo took my hands and smiled down at the mess I had made of his clothing, letting me know I didn't need to worry about it. "I came because you and I needed to have a better good-bye."

Logan was eavesdropping and shouted up from the hole. "But you'll help us dig, right? Since you're here anyway?"

Leo was always a little too aware of what it would mean to break the law. I didn't want to ask him to do something he was uncomfortable with. "Do you know what we're doing here, exactly?" I motioned to the grave.

Leo looked like a thousand pounds of rocks had been lifted

from his shoulders by just being able to have a regular conversation again. Well, as regular as it can be when you're talking about digging up a coffin.

He stood up and pulled me to my feet. We walked to the hole and he jumped in, taking the shovel from Logan. He said, "I know enough to know that I don't want to know any more. Plausible deniability."

Leo and I went to work while Georgia chattered away, trying to break a tension that was already dissipating, and Logan held the flashlight. Somehow, after everything, it felt right to have Leo here with us helping to finally put all of the pieces of my family's past to rest. He had known both of my parents and had had to watch them pass away. Having him here for this peculiar last bit of family business seemed like the only way for him and me to really end, to really say good-bye.

Graham eventually pulled up in a huge truck. A dually with spotlights on the top and an enormous winch on the front. He looked like he had just been dragged out of bed.

Logan introduced him to her mother. Georgia was making a point to try to brush the dirt off her face and out of her hair before saying hello. Some people have Sunday dinners to get to know each other; we meet the new boyfriend in the middle of the night while covered in dirt.

After a cursory handshake and a quick introduction, Graham and Leo were digging together in the hole. They were easily doubling the pace we had been able to maintain mere moments ago.

Graham and Leo spoke in that easy lighthearted way that men are able to, no matter the awkwardness of the situation.

Their banter stood in stark contrast to the events that were un-folding and to our particular environment at the moment.

I also noticed that more than a few of the questions Graham was asking were related to Leo and me. More to the point, where our relationship stood and where he saw it going. *So when are you and Olivia heading back to Maryland?* Things like that. Graham was on a fact-finding mission. I knew that Elliott would never have asked him to do that. I looked over at Logan.

"Lo, will you come to the water with me and help me for a sec?"

Before I had a chance to say anything she was defending her-self. "I just asked Graham to, you know, see for himself that like the wedding is canceled and everything."

"This isn't your place. It isn't any of your business." I squat-ted down on the bank and rubbed my hands in the lake. The cool water burned my blistered palms.

"Don't be mad at me, Aunt Liv. Anyone can see that you and Elliott belong together. I know it's a total mess right now, but he'll come around. Graham can help. You just have to make him understand."

"I don't think so, Logan. It's really bad. What I did to him? Lying to him like that? Look, I get what you're trying to do, but really just stay out of it." She looked like a wounded puppy. Why was I taking this out on her? "I'm sorry. I'm just a mess right now. I don't mean to be such a bitch."

She gave me a hug and said in my ear, "It'll be okay, Aunt Liv."

Hearing her little voice say that made something inside me shatter. She really thought everything with Elliott could somehow work out. I wanted to believe her, but every instinct I had told me she was wrong. I held her tighter. "I'm so glad you came down here with me."

"Me too." Logan left to go back up to the cemetery as Georgia made her way down to me.

Georgia sat next to me quietly rinsing her hands off. Then the clouds broke again and you could just make out the far shore of the lake. She said, "It's really beautiful here. I would love to see it in the daytime."

"When you're not busy with a grave robbery?"

She laughed. "Yeah."

I stood up and stretched my sore back, which creaked and popped with every movement. Georgia stood up next to me and put her hand on my shoulder. "It's kind of amazing what Elliott was able to figure out. We owe him a lot."

"I can't talk about him, Georgia."

She nodded. "Well, when you're ready."

It was almost four in the morning when Leo's shovel hit something hard. We all four jumped, startled that we had actually found something. It took another half hour to dig around the edges enough to uncover the full lid of the vault.

The vault was constructed of concrete and had two loops on the top made out of steel rebar that were used as handles. Graham and Leo debated attaching a pulley to one of the tree limbs to use as leverage to lift the lid but then decided that they ran the risk of pulling the whole tree limb down. In the end they decided to attach the loops of the vault lid directly to the winch on the front of the truck and try to raise it up enough for us to get the coffin out. We had no idea if it would work but we were running out of time.

We ran a large chain through the two loops on the lid and then attached that to the hook on the truck's winch. We all moved away from the edge of the grave and then started the winch.

The first grinding sounds of stone on stone echoed up as the concrete lid began to drag slightly across the concrete vault. The lid was not actually lifting up, but rather was being pulled askew and rotating up slightly as if hinged on the side. We were shouting at each other over the rumbling motor of the winch trying to decide the best way to get the casket out. It seemed as if the capacity of the winch's motor was reaching its limit. When the lid was finally lifted enough for us to peek inside we stopped the winch and locked it in place.

We all peered down into the small opening of the vault and shone our flashlights in to get a glimpse of what was waiting inside.

We spotted a wooden box. It was heartbreakingly small.

Lying on my stomach in the dirt, shining our light onto this tiny coffin, it finally occurred to me that this little boy, little Oliver Jones, was our half brother. And I felt an even larger sense of obligation to his welfare.

Leo and Georgia were debating moving the chains to try to get under the whole lid and lift it up. Leo said there was no way the motor had enough torque to lift it all the way off the vault. I didn't think it would work either and as the sky in the east started to glow a faint yellow color, I knew we didn't have time.

The wedge of opening between the lid and the edge of the vault was about twenty-four inches. I thought we could squeeze the casket out. You could tell that it wasn't one of those enor-

mous, elaborate coffins with a curved lid. It was a simple flat
wooden box, the lid nailed shut. Unadorned and so very small. I
thought it would fit.

It had to fit.

"We can pull it out. We'll just stand on the very edge of the
vault and lift the casket out. I'm pretty sure it can squeeze
through."

Leo and Georgia were both starting to disagree with me but
I didn't think we had time for a debate. I was already climbing
carefully down into the hole and Logan was following my lead
on the other side.

I reached my arm in and managed to get my fingers underneath the bottom of the casket. Logan did the same on her side.
We worked it over toward the edge of the vault and then were
able to get our other hand in to help lift. We managed to lift it up
but we needed just a tiny bit more space to pull it through.

Graham saw that we were struggling and rushed over to the
winch. The motor started up and the cable pinged as the winch
pulled it taut. I wasn't sure if the motor would be able to lift any
more. Or if the whole thing would snap bringing the concrete
lid down on our arms.

Leo yelled over the sound of the motor, "Not too fast! The
lid could shift and crush their hands!"

Logan and I both looked at each other with a quick terrified
glance. Crush our hands? We made one last heave and the side
of the casket was freed. Leo and Georgia both reached down to
help.

Leo screamed, "We've got it! Climb out of there!"

Georgia and Leo pulled the small box up to ground level as I scrambled out of the grave, which was getting more and more difficult as the hole had gotten so deep. Logan was still in the hole. She shouted up, "Hang on! I see something else."

Georgia dropped back down to her stomach yelling at Logan to get her hands out of the vault before the winch gave way.

Logan had her entire left arm inside the vault, straining to reach whatever she had seen in the dark recesses of the box. I could tell by the way she was grunting that it was heavy. When she got it out of the gap between the edge and the lid of the vault she caught her breath for a second and then handed it up to Georgia.

Georgia put the metal box to the side quickly and then helped Logan out of the hole.

When we were all back up on the ground we moved away from the edge and signaled to Graham to reverse the winch. It moaned and creaked as it went to a full stop and then slowly started in the other direction, lowering the lid back onto the vault. It sealed back up with a deep thud and we all closed our eyes with a simultaneous sigh of relief.

The five of us, dirty and sweaty and tired, walked over and stood around our prize. Our little wooden treasure box that we had spent all night freeing from the ground. This symbolized the end of that life for my mother. The end of Janie Jones and Huntley, Georgia. All packed into a tiny wooden box.

Graham pointed to the small metal box next to it. "What's that?"

We all shrugged. We had no idea what that metal box was.

Logan picked up her shovel and said, "I call the first shower when we get home."

THIRTY

Leo gave me a sympathetic pat on the shoulder as he walked back and started filling in the grave. The rest of us fell in line with our shovels putting the dirt back where it came from.

It didn't take nearly as long to put the dirt back in as it did to get it out. Although it didn't exactly fit either. We had a huge mound of leftover dirt. It was almost sunrise and we needed to get out of there before anyone came by. We did not have time for expanding dirt. We ended up spreading it out around the base of the oak tree and covering it with pine straw.

We tucked Oliver's casket into the back of my car wrapped in a plastic tarp and then did the best we could to cover our tracks. When we finished it was after six thirty and the sun was up enough that we could see very clearly without our flashlights.

I took one look at my clothes and my hands and my legs and started walking toward the lake. I was covered in dirt. Dirt from an actual grave. It was all over me. In my hair, my mouth, ground under my fingernails.

Georgia called out. "Where are you going?"

I just pointed to the water.

When I got to the bank I ran into the lake and dove under the water. I stayed under as long as my lungs would let me and then burst up for air. Georgia was right behind me. When she came up she was laughing.

"I can't believe we just did that."

I couldn't believe much of anything. "I can't believe he was actually in there. That it's all real. I thought we were going to keep digging and there would be nothing there."

Georgia was scrubbing the dirt off her hands. "William is not going to believe all this." I knew her husband, William, would be most upset at being left out of the dig. She added, "I'm glad it didn't smell like a dead body."

"I can't believe you just said that." My shoes felt squishy filled with the muddy lake water. I reached down and took them off then threw them on the shore. Georgia did the same. Then I took off my socks and my watch and threw them next to my shoes. I was making a pile of garbage.

Leo had walked down to the edge of the lake and was rinsing his hands in the water. He said, "William is going to be so pissed that he wasn't here for this."

I had to laugh. "Georgia was just saying the same thing."

Leo smiled at me; all the things we needed to say for the moment had been said. He stood up to leave, to walk back up the hill to where his rental car was parked in the shadows. Yes, maybe someday we would be able to be friends. He waved to us over his shoulder, walking away without a word. I just watched him as he became smaller in the distance and then drove off into the first hazy break of dawn.

Georgia was taking off whatever bits of clothing she could safely toss too. I reached into the pocket of my shorts and pulled out my new cell phone. I had forgotten about that. I held it up and watched as the water drained out of it. I just tossed it over my shoulder into the lake.

I floated on my back and looked at the bowl of mountains cradling the water. I said to Georgia, "Do you think Mom . . . I don't know, ever got over it?"

"Obviously not." Georgia was squeezing the water out of her hair. "You did a good thing here, Livie. I mean finding him and figuring all of this out. You got to finish what Dad was trying to do for her. It's good we know it now."

I said, "Elliott figured most of it out."

I wasn't sure what her thoughts were about Elliott, but for some reason I didn't want her to blame him for my breakup with Leo. I said, "It wasn't his fault. I mean everything that happened with Leo and me. It wasn't because of Elliott."

She was making a big show of digging the dirt out from underneath her fingernails clearly unsure how to handle this phantom man named Elliott. "I know that, Olivia. You've had doubts about Leo for a while, whether you knew it or not. He did too. It just took some time away from each other for you two to see it. I know that Elliott wasn't a part of that. I wouldn't hold that against him."

It was either brought on by sadness or exhaustion, but I started crying again. I said under my breath, "I don't think it really matters anymore."

She didn't seem to have heard me. She asked, completely off topic from my love life, "What do we do with the body now?"

I shook off my tears. I had been thinking about the second half of this little excavation while we were digging. Buddy had planted the idea in my head when he said we could legally move the body ourselves, in our own car. "I think we just take the casket straight over to Mary Frances at the cemetery and tell her we are burying him in that grave next to George."

Georgia agreed. "We should have a proper funeral for him."

Logan yelled down to us. "Graham's going to drive me back to the house."

Georgia called back up to the two of them. "Be careful driving, Graham. I know you're tired."

Logan rolled her eyes. Graham said, "Yes, ma'am."

I would have checked my watch for the time but I had already tossed it. "The funeral home won't be open for hours. What now?"

Georgia said, "Showers and sleep. Lots of sleep."

We got back to the house and showered in a haze of fatigue. No amount of water or soap could get the stains of the red Georgia clay out of our hands and the smell of dirt out of our hair. I finally gave up and collapsed in a wet steaming heap on the bed for a few hours of sleep before Georgia and I took the tiny casket to the cemetery.

Mary Frances was very kind about us pulling in with a new addition to their cemetery. I had to believe that it wasn't every day that two women pulled up with a filthy dirt-caked casket in the back of their car and asked to have it buried, but you would never know it to look at Mary Frances.

We had copies of little Oliver's birth certificate and death certificate. We had the letters from our father about moving him to the Rutledge family graveyard and his plans to have his final resting place be the Jones family plot in the cemetery. We gave her our proof of little Oliver's lineage so that he could rightfully be buried in the Joneses' family section with his father. I was tossing papers at her so fast she was having a hard time keeping up. I mentioned quickly and offhandedly that we had the permit from the disinterment but I had left it at home. I was becoming quite the accomplished liar these days.

We made the necessary arrangements for the burial to be held the next day. When we handed Mary Frances our credit card to pay the bill she went over the line items one last time. She was going to explain the cost of the vault to us, in case we didn't know about the policy to have each casket placed in a vault. Georgia held up her hand indicating that we were fully versed on the topic. Then Mary Frances pointed to the charge for the "grave opening and closing" and explained that was the fee for the men who dug the hole.

Georgia smiled as she signed the bill. "A backhoe is worth every penny."

Mary Frances misunderstood the comment and thought Georgia was feeling blue about the idea of the grave being dug. She patted Georgia on the hand and then looked at me and said, "Bless her heart."

With that Georgia and I broke into a fit of inappropriate giggles that we could not control. We were punch-drunk and exhausted and laughed in that unhinged way where you can't control it. Where your eyes water and your nostrils flare and your face turns red. We laughed the whole way back to the house.

When Georgia and I walked in the door we found Logan and Graham in the kitchen. I asked, "What are you guys up to in here?"

Graham held up a carrot and a knife. "We're making a lunch."

I turned on my heel. "Scary."

Georgia and I packed up some of the research into boxes to make room to sit down and eat. The four of us sat around the dinner table eating an enormous salad and overly buttered French bread while rehashing everything we had gone through the night before. We all had that nervous energy associated with a shared traumatic experience. We had the need to discuss each tiny bit of it ad nauseam in order to process the whole encounter.

Graham was particularly enthralled with the winch on the truck he had borrowed and he kept re-creating the noise it made as it pulled the lid free.

Georgia said hypnotically, "I can't believe we pulled that off."

I found the stem of a bell pepper in my salad and held it up. "Do you mean digging up the grave or eating a meal prepared by Logan?" Logan fished an ice cube out of her tea and threw it at my head.

Georgia ignored us. "I was referring to the grave thing."

Logan said for the fifth time, "I wonder what's in the metal box."

The small box that had been buried in the vault with Oliver's casket remained on the coffee table, covered in dirt and locked up tight. It was a black-painted metal box that Logan had declared was the exact same size as the shoebox from her Ugg boots. Apparently there is the English method of measurement, the metric method, and then Logan's shoebox method.

There were deep scratches and dents all over the dull, black surface of the box. Where the paint had been scratched off, dark red rust had formed.

The hinged lid of the box was locked with a silver-keyed lock. Looking at it made Logan mention again that she, and she alone, had spotted it and recovered it. Graham was talking on top of her about the hoisting powers of the winch. The rest of us were yawning. We were four very tired and punchy people.

We tried in vain to open the lock, but we didn't have any tools, we were all exhausted, and our hands were sore and blistered. We decided to deal with it after the burial in the morning. We'd blow it up if we had to, but we would get it open.

It wasn't even three o'clock in the afternoon, but the four of us were ready to call it a night. As Logan walked Graham out, I followed them to the door. I called after him. "Graham, you know you can't tell anyone what we did last night, right?"

He and Logan shared a look. He said, "Yes ma'am, I know."

I knew what that look meant. "Did you already tell him?"

Logan answered for Graham. "Elliott had a right to know. He's the one who figured everything out."

My hand instinctively went to my pocket for my phone. I had

forgotten that I had lost another one to the waters of the lake. I couldn't explain my urgent need to see him considering the fight we had had, but it was immediate. He knew that we had found the baby, that he was right about everything. For some reason I had to talk to him about it. I felt awful that I hadn't been the one to tell him. I turned to Georgia and said, "I'll be right back."

When I got to Elliott's house he was sitting on his porch, waiting for me. Somehow I knew he would be. On the way over there I had realized the improbability of Graham being able to get his hands on a truck with a winch in the middle of the night. That had to have been Elliott's doing.

I wasn't sure what to say, where to start. Elliott's eyes were red rimmed, as if he had been up all night. It made them look even more green. My stomach hurt to look at him. I made my way slowly up the stairs, the two of us locked in a silent stare.

Finally I said, "Thank you for sending Graham with the truck. We couldn't have gotten into the vault without it."

He didn't answer; he just nodded.

"Where did you get it?"

"It's Jimmy's. He let me—Graham borrow it."

I dared to move closer and took the last step onto the porch. "How did you know about Oliver? How did you figure it out?"

It took him a long time to answer. "I'm not sure. It just hit me when you said that thing about being a good boy, that you would cook me dinner if I was a good boy." I felt queasy as he said that, remembering the fact that I wasn't able to cook him dinner because I was busy having all of the lies I had been living blow up simultaneously. He continued. "I realized that we had never looked for a baby being born after they were married. It all seemed to make sense. It was the only person I could think of that would be so important to Janie that your father would go to all that trouble to find and to move."

"Did you know I would do it? I mean, go in and get him out?"

"I thought you might. You knew your father was never able to get permission to move him. I wasn't sure you'd actually go through with it though."

"I'm sorry, Elliott." I couldn't think of a single other thing to say.

Elliott kept talking as if I hadn't interrupted him. "But I guess, well I guess I thought that I had pushed you away. Pushed you to the point where you would want to get out of town as soon as possible. Look, I feel . . . I feel really awful that I said that about your mother. I know that hurt you. I'm sorry for that."

That comment about my mother had hurt me, but maybe it just hurt because it was accurate. I said, "It's true though. She had a whole life she never talked about, and then there I go, following her lead and lying to you."

He was wringing his hands together. "I know you weren't . . . I know you didn't keep it from me to be cruel." Elliott stood up and I leaned back. I was pinned in between him and the porch rail. "Olivia, how could you not tell me? How could you keep that from me?"

I was trying to hold on to calmness and reason, but it wasn't working very well. I just had to fall on my sword. Apologize. How could I have handled this so badly? Warm trails of tears rolled down my face. I kept brushing them off with the back of my hand but I was having trouble keeping up. I was so tired, and hurt, and upset. "I didn't know how to tell you. I wasn't doing it to hurt you."

"I was just so stunned. I don't understand. I didn't mean to blow up at you like that. I should have . . . I should have given you a chance to explain but . . ."

I put my hand on his chest to quiet him so I could speak. Taking in a deep breath I tried, unsuccessfully, to stop crying. "I know I messed up. I'm so sorry. I'm sorry I didn't tell you about Leo. I was just . . . scared. I think I was afraid that if I said anything . . . that you wouldn't understand. That I would lose you." I shook my head. I wasn't saying any of this right.

Elliott stood there for a long time looking over my wrecked body. He was completely still and silent. Finally he took both my hands in his and rubbed them lightly. He could feel the calluses and blisters on my palms.

I said, "You told me that I ruined this before we even got started." I didn't want to believe that. I wanted to believe that this was our first fight, not our last.

"I was . . . shocked. I saw you two in there—"

"I know it was my fault for not telling you. I knew from the moment I met you that it was already over with Leo. I just didn't know how . . . Then so much time had passed, so many things happened with us. I didn't know how to go back." I broke off, not knowing exactly what to say. He was still holding my dirt-stained, aching hands. I said in a hopeful whisper, "You didn't push me away."

"I didn't?"

"No. I'm the one in the wrong here."

"Yes, you are. You're in a lot of trouble." He put my hands to his lips and kissed them. Very gently. "Why didn't you wear gloves?"

I smiled a little. My tears had stopped but my voice was still choppy. "I know. I didn't think of that. Elliott, you have to know . . . how I feel. I can't pretend this didn't happen but maybe we could just start over? Are we . . . are we going to be okay?"

He made one small movement, a slight shrug and nod, and then took me in and held me tight to him. I could feel the flood of relief take over. He whispered in my ear. "We have to be. I don't know what else to do. You have a lot to tell me, but we'll be okay. Right?" He kissed my neck and behind my ear. "What choice do we have?" I ran my sore, blistered hands through his hair and pulled his face into mine to put a stop to all this annoying talking.

We had a few blissful minutes of making up and then I realized that some of the neighbors were starting to stare. Elliott led me inside. "How about some coffee, Liv?"

First of all, I loved it when he called me Liv. Second, I didn't care one bit about coffee at the moment.

I held his hand, following him to the kitchen, where he lifted me up to sit on the counter. He began filling the pot with water. I told him that as soon as I had the energy I would start at the beginning, tell him everything about Leo. Everything I had been holding back.

He stood in front of me and said, "I think we should take things slowly, especially now, after everything."

I wrapped my legs around his waist pulling him closer to me. I let my head fall onto his shoulder and rub his rough unshaven cheek, letting my hair catch on the whiskers.

Elliott gently traced the length of my back as he kept talking. "We need some time I think. I don't want you to regret your decision and I'm worried if we rush into anything you'll feel conflicted."

Why was he still talking? I kissed his ear, down his neck. I breathed him in. He said something again with the word "slow." I was going as slowly as I possibly could. It was taking every bit of self-control I could muster not to tear the jeans off his body.

He said, "We should probably take some time . . ." He halted as I ran my hands down his back. "To . . . to sort out everything that's happened since you got to Tillman. That would . . . that would be the smart thing to do."

The thin T-shirt that I was wearing was gapingly large. The neck of it fell from my shoulder. He kissed me on my collarbone and lifted me off the counter.

I pulled him out to the couch and fell on top of him. Finally not having to stop, finally not being interrupted by Logan or thoughts of anyone else.

Then he flipped us over quickly, landing on top of me and pinned my arms above my head. Laughing he asked, "Are you listening to me at all?"

"No. Why do you keep talking?"

"I just said we should take things slowly."

I said, "I honestly don't think I can go any slower."

"That's not what I meant."

I stared into his eyes for a long time trying to think of which words I could use to best make him see my point of view. The words didn't come. Maybe this was an argument better won by actions anyway. I leaned up to kiss him.

I didn't have to put too much effort into changing his mind about that stupid waiting thing.

I got back to the rental house the next morning. I was sitting on the couch when Georgia came out from the bedroom. She put her finger to her lips and shushed me to let me know that Logan was still asleep.

It occurred to me that Georgia didn't know that I had spent the night out. That I had been with Elliott this whole time.

She whispered, "She's still sleeping."

"Don't worry about it." We had to get ready for little Oliver's funeral but we had time. "She can take the third shower."

Georgia nodded, agreeing with me. "Was that the best sleep you've ever had? I think I was out by four o'clock yesterday. Did you sleep through the whole night?"

I wasn't sure how to answer that. I had slept, a bit. For maybe an hour? Maybe less. There were bits of time cobbled together where I slept with my head tucked into Elliott's shoulder while he rubbed my back or snored gently into my neck. Those moments didn't last very long as one of us would always seem to wake up and need the other one to be awake too. We talked for hours, whispering into the dark, and when we weren't talking we were busy doing other things.

To answer Georgia's question I said, "I slept a little bit." But I had a stupid love-struck grin on my face, giving me away.

Georgia shot up and shouted. "Oh my God!" She remembered that Logan was sleeping and sat down again. She said in a scolding whisper. "Did you stay at Elliott's last night? Did you sleep with him?"

"Well, we didn't *sleep* that much."

She hit me on the shoulder nearly knocking me off the couch. Then she stomped into the tiny kitchen and pointed to the floor at her feet, demanding that I follow her in there. She closed the small swinging door so that if Logan woke up she wouldn't hear us. We huddled in there whispering. She said, "I can't believe you! You've been broken up with Leo for what, a day?"

Was it that recent? Wasn't it a lifetime ago? "I know. I thought you were on my side. You said you would support me."

"I meant I would support you being alone. Not running off with this other guy you just met. You can't just rush into this! You need to take some time to sort things out in your head."

"Rush into this? I'm already *in* this. I've been *in this* since I met him. God, you sound like him."

"I sound like who?"

"Elliott. He was saying all the same things. That we needed to take it slow and take time to deal with all of this. Especially since he hadn't known about Leo. He was worried that I was conflicted. He thought it would be best if we waited before . . . you know."

"Hold on. So he wanted to wait and you . . . "

I bit my lip trying to keep that dumb smile off my face. "He was pretty easily persuaded."

"Olivia! You can't do that!"

"I kind of already did." I knew every one of Georgia's gestures and intonations, and one look at her told me that she did not approve. At all. Normally having my older sister so obviously disappointed in my choice would be a bit upsetting but today it just made me laugh. "I know this seems strange to you and too soon and too reckless. Well, maybe it is, but I don't care. Georgia, I'm . . . I'm in love with this guy." I had my hands strapped across my stomach trying to hold it in. "And I just don't see how time is going to change that. I've never felt like this about anyone. Ever."

Georgia softened. She brushed the hair out of my eyes, like our mom used to do. "But everything's such a mess right now. What if you get hurt?"

I shrugged. "I don't care. I would rather throw it all in with Elliott and risk having my heart broken than slow down or be reasonable. I don't want to wait. I don't want to do the right thing. I don't want to be rational. I just want to be with him."

She sat down on the small metal kitchen chair and pulled her knees to her chest. "That doesn't sound like you, Livie."

"I know. Maybe this is the new me. Maybe I dumped the old me in the lake."

"So you . . . you really love him?"

"Yeah, I really do."

"What does this mean? What are you going to do?"

What a strange question. *What am I going to do? I'm going to spend all the time I can with him, of course. I'm going to meet his family, finally, and make them like me. I'm going to cook him breakfast. I'm going to tell him every thought I've ever had and everything I've ever experienced so that he'll be the one person who knows everything about me. I'm going to hold his hand when he gets scared. I'm going to sing lullabies to all ten of our children.*

I said, "I don't really know." Because the truth was I didn't really know. I had a lot of very pesky realities that I was going to have to deal with. Not the least of which was the fact that he lived in Georgia and I lived in Maryland. That's a long way to go to cook someone breakfast.

Georgia felt compelled to point out some of the logistics involved with this reality. "I mean if you're serious about him then what, you'd quit your job? Move down here? Change your whole life? You couldn't do that."

I knew she was just looking out for me. And she probably didn't want me to move so far away from her and her children. But in light of everything we'd learned this summer it was hard not to laugh in her face. "Gigi, that's exactly what Mom did. She walked away from an entire life and started a new one."

"You can't use that as an example. Her first life died. Burned down. Drowned. Yours didn't."

I didn't want to talk to her about this anymore. I was working on an hour of sleep and some kind of contact buzz from my night with Elliott. I gave her a tight hug and then moved to the kitchen door. "I'm going to get ready for the funeral. I'm taking the first shower."

She gave me one of her wry smiles. "Good, because you smell like sex and mud."

THIRTY-ONE

Georgia, Logan, and I had planned a small private burial for Oliver and our mother at Huntley Memorial Gardens. I got ready quickly and then left Georgia and Logan in the house while I wandered down to the lake.

The lake felt different in the mornings. The air was surprisingly cool and breezy. It smelled of fresh grass and blooming flowers. Later, I knew, the lake would feel hot and sticky, the surface of the water would be alive with skimming bugs, and the air would be filled with the smell of suntan lotion and the sounds of motorboats. I sat back and tried to enjoy this fleeting moment as the sun began to burn the mist off the rise on the opposite bank.

Eventually Georgia found me and made me come back up to

the house to zip up her dress and fasten her bracelet and check her hair. I didn't think she actually needed help getting ready; she just didn't want to be alone as we dressed for yet another family funeral.

Georgia asked, resigned, "So when do I get to meet him?"

I caught Logan's eye and I could tell that she'd been acting as the Olivia-Elliott advocate the whole time she'd been alone with her mother. I said, "He's coming over in a little bit to set up for the reception."

"Who is coming to this reception? We don't even know anybody here."

Logan started counting off names on her fingers. "Elliott, Graham, Jimmy, Betty, Laura and all the other people from camp, Maggie—"

Georgia cut her off. "Okay, I get it. You two are locals now."

I didn't want to push her, but I had to ask. "And you'll be nice to Elliott, right?"

Georgia looked put out. "Yes! Why do you guys keep telling me to be nice to him? When am I not nice?" I had to kick Logan to keep her from answering that question.

I waited out on the front step for Elliott so that he and I could have a minute alone before he was subjected to Georgia's inquisition. He turned the corner onto my street and our eyes locked. We both smiled. When he reached the front porch he put down the bag he was carrying and sat next to me.

I said, "Hi."

"Hi."

"Do you want to talk about it now?" I asked.

He took my hand and held it tight in his lap. "About what?

About the fact that you're a blanket junkie and you stole all the covers, or the other 'it'?"

"I meant the other thing, but now that you mention it, I wouldn't have had to steal the covers if you didn't keep the room so ridiculously cold."

"You are completely intolerant of changes in temperature. You know that, right? And you fall down a *lot*. What have I gotten myself into?"

"I'm a lot of trouble. You may not want to get stuck with me."

"That's where you're wrong. I do want to get stuck with you." He pulled me to my feet. "Come on. Let's go get this over with." As I walked into the house holding Elliott's hand I felt overwhelmingly blissful and happy, utterly calm yet tremendously excited. It was that same strange mix of emotions that I felt they should really have a name for. It occurred to me then that they did have a name for it, and I was more convinced than ever that I was, in fact, stupidly, girlishly, giddily in love with Elliott Tate.

We found Georgia in the kitchen pretending to be busy and pretending to be unaware of the fact that Elliott was there. I introduced the two of them. They both stood their ground for a long tense minute. Then Elliott smiled one of those huge, face-engulfing smiles and he went to Georgia and gave her a bone-crushing hug.

"You have no idea how nice it is to finally meet you, Georgia."

It would be so very hard not to like Elliott. She laughed and hugged him back, saying grudgingly, "It's nice to finally meet you too."

I left them alone in the kitchen to talk for a minute, which was probably not very nice of me, but they needed to get used to each other. They might as well get started.

I was packing up the stacks of research and printouts when Elliott came up behind me and circled my waist. "See? Nothing to worry about."

"Who said I was worried?"

He laughed at that. "Yeah, right. Hey, I have a surprise for you."

"I have really grown to hate surprises. What is it?"

He pulled an enormous pair of bolt cutters out from the canvas bag he had brought with him. I said, "You shouldn't have?"

He cocked his head as if I were an idiot. "It's to cut the lock off that box you told me about."

"Oh! Brilliant!" There was a knock at the door. As I went to answer it I said over my shoulder, "We'll open it as soon as Graham gets back."

I threw the door open. Emory and Maggie Bryant were standing on the front step.

"Oh. Hi there. I . . . hi." I didn't want Emory to think that he made me nervous, but for some reason he did, and the last time I saw him I was bleeding out all over his backseat. I decided to just turn my attention to his wife, Maggie.

She smiled at me and I felt myself calm down. "Hello, Olivia, I hope we're not intruding. I wanted to check on your stitches, and Emory . . . thought he'd come along with me."

"That's so nice. Come in, please."

I led Maggie and Emory into the cottage and introduced them to my sister. Emory was looking around the room, taking it all in. I tracked the movement of his eyes as he searched through all of the pictures and maps and articles scattered around the room. He was looking back and forth between the Vietnam pictures of Oliver with his buddies and the wedding photo of George and Janie.

Maggie brought me into the kitchen where she subjected me to a thorough examination of my head wound. I said, "I understand you're a veterinarian. I feel terrible that Elliott made you stitch me up." I thought back to the desperate look on his face when I had gotten hurt. The way he held my hands to keep them from shaking.

Maggie shooed that away. "Don't be silly. I don't mind at all. It's actually nice to be able to have a patient that can talk back now and again." She was finished. "It looks good. No sign of infection."

As we walked back in to join everyone else, I overheard Emory giving his condolences. Georgia and I glanced at each other, each one silently willing the other not to give away anything about our illegal late-night operation.

I repeated what Emory had said. "You're sorry for our loss?"

He looked at me with that same intense stare that he had from the day we met. "Yes, I understand you're scattering the remains of your mother today." I felt a wave of relief wash over me. Then he added, "And burying her son."

How in the world had they known about Oliver? Maggie suddenly looked nervous or anxious. Emory walked to the Wall of Discovery and pulled down the photo of Oliver on his boat in Vietnam, staring at it. I kept seeing the name Bryant in my head. The tumblers were clicking into place in my brain. Of course. I looked at Emory and asked, "When did you change your name?"

He didn't answer; he just looked at me. I had guessed correctly.

I took the photo from his hand and flipped it over. The names written there were: Me, Whitey, Johnnie, Turk, and Slim.

"You used to be called Johnnie, right? Johnnie Bryant. Is Emory your middle name? You served with Oliver in Vietnam and then what? Did you come back to Tillman with him when you got out?" The muscles in his face froze. He didn't say anything. I looked at the picture again. It was hard to see the face of Johnnie in the pictures because of the harsh shadow cast by his floppy hat, but I knew it must have been him. I said, "Your name was written on the coroner's report too. Johnnie Bryant, eyewitness. Were you the last one to see Oliver alive before he committed suicide?"

The room was deathly silent. I could tell that the others had followed my train of thought to figure out how I had reached my conclusions.

Finally Emory said, "No. I wasn't the last one to see him alive; that was George. I was the one who found him though. I knew he'd be in the lake. I tried to get him help; we all did. I'm sorry to say that he was very seriously depressed. He was unstable even before we came back stateside."

I felt my knees go out and I plopped down on the couch. I glanced at Maggie and saw a look of compassion aimed at Georgia and me. Was this why she had brought Emory to my house, not to check my head or give us condolences, but to answer the questions that we didn't even know we had?

I turned back to Emory. "So you knew my mother? You knew Oliver and George? You even stayed at their house, didn't you? You were staying at Rutledge Ridge when Oliver died. Why didn't you say anything? Why didn't you tell me?"

Emory sat down, clearly emotionally exhausted. He and Maggie shared a silent moment and in it she gave him the strangest look. She said, "I'm going to Betty's. It was nice to see you again, Olivia." She waved at the others, manners and decorum trumping the obvious growing tension in the room.

When she was gone Emory cleared his throat. "I didn't say anything because this was my story, and I didn't think you had a right to it. I don't think it's any of your business."

Georgia spoke up. "Then why are you here now? Did your wife make you come?"

"Maggie? No. She didn't know anything about it till last night when Buddy came over." I was getting ready to demand that he tell us what the hell he was talking about, but Georgia put her hand on my shoulder to shush me. She had a husband and three kids so she was more experienced in the art of hearing a confession. She realized the bounty to be had by waiting patiently and quietly.

Emory started talking and he didn't stop for almost an hour. As soon as we had left Buddy's house on the night of the covert operation, he had stormed over to Emory's. He told Emory that even though it was foolish and stupid, Georgia and I were bound and determined to find out everything we could about our mother. Buddy and Emory were the only two people left in this town who had known Janie. They were the only ones who could tell us anything else about her time here. Buddy told Emory that if he didn't share his story with us then Buddy would do it for him, probably in a very unflattering light.

Emory did a decent impression of Buddy, repeating with a drawl, "They already know about the damn baby. They might as well know whatever else you can tell them." He went back to his normal voice. "I guess Buddy thought I could fill in some blanks for you, after George and Oliver died, but before she met your dad."

So Emory began to tell us his story, starting with his tour of Vietnam when he met Oliver. Jonathon Emory Bryant, or Johnnie, and Oliver were the only two men on their boat to make it back to the States. He mentioned some river they patrolled, but I didn't know enough about Vietnam for it to register. He talked about how dark the nights were, how long they lasted. How the attacks would come randomly at you from small fishing boats, thick muddy banks, or women and children. The river was out to kill them from the moment they got there. To live through it, to fight back, meant killing. That was war; that was the job. Only Oliver couldn't take it. It broke him. He wasn't able to settle it with his own moral compass the way the others could, because he didn't really want to survive in the first place. He hadn't for a long time.

Emory made it sound like Oliver had serious suicidal tendencies. I wished I could have defended Oliver, but knowing how it ended I had to admit Emory was right.

Emory had come home with Oliver to start a boating and fishing business on the lake. They weren't stateside long when Emory realized that Oliver wouldn't be able to make it work. By the time they got back to Georgia he was too far gone, too desperate for the long fight to be over.

Emory talked about how awful it was for George and Janie

after Oliver died. When he mentioned that Janie was pregnant and expecting the baby I heard a sniffle from my sister. All of our emotions were raw, even Emory's.

Emory jumped around in time, telling us bits about Oliver in Vietnam and then some pointless fact about the house on Rutledge Ridge. He said several times how nice George had been and how welcoming Janie had been when he arrived with Oliver. This whole thing was obviously a story that Emory had never intended to tell. He had not run through it in his mind, practicing the way to weave it. It was just spilling out in fits and starts, disjointed and at times incoherent.

He didn't seem to want to talk about the baby, but he made himself. Emory said that he had looked just like George, the same eyes, the same coloring, the same smile. He said that Janie was so wonderful with the baby, so loving, so attentive, so in awe of him. Then he stopped himself from thinking about little Oliver and what it all meant. His mind bounced to the fire and about how difficult the cleanup of the site had been. His eyes kept going to the black metal box as he spoke. It was sitting in the center of the table, locked tight. He would stare at it unblinking as the silent minutes stretched out. He talked about the fact that nothing from the house could be saved. Saved. That pulled his mind to the moment when they finally found Janie in that boat on the water. Every boat on the lake had been sent out to dredge for Janie's body, sure she was gone.

Emory said, "When we found her, in that boat, and she was okay . . ."

He was quiet for a long time. That's when I realized. He was in love with her.

"Emory, did you . . . did you have feelings for her?"

He laughed at my stupid choice of words. "It was a long time ago, but this is still painful for me." I didn't think he wanted to answer the question, but he had gone this far. "Yes, I had *feelings* for her. I loved her." He deflated back into his chair, having said that out loud, and rubbed his face until it was red. "I really did love her. After George and the baby . . . She was so hurt, so fragile. I truly thought I could make her whole again. I think I could have made her happy. She would have grown to love the marina, and maybe me, in time."

"Did you . . . Were you planning to marry her?"

He nodded. I was stunned. How could my mother have been involved with someone like Emory? I was starting to realize that Buddy might have had a point when he questioned the wisdom of trying to uncover *everything* my mother had done.

Emory explained. "She said yes. It was more than two years after George and Oliver. She wasn't herself again yet, but I thought she had made progress. I guess if I were being honest I would have to admit that she wasn't exactly in touch with reality. She was still so quiet, almost catatonic at times. She pretended to come out of it for the sake of the people around her, but even then she hardly ever spoke more than a few words and she barely ate anything. Her mind wasn't right. She was not a whole person when she left."

"Left? What happened?"

"She was just gone one day. She didn't take any of her new things that we had bought. She left a note on the door and that was it. It took me weeks to find her."

Georgia asked, "What did the note say?"

"It said, 'I'm sorry. Cancel the wedding.' That was it."

I wondered where she would have gone. This would have been years before she met our father. "Where did she go?"

"She checked herself into a hospital. A sanitarium."

"Mom was in a mental hospital?" I felt Georgia's hand light gently onto mine.

Emory continued. "When I finally found her I wanted to get her to leave with me, but I couldn't even get her to see me. Her doctor said that she had a break with reality; she couldn't cope with what had happened. That's when I realized that she had never really felt about me the way I had felt about her. It wasn't long after that when the notices started coming about the fore-closure. She didn't care about any of it, her property, her estate, or me. She gave all of her money to Buddy's son, Nate, and it was a substantial amount of money. I guess I was still angry with her and hurt when I bought the land out from under her. I honestly thought she would come back here. If not to me then at least to the lake, to the area. This place was so much a part of who she was. I always thought I would see her again. Anyway, a few years later Maggie moved to town." He shrugged not wanting to tell us that part of his story and knowing we didn't have the right to ask about it.

Georgia, Logan, Elliott, and I had been made a bit catatonic ourselves at discovering that Emory had been in love with her. I didn't for a second believe that she had loved him back; she just didn't know what else to do in the moment. In some strange way it reinforced my belief that she honestly loved our father. She wouldn't have married Adam Hughes otherwise. Somehow they found each other and loved each other enough for her to want to live. Enough for her to want to try again with life.

None of us seemed to know what to say. I thought back to

how strange Emory had acted since the first time he laid eyes on me. Now it all made perfect sense, considering how much Georgia and I looked like our mother. Then I thought of how kind he had been when I got hurt, rushing me to Maggie to get stitches.

I put my hand out. "Thank you for coming here. I can tell it wasn't easy for you."

He smiled and we shook, awkwardly. He stood to leave. "I guess if you have any other questions, I'll answer them."

I said, "Because Buddy is making you?"

Emory smiled at that. "Yes, Buddy is making me."

Logan spoke up. "Can I ask why you took the pages from the map book in the library?"

Emory seemed to consider that for a second. Probably trying to decide what the consequences would be of admitting to it. "There were some notations on there about the tax deed that would have led you to me. I just didn't want you coming to me asking a lot of questions about her."

Elliott asked, "What about the missing journals from the Fells?"

He seemed genuinely confused. "I don't know anything about any journals. But, I will tell you this"—he looked back at the box on the coffee table—"when we found Janie in the lake that night, the night of the fire, she had that box in the boat with her."

All eyes turned to the box as Emory left. Georgia wouldn't let us open it yet; we had to leave for the cemetery. She promised, as soon as we got back we could see what was inside.

THIRTY-TWO

As I took the winding country road that led to Huntley Memorial Gardens I glanced in my rearview mirror at the urn containing my mother's ashes. Logan had buckled it into the seatbelt next to her. I really missed her. I wondered what she would think about the fact that I had canceled my wedding to Leo. I knew she had liked him. But she had canceled a wedding to the wrong person, hadn't she? Granted, in spectacularly more dramatic fashion than me. I figured she would understand. And I think I had finally come to understand what she meant about needing someone in order to breathe.

The memorial service we had had in Maryland for our mother when she passed away had been so difficult. It was sad and hard and busy. It was full of everyone else's expectations and needs for dealing with their grief, their desire to say good-bye. None of it felt as if it had, in any way, helped me deal with her death.

But this send-off, this good-bye, felt like a complete catharsis. We three girls, Janie's girls, were going together to say our farewell and remember the woman she had been and the life she had lived. The whole life she had lived. The life she had lived with George and with Oliver. The life she had lived with our father, Adam, and with Georgia and me. The life she had gotten to live with her grandchildren.

We carried the urn across the cemetery toward the tent set up in section 30. Underneath the tent was the small casket that we had wrestled from the ground. It was covered with a white satin cloth and behind it stood an enormous wreath of white lilies.

Mary Frances was waiting for us, wiping sweat from her forehead with the back of her pudgy white hand. I said, "Everything looks lovely, Mary Frances. Thank you."

"You're welcome, dear. You know Betty Chatham insisted on doing the flower arrangements for you. So fortunate." She set her gaze on the flowers as if they were made of bacon. "Betty's the head of the Altar Guild you know." I could tell that we were to be as impressed about that as we were supposed to have been about her presidency of the Tillman Garden Club.

Georgia looked at Logan and me. "What's an Altar Guild?"

Logan answered under her breath. "They do church flowers and stuff. Betty Chatham is like some kind of competitive florist."

Mary Frances asked, "Would you like us to say a few words, or would you like a moment alone to say your good-byes?"

Somehow I had been designated as the spokesperson for our

crew. "Could we lower Oliver into the grave, and then take a few minutes?"

"Oh, of course." Mary Frances gave a signal to a groundskeeper and Oliver's little casket was slowly lowered into the ground. Then they stepped back a few yards and pretended that they couldn't hear anything we were saying.

Georgia, Logan, and I stood over the edge of the grave, peering down into the hole that held Oliver's little casket. It was right next to George's grave. They were finally together again.

The air was still and quiet with just a faint buzz of insects in the tree line. I glanced at Logan, then to Georgia. I said, "I'm glad they're all going to be together."

Logan took something out of her bag and let it fall into the grave. It was a small stuffed bear. She shrugged. "I remember when Will and Adam were two years old." Georgia put her arm around her and pulled her in for a hug. And as some kind of miracle, Logan hugged her back.

Georgia took the lid off of the urn and the two of us looked at each other. Our mother was finally, forever, going to be laid to rest.

We held the urn together and sprinkled half of the ashes into Oliver's grave. Then we sprinkled the rest over George's.

"Love you. We miss you," said Georgia.

I said, "Bye Mom. I hope you're happy. Wherever you are."

Logan linked an arm in each of ours. We stood there each silent, each with our own thoughts. I think we were all three crying.

There was a slight sniffle and we all glanced over to see Mary Frances standing as still as was possible considering she was currently dissolving into a puddle.

Logan took a deep breath and said, "Bless her heart."

Georgia cracked first, but as soon as she was going we all started laughing. We laughed through our tears as we made our way out of Huntley Memorial Gardens.

We headed back to Tillman feeling nostalgic about our mom and telling Logan stories from our childhood. I had felt like we'd lost some of that when we found out about George and Oliver, but we hadn't. Not really. It was all still there for us to remember anytime we needed it. There was just more background to the story than we realized before.

Our little rental lake house had been transformed while we had been gone. Betty Chatham had brought in yet more flowers and tidied up the living room. Someone had catered a lunch so the dining room table was overflowing with food. There were platters of tiny biscuits with honey ham tucked inside and bowls filled with pasta salad and fruit salad and some kind of corn salad. There were elevated plate stands stacked with brownies and cookies and tiny pies. I was trying to figure out where it had all come from when I spotted a note tied to a pitcher of iced tea.

It read:

> *My dear Olivia, I'm sorry I couldn't tell you about the baby. I hope you can understand why. I would never hurt your mother or open one of her wounds. It was an unspeakably horrible time for her. But I can see that by discovering him you were able to bring the family back together and I know that somewhere she is now at peace. I hope you don't mind that I sent some refreshments for the reception. Please call me anytime. I promise that this time I will answer. Much love, Florence*

Before the reception was in full swing we had one last errand. Logan, Georgia, Elliott, and I hurried to the screen porch to open the black metal box before any more reception guests arrived.

Elliott cut the bolt and Logan pried the rusty box open. Inside was a bundle wrapped in stiff, dirty molded canvas and tied with twine. Georgia unwrapped it and laid the bits of treasure out on the table.

We all picked up something as the items spilled out from the wrapping. I held up three small books. "The missing journals from the Fells."

Elliott asked, "Why are they in here?"

I flipped through one of the volumes and stopped on a page. It had the same ink notes scrawled across it that I had seen in all of the other journals that had belonged to our grandfather. Notes about cases he was working on. But on top of the notes, on most of the pages, someone had scribbled with crayons. I said, "Oliver used them as coloring books."

Logan pulled out a small velvet box and snapped it open. Nestled inside was a platinum wedding ring. The band was richly engraved with scrollwork and the oval-shaped diamond sat on a delicate filigree crown. We all recognized it from the wedding photos of Janie and George. It had been her mother's ring. Janie had worn it when she married George.

I pulled the ring from the box and stared at it, turning it over and over, committing it to memory. Then I took Logan's right hand out and put it on her finger.

Georgia said, "Are you sure you want Logan to have it? You don't mind?"

I wiped the tears away. "Of course I want her to have it. And so would Mom."

There were other things in the box, documents and letters. Random things. There was a copy of George's will and of Oliver's birth certificate. There were a few pictures, but they had been damaged over time with water and mold and were difficult to see. There was a baseball, which must have meant something special to George. There was a military medal of some kind and I held it up to see if Elliott recognized it.

He said, "I think that's the Navy Cross. For valor."

I turned the medal over in my hand. Its ribbon that had once been blue and white was now a uniform gray. "Valor in Vietnam and then he kills himself as soon as he gets home. So sad."

At the bottom of the bundle was a very tarnished silver baby spoon.

Georgia had been opening each piece of paper and glancing at it before moving on to examine the next one. She handed one to me. It was the missing page from the coroner's report of Oliver's suicide. The eyewitness interviewed hadn't been Emory; it had been George. Just as Emory had said, George had been the last one to see Oliver alive. He had called the sheriff when Oliver didn't come home one night. I didn't read the rest of the statement; I knew how that story ended.

There was a stack of letters bound together with a frayed ribbon. We just put it aside, knowing somehow that they were love letters from George. None of us wanted to intrude into those memories any more than we already had. At least not today.

There was one loose letter among the bundled pieces and

yellowed envelopes. Georgia said, "This one has Mom's handwriting."

I nodded to her. "Read it."

Logan, Elliott, and I held our breath as she read the small handwritten note.

> *George, I'm lost. I don't know how to live here without you. Everything is gone now. The things that were left here don't make sense without you. I don't want it. I don't want this life without you and Oliver. How could you go with him and leave me here? Why did God pick you to go and not me? It's not fair. It hurts too much. This is my punishment. I burned the house down and Nate got hurt. It was all my fault. I can never forgive myself. I just wanted it all to disappear. Then I went out to the lake to finish this. How did your brother do it? I'm ashamed that I wasn't strong enough. I couldn't risk damning my soul to hell and not seeing you again. I will be with you and the baby again. Wait for me. Your Janie.*

Our eyes moved around the group, each meeting one another's. Finally I said, "That's the saddest thing I've ever heard."

Logan was shaking her head, "I can't believe she burned the house down on purpose."

Georgia said, "No wonder she had to go to a mental hospital."

Logan held her hand out and was staring at the ring. I wondered for a second if she thought it was cursed. Then she said,

"At least she got to spend her whole life with him. You know? Before he died, I mean. They had like twenty-five years together, right? And she was happy with Grandpa Adam, wasn't she? She made it. She pulled through."

Elliott said, "She must have had this box with her that night to keep a few things safe from the fire."

The fire. I started to wonder if that was why she had wanted to be cremated and I stared at the now-empty urn.

My attention was pulled toward the inside of the house where more reception guests had started to arrive. "Lo, Graham just got here. Will you two hold down the fort for a minute?"

"Sure. What are you doing?"

I picked up the urn and looked at Georgia. "Want to go give this a burial at sea?"

"Yes!" As Georgia and I made our way down to the lake she called over her shoulder, "Elliott, come with us. We need a good throwing arm."

We stood looking out at the waters of the lake. The entire town of Huntley was under that water. The old streets and stores and houses. I wanted some tiny part of my mother to be put into the lake too, even if the only thing we had left of her was the last vessel of her remains.

I handed the urn to Elliott; he asked if we were sure. I had no idea what else one would do with a used cremation urn. He wound up and launched it out into the water. It sailed in an arc and landed in the cove. I imagined it sinking slowly down to the bottom of the lake. Perhaps settling on some lane where she and George used to walk as children, or on the old site of some long-forgotten patch of grass that afforded the best view of the river.

Maybe near a tree that Janie, George, and Oliver used to climb as children.

Logan called down from the house, "Mom, come up here and meet everyone."

Georgia looked at me with a most shocked expression. I said, "I can't believe she wants you to meet people."

"I know. Usually she's trying to find ways to lock me in the basement."

Elliott and I were left alone on the muddy bank of Lake Huntley. He put his arm around me as we watched the circle of ripples in the water that had been made by my mother's urn.

Elliott turned to face me and said, "Olivia . . ."

"Yes?"

He ran his hand through his hair. He knew I considered that one of his tells, and he smiled at me as if I'd caught him thinking. "I'm not sure where to start."

"Start what?" I felt my stomach drop. Where was he going with this?

"I just feel so bad saying this. I know it's not really fair."

"Just say it then."

"Liv, you haven't been here long. What? A month?" It had been five weeks and two days, but I didn't say that out loud. He said, "I know you're done here. You've finished what you came to do." There was a palpable panic settling into the pit of my stomach as he kept talking. "It's not fair of me to ask this. You have a life in Maryland and your job and your family. But Liv . . . Look, I *do* know how to live here without you." He was echoing my mother's letter. "I've done it for a long time. But I don't want to anymore."

I surprised myself by hitting him. "Dammit, Elliott! You just"—punch—"scared me"— slap—"to death!" Shove.

He started laughing. "I just told you I want you to stay here with me and you start hitting me. This is not an auspicious beginning."

"I thought you were trying to tell me good-bye."

"You're so crazy. How could I let you go now?"

I said, "Then what was all that about us not knowing each other very long and feeling guilty?"

"I do feel guilty. I'm being selfish by asking you to stay here with me. I know that. But you know I can't leave. My dad, my family, the paper. I've worked so hard to get it running. But what about your job? Your family?"

It all felt so easy now. "I'm quitting that job and I'll always have my family." That little sideways smile of his that I really liked was beginning to form. I said, "I don't want to be anywhere without you either."

"You'll stay with me?" he asked.

"Yes." It came out as a whisper.

"I'm so glad you said yes. You would have been so miserable if you had left me."

I laughed. "Oh, really?"

"Really. You know you're in love with me."

"I do. I do know that. I wasn't aware that you knew it."

He said, "I'm very perceptive."

"So you keep telling me." I asked, "What do we do now?"

"Now? Now we fight over the covers. I will probably let you win, because I'm a gentleman. I will install first aid kits all over the house for you since you're such a klutz." I hit him again playfully, but he just kept talking. "I will cook you dinner and you can make me coffee. I had to meet your sister so you'll have to meet my mom. She'll want to get to know this girl I've fallen for and can't seem to live without." He shrugged. "I just want to be with you."

I asked, "You do?"

"I do."

We leaned in to each other and I kissed him until the last ripples made from the urn traveled across the water to the edge of the bank. They resolved themselves in a tiny wave over the red Georgia clay. One decision in life can roll out like that, travel out through time and place, until it has changed, ever so slightly, everything in its path. Our mother's secret had been one of those ripples, cast out onto our world. I did not regret coming here and diving in. I did not regret knowing her in a way that she had never intended. Everything in my life had changed because of it, because of my decision to come here. But they were my changes and my choices. I was the one causing the ripples, no longer the one merely in their path.

ACKNOWLEDGMENTS

I am most indebted to Caroline Upcher, freelance editor, published author, and deliverer of copious red-ink admonishments. Caroline is the single greatest factor in this book being finished and published, and I owe her and that red ink a great deal of thanks. I have never been more grateful to someone for scolding me in a British accent.

My amazing and kind agent, Marly Rusoff, who has ruined my perception of things by making me believe that everyone in the publishing world is generous and friendly. I also owe a thank-you to Michael Radulescu for his help with all of the logistics along the way and to Julie Mosow for her honest critique and thoughtful edits.

I will be forever indebted to my editor at Harper, Claire Wachtel, who took a chance on a new author and guided me with her subtle notes and keen insight, improving the entire manuscript. Also a big thank-you to Hannah Wood, associate editor and accomplished hand-holder.

To all of my friends who have always supported my strange endeavors. My Burke Girls: you don't tell and I won't tell. My Clemson friends: you can't tell because you don't remember anything. Playgroup: thank you for not judging all that may or may not have happened. My Blog Tribe: you were the best and safest place to learn how to write. My friend and photographer Jo Reeves, who put up with way too many photo shoots because I hate getting my picture taken. Card Group, especially Lisa with her endless tales of the South. And to all the soccer and school and karate parents with whom I spend way too much time, thanks for always making it fun.

To my early readers, who were always very supportive and encouraging even if they were probably lying: Laura Heard, Jules Johnston, Becky Mautner, Darcy Mayers, and Travis Ward.

And of course my biggest thank-you goes to my family. My sister, Julie, who approaches everything with the enthusiasm of a puppy. My mother who has told me my entire life that I could do anything. Except that one time when I wanted to try out for the seventh-grade chorus.

My sweet, neurotic husband, Scott, who is the best dad and the worst cook, and didn't flinch when I gave up doing laundry about ten years ago. My oldest daughter, Tempel, with her wry wit, endless empathy, and mad gaming skills, who is never afraid to taste any food, but is still wisely afraid of zombies. My baby,

Parker, who has a lust for life and being silly, who can somehow run faster than her dad and organize better than her mom, and makes the sweetest and most creative birthday cards ever. Thank you for asking me to stop writing about you in my blog, which forced me to start writing fiction.

ABOUT THE AUTHOR

CAROLYN DINGMAN lives in her adopted hometown of Atlanta, Georgia, with her husband and their two daughters. *Cancel the Wedding* is her first novel.